GIRLS SAVE the WORLD iN THiS ONe

Also by Ash Parsons

Still Waters

Holding On to You
(previously titled *The Falling Between Us*)

GiRLS SAVe the WORLD iN THiS One

ASH PARSONS

PHILOMEL

PHILOMEL BOOKS
An imprint of Penguin Random House LLC, New York

First published in the United States of America by Philomel,
an imprint of Penguin Random House LLC, 2020.

Visit us online at penguinrandomhouse.com

Library of Congress Cataloging-in-Publication Data is available.
Printed in the United States of America
ISBN 9780525515326
1 3 5 7 9 10 8 6 4 2

Edited by Kelsey Murphy.
Design by Jennifer Chung.
Text set in Adobe Caslon Pro.

With love for:
AAK! Productions—(Ames, Kel, K-10—
Stay cool and have a great summer! LYLAS!)

Kari Bakken—never forget RAVEN fics.
Thanks for taking me to Dragoncon!

And for Jennifer Taylor—BFFL

$$\begin{array}{r} 2\text{Sweet} \\ + \ 2\text{Be} \\ \hline 4\text{gotten.} \end{array}$$

Thank you, friends. xxoo

1

We're never going to make it. This is it. My life is over.

In the days and months that follow this tragedy, when they speak my name, they'll say in hushed tones, "She died as she lived: full of complaint and bile, mere inches from her goal."

Mom twists to smile at me in the back seat.

"See, June? The doors aren't even open yet!" she says.

My best friend, Imani Choi, is riding shotgun, and it's good because this way my mom can't get the full force of my eye roll.

"I know they're not open yet, Mom. That's not the point."

Outside the convention center, there's already a snaking line along the sidewalk up the street and around the corner. A milling press of hundreds of early birds waiting to get in.

ZombieCon! is the biggest thing this town has ever seen. For the first time, it feels like the new convention center might reach its capacity, at least in the exhibit hall and ballroom. They're saying up to ten or even fifteen thousand people are projected to attend the con!

"Look at that line," I moan.

"I'm sure we'll be fine," Imani says.

I take a deep breath.

It's not Imani's fault we're not already in line for *Zombie-Con!* Even though we'd arranged to spend the night together, and said we'd get here before sunrise, and even though I'd texted Siggy last night, to remind her again of the importance of getting here early. And even after I had set two alarms, and set my mom's alarm as well.

We're still running late.

It's Mom's fault. She laughed this aren't-you-cute indulgent laugh when I told her to get moving this morning, that the early bird catches the worm, the world isn't going to wait for you, rise and shine, all those nagging things she says to me every morning to go to obnoxious school. But now the one thing that I really want, the one thing I'd worked for, well, the one *fun* thing, and Mom had the nerve to say, "Hold your horses, I need coffee."

Then she moaned and complained, leaning against cabinets and counters, imitating me on school mornings. Paying me back for how hard I am to get going most mornings, and laughing like it was so original.

And as if that wasn't annoying enough, after coffee, and after Imani finished putting on her makeup (which she doesn't even need because her brown skin is flawless), on top of all that,

I had to listen to Mom ask Imani about the colleges she would apply for if the early decision one didn't work out. Which, I know, is the single issue that stresses Imani out so much, even if she's used to parents asking about it because *they all ask*.

Then Mom continued asking about other scholarships Imani might apply for (she's already got one sponsored by a local law office) and Mom kept going, *Do you know if Siggy is planning to take the SAT again? June is, you know that already, next Saturday, and maybe if there's time while you're standing in line, you could help quiz June on the test-prep app* . . . on and on and on.

I just kept quiet in the back seat. We were almost there; I'd worked for this day all summer, saving all my summer jobs money that didn't go toward gas. Between summer school and my jobs, my white skin barely even tanned, because I barely went outside during daylight, it felt like.

So I'm determined. Nothing but *nothing* is going to ruin today, not even the Math Booster app.

And not the fact that I'm retaking the SAT for the third time next weekend.

And not the fact that I'm not sure any college is going to admit me if I fail math again.

Someone has to let me in, right?

Right?

And not the fact that it doesn't really matter if I do take

the SAT again. My score isn't going to improve. We all *know* I have a learning disability. In math and math-y things. So why do I have to keep banging my head against this wall?

And not even the fact that there's a massive zit in the crease of my right nostril—and it looks horrible and hurts, too—on this day, this one day, when I'm going to take a million pictures and when I even have a coveted photo op with one of the stars of *Human Wasteland*.

The photo is the pièce de résistance of this, my first con experience.

The car line for the drop-off circle creeps forward, and Mom finally changes the subject from college and the SAT.

"Has your mom had a longer commute with all the protesters?" she asks Imani.

Imani's mom, Naomi, is a civilian contractor on the nearby army arsenal test range. There's been talk recently that USAMRIID (the US Army Medical Research Institute of Infectious Diseases) has established a field office at our arsenal, which would make sense if it's true, because Senoybia is also within an easy commute of the Centers for Disease Control in Atlanta.

But a lot of people don't like the idea of the army medical research field office on a test range, and so there's been an influx of protestors outside the arsenal gates.

"No, Mom says the drive time is about the same," Imani

answers. "But last week she dropped off two boxes of donuts on her way in: one for the protestors, and one for the military police at the gate."

"I just love that," Mom says. "So diplomatic and thoughtful."

Imani quirks a smile at Mom.

"Well, everyone also waves and gets out of the way for her now," Imani says.

Mom laughs and turns onto the road that runs along the front of the convention center drop-off circle. She whistles low. "Wow. That's a lot of people."

"I told you it was a big deal," I say, the words snapping between my teeth sharper than I mean, but would you *look* at that line?

"I know," Mom says. "I mean, I knew. But still. Wow."

Outside the car window, the rising sun tinges the silhouette of the convention center a pinkish gray, like a Hollywood backdrop only not in LA but here, in basic, boring, nice-place-to-raise-kids Senoybia, Georgia.

I'm not joking, they actually put that in the tourism brochures and on, like, the town website and stuff. Not that it's dull, just that it's a great "family town!" And stuff like "Slow down! Give Senoybia a try!"

It's a nice place, sure. But I can't blame anyone, Imani especially, for looking forward to graduation and college.

Our high school is like only 10 percent students of color. It's embarrassing how white it is.

So, I am excited for Imani next year, no matter where she goes, or how far away, because I know she's really looking forward to a larger city, and being around more people like her, black or Asian or biracial, and being in a town that isn't quite so Mayberry.

I mean, I'm looking forward to that, too! For my own self. It's just . . . I'm not entirely sure I'm graduating. Or getting into a college.

Anyway, it's a miracle that *ZombieCon!* is even here. I'm serious, it's like a gift from the fandom gods just to me. *ZombieCon!* travels around the country, but it usually only hits the really big cities. Your Los Angeleses, your Houstons, your Chicagos, your New Yorks. Not my Senoybia. But there had been a contest, with the tagline: "Is your city A WASTELAND?" that encouraged fans to petition the fanfest, and tell them why *ZombieCon!* should come to their town. I boosted the posts nominating Senoybia, and so did Imani, and Siggy. Blair did, too, back before I learned about what she did. When I still thought she was my friend.

Even thinking of her name summons a particular pain. Still new. Betrayal. This is what it feels like: shame, anger, and hurt, like sandpaper made of shattered glass, rubbing under your skin.

I shake my head to stop thinking about her.

Anyway, Senoybia won the contest, and our convention center was approved as the location. It's big enough, and new enough, and there's even a luxury hotel attached to the convention center by a skyway. I mean, they want you to call it a skyway, but really, it's a bridge-tube like the kind hamsters use. Ridiculous to even have it, of course, because on most days the traffic in downtown Senoybia is downright sleepy, sluggish, and otherwise nonexistent. A child could literally play on the street and be fine, most days.

Mom turns into the convention center drop-off circle and puts the van in park.

I have my safety belt off and the door open before Imani can finish saying, "Thanks for the ride and the spend-the-night, Mrs. Blue."

Imani and I get out onto the sidewalk. I adjust the neckline of my favorite olive green shirt. It's just the right amount of slouchy-and-stylish, with a wide scoop neckline that falls off one shoulder, so I always wear a wide-strapped black tank top underneath. Plus the olive color looks nice against my brownish-reddish hair. So that's a plus.

"You're welcome, sweet girl!" Mom puts the passenger window down and leans over to call to us. "Have fun! Stick together! See you at midnight!"

Imani gives a big nod and a little salute.

It's not Mom's fault she's hopelessly uncool. Or that she likes my friends and spends entirely too much time talking to them. I mean, I like talking to them, too, they're *my friends*.

Okay, but it was nice of her to offer to drop us off so we wouldn't have to spend an extra ten bucks on parking.

"Thanks, Mom!" I yell, and wave.

She blows me a kiss and eases back onto the street.

Imani smooths her crisp white tunic. She's so cool. She looks like a fashion blogger or something, her legs long and slender in black leggings, with sparkly black sneakers and a coral cropped jacket that matches her nails.

I look cute, too, and actually *feel* it. I'm short compared to Imani, and I'm not model-slender like her. I'm average, I think. Normal. Rounded. Some days I don't feel so good about my shape, but today I feel lush and curvy, wearing my favorite shirt, ripped skinny jeans, and red high-top Converse.

Imani gives me a smile, and I can tell she's thinking the same thing.

We look good.

Now it's really starting. I have a whole day to spend with my friends, with my fellow fans, with zombie and apocalyptic horror lovers from all over.

ZombieCon! The Ultimate in Undead Entertainment starts now!

2

ZombieCon! The Ultimate in Undead Entertainment will start once we get inside. Now we're walking along the massive line of people already waiting for the doors to open.

"Sorry about all the college questions," I say.

"It's okay."

But when I glance at her face, a frown has stitched in between her eyebrows.

"You're totally getting in. You know that, right?" I say.

"Harvard has a five percent acceptance rate, June." Her voice is gentle, but resigned. "Less, actually."

"Well, if they don't take you, they don't deserve you!"

Imani smiles a little.

"Seriously, Imani!" I loop my arm through hers. "You're so badass. You're going to get in somewhere amazing, and they're going to pay you for the honor of having you as a student."

Imani lets out a tight breath, almost like she's been holding part of it, holding a slight catch of breath deep inside her lungs, holding it inside forever, waiting, waiting, just waiting and hoping.

She gets straight A's. She kicked the SAT's butt so hard it couldn't sit right for a week.

And school can still sometimes make her so anxious she calls me in tears or on the verge of them. When that happens we end up watching Bob Ross paint some happy trees together while we talk about life *after* college. What different places we might live. What kind of pets we might have. What we might name our pets or our kids, if we have them. Places we might travel. People we might know. People we might become.

The whole wide world outside of school.

The weird thing is, Imani actually loves school, loves learning, loves working on projects and papers. It's just grades and class rankings that make her miserable.

"Listen, let's take the day off from it," I suggest.

Imani's eyebrows lift, but she's got an amused look in her eyes.

Since we almost always know what the other is thinking, I can see she's already there with me.

"The day off from college applications and acceptance stress. Imagine." Her eyebrow quirks up like a punctuation.

We smile at each other, these huge Cheshire grins.

"Deal."

We shake hands to seal it.

"There's the end of the line, I think," Imani says, pointing with a coral-colored nail.

Did I mention she's gorgeous? While our relationship is purely platonic, it doesn't keep me from admiring how beautiful she is. Beauty is just beauty.

And Imani is every bit as beautiful on the inside.

By which I mean she's a really sweet, wonderful person.

Not that her insides themselves are beautiful. Which sounds weird and serial-killer-y when you think about it.

Imani hooks her arm with mine again. "This is going to be so much fun, June."

I smile back, even though we're *still* walking to the end of the line.

"Everyone coming to Senoybia for the con, it'll be like our town has imported a town!" Imani says.

"A town full of zombie fans!" I chirp back. I can't help it, I give a little jump of joy.

"And just look at this line!" Imani murmurs, squeezing my arm.

"It's long," I groan.

"No, I mean, it's *diverse!*"

She's right, and I can't believe I didn't notice before. The line is full of all different kinds of people: all different skin tones, all different body types.

I smile at Imani and her happiness just beams into me. I feel like I could levitate from it.

There's a whole wide world, waiting out there, and for

today it's almost like there's a whole wide world here, too.

We've passed a million or so people, it feels like, and at least half of them are cosplaying. Some of them are dressed like characters from *Human Wasteland*, but there are plenty of other horror movie characters, and zombies galore; I've counted at least three zombie Spider-Men.

It's going to be the perfect day. First and foremost: I have always loved zombies. If there's a zombie movie, I've probably seen it, and if they make a new one, I'm going to see it.

It all started with the first zombie movie I ever saw. It was on TV late at night on Halloween, and my mom *definitely* didn't know I was watching it. Mom hates scary things. I think it's kind of linked to how she's a kindergarten teacher, like everything is optimism and respect and fairness and love with her, which is nice, but you know. There's more out there, right? Good and bad. We can't stay in kindergarten forever. Generally speaking. I guess my mom found a way.

But it's so stinking cute when her students see her, like if we're in a restaurant or a store, their eyes go wide like they've seen a celebrity, and they'll run up calling "Mrs. Blue! Mrs. Blue!" with these high little voices, and she'll lean down to hug them, and I don't know why but sometimes it makes me want to cry.

My dad likes scary movies okay, he likes mystery more

than horror, but they overlap a bunch so we can sit and watch those together. Dad is the director of our public library, so he's definitely more cool and up on trends and stuff than my mom. Last week he even brought home an old library DVD of the first zombie movie I ever saw, the one I watched on TV all those years ago.

Fight the Dead. Changed. My. Life. It's about a zombie outbreak happening and a group of people holing up in a gas station trying to survive the night. Even though it was in black-and-white, it was terrifying! And thrilling! And I felt like it was telling me something deep and true when I saw it, even though zombies aren't real, because of how that group of people acted once they were in the gas station.

My favorite was the scared girl, who everyone kept discounting and who just kept surviving, impossibly, until the very end.

Weirdly, I really like the idea of them: zombies—these horrible, terrifying, inexorable things, animated corpses that want to devour you. Seriously scary, primal stuff.

But more than that, I like that zombies are clean. Not physically, because ew. But, like . . . emotionally.

They *only* want to eat you. They don't want to hurt you, or torture you. Pain is just a by-product of how they want your meat. They're not sadistic. They're just hungry.

Zombies are basically human sharks.

If the sharks were also dead. And if a shark bit you and you then were destined to become a shark.

Okay, so not really like sharks.

"Have you heard from Siggy?" I ask as we get in line.

"She's still got plenty of time." Imani glances at her phone again.

I love her, but our other beffie, Signe Larsen, has absolutely no sense of time. She doesn't get how long it takes to get somewhere, how long she needs to get ready, how long she needs to do anything, hell, how long she needs to watch a minute go by.

But the thing is, when Siggy finally arrives anywhere, she's so cute and funny and so apologetic it's hard to stay mad at her.

Hard, but not impossible.

Imani slides her phone back into her tunic pocket. "Siggy's going to be late but not late-late. She loves the show as much as we do."

We're all mega fans of *Human Wasteland*. It's the best show on television, and I am completely obsessed with it. It's why *ZombieCon!* even exists.

Me and my three, well, two, best friends have watched literally every episode of it together, live when they air. It's our thing. We write and read fanfic, we tweet at the show writers and actors and costume designers and just about everyone involved with the show. And of course the other fans, which is *so much fun* because you get this feeling in your heart, as you watch with countless other fans, this expanding, growing, glowy feeling. This feeling that there's so much more out there, there's a whole world of people, and they're so into the same thing you are, and that makes you feel . . . loved, somehow. Like you belong. A really buzzy, shared, beautiful feeling.

Have you ever discovered something that made you feel . . . understood? Somehow called to something in you, and made you long to be a part of it, even if that was absurd and impossible, but even so it just . . . resonated with you, somehow?

That's how *Human Wasteland* made me feel the first time I watched it, and every time after.

Part of why I love it so much is because it doesn't try to pretend that bad things don't happen. And yet it also highlights hope, love, and a community of chosen kinship as ideals. This big found-family of survivors who have their differences and yet in the end have to get along. The show asks big questions about what kind of world we want, and what kind of people the survivors have to be, how they've had to change over the course of the zombie apocalypse.

Like my favorite character, Clay Clarke, the army ranger's surrogate son. Clay is played by Hunter Sterling, an actor only a year older than me.

Which I know, because I looked it up. Like I said, I'm a mega-fan.

I have a full-size poster of Hunter as Clay hanging on the back of my bedroom door. Which is how I know exactly what pose I'll strike when we have our group photo op with him at the end of the day. I took a bunch of selfies with the poster, trying different poses, expressions, and outfits. By the end of it, I was just being funny, because I was holding different props, and cracking myself up.

Which, let's face it, was infinitely more fun than studying for the SAT. Which is what I was supposed to be doing at the time.

My favorite selfie, which is now my lock screen, was the one where I put on my dress from the junior prom (what a disaster that was—do not ask). I held on to a bunch of silk flowers I swiped from the dining room table, holding up my other hand like a beauty queen waving, with her dirty and intense date glowering behind her.

I amuse myself. But if you can't laugh at yourself, who can you laugh at?

We're still not moving, but it's only going to be a few more minutes before the convention center doors open officially.

I text Siggy again, then crane my neck around, looking for her white-blonde head.

"She should have spent the night with us." Imani says what I'm thinking.

"I tried, but she was with Mark."

"I know. I should have insisted, I'm sorry." Imani is the benevolent ruler of our trio. If Imani wants something, she usually gets it. All she has to do is turn the full power of her smile on you, and yeah. Goner.

"I mean, that would have worked," I say. "Swear to God, Imani, I don't know why you don't use your powers of persuasion more."

I place a hand over my heart in a solemn vow. "If I had your skills, I would talk Mrs. Casey into passing me."

"That's *wrong*, June!" Imani is laughing, but this is it: the taproot of who she is. Imani is Principled. She believes in making a better world, in making fairer rules, and she believes in the supreme power of hard work above everything.

Me? I believe in the supreme power of accepting your limitations, and adjusting your target accordingly.

Imani's an older sister, too, so that's in there. She's always been the responsible one, especially compared to her kid sister, Tishala, who is in the eighth grade. Tishala is impulsive, hilarious, and a total pest.

Obviously, Imani loves her lots. Even when Tishala breaks into Imani's makeup. Right now, Tishala is completely into doing these epic fantasy and sci-fi photo shoots, most often with herself as the model, although she's used Imani and even me sometimes. And she's into special effects makeup (as long as it's beautiful. She's not into zombies or gore, which is why she didn't pester us to come to the con, thank goodness).

My older sister, Summer, went to college last year, and my parents' single-minded focus on me ever since has been . . . well, it's been *a lot*.

Tishala's gonna have a *big* adjustment next year when Imani goes to college, let me tell you. I don't know if she realizes how much Imani does for her.

"You can't just talk someone into passing you," Imani says as we take a step forward.

"It would be for the greater good!" I argue. "Trust me, Mrs. Casey is as sick of explaining quadratic equations as I am of never understanding them."

This is my second time in Mrs. Casey's class. It's exhausting having a learning disability and trying to make everyone see that I'm never going to "get it" no matter how "close" it looks like I am.

Or that it doesn't matter how many times I take the SAT. I'm just going to psych myself out; clench up; get that old familiar feeling; hello, anxiety, my old friend; and just . . .

Whiff. Spectacularly. And extra time to take the test won't fix that. No accomodations can.

I glance at my phone again. The doors will open in just a few minutes.

Imani notices my glance at the time.

"Siggy'll be here," she says. "Any minute now. Mark will probably drop her off at the circle, right when we get there."

Annoying Mark. Annoying Mark Carson. Annoying Mark Annoying Carson.

He's okay, if you have to deal with boyfriends, I guess.

"If I'm being honest, I wanted to have you to myself," Imani says, with that sly side-smile that makes it feel like the sun is rising in my heart.

"I liked that, too," I say, and there it is, my doofiest smile, the one where I tip my chin unconsciously, giving myself jowls and creepy eyes. This is not a smile I ever intend to unleash, which is why I generally only know I've done it when I see the picture afterward.

Also this smile is another reason why I practiced for the photo op with Hunter's cutout.

Imani says I look great in every picture, that I always look "cute" or "so adorable," and I'm like, sure, Imani, sure, because best friends are supposed to say those things.

But Imani hates lies, too, so maybe she means it? Still, I don't want to make *that face* in my picture with Hunter.

"Let me try calling her," Imani says. She holds her phone to her ear.

We start moving forward. Either the doors are open or the people in line in front of us can see activity behind the glass doors and we're all pressing forward like Black Friday shoppers.

"She's not answering," Imani says, lowering her phone.

"Aaaaaaaarrrrghhh, Imani!" I groan, grabbing at my chest. "The doors are getting ready to open, the time is now, the moment's arrived or it's about to arrive, the train's leaving the station, the boarding gate is closing, Elvis is at the fire doors . . ."

"Deep breaths, June," Imani says, and she quirks that smile at me again. "It's a good thing Siggy hasn't answered. It means she's almost here."

"What?"

"You know, she feels bad so she doesn't want to pick up the phone. I bet she's almost here."

The doors are definitely open now. We take six steps forward.

"This is supposed to be our big day." I can't stop the worrying once it starts. It just keeps getting bigger. "It's already been screwed up 'cause we were late, and we'll be even later to the opening session—"

Imani gives me *the look*, but I don't stop.

"How are we supposed to make Special Memories without Siggy?"

Special Memories is what we call any big shared event, a joke from the yearbook pages that read *Special Memories* and are always a collage of pictures: friends sitting together at lunch, a teacher pretending to strangle a student, groups clustering together for a friendshot, the band in formation on the football field, various team members flexing or high-fiving or holding up number-one fingers.

I'd sold this whole day to the group on that big bonding premise: *Let's Make Special Memories.* That this is our senior year, and we've been friends since elementary school, and now we're just supposed to leave each other after graduation? How do you just do that?

I remember meeting Imani and Blair in kindergarten. Imani is still my best friend, even if Blair isn't.

But I remember meeting Imani over those little multi-color plastic bears. Green and yellow and red and blue, you were supposed to use them for counting, but I gave them all names and arranged them in groups and Imani loved that.

I remember she looked at me, eyes wide, and she said, "You're making them *families?*" like it was the best idea and no one had ever had it before.

She can still make me feel that rush of embarrassed pride, because I'm not that clever, but she likes the way I think sometimes, I guess.

How are you supposed to let go of Imani?

And how are you supposed to let go of Siggy, who we met in third grade when she moved to our school, who makes us laugh so hard, who is such an outrageous flirt, or was before she met Annoying Mark.

It makes my shoulders tight to think about graduation. To think about next fall when we're all separated, to think about moving on, moving out, what if I can't hack it? What if no one else likes me? Just these girls I met in elementary school, and the rest of the world doesn't care. Or worse.

What if I'm fundamentally unlikeable, and I drive everyone away with questions like this?

How do you stop asking questions?

Okay, so even if I do let go, or if they go anyway, which they will, no matter if I'm ready or not, how am I supposed to start over without them?

It doesn't matter if Siggy makes me so annoyed sometimes with her boyfriend and her occasional insensitivity. It doesn't matter if Imani can be frustrating with her grown-up seriousness, and it doesn't even matter that Blair—

A knife twists in my heart at the name.

Okay, so it still does matter about Blair, duh, don't be foolish, June.

I'm not going to let her ruin this for me. For us.

"June, I feel like you're getting caught in it," Imani says gently, and her hand touches my arm.

Sometimes I get too worked up. My mom calls it anxiety, Imani calls it "getting caught," and I call it being a normal, rational person who can see all the ways everything can go wrong.

"She's on the way," Imani says. "Deep breaths."

I gulp down air, take deep breaths, and nod at Imani.

"It's not just Siggy. What is it?" Imani asks.

She's got Spidey-level insight with me. And I do with her, too. We can always see when something is bothering the other, or when the other is upset about the thing underneath the thing.

I wave my hand at the world.

"It's everything," I say. "Blair and Scott. And graduation and stuff."

Imani nods and pulls me into a hug, giving me a big squeeze.

It calms me down, and I squeeze her back to say thanks.

And I really do feel better. Just like that.

The line moves forward, and we step around the edge of the building. I can see the doors and the large *ZombieCon!* banner designed like a biohazard warning. Above it is a massive promotional sign for *Human Wasteland*, as big as a billboard, unrolled from the top of the three-story convention center. The main cast stares out at us from the sign, worry lines furrowing their brows, sweat staining their very close-fitting and/or strategically ripped clothes, their eyes intense with everything they've seen.

Oh my God, I love this show!

A separate banner hangs below it, the tagline for this

season, written in letters three feet tall: WILL YOU SURVIVE . . .

It can be a question, but they write it like an unfinished sentence because it has more impact that way, sounds like an imperative statement, use your will, choose to fight, because one of the themes of the show is what will it take to survive?

Will you survive . . .

A jolt of happy adrenaline dumps into my veins, and I turn and grab Imani's arms. And something I love about her (and Siggy, too, if she was here, dammit, I'm going to throttle her) is we know each other's thoughts almost instantly, and even though I was just worrying, Imani is with me immediately right now, a jolt of pure excitement, as we scream at each other.

"*ZOMBIECON!*"

We're here, it's our senior year, graduation is seven months away, and we will be friends forever, no matter what. This day is going to be one of those *Special Memories* we always think about, think back to, and we'll have the photo op with Hunter Sterling at the end of the day to prove it was the best day ever. Nothing's going to stop us. It'll be the perfect day, maybe the best day of our entire senior year.

Forget prom.

Forget graduation.

We're at *ZombieCon!*

3

*A*fter taking and posting multiple selfies with the banners behind us, Imani and I start rehashing our plans for the day: listing who we're going to pay for their autograph, who we might pay for a selfie at their tables, what we might buy for souvenirs. We strike up a conversation with the people in front of us, two girls and a guy, sharing the latest fandom gossip about the current showrunner, who is doing a great job with the show but seems to be a bit of a jerk at cons, and talking about the newest characters on the show.

"Man, it's too bad our friend Siggy isn't here, Linus and Annie are her absolute favorites," Imani tells them.

As we get closer to the doors, the energy of the crowd picks up; you can feel it building like a wave. It's good-natured, excitement and eagerness, but nobody's pushing or shoving. It's that elevated, amped-up feeling from our community of fans. Everyone here loves the same thing.

Pop music blares from the radio station van parked on the side of the convention center. The local reporter stands interviewing people in the line. She pulls over a rowdy group who roar just like football fans in a stadium when the camera sweeps over them.

Now I can see the doors and more importantly the security checkpoint in front of them that's slowing everyone down. A bag check area, a metal detector, and a pat-down station. Beyond them is the main entrance to the convention center: a three-story, semicircular glass wall arcing out toward the street, with five sets of double doors set at regular intervals along its round edge.

"We could just go in and meet up with Siggy inside," Imani says, twisting her *ZombieCon!* badge on the shoestring-style lanyard around her neck.

I glance at my phone. Still no texts.

"No, we need to wait," I say.

"We have phones, June," Imani says. "We could just meet up inside."

I can feel it, too. The open doors, so close now, are pulling at me like they have hands, gently tugging. I can smell the slightly chemical newness of the inside—the walls, the carpet, the air conditioner, urging so many wonders within.

"Imani, we have to wait. Yes, she screwed up, and yes, we're going to kill her, a little, when she gets here, but we can't just go in without her. No friend left behind! Fight together or end alone! We have to decide right now who we are. Do we leave people behind? I say nay! We wait! All together or none at all!"

"Sweet lord," Imani groans, laughing. "Juuuuuuuuuuuune. We have phoooooones."

But no, I will not be swayed. This is how a day gets ruined. These little compromises and I'll-meet-you-laters that turn into meeting-you-not-at-alls. The next thing you know you spent the whole day apart, planning to meet up "sometime."

Besides I can feel the oratory loading up in my brain, almost like there's a swell of inspirational music underneath it. So, I lean into it, tenting a hand on my collar bones in affront.

"Do we leave her behind? Our time-challenged friend? Who, need I remind you, we have known since Mrs. Raspberry's class? Do we abandon her to the chaos of this line alone?"

We edge forward. Now only two groups of people stand between us and the security point.

My hand lifts into a rallying fist.

"Or do we wait? Yes, wait! For waiting for a friend is the most noble thing one can do! Do we wait, though we will be pissed off at the waiting, or do we abandon our posts?! Nay, we do not!"

"Go inside!" some rando in the line behind us yells, and people laugh.

"You, sir, will be the first to go when the zombie apocalypse comes," I yell back.

"Nah, I'm a survivor!" the guy yells. His skin is dark brown and his eyes are warm with a *we're all here to have fun* light. He's wearing a T-shirt with a zombie chasing people that reads ZOMBIES HATE FAST FOOD.

"Okay, see you at the end, then!" I yell back, because if he's a survivor then I'm a survivor, too.

Everyone chuckles along, and we all turn back to the front of the building as the line moves up again. We're next.

"Seriously," Imani says, still chuckling. "What are we gonna do? Siggy has her badge, she can meet us inside."

I turn to the bored-looking guard standing to the side of the checkpoint.

"Excuse me, we're waiting for our friend. Is it okay if we just wait here? Then when she gets here we can go in?"

"Knock yourself out," he says.

Imani and I shuffle off to the side a little, and I wave a hand in front of us. It takes only a few repetitions of "Go ahead" and "We're waiting for a friend" before the crowd gets it and we can just stand there grimly, smiling these pained smiles, and nodding as people give us generally sympathetic looks, as if we're orphans asking for more gruel.

"Oh, no. Okay, June, don't look." Imani's voice is first

hushed and tight, then hushed and soothing, and that's how I know what it is.

Or rather who.

"Just look at me. She hasn't seen us, and we don't have to see her either. Not if you don't want to."

I knew she was coming. Her and Scott both. I knew that. I know that.

"Scott's not with her," Imani murmurs, reading my mind like always.

That pain that wears Blair's name lances through my heart again. Betrayal sharp as a sword. What it feels like to lose a close friend. After years. Because they were never your friend at all, it seems.

Shame and heat burn through my veins and I have to pretend now, that I don't feel this either, this particular self-hatred of being so, so, so *stupid*.

And not about math, which, I already knew.

But a new kind of stupid. A stupid about people, when I thought I was good at them.

I know I'm not supposed to say that word. To use it. I know my mom would hate it if she knew I thought of myself that way. I know it's a bad word, and inaccurate, and wrong.

But nothing else captures the way I feel. The worthlessness and shame of being . . . that.

"It's okay," I lie. "I'm fine."

And so, I look around, even though Imani has twisted in front of me slightly to shield us.

Blair Whitley walks alongside the slowly snaking line. She's taking long strides, like no one is going to stop her, not ever, why would they?

Her smile is tight on her face, like all her smiles are. Tense, forced, tightening her eyes and showing sharp teeth.

She's pretty in the whetted way of a knife. Her honey-brown hair is wavy, like she might have used hot rollers this morning. Her eyebrows are perfect arcs accenting her freckled white skin.

Before I can wonder where she's going in such a rush, when the line is so slow and we're all just standing here like cattle, I see it. Around her neck.

A VIP badge on a deluxe, collectible, blood-spatter-design ribbon lanyard.

Air whuffs out of my chest with a sickening thump.

I mean.

Of course.

"Is that a VIP pass?" Imani murmurs. "Good lord. They cost what, a grand?"

I nod, and make myself look away from Blair.

"Or more. Depending on which level you buy."

We were all supposed to go to *ZombieCon!* together.

"She must have upgraded," Imani says. "I guess her parents coughed up the cash, as always."

I feel an old surge of protectiveness, the light-tracings history of our entire, complicated friendship.

"Can you blame her?" I ask. "Especially since she knew she wouldn't be coming with us."

"Don't you start punishing yourself." Imani's voice is a gentle reprimand.

I just shake my head.

I can't help it. I met Blair in kindergarten, too. She used to play with me and Imani; they'd fight over me. Hard to believe, right? But I think it was because I used to be happy to play any game they wanted, not because I was so great or anything.

On the playground Blair would pull on one arm and Imani would pull on the other and they'd both be laughing and pulling at me, saying, "She's my friend! She's my friend!" and I would be laughing, too. I'm not going to lie, it felt pretty good to have them fight over me. But I'd say, "We can all play together!" and "I'm both your friends!" Which didn't quite make sense grammatically, but I knew what I meant.

And eventually I was both their friends. We were like the Three Musketeers, *one for all, and all for one!* And when Siggy came to our school in third grade, she became our fourth musketeer. We would hang out together in our group of four, or we'd break off into pairs, or trios, but usually we were all together as much as possible, sitting together at lunch every day, meeting up in the courtyard at break, and we might make friends outside of our musketeering but we always knew that we four were the closest of friends and the "core" group.

I'm close friends with a few juniors and sophomores because of how I had to repeat first geometry and then algebra 2. Imani has two other tight friend groups, one with the student council kids and the other through the Multicultural Club (I'm in it, too, but I don't go as much as Imani because I have tutoring after school. Right now the club is putting together an anime film festival). Siggy is hella into Botany Club and is of course close with Mark's friends. Blair is big in the AV Club and the newspaper, and has other friends in those groups.

But for all of these other friendship circles, we all always knew that Imani, Siggy, Blair, and me were the innermost circle. The base. The core.

And for me it was like each of them saw something different in me, and more than that called something else to the front.

With Blair it was intensity. She made me feel so immediate, a little unsafe, a little thrilled, being around her like being on a roller coaster that hasn't been tested.

I don't know what she liked about me. Whatever it was, I guess she didn't like it all that much, in the end.

We were all still friends until a little over one week ago, which is when I found out that Blair had gone behind my back to go out with the guy I was dating. And when I say "dating" let me unpack how pathetic this all is, because Scott's the one guy I've ever actually gone on a real date with, okay? And he's only the second guy I've ever French kissed, and the second French kiss total. (When we kissed the first time at least. We kissed a lot after that.)

I mean, it's not pathetic to not date. Plenty of people don't date, and they don't want to. And that's great!

It's just that I really want to. Despite all my complaining about Siggy and Mark. And my teasing Imani when she was with her ex, Ryan, who graduated last year.

Despite all of that, I just really, really wish I had a boyfriend, too.

High school for me has been one long, unending series of secret crushes from afar or boys who "think of you like a sister," and I'm not good at flirting or any of it.

But then there was Scott! And we *were flirting*, effortlessly, and he was so fun and funny and when he looked at me, I felt like he saw me and saw someone awesome at the same time. He doesn't go to our school; he actually lives in Peachtree City, which is thirty minutes away, and so it sort of gave me hope, too. That maybe boys just don't like me *here*, but when I get somewhere else . . .

Anyway, we met at a comic shop event in Peachtree City. One of the artists for the comics adaptation of *Human Wasteland* was there signing. Scott started talking to me, about the show, about zombies, and the podcast he wanted to start, and we just clicked.

Scott was the first guy I really liked who liked me back. And okay, so he wasn't my official, exclusive boyfriend. Not in that "going together" or "it's serious" way, but I thought we had that potential. And it sucked that I got him so wrong, and that he was a two-timing jerk, but it hurt so much more because Blair was my *friend*.

Or so I thought.

Needles sting the corners of my eyes.

Blair has reached the separate VIP security station. She's opening her purse for the guard, smiling and talking to him.

Okay, I better look away, because I don't want to cry, and I definitely don't want her to see us here in the damn plebe line, and I don't want to miss her at all, which I do. Even though I hate her with the fire of a thousand suns that are also on fire and in a volcano. In space. A space-volcano.

I don't want to think about how she really, really, really.

Really, really, really. Really. Didn't care about me or my feelings.

And that she didn't hesitate to hurt me.

Because she didn't think about me at all.

When I called Imani, crying about Scott and Blair, Imani picked up Siggy and came to get me immediately. We all went to Imani's house, and I sobbed my heart out.

"That's horrible," Siggy had said, her voice absolutely aghast, and I knew she was thinking about how it would feel to stumble upon Mark in one of their favorite places with another girl.

Or worse, how it would feel if that girl was Blair.

"I can't believe Blair!" Siggy added, her eyes blazing.

"Maybe it's some sort of misunderstanding," Imani offered.

"Sure," Siggy scoffed. "They went on a picnic in the park and were making out *by accident.*"

Imani had turned to look at me, her eyes glistening, reflecting my hurt. "I'm so sorry, June."

I hiccupped, and blew my nose. "I can't believe I didn't even suspect it!"

Imani had leaned forward then, and given me the biggest, tightest bear hug. Like she wanted to save me from something that had already happened, like she wanted to fix a bird's broken wing, or tape a butterfly back together.

Siggy leaned in to hug me, too, and when she leaned back, fury sparked in her eyes.

"It's not right," she'd said. "How would either of us feel, Imani, if Blair had done this to us?"

"Horrible," Imani breathed. "The worst."

"We should teach her a lesson," Siggy said. "Give her the cold shoulder. Just for a little while."

"I don't know . . ." Imani's voice was sad and raw, but she didn't let go of my hand.

So we talked about it. We sounded like parents, talking about putting a toddler on the naughty step.

But I was angry, and I was hurt, and Siggy was angry and hurt for me, and Imani just wanted me to feel better. So we agreed. Two weeks of no contact.

The four musketeers, now suddenly only three.

We've been giving Blair the cold shoulder for about a week. Less. None of us talking to her, moving away from her at lunch, not taking her calls, blocking her texts.

It feels harsh. It also feels pretty good in a twisting, dark way.

When it feels more twisting than good, I tell myself it's not forever.

I duck, giving my head a little shake so some hair falls in front of my eyes. I'll pretend I can't see her.

Imani's whispering soothing things, and we're just curled

in the general direction of *away from Blair*, trying to make ourselves small, and that's when I hear Siggy's voice, shrill as a band saw.

"Haaaaaaaay, sexaaaaaaaay ladaaaaaaays!" she calls.

"Kill me now," I whisper to Imani, but we turn, and I can feel, without looking, not only everyone in line watching our friend finally arrive, but the call reaching out and catching Blair's ear. I can feel Blair's head swiveling like a tank gun. Her eyes sweep over us.

I have two choices: I can turn and look at Blair, let her know I see her and that I know she sees us, or I can keep pretending that I don't feel her watching. That I can't see out of the corner of my eye, how she's stopped and is watching us.

Siggy dance-walks up to us, with her hands out, palms up, and her head pigeon thrusting on her long neck. The move of one of the guys in that viral dance clip "when you run into your friends."

It's hilarious, and it makes me laugh even though she knows we've been waiting for her. One thing I will say about silly, skinny Siggy, she knows how to apologize, how to make an entrance, and how to make you laugh all at the same time.

"Forgive me, babies?" she says when she reaches us. "I'm sorry. I'm hopeless."

"Should have been your middle name," Imani says, but she's smiling, too.

Siggy's dressed in her usual boho-chic style. She's wearing a halter-top capri-length jumpsuit, gentle blue like her eyes. Her white-blonde hair falls in a sheet over her tan bolero jacket. Chunky ankle boots with peekaboo toes and a long bag-of-cloth purse finish out her look.

"You look so great," I tell her.

Siggy smiles and does a little dip, like a curtsy. Her dangly earrings glitter and bob hypnotically.

I can feel the weight of Blair's eyes on me, like a finger flicking my ear. Hot and stinging, and definitely something you ignore.

"Can you believe it? *ZombieCon!* Finally!" Siggy looks at the banners above our heads.

Honest excitement burbles up in my chest again, along with something darker, an *I'll show her* that seeps out toward Blair. I grab Imani's hand and Siggy's hand.

Imani immediately grabs Siggy's other hand, and our hands are twined in the middle of us, and I scream, as loud as I can, because we're here, and I'm not going to let Blair ruin my day, or Scott, or the SAT, or my zits, or *any of it*.

And Blair should see that we don't miss her, even if we do.

"*ZombieCon!*" I shriek, and Imani and Siggy scream and we jump up and down, laughing and screaming "Ahhhh!" and bouncing like a bunch of excited circus poodles, and there Blair is by herself, because she showed her stripes, didn't she? And Imani and Siggy are on my side.

Karma.

Eat your heart out, Blair, I think, even though it feels dark and I feel a bit queasy with it. Gross and kind of like I can feel my heart shrinking and it's not a good feeling. I still think it, anyway.

You shouldn't have hurt me.

Who am I kidding? She doesn't even care about me. I'm just trying to make myself feel better.

It works.

Because we're still here, the three of us, and it's finally *ZombieCon!* day, and it's going to be amazing.

It's going to be the best day of our lives, no matter what.

4

ey, look, your friend arrived," the security guards says, in a tone like maybe he hadn't noticed even though we were all just screaming. His sardonic asshole setting is indecipherable from flirting, really.

He aims a smile at Imani, confirming it.

"Yes, she did!" Siggy says, and we ease back into the line, show our badges, get our bags searched, and walk through metal detectors before that's it, we're *in*!

The atrium is a large glass-walled semicircle, three stories tall. If you look up you can see the second-floor lobby railing cutting across the bottom edge of the circle and the third-floor railing above that.

We walk forward, craning our necks to look at the floors above us, taking in all this modern steel and glass and gleaming tile.

In the center of the atrium is a massive water feature. It looks like a hulking volcanic rock—the top stretches almost to the second floor. Waterfalls spill down four different sides, pouring in a loud rush from the bowl at the top.

"A bit tacky," Imani says, even as we stop to admire the waterfalls.

"Noooooo, it's beautiful," I say.

"I love the orchids and the ferns. And the moss," Siggy says. "I feel like we're in a huge, fancy greenhouse."

"So, you feel right at home," Imani says, and I start coughing because it's funny, and also true because Siggy's house is simply covered with plants. Like every surface, window, and corner is bursting with green-growy things. Her mom, Lene, is an earth-mother type. She's got white-blonde hair like Siggy, but she's shorter and plump and gorgeous. She's got the greenest thumb—so much so that it's almost magical. I swear she can look at a droopy or yellowing plant and know precisely what's wrong with it. I think plants perk up when she walks into the room.

Siggy gets her height from her dad, Harald, who, honestly, looks like a Viking or something; he's this burly tall guy with red hair and a bushy beard. He's so nice, though, gentle and boisterous both, with a hail-fellow-well-met laugh and whose favorite pastime is building miniature ships with Siggy's little brother, Aksel.

It'd be pretty funny to hide one of their pirate ships somewhere in the massive water feature in front of us, tucking it into a fern for only observant people to find, like an Easter egg.

I tip my head up, taking in the tremendous size of the volcanic rock in the atrium.

"How'd they even get this big hunk of rock in here?" I ask. "They must have wide-loaded it down the interstate like a mobile home."

Imani laughs. "I'd like to see that. But it's poured concrete, June. Mom showed me a time-lapse video of the company that set up the molds and everything. They designed it with all the planters and maintenance panels and stuff."

"Oh," I say, and feel a bit disappointed that it's not actually volcanic rock, carted all the way here from somewhere far away and sunny.

Then I picture a crew of construction people working on this one, beautiful thing, carving out places in concrete for hothouse flowers to grow.

"Can you imagine having that as your job?" I yelp. "Designing waterfalls! That would be so cool!"

Imani laughs, but it's the warming kind that makes you feel like you're lying in a patch of sunlight.

"Don't ever change, June," Imani says. "You see the good side of everything."

She takes my arm and leads the way around the water feature.

Once past the huge rock, you can see the escalators that reach to the second floor, and then the third-floor escalators rising above that. Here the line of people entering the convention center splits into groups either heading to the open doors on the ground floor that lead into the exhibit hall, or riding up the escalators to the ballroom.

"Okay, let's review," I say as we wait in line to get on the escalator to the second floor.

Siggy claps, and Imani rolls her eyes.

"Ground floor?" I ask.

"Exhibit hall! Vendors! Autographs! Photo ops! Snack food!" Siggy rattles off the list like an A+ student.

"Good! Second floor?"

"Ballroom! Interviews and panels! Smaller panels in the banquet rooms! Dance party in the ballroom tonight!" Siggy says all in a rush.

"Excellent!" I praise her as we step onto the escalator.

"You forgot skyway to the hotel for lunch," Imani says drily.

"Imani! You *were* listening to the orientation!" I tease her, but it's all in fun. Imani is excited to be here; she just didn't need the floor-plan prepping.

"Last but not least, third floor!"

"No con activities! Go up for extra bathrooms if there's a big line!" Siggy says.

"Excellent! You pass with flying colors," I say.

Directionally, Siggy is hopeless. She couldn't find her

way out of a paper bag, but she's as ready for this con as I can get her, and anyway we're using the buddy system today.

We step off the escalators on the second floor and walk to the ballroom lobby area, funneling into a pack of people moving into the ballroom for the opening session.

ZombieCon! is being opened officially by Hunter Sterling.

"Don't forget to breathe," Siggy instructs me as we catch a glimpse of the huge screen hanging over the stage. Hunter's character, Clay Clarke, stares out at the audience.

"Who needs to breathe when you can see that face?" I reply.

"Imani, slow down, June is hyperventilating here," Siggy calls to Imani in front.

I'm not, but I did just bump into Imani because I was looking at the screen instead of where I was going.

Once we're through the doors, the ballroom buzzes with voices and excitement. There's row upon row, easily twenty or thirty, of padded metal chairs set out in three sections facing the stage.

Imani doesn't stop to get her bearings or scan the rows of chairs for a group of three seats; she just walks immediately to the left, and then straight up the farthest of three aisles toward the front of the hall.

I don't even question it. After practically my whole life

with Imani as my best friend, I can say without a doubt: that girl always knows where she is and where she's going. It's like she has a built-in compass or GPS. And she never gets vertigo or dizzy either; even when we rode the World-Famous Zip at the county fair she just laughed and laughed and walked right off it like it was no big deal.

Meanwhile I was stumbling to one side or the other like a person with an inner-ear disorder who had just ridden a ride that should only be used for astronaut training.

I follow Imani through the ballroom, which is already almost half full with audience members, people with the same idea as us: get here early.

I spot a clump of other kids from school as well as our English teacher, Ms. Guillory. Judging by the bright red shirts just past them, there's also a bunch of college students from Georgia State here.

A zombie-fied group of cheerleaders, six guys and girls in ripped and stained cheerleader clothes and zombie makeup, stand on their seats in front of the red-shirts and lead a UGA cheer.

I'm surprised at how close Imani is getting us, and I turn and stare across the room at the other two sections of seats, which are fuller. Will our view be blocked? Why are these seats not as crowded?

Imani gets us in what feels like the thirteenth row, not

bad at all, especially when you consider that the first five rows of each section are reserved for VIP badge holders and official photographers.

"Wow, Imani, got magic much?" Siggy says as we sit. "How'd you know these seats were here?"

"Disney trick," she says, flashing a shy smile at us. "Always cut left as far as you can."

Imani's family is amazing. Her mother, Naomi, is an aerospace engineer, and her dad, Sejun, is a history professor. Because of the nearby army arsenal and all the civilian contractors that work with them, they moved up here for Naomi's job from Florida when Imani was a baby. But when they lived in Florida, they fell in love with Disney World. And I mean, they are fanatics—they go at least once a year. Their house is this faintly ridiculous but also cool combination of museum reproductions and Disney World figurines.

Naomi is African American and is gorgeous like Imani— but Naomi has darker brown skin and wears her hair in a tight, short afro. She looks like a high-fashion model, too, with her style. Vibrant colors and what she calls "accent pieces," which means the most perfect-looking, distinctive piece of jewelry you ever saw. She's an amateur genealogist and has traced one branch of her family back to Kenya, so she's collected a lot of jewelry from there: beautiful, bright beadwork or carved wood pieces.

Imani's dad is just as good-looking, for a dad. He's Korean American, and currently teaches at Emory. He's an avid video gamer and it was probably through watching playthroughs with him that Tishala got into her sci-fi cosplays in the first place.

Fortunately, Imani's dad thought that the cosplay stuff was amazing, and he gave Tishala her first camera setup. Now Tish constantly works on her photos, planning them, building the costumes, props, and looks, and pestering anyone around (usually Imani) into helping.

Next to me, Siggy flops into her seat.

"These seats are great! See, I didn't ruin everything!" Siggy says, and she smiles at me and Imani, a happy, relieved-of-guilt look in her eyes.

"Well, it was a close call," I grumble. Because really.

Siggy leans into me, then puts her head on my shoulder.

"I'm sorry. Can you ever forgive me?"

"Maybe. Since you're cute."

Which, hand to God, she is. And she's so narrow. As in her actual bone structure is slender.

Elfin. She's built like a twig.

A really cute twig.

"Why were you late anyway?" Imani asks Siggy, across my lap. "Did Mark hear about the early decision?"

The big drama of Siggy's life currently is whether or

not she and Mark will end up at the same college next year. They've both applied early decision to Oglethorpe. Siggy is sure to get in. Mark . . . maybe not.

Siggy shakes her head. Instead she sits up and pulls on a lock of her hair, stroking it while tipping her chin down and looking at us through the tops of her eyes. Her eyebrows waggle.

"Forget I asked," Imani says. Her tone more resigned than annoyed.

She has more patience than me when it comes to Mark and Siggy.

"Seriously?" My voice is harsh, because now I'm a bit mad. Annoying Mark Annoying Carson.

"Yeah, but when you fall in love, you'll understand," Siggy says, immediately defensive.

Imani puts a hand on my shoulder as she feels me bunching up.

"It's okay," Imani says. "She didn't mean it that way."

Siggy immediately turns doll-wide eyes at me. "Did that sound bad? I didn't mean it like that!"

I know she didn't, but it's hard not to feel self-conscious about being the only one in our group who hasn't had an actual, committed-and-into-me boyfriend. Someone exclusive.

Especially because I would really, really, really love to be in love. To be in a relationship like that.

And because of what just happened with Scott. And Blair.

Siggy didn't mean to hurt my feelings. And I shouldn't have sounded so mad about Mark. She already knows I don't like him that much.

That's not entirely my fault because I didn't realize that they were going to get back together the first time they broke up. Or the second time. Also, you know, the third time.

I'm a slow learner, okay? I think I've put that on the record already.

Now when they break up, I just listen to her cry about him and don't tell her what I actually think. Because they'll just be getting back together in a few hours or the next day.

"It's okay," I say. "We're here now, and that's all that matters."

"Thanks, June," Siggy says.

"All together or none at all," I mutter.

"Don't start that again!" Imani says.

We start laughing as Siggy asks, "Don't start what?"

5

The music playing from the massive speakers onstage changes. I glance up but the stage is still empty.

The ballroom is a huge multipurpose room that can be easily reconfigured for different uses. There's even a semi-circular balcony above the entryway, accessed from the third floor. For the con, on the main floor of the ballroom there's a massive, tall stage that's been erected in the rear center of the room, opposite the main doors.

Next to me Siggy is trying to scoot her chair to the left a bit. She grunts with the effort.

"Help me, June," she says, tugging on her seat and lunging at the same time.

"What are you doing?" I ask.

"We're sardines. I'm just trying to get a teeny bit more room."

I try to scooch my chair in the opposite direction.

"It won't work." Imani points at the row of chairs in front of us. All the seats are those fancy, cushioned metal kind that stack.

I still don't see why they won't move.

"What?" I ask Imani.

"See the clips?"

Then I do see them, on the back legs of the chairs in front of us: locking clips that allow convention center workers to place the chairs in rows that make it impossible to spread out and ruin the carefully laid-out aisles.

"Sorry, Siggy, looks like we're trapped," I say.

Siggy huffs in frustration but soon gets over it as the music gets louder. We crane our necks trying to see if anyone is getting ready to walk out.

Onstage there's a sofa and two easy chairs, talk show style. Behind them the stage is decorated with rubble, and even a rusted-out car chassis.

Zombie apocalypse set dressing.

At the side edges of the stage, long black curtains hang behind freestanding chain-link barriers. The chain link isn't anchored to the floor, and it doesn't run all the way from the stage edge to the wall, but the fencing gets the point across: behind the curtains is off-limits.

Behind the car chassis and rubble is another huge black curtain pulled closed along the back of the stage. Hanging in front of it, above the scenery, is the massive video screen. Since we arrived in the hall, it's simply been playing a repeating slow-motion reel of the stars of *Human Wasteland*, dressed as their characters, turning to or away from the camera, looking heroic, stoic, and some other word that rhymes with "-oic," probably.

And sweaty.

There's no air-conditioning in the ZA.

The lights flicker, then dim, and the screen immediately cuts to the main character, the army ranger Captain Cliff Stead, played by actor James Cooper. He's handsome in a grown-up way, with a strong jaw, intense eyes, and beautiful brown skin. His hair was in a military buzz cut when the first season started. On the show he's searching for his family, but he's managed to cobble together a ragtag group of followers, including my favorite, Clay, who's been out looking for his own dad.

The audience screams raw-throated approval as Cliff speaks.

It's the scene from the first episode, the one when the characters first realized what odds they were facing.

"I may not know how this happened," Cliff says, his voice intense as he looks around at the others in his group. "Hell, I don't know what those things are or if they're everywhere. It doesn't make any sense, but it's our reality now."

His jaw tightens and he glances at Clay, who's looking up at him with luminous green eyes.

Hunter was so cute even then.

He's gotten taller and cuter in the past two seasons.

Cliff drops his eyes in shame. "I don't know anything. I don't even know where my son is."

He swipes at his mouth, a pulling motion, like he's trying to pull off worry, trying to wipe away fear.

He looks up, and a new determination is in his eyes.

"But I know one thing. I know what I'm gonna do." He looks around to the others. "I'm gonna fight."

In the ballroom, the audience whoops a *hell yeah!* sounding yell.

Clay steps forward, the first of the group to reply. "Me too." He looks around at the others. "We have to fight together. Or end alone."

The audience cheers a *damn straight!* kind of cheer.

Cliff looks at Clay, and gives him a tight, proud nod, as the others all promise to fight.

Then the scene cuts, and I realize it's a compilation of greatest hits, Clay's best scenes over the first three seasons.

I scream louder than anyone.

The new scene is when I went from thinking "He's cute" to "He's the most precious cinnamon roll and must be protected." And, in my opinion, it's the best episode of the second season, when Clay goes rogue against Cliff's orders. Clay's committed to doing his shift as perimeter guard, even though Cliff told him not to, because Clay wasn't looking so hot. Because he was sick! But he was just too damn stubborn to accept his own helplessness, and he didn't want to be just a kid, so he went anyway. And while he was out there on patrol he thought he heard a child calling for help, so he started searching the woods, going farther and farther out, sweating and shaking and just a mess, and what he didn't realize was, his fever was so high he was having auditory hallucinations.

And. AND, AND!

The child he heard crying in the woods turns out to be himself. So when he finds this bedraggled bundle in the woods, you think, oh sweet lord, it's a zombie. He's going to die because he's so sick and he's not thinking right, ohmygoooooooood—

And then he touches the thing and turns it over and he sees a little kid and it's HIM.

And the little kid that's him says, "Why did you leave me?"

And that's how we start to get an idea about his backstory: That the dad he's been searching for all this time maybe left him? Or something worse? We don't know; it's one of the big mysteries of the show.

The scene cuts to when Clay was accidentally shot while he was trying to get back to camp. The newbie guard on duty stammers apologies as Cliff runs down to the boy (fortunately only winged by the bullet).

Cliff puts pressure on the wound, murmuring, "It's okay, son. I'm here."

And omg, *my heart*.

The next clip is Clay and Sugar, his short-lived love interest. I mean that literally. She was a zombie by the end of her second episode.

Tragedy follows Clay Clarke, I'm telling you.

Clay and Sugar kiss tentatively over heartbreaking music. Then it cuts to him crying, whispering, "I love you," to her dead, post-dead, post-zombie-transformation-and-now-dead-dead body.

It's the zombie apocalypse. Falling in love is the most ridiculous thing you can do.

After the scene with Sugar, it's a kick-ass compilation of Clay's zombie kills, or his big moments when he had to step up, to become a leader, even when he's just a kid, and nobody thinks he can do anything. But he does, he proves himself again and again. There's the clip where he breaks into the veterinary office to get the antibiotics, then as a zombie is coming at him, Clay just whirls and stabs it in the eye, straight up. *Crunch*.

He's so cool.

Then it's a scene where Clay's running, sliding under a parked eighteen-wheeler, and moments later there's shuffling zombie feet all around him and it's intense. It's so intense, but you can't always fight.

The lights come up, and Michaela Robinson walks out onstage. The bright blue of her dress pops under the stage lights and against the dark brown of her skin. Her signature long dreadlocks are pulled into a low ponytail.

Michaela's the host of the post-show that airs every week right after *Human Wasteland*. She's perhaps the biggest fan out of all of us, completely freaking out over every surprise story development, and talking fan-theories at length with the cast or show writers she has on every week.

We all scream in excitement and welcome.

"Hello, Senoybia!" Michaela yells into the walk-around mic. "You lucky town! How many locals are here?"

We scream, and it's a vocal, super-excited minority. Most people are from neighboring towns, or even Atlanta.

"Yeah! I see you! I think the whole town is here today!"

We cheer again, and I spot Blair, sitting front and center in the third row, the VIP reserved section.

Ugh.

But once I see her it's hard not to. So I reflexively look to see who's sitting next to her. On one side it's an older guy I don't recognize, and on the other side it's a lady.

Huh.

I wonder where Scott—

Nope. Nope. No.

I'm about to see *Hunter Sterling*. I am not thinking about Blair and Scott.

"You've just seen the highlights of one of my favorite

characters, and he must be yours, too, because here you are! And so without further ado—let's just bring him out. Ladies and gentlemen, and others . . ." She winks out at us, and since we got such good seats we can see it, but even the people in the back can see it, too, because there's a camera stand in the middle of the ballroom, broadcasting a simulcast close-up onto the huge screen hanging over the stage.

"Please give a wake-the-dead welcome to HUNTER! STERLING!" Michaela yells.

Rock music plays, heavy guitars and snapping percussion, and he walks out, and oh my lord, he's so gorgeous. I mean it. How is it legal for anyone to be that good-looking? It shouldn't be possible.

Unconsciously, I sigh, an actual cooing, silly damn sigh, but I can't help it and honestly? There's kinda a quiet whooshing sound, and I don't think I imagined it, so we're all doing it. All sighing, or catching our breath, or just gasping maybe.

We're thirsty. For oxygen.

Hunter is impossibly gorgeous. His skin is white and his hair and eyebrows are nearly jet black. His eyelashes are so thick it's practically indecent. He's got a lanky slouch, and he moves with this amazing, boyish looseness. The kind of movement that is spontaneous but looks like a pose for a magazine shoot.

Hunter stops a few times as he crosses the stage, holding

up a hand to acknowledge us as we scream our heads off, and I swear to God he looks right at me, and he's smiling that gorgeous half smirk that always manages to look both a little shy and completely sexy, and would you look at his cheekbones? And his jaw? And his light-green-hazel eyes? And I grab Siggy's and Imani's hands and we scream our heads off some more.

"He looked right at you!" Imani yells in my ear.

"HOTNESS!" Siggy shrieks at the stage, but Hunter has moved over to the sofa, so he probably can't hear her.

He gives a couple more waves, then sits down. Michaela hands him a mic.

"Thanks, thank you," Hunter says to us. So, we scream some more.

Michaela waits a moment, then she starts speaking over the screams, and everyone gets quiet quickly, so as not to miss a thing.

"Here we are, and this is your first session, and this is your first fan con, too, is that right?"

"Yeah." Hunter smiles out at us and it's like he's apologizing, showing us his nervousness, and that's the quality I love about him as an actor, and in his role as Clay, because he's got this openness, this vulnerability.

It comes through, even when he's stabbing a zombie in the eye with a screwdriver.

"I mean, aside from Comic-Con, which the show does a whole big thing for, but like this? No, I haven't."

He waves a hand, and I know exactly what he means.

I want to tell him this is my first fan convention, too. We have that in common.

But of course, what Michaela means is that all the other actors on the show, and tons of actors on other shows or from movies with big fandoms, well, they do this actual circuit of fan conventions. They just rake in the money, from autographs and photo sessions, and selling headshots. It's wild to think about all the people they meet.

But it's awesome to think about all those people, too, all over the country, who love the same things that you do. Or who love other things, *their things*, as much as you love your thing. God bless fandom, forever and ever. Amen.

"This is your first time to do meet and greets? To do photo sessions?" Michaela asks.

"Yeah, so go easy on me, okay?" Hunter says, with that little, shy half smile, to us, and I promise myself right then and there, I promise myself in my heart, that I will *be cool* when I have my photo op. I will.

It's got to be a *Special Memory*, after all.

6

Michaela and Hunter have a little back-and-forth onstage about the show, about the fandom, about the best-part-of-the-show-so-far, and then Michaela says, "Okay, does anyone have a question?"

And like a jackrabbit, I'm up, along with people all over the ballroom, even while Michaela and Hunter continue talking onstage.

"Attagirl, get in there!" Imani whispers as I climb over her lap.

Siggy whisper-cheer-screams for me as I'm climbing over laps like a hurdler, then I'm in the aisle hustling to the line already forming.

I actually do have a question—it's about something it felt like Hunter was almost going to say in an interview, but the interviewer moved on before he said it. The interviewer had asked why Hunter identifies with his character so much. Hunter had started in, his usual boilerplate answer about Clay's vulnerability and toughness, but then he started to look contemplative and he said, "Clay's a searcher, you know? And I feel like I'm searching, too."

And then the interviewer *did not ask* what Hunter is searching for! So that's my question. That's what I want to know. And I feel . . . an affinity toward that unanswered question. To the idea of searching, and to Hunter as a searcher, because sometimes I just get this yearning inside. Like a longing. Like I'm missing a part of myself, almost. This big, nameless feeling like there's something out there in the world waiting just for me, somehow. And if I could figure out what it is then I wouldn't be scared that I won't ever find it. And I won't be as scared about graduation, or what's next, or any of it. Or if I still get scared sometimes, it won't be as big, the not knowing, because I'll know about this other part. This part that's mine.

Also, and this might be corny, okay, I admit that, but I feel like by asking my question, maybe I'll let Hunter know that I recognized *him* in that moment, you know? That he's not just an actor, not just a show pony, but a person with something to say.

I don't know. It's ridiculous.

I still want to know the answer.

I'm the sixth person in line, but that's okay, I saw online they usually take at least ten questions. And I also know from watching the sessions with some of the other actors that most of the questions are either about their personal lives, their pets (Hunter has a dog, a super-cute mutt named Best Rex, so I bet someone asks about him), or it's not a question at all and is instead a fan wanting to talk about a show theory or something.

Okay, yes, I spent a lot of time researching for this. Like, a lot. Hours, even. My dad said I should use my powers for good but he was just kidding, really.

Since I'm the sixth in line that means I'm almost guaranteed to get to ask my question!

Then I see a second mic in the next aisle, and I realize if they alternate, and if they stop at ten, I won't get to ask my question

But maybe, just maybe . . .

Michaela starts cuing the stagehands holding the mics, and I'm listening but it's kind of hard to hear over the thuds of my galloping heart. I'm inching forward, and no one has asked my question, and then they get to the eighth person.

And she ruins it for everyone.

"Hi, I love you. My question is . . . can I get a hug?"

The reaction of the audience is split, one part groan of annoyance, and one part get it, girl.

Hunter laughs and his hand comes up and pushes the hair down over his eyes, a nervous gesture, but he says, "Sure." He hands his mic to Michaela and hops off the stage and trots up the aisle. The girl steps out in front of the mic a few steps, and Hunter is there, just a few feet in front of me, and he gives her a hug, a little awkward, bending down, but he smiles and he doesn't hold her like he really resents it, he just gives her a quick squeeze, and she asks to take a selfie, and he does and—

Fortune favors the bold, I guess.

I am so jealous of her. And so mad at her.

Hunter trots back up to the stage and everyone is screaming, and I see Hunter say something to Michaela, and he's smiling, but then Michaela says something about what a great crowd we've been, and thanks so much for opening the con, Hunter. Hunter says, my pleasure, thanks, guys! And he waves and scoots off that stage fast before anyone can ask for another hug.

It's over. I didn't get to ask my question. That's it, there won't be another chance. Photo ops move so fast I won't be able to ask then, and besides I don't want to monopolize the time because Siggy and Imani and I pooled all our money together for it.

I didn't get to ask my question.

I still feel a little shaky from the adrenaline dump, and a little empty like a balloon drifting down to the floor.

Onstage Michaela is saying don't go far, the next event is a panel featuring some writers of the show, and after that is the zombie makeup team, don't miss it—

But all around me people are grabbing their things and making their way out, brushing past those of us who rushed out to get in line and are still standing in the aisle.

Imani and Siggy are making their way toward me. Imani has my mini backpack slung over one shoulder.

I'm struggling to keep from feeling furious at that girl, wondering if the session would have gone on longer, if I would have been able to ask my question, and also wondering if he smelled good and if that girl can die happy now that she got a selfie and a hug.

Ugh.

"Ugh," Siggy says as they reach me.

"Ugh." Imani hands over my backpack and starts to lead the way out. "That's so unfair!"

"Yep," I say, but they know how I feel already; they heard me practice my question all week.

We step out into the airy hallway, and file onto the down escalator.

"Okay, we're not going to let that ruin our day but can I just say, that was so much BS." Imani runs a hand over her side-sweep of wavy hair.

"It was," I agree. "I'm just gonna be in my emotions about it for a little bit more."

"We still have the photo op," Siggy says. "Maybe you can ask your question then."

"Yeah," Imani says.

"That's for all of us, though," I say. "It's okay, I promise."

I say it because I can see that they want to push the issue. They want to swear that they don't mind and I should ask my question at the photo op.

But the photo op isn't about me asking my question. It's just a quick moment, to memorialize our day, and beyond that our friendship (and how much we love Hunter and *Human Wasteland*), and I'm not going to change that.

"The photo op is going to be great!" I continue. "I can't wait until we're all there together."

We step off the escalator and walk forward, past the floor-to-ceiling exterior window wall and around the volcanic rock waterfalls to the bottleneck forming at the center set of exhibit hall doors.

"I just hope I can act cool during it, and not become a complete dork," I say.

"You *are* cool," Imani says.

"Thanks, Mom." I roll my eyes at her.

She thwaps my shoulder, laughing. "Stop that, young lady."

"June, you really are, you know." Siggy adjusts the side-tie of her jumpsuit while we wait in line. "You're cool and awesome and hilarious, too."

"Aw, stop." I feel my eyes start to well up. "You're fun and beautiful and you have such a free spirit, Siggy."

Imani gives a polite little cough. *Ahem.*

I turn to her, smiling.

"And you're absolutely brilliant and loyal and your convictions are such a force for good, Imani," I tell her.

Imani loops an arm around me.

"June, you've got the best sense of humor, you're so smart no matter what you say, and you have the biggest heart of anybody I ever met."

"Stop, I'm gonna cry," I say.

"Too late," Siggy says.

"What are we gonna do next fall?" I ask.

"I don't want to think about it," Siggy says.

"We'll talk all the time," Imani reassures us.

Siggy swipes her fingers under her eyes. "Aw hell, why don't I ever have any Kleenex?"

Imani hands us tissues out of her purse and even has to dab at her own eyes.

We all stand in line, in our little trio, dabbing at our eyes and honking our noses and saying *I love you guys so much* and *Stop talking, okay? I'm still crying* and Siggy starts humming the theme from *The Golden Girls* and that gets us over the emotional hump.

We inch forward, waiting to show our badges to the door guards. Behind us, there's a ruckus, a person shouting "Whoa!" and laughter.

I turn and there are two people in head-to-toe hazmat suits pushing through the crowd, holding up some kind of scanner, sweeping it at people.

Imani laughs, and she lifts her phone for some pictures.

"Weirdos," Siggy laughs.

"No, it's cool!" I half wish I was cosplaying, but then decide I want to experience my first con as *me*.

In front of us, two zombies, a man and woman, sink a little when they see the hazmat guys.

"Ruh-roh, they're coming for us," the man zombie says, smiling at me. I guess because he heard me say the cosplayers were cool.

"Don't let them get you, babe," the woman zombie replies. Her makeup is so cool. There's a gaping bite mark in her neck, her skin looks positively necrotic, and her eyes are clouded with milky cataracts.

"Wow, you guys look *amazing*," I say. "Can we take a picture with you?"

"Absolutely!" she says, so we get in the exhibit hall and slide to the side. I ask a man to take our photo, and the three of us act scared while the man and woman strike hungry-zombie poses at us.

"Thanks! Have a great day!" Imani says. The man groans and makes these wet choking noises, and the woman lets her head fall forward as she starts shuffling away.

The man stumbles after her, takes her arm, and steers her down the first aisle on the right.

They hold hands, and stumble-shuffle away. People all around are laughing good-naturedly, taking pictures of the zombie couple.

"True love, you guys," Siggy says. "Till death do they part. And then not even then."

"Those sweet kids. I hope everything works out for them," I say.

"They're already dead," Imani says. "What's the worst thing that could happen?"

7

We start wandering into the center of the massive exhibit hall, just wandering at first, then I remember our schedule and turn at the middle aisle to cross to what will be the biggest celebrity autograph line.

"Wow, I feel like a rat in a maze," Imani says.

"Sure, but an *awesome* rat in an *amazing* maze!" I say.

"Just as long as we don't get shocked or anything," Imani says.

"Bad things happen in mazes," Siggy groans in a creaky voice.

I've never seen so many T-shirts, fan art posters and paintings, jewelry, and 1940s-style pinup dresses and pleated skirts made of comic-book-printed fabrics. There are books and comics tables, and so much more, we've barely scratched the surface of everything there is for sale.

The aisles are separated not just by the rows of tables and shelving and display racks in each booth, but also by tall black curtains that act like a wall between rows of merchandise.

On the *ZombieCon!* map the layout of the exhibit hall was styled to look like the Red Cross symbol, but with one wide center aisle bisecting multiple rows.

In the middle of the exhibit hall where the center rows meet the center aisle, there's a hub of sorts. It's a large, elevated square stage surrounded by folding-chair rows and food and beverage carts with tall round standing-tables. When I find the hub, I can turn left to cross to the left wall of the hall, where the biggest star of the show will be for most of the day. The other show actors take shifts at nearby signing tables only, and the less famous, B-movie actors are at a separate signing area called Autograph Alley, which is on the opposite side of the exhibit hall.

But I know from my research that the line for the lead actor, James Cooper, will only get longer as the day goes on, and since we don't want to spend all day waiting for one autograph, our second stop of the day, and our first stop in the exhibit hall, is to go see if the line for James is still doable or not.

We reach the hub. On the elevated stage are a few armchairs and stools, as well as a black-tablecloth-covered table with a mixing board, mics, and headsets. Throughout the day, fandom podcasters are going to be recording new shows with the cast and crew of *Human Wasteland* as well as the other horror genre actors and authors at *ZombieCon!*

There's a schedule posted on a stand beside the stairs up to the hub stage. I pause to look at it in spite of myself. The podcaster schedule didn't get finalized until this morning.

"Keep moving, June," Siggy says.

"I am, I just want to make sure when to avoid it here."

Scott's show is on the schedule, in under an hour, at 9:00 a.m.—*Wasteland Stans*. Good to know.

Yep.

Good to know.

Feels good to know.

Yeah, knowing is great.

It doesn't at all feel like my heart is shriveling into a dusty, dry bag of sawdust. Sawdust and shame.

Nope. Not at all.

I force a smile at the others.

Scott's podcast doesn't have a big following, but he scraped together the money to be on the roster and talked his way onto the stage.

Bully for Scott. I never said he wasn't charming.

"Screw him." Imani takes my arm again and turns me toward the next stop.

Siggy takes six steps in the opposite direction before realizing she's going the wrong way and rushing to catch up with us.

"His obnoxious show would totally suck if it hadn't been

for all your ideas," Siggy pants as she draws even with us.

"I'm not even thinking about it," I lie.

We hustle across the hall to James's signing area.

When we arrive he's already up there signing. His security stands nearby, along with his assistants, taking cash, it's all cash only, for the autograph. And they're selling headshots and production stills, for anyone who hasn't brought a specific thing for him to sign.

James's autograph tables are on a platform, so we can watch as each autograph seeker approaches him.

Even though I know I'm here? And I know he's here? I know that they're all here?

I still experience an adrenaline dump. My heart judders and I have to take a few deep breaths.

James Cooper is right there. Captain Cliff Stead is right there. He's wearing sunglasses indoors, which looks more cool than odd, and expensive-looking jeans and a tight black T-shirt.

Siggy makes a little chirrup and I know she's thinking the same thing.

He's right there.

"What do we think of the line?" I ask.

"Totally doable, let's get in there," Imani says, her eyes bright with interest and excitement. James Cooper is the main actor Imani wanted to meet, because Captain Cliff

Stead means so much to her. He's African American and the star of the show, and Cliff Stead the character is not only the leader of the group of survivors, but he's also a deeply human, principled person.

Imani leads the way into the line, which starts inching slowly forward.

We start checking our hair and adjusting our clothes like a trio of nervous birds preening. Imani pulls down the cuffs of her coral jacket and smooths her white tunic. Siggy fluffs the blonde sheet of her hair and checks the legs of her blue jumpsuit. I pull at the scoop neck of my olive shirt, billowing it out so it falls just right.

Onstage James laughs, and man, he's got a great smile that just lights up his whole face. Dazzling.

"Okay, okay." Siggy lifts her hands up and takes a deep breath. Then she exhales and pushes her hands down.

"Y'all are adorable," Imani says, smiling at us. She cocks a leg, resting a sequin-sneakered foot, toe-down, like she's not nervous at all.

"Don't act too cool for school," Siggy says. "You know you're excited."

Imani cocks an eyebrow.

"Give yourself over to the feeling," I urge her. "Fandom freakout. One of us! One of us!"

Apart from hanging out with us, Imani's very favorite

things are: 1) listening to the first responder scanners on the Code Blue app and 2) watching C-SPAN political broadcasts and commentary shows. She'll probably go on to become a DA or congresswoman or something, I am not kidding.

Which will be great for all of us! But sometimes I worry about her. I don't want her to lose her sense of fun in Being Serious.

Imani's straight face cracks as a huge smile spreads across her face.

"You guys," she whisper-screams. "That's James Cooper!"

We whisper-scream back.

As the line moves forward, my view of James gets better, and he's actually so much better looking in person. How is that possible? Especially with this hideous fluorescent lighting?

Maybe it's because he's smiling at each autograph seeker, and doesn't seem rushed at all, and he just seems so nice.

Also because he's movie-star gorgeous, of course, with a lean, muscular build, and when he smiles, man, those *dimples*.

He's actually hugging people across the table.

"Quick survey: Will you ask for a hug?" I ask.

"Yes!" Siggy yelps.

"Yes!" Imani says.

"I want to know what he smells like," Siggy says.

"Ew," Imani says.

"I'm conducting a study," Siggy says.

"Double ew."

"Smell is an underrated sense," Siggy says.

"You smell like thirst and desperation," I say.

"Whatever!" Siggy gives me a play-shove. "At least I didn't go dry-mouthed when Hunter got onstage."

"Quick survey: who wants to change the subject?" Imani says. But she's just playing with us.

As we draw closer to the front of the line, a flock of butterflies flutters in my chest. A herd? A gaggle?

What's the collective noun for a group of butterflies?

I think it should be an anticipation. An anticipation of butterflies nestles in my chest.

While we've been creeping forward in line, a few VIP pass holders have used their exclusive cattle chute to jump to the front. But so far it has only been a few of them, so it's easy to ignore it.

Until Blair walks up.

We all see her at the same time, but no one says anything.

It's petty, but I don't want to watch her get her autograph or anything, so I put my back to the stage.

There's an uncomfortable moment of silence, and I can't help it, it hurts again. It shouldn't. It's been over a week already, basically, and it's not like Scott and I were in love or anything. He was a guy I was dating, he was *a* boyfriend, not *my* boyfriend.

Still, I feel poisoned by the hurt, and by my anger at Blair.

"I should just forgive her already," I murmur. "I feel guilty that I can't."

"You're entitled to your feelings," Imani says. "Even your pain." Her voice is gentle, accepting.

"But I haven't even let her explain."

"What could she say?" Siggy's voice is firm. "It wasn't confusing. We all knew what he meant to you."

"I know, but—"

"He lives thirty minutes away, for God's sake." Siggy shakes her head. "She had to *work* to go behind your back. It's not like they were in the same class every day."

It hurts so much. Even though Blair and I have always had a weird-intense friendship, the kind with sparks and sharp edges at times, we've always been close, too.

We've been friends forever.

And friends don't just date the same guy their friend is dating, even if their friend and the guy aren't exclusive. It's an unwritten rule of friendship that everyone knows. You don't just date the guy that your friend has told you about, breathlessly, rhapsodizing, reading aloud her text conversations with him, so excited and so clueless.

I know I've played my part in our little friendship spats

before now. My mom always says there are three sides to a story: mine, yours, and the truth.

But maybe that's just a saying suckers tell themselves so they feel safer about all the other people in the world.

I keep trying to tell myself I'm over it. That I'm better off without both of them. But the hurt, ashamed feeling won't go away.

It's a total zombie. Because the feeling just keeps coming back alive and will not stay dead—as much as I want it to.

"She's going now," Imani says.

I don't look. Next to me, Siggy holds up a hand, a reflexive wave back to Blair.

Habits die hard, I guess. Even though we're all mad at her, we all miss her, too. I know. I live with myself, so I miss talking to Blair, too. I miss her like a limb.

I don't like the way that feels, acknowledging that.

Surely I don't miss her like a limb. More like an appendage. A toe. Or a finger.

I don't miss her that much at all.

The line creeps forward and we finally do manage to forget about Blair and Scott again, and talk about the show. We rank our top five episodes across the three seasons that have aired so far. Siggy practically dances in place when she talks about the new characters, Hugh and Shella, played by Linus Sheppard and Annie Blaze and who Siggy ships like

FedEx. They were added to the last three episodes of season three, and a huge fan campaign has sprung up during the hiatus to demand more storylines for them.

Before I know it, we've reached the front of the line.

I thought long and hard about what I wanted to get the actors to sign, and who I would pay for an autograph. To be honest, most of the money I saved over the summer went to the ticket and the photo op. But I have a bit extra and I can pick and choose who I want. I just can't also afford to buy their headshots.

So I got all my fan magazines, some archive glue, and one of those little photo scrapbooks from the hobby store, and I made a collage page for each actor I know I want to get. And I left blank pages next to each one, so they can sign there, and it'll be perfect.

"We're next," Siggy says.

Imani and I let out muffled shrieks.

Imani buys a black-and-white headshot of James Cooper, and so does Siggy. I get out my autograph book, and we wait patiently as the lady in front of us gets an autograph, gets a hug, and gives him a stream of things she's brought in gift bags, and gets another hug.

When she's finally done, she turns and pumps both arms in the air, like she's just finished a marathon.

Then it's Imani's turn, and without thinking, we all kind of press forward together.

Also Imani is squeezing my hand so tight I think she's forgotten she's doing it, so she just tugs me along with her.

James smiles, and omigod.

He is really, really hot for a dad-aged guy.

"You all are all together, huh?" His voice is rough like an old quilt, okay, or something like that. A warm burr-type noise. Scratchy but warm. Like a thistle in a patch of sunny grass. I'm thinking about it too much.

"Yes," Imani says.

Siggy nods. "We're best friends."

I smile. I feel like my face is all teeth, weird, dry teeth.

"Okay, well, hi," James says.

"Good morning," Imani says.

"Hey," Siggy says.

"I love you," I blurt out. Blood rushes into my cheeks.

I want to sink into the floor.

"Thank you, I love you, too," James says, easily, fluently, because he does love his fans, anyone can see it. And he unleashes that brilliant smile at us again. Then he's reaching out over the table, and Imani automatically sticks out her hand like she's going to shake his, like this is some kind of receiving line at a wedding, or like she's going up for a job, and he doesn't see it because he's already leaning over the table and he gives her a hug.

It mostly doesn't look awkward, even though one of her

arms is basically trapped against her chest and the other is patting the side of his ribs.

James leans back and asks Imani if she wants him to inscribe her picture, which is definitely not something he does for everyone—and she says yes and spells her name. He chats with her as he signs and then hands the photo back to her.

Then he turns to Siggy, who lets out this high-pitched giggle the minute he leans over the table to hug her.

Siggy octopus-wraps her arms across his broad shoulders and presses her nose into the collar of his shirt.

Then he has let go and she's talking to him as he's signing, but I can't hear what she's saying because all I can hear is my own hyperventilations and my heartbeat.

Then it's my turn. Imani and Siggy are standing just a few steps past the center of the table, waiting for me without going down the steps.

"Hello," James says, smiling at me.

"Hi there, hello, howyadoin, hey," I reply, and want to clap my hand over my mouth.

Not. What. I. Practiced.

He leans forward and I lean forward and the table is between us but we're still hugging and really, it's perfect, it's the perfect scenario. Have I ever hugged before? Has a hug ever felt so warm? So personal? Even with the rounded edge of a table pressing into my thighs?

Get a grip, June.

I've let go before I realize I forgot to notice what he smells like, but everything's moving too fast, so I look down and he's signing my autograph book, across from the page with the collage of his character, and he's flipping through my book, smiling at the actors and actresses I've made pages for, I guess, 'cause he laughs and the next moment he turns and says something to one of his assistants, and the guy nods and starts messing with the tables.

"You and your friends want a picture?" James says, and I swear to God he holds out a hand at me, like a prince inviting me onto the ballroom floor, or like a hero saying *come with me if—*

"I want to live!" I say.

Oh. My. God.

James doesn't bat an eye, that I can see, I mean, I'm sort of understanding those sunglasses now. He just gestures to the gap in the tables that the assistant made by pulling one back.

Imani lets out a cheer and hands over her phone to the assistant. Siggy makes a noise like a hiccup crossed with a sneeze, like Pikachu, and I thankfully don't know what noise I make as James Cooper drapes one arm around Siggy and me and places his other around Imani and we all smile for the photo.

Then we're saying thank you, I tell him I love him again, and before we're even down the steps we're yelling and looking at the picture.

I'm doing the chin thing but at least my eyes are open.

Imani sends us the picture and we all post it, and basically write a hymn of adoration on the spot for James Cooper, how nice he was, how lovely, how very sexy, and how we always liked him, didn't we? But we didn't KNOW before but now we KNOW and so we are going to need to rewatch some of his best episodes this week, right?

As we talk, we're walking to the next stop on the itinerary, the main antagonist's autograph line, but when we get there, Cuellar's line is already too long for me. Especially if I'm going to get another autograph I really want and have a chance to look at some of the merchandise.

Besides, he's no James Cooper.

Siggy and Imani agree. If they didn't I would wait with them, but we're all a bit too hyped to stand in another line anyway. We start walking through the rows, zigzagging our way to Autograph Alley, stopping to look at all the amazing stuff on sale as we go.

Siggy buys a Nordic-looking tarot card deck. Imani buys a *Human Wasteland* official T-shirt and an ornate crown for Tishala's next photo shoot. I buy a necklace with a teeny bell jar suspended from it. Inside is a miniature scene of a tombstone, grass, tree, flowers, a bench, and a crow sitting on the bench.

The exhibit hall is getting more and more crowded; you can feel a surge of excitement, moving in the air above us like heat lightning.

At the bottom of one of the rows, a girl is sitting on the ground like she collapsed there, a spill of bags and posters strewn around her. A small crowd has gathered to watch or help, offering water, a hand up, a tissue for her very, very bloody nose.

"I'm fine," the girl says, voice muffled from behind the Kleenex. "I just got a little light-headed."

A *ZombieCon!* employee arrives with a paramedic. They crouch next to the girl.

"Let's keep moving," Siggy says. She gets queasy about blood, and it does feel weird staring so we ease past the girl and start down the next aisle.

After we get a little farther Imani turns and points at a table. A framed picture stands on a wire rack. In the picture, an anime character rocks back with a shooting nosebleed. It's an image I've seen before in anime and manga to show something like how that character's mind is being blown by the beauty of another person.

"I know who that girl just met," Imani says. "James Cooper."

8

Autograph Alley, where the B and C movie stars will sign for most of the day, is at the edge of the exhibit hall. The alley is opposite a wall of windows. They're not as big as the ones in the atrium, and they are tinted more, but they still let in enough light to break up the fluorescent glare.

I realize my eyes are actually tired when I look at the windows. James Cooper's indoor sunglasses make more sense now.

We stop at a vending machine tucked in the corner for some drinks and then walk to a cluster of upholstered chairs set against the windows.

Imani flops into a chair.

"How am I so tired already?"

"'Cause you got up at five a.m.?" Siggy asks.

"Lightweights," I tease them.

"Isn't your next stop just right there?" Imani asks, pointing down the Alley. An unbroken line of tables covered in black tablecloths face the windows. Celebrities stand behind the tables, talking in pairs or small groups, or interacting with fans. Every four or five feet a different *ZombieCon!* banner hangs against the curtain wall behind the tables, showing who the celebrities are and what they are famous for, in horror specifically, in case you didn't already know.

"Yeah. She's gonna be down there somewhere," I say, but I don't try to pick her out of the motley assortment of people standing or sitting behind the tables. For one, that doesn't really feel like the right way to see one of your faves for the first time, just squinting at a legend from a cushy chair, for God's sake. For another, I'd rather just not anticipate her until I'm standing right there.

Janet O'Shea, scream queen extraordinaire, Mother of Zombies, and one of the original stars of the first, most iconic zombie movie of all time, and also the first zombie movie I ever saw: *Fight the Dead.*

She's here!

Siggy flops into the chair next to Imani. "Why don't you go get her autograph, and we'll wait here." She twists off the cap of her bottle.

"Good idea," Imani says. "I'm gonna send Tish a picture of her crown. She's going to love me forever. What should I ask for in return?"

"Less photo shoots?" Siggy offers, but we all know that Imani actually treasures their sister time together, helping Tishala get just the right image.

"Maybe she'll have to clean our bathroom for a month?" Imani says.

"Bingo," I say.

"Where is Tishala, anyway?" Siggy asks Imani. "She didn't try to tag along with you at the last minute?"

Imani smiles. "Nope! Mom had my back. She offered to take Tish out on a 'girls' day.' Lunch and pedicures."

"Oh, that's sounds nice!" Siggy smiles brightly.

Imani snorts. "Well, Tish turned it into a craft store spree instead of a pedicure, and driving around looking for new locations to take pictures rather than lunch."

"I'm guessing your mom doesn't really mind," I say, and Imani smiles and shakes her head.

"That girl is a mess," she says fondly.

"Go on, June," Siggy says to me. "We'll stay here and I can check in with Mark. Win-win."

I would feel braver if my friends came with me, though.

"Go ahead," Siggy says, smiling. "You're going to love her."

Which is a funny thing to say, but exactly right, because I already do love her. Even though her character is mostly the quintessential helpless-girl, and even though she doesn't make it through the zombie apocalypse (none of them do, that's the way it goes), she at least makes it through the night, holed up with a bunch of desperate strangers in a lonely gas station.

And she's one of the only female characters in early horror who isn't a Madonna or a whore. And let's not get me started on that horrible trope, which makes me so mad, and is a shortcut lazy storytellers take. As if a woman's value is reduced to if she has sex or how often. Ugh.

Which is another reason why I love Janet O'Shea in *Fight the Dead* so very, very much.

She's not a mother, not a lover, not a daughter. At the start of the movie she is shown on the phone, telling someone (presumably her boyfriend) that she's not pregnant. It's just a quick moment, but absolutely groundbreaking. After that, once the zombie apocalypse starts, she's just a scared girl with big blonde helmet hair, looking out of her depth always, but holding in there somehow. Realistically. Authentically.

And she's one of the last ones to die. Which is pretty good if you're trapped in the zombie apocalypse. It's all you can hope for, really.

Fight the Dead came out in 1968, when Janet was twenty-one. That makes her kind of old now; she's in her seventies I guess, but in her pictures on the *ZombieCon!* website she looks spry. Or whatever word you use for a cute older lady. Like a fairy godmother. Except thin and with a cute pixie-cut hairstyle.

I leave my girls lounging and looking at their phones,

and I walk down the one-sided row—windows all on one side, tables on the other.

If I'm being completely honest, I'm a little scared to go talk to Janet O'Shea by myself. It's not that I think she's going to bite me or anything (har!) and it's not that I think she'll be mean.

It's just . . . I feel safer. I feel stronger. I feel like a better person with my friends around me. Because they're so awesome! And if they like me, it shows I'm all right, right?

Or at least it camouflages how not-cool I actually am, comparatively.

Imani and Siggy, and Blair, too, before everything happened; they all hated it if I'd say that sort of thought out loud.

But it's the way I feel.

Ugh, next year is going to suck so hard. How am I supposed to just start over? Sixth grade was bad enough, when we were split into different teams, and somehow I was the only one who got on the Cool Cats team, and they all got Flamingos.

My feet keep walking, and I'm going down the aisle, and even though there are other people here, well, it's just not that crowded, and I start to feel bad for walking past these other actors. It's like they're animals in cages, on display. And when I make the mistake of glancing their way, I get glimpses of friendly smiles and tables with headshots and Sharpies, and these floor-to-ceiling banners telling you who they are and why they're important to the horror movie world.

I start saying hi and giving these little apologetic waves, which I hope sort of encapsulate that I think they're all awesome but I'm just a kid and don't have enough money for all their autographs.

There she is. No one is waiting at her table. Janet O'Shea stands behind it, cute white-and-gray hair in a Peter Pan cut, and a smile that reaches her eyes. She's tiny! She's sweet, I can just tell. A booth-wide banner hangs behind her, with her black-and-white picture from *Fight the Dead* looking out from her most famous scene: when she first sees the zombies in the park. And her obnoxious brother makes fun of her fears; when she sees this shambling form coming toward them, he tells her it's a wino. He makes fun of her! Saying, "There's no stopping them, Vivian!" and then *CRUNCH* he gets bit.

Serves him right. Listen to your little sister's gut, am I right? Women have more of a sense of self-preservation. Our Spidey senses are just attuned to these things. To danger.

A loud bang draws my eyes to the end of the hall and the emergency exit. A skinny white man in a T-shirt and jeans is messing with the two solid aluminum doors. The doors are the kind with the long horizontal metal crash bars in the middle that you push to get the door to open.

The man works at the bar of one door with a screwdriver.

At his feet a shabby backpack with a large Mickey Mouse patch spills other tools onto the floor. He's not in a uniform, but he must be a maintenance guy.

Or something.

"Hello, dear," a woman's British voice says, and I look back at the table.

Janet O'Shea is smiling right at me.

I still turn around to look behind myself, like a fool. Ugh. Be cool, June.

Janet O'Shea's eyes are lively, like they actually sparkle.

"You're Janet O'Shea," I say.

She knows who she is, June.

I wish the earth would just open up and take me down into sweet oblivion.

"You know you're Janet O'Shea, of course," I say quickly, waving my hand.

Oh God, did that make it sound like I think she has dementia or something?

Janet O'Shea laughs.

"Yes, I suppose I do."

"I love Vivian," I say. "I love *Fight the Dead*."

"Oh good, me too." Janet O'Shea leans forward. "I don't understand it, but there's always been a faction of people who simply can't stand Vivian. They find fault with everything she does in the movie."

"I bet mostly they're men, right?" I say.

"Yes."

Honestly, who would have a problem with Vivian? She's just a girl doing her best, and she has the pragmatism to kill the jerk who gets bit at the window.

Well, okay, so jerks might take an issue with her, back in the day. Just like they did with the other lead—a black man in the sixties.

Racism and sexism, still here, still the same ugly story.

Some people just can't stand it if anyone else ever gets to be the hero.

"Well, screw them." My voice comes out firmer than I intended.

Janet laughs, and it just lights up her whole face.

Actors are something special, man. I think I finally understand what charisma is. I mean, I know Imani has it, but I also remember how she used to pick her nose in first grade when she thought no one was looking, so she has that to overcome, there.

"Screw them indeed," Janet says.

With her posh accent, it actually sounds like a pleasantry. A bit of chitchat. Like *Hello, good day. Cheerio, pip pip. Screw them indeed.*

The guy at the end of the hall is checking one of the doors, jumping at the crash bar. It won't open. He starts working on the other one.

Maybe he has to lock them both and then unlock them. To get them to open right or fix whatever the problem is.

"Would you like an autograph?" Janet O'Shea asks.

"Yes!" I yelp, and she laughs, this beautiful rich laugh like a Disney villain, except it's nice, and I think she's probably my favorite actress ever, now that I've met her.

I pull my autograph book out of my bag, and I dig out the autograph fee (less than James Cooper's but still, it's a service and she's got to pay for this booth). As I reach out to hand it to Janet, this white lady just barges up from the table next to us and pushes in front of me.

Her backpack bumps into me, knocking the bills out of my hand.

My autograph book falls open to the ground, crunching two of the pages.

"Janet O'Shea!" the woman says, but she's reading the banner and pretending to know who it is. Her lips are shiny, like they're coated in grease, not gloss, and her whole look is a bit brittle, like her demeanor.

Janet smiles. "Hello, excuse me, but I was about to autograph for . . ." She holds her hand out at me, but I step back, shaking my head so my hair falls in front of my eyes.

"It's okay," I say. "Go ahead." I bend to pick up my book.

The woman turns her chicken-grease smile at me. "Thanks!" Then she's pulling out about five collectible figurines, miniature Vivians in unopened, plastic packaging.

She slaps money on the table to cover the cost as Janet O'Shea signs her name on each.

The woman picks up the memorabilia and moves down to the next table. Without saying thanks. Or goodbye.

Janet shakes her head at me.

"She's going to sell them online. I guess that's her pre-rogative, but she's not really here as a fan, you see."

"That's cool, though, that your autograph sells the figurine better."

"I used to ask if they wanted anything inscribed, but now I just try to get it over with," Janet says. "Listen to me, I sound awful. She paid for my autograph, she got my autograph."

But I think I understand her anyway, or at least I know why I wouldn't like it. Something about it just felt gross, just a transaction, with no humans underneath.

As the autograph lady makes her way down the line, you can see that some of the actors know the drill. They don't even stop talking to each other, just take the money, count the items, sign the items.

The guy at the double doors is packing up his tools. He's dressed in a faded Nike T-shirt that shouts JUST DO IT. There are pronounced circles under his eyes, and he's unshaven; not in a deliberate way but more like he's been working too hard, and is too harried.

He doesn't really strike me as a maintenance guy, actually. He just seems . . . ill at ease. Jumpy, somehow. Hurried.

The guy drops his Mickey Mouse patch backpack, spilling screwdrivers and a water bottle, a massive sheaf of paper bound in black binder clips, and a wide, double-sided breathing mask—the kind with two filters set at either side of the mouth.

He stoops to shove his things back in his bag and then he looks up, and sees me watching him.

He makes this strange expression at me, partway between a wince and a smile, almost like an apology.

Or like guilt.

What's he doing with the doors, anyway?

"Well, she's gone now, and it's just us Vivian fans again," Janet says in a bright voice.

I turn back to Janet and smile. She helps me smooth the crunched pages of my autograph book on the table and then she signs it, remarking over the collage of Vivian. Then she asks about me, what grade I'm in, what my favorite subject is.

I love her even more, because she doesn't ask what my plans are after graduation, like everyone else does these days.

Then, because she is so cool, she offers to take a selfie with me, and doesn't even charge me for it. Then she gives me a hug.

"Do you know the thing I always loved about Vivian?"

she asks. "She wasn't a badass. She was just a girl in this world. But she trusted herself, when it came down to it."

Janet O'Shea puts her forefinger under my chin, giving it a little lift, and I don't even mind. I feel like a little kid, and I'm fine with it.

"You've got to trust yourself, all right? Trust yourself."

"I do. And when I don't, I will." And like everything I want to say, it comes out a mess, with the jumbled-up syntax of a Martian. But it makes sense to me.

And I'm going to trust that it makes sense to Janet O'Shea, too.

9

When she sees me walking back up from meeting Janet O'Shea, Siggy stands and does a little victory dance for me, pretending to spike a football on the ground, waving her knees in and out, holding up a number one finger and making a crowd-goes-wild cheering noise.

She rushes up to me, pretending to be speaking into a microphone.

"June Blue! You've just met one of your favorite actresses of all time," she says.

"Correction: my favorite actress," I say. "She's my favorite actress."

"You've just met your favorite actress ever! What are you going to do now?"

Imani butts her head over the pretend microphone.

"We're going to Disney World!" she cheers.

"If by 'going to Disney World' you mean going to another session and then a podcast, then yes," I say. "Because that's next on the schedule."

As we meander back into the exhibit hall, I show Siggy

and Imani the selfie I took with Janet, post the selfie, and show them my autograph book. Siggy says Mark was asleep when she called but happy to hear her voice (they're such dorks), and Imani says Tishala is completely in love with the crown, showed their mom the photo, and they've already started building a "look" around it.

The live podcast we want to see, *The Undead Listen*, is going to be on fifteen minutes after Scott's. If we time it right, we probably won't even see him.

Which is how I want it. Today isn't about Scott. It's about *Human Wasteland*. And zombies. And why we love to be scared by them.

I've read some articles online that say that horror trends reflect our fears as a society. How the scary movies and stories that take hold in popular culture show us something about what we are afraid of or are grappling with.

Some people say that zombies represent our fear of "the other." That zombies represent xenophobia, fear of the outside world, of being overrun by a horde intent on taking everything we have, even our lives, even our meat.

But I don't think zombies ever meant that. Or just that. Because look at the movies. I mean, just look at *Fight the Dead*.

It was made in the late sixties, in a time of huge social upheaval, and the heroes are a timid white girl and a strong black man. The dead keep coming, they have been fundamentally changed, and the two heroes hole up in an abandoned gas station with other people—and in that moment, in trying to survive the night, they have to confront each other, confront prejudice, fight to even have a say about what they should do in a life-or-death circumstance.

In the end, death doesn't even come from the zombies.

And this is what I think *Human Wasteland* understands about zombies, and about horror. What do zombies stand for? They're not even human anymore.

That's what zombies are: a loss. A loss of someone you thought you knew. More than that, a death. And then a transformation.

Into a monster.

I don't know. Looking at the world sometimes, zombies make more sense than people.

We slowly walk through the aisles of the exhibit hall, passing countless tables of merchandise, and specialty shops. There's an honest-to-God tattooist giving horror hounds tattoos; his book is impressive and I can't say I'm not tempted, but my mom would kill me.

But maybe I could get my nose pierced?

We keep going and in the next aisle we see the zombie couple again. They've gathered a small crowd outside a specialty makeup booth.

The booth sells all kinds of makeup, but obviously the big hit is the various bite wounds and zombie effects.

The zombie couple are clumsily dabbing makeup on each other, rough swipes of neutral tan that look ridiculous, like the worst mortician in the world just gave up on making their corpses presentable.

The booth owner, a middle-aged white woman with dyed-bright magenta hair, good-naturedly takes the makeup out of their hands, gently turns and pushes them away.

"Go on," she laughs, shooing them.

The man zombie winks at me as the woman zombie grabs his arm and together they careen to the next booth.

The crowd that had gathered starts to disperse.

Imani examines the makeup artist's photobook, exclaiming over the beautiful-but-scary evil queen makeup, ominous threaded silver veins edging up her neck and onto her jaw under dark skin, special-effects red-iris contacts, the hint of blood edging the model's mouth.

"Can I take a picture of this?" Imani asks the woman. "It's beautiful and my little sister would love it! She's really into cosplay and fantasy makeup and stuff."

The woman agrees and Imani shows her some of the pictures she's taken of Tish in various makeup and costumes.

"Oh, I love her!" the woman says, swiping through more photos. "She's amazing! Give her my card, tell her to email me saying I talked to you at the con, and I'll give her an online discount code."

Imani thanks her and slides the card into her jacket pocket.

Another woman wearing special effects makeup stumbles into the booth. Her skin is more sickly looking than actually necrotic, almost gray and with a sheen like she has a fever. On one side of her jaw there's a large, oozing bite wound.

"That looks great," Imani tells her.

The woman doesn't acknowledge the compliment. She's staring fixedly at pictures of legs and arms, covered with fake tattoos or flowered wreaths.

"She looks great," Imani says, turning to the makeup artist. "Great work."

The makeup artist shakes her head.

"I didn't do it." The makeup artist sighs. "I wish, though. Look at those edges. That's next level."

The bite prosthetic, torn meat and gore, is flexible, moving with the slight opening and closing of her jaw, undulating, almost, under the twitching of fine facial muscles.

The makeup artist moves forward, studying the effect.

"Who did your makeup?" she asks. "That looks real."

She reaches out to the woman's arm.

The woman with the bite effect jerks her arm away,

violently. She stumbles back, confusion in her eyes.

She shakes her head, like she's trying to clear it. Then she spins on her heel and runs away from us, pushing through groups of people, until she reaches the end of the aisle and turns out of sight.

"Oooooookaaaaaaay," the makeup artist says.

We laugh a little, and shrug at her.

The makeup artist picks up a few brushes that fell out of her apron when the woman jerked away.

"I just wish really committed cosplayers would give you some sort of sign," she says.

• • •

We leave the exhibit hall and go back up the escalators, then down the hallway that leads to both the hotel skyway and the smaller banquet rooms. We stop at the second banquet room for a session called "Apocalyptic Preppers."

We all agreed it would be interesting, but Siggy was the one who really wanted to check it out. Which surprised me, but she's really psyched to tell her dad about it. Harald isn't a prepper, for the record, but he likes to watch that reality show about them.

We step into the back of the room and scan the audience, getting our bearings for a moment before deciding where to sit.

"It's pretty bright in here," Imani murmurs. "Compared to the rest of the con."

She means there's mostly white people in the banquet room.

I had just been thinking the same thing.

Siggy turns on a dime. "Let's go to the author panel instead. That looked cool!"

"No, it's fine," Imani says. "Just, you know. Noticed."

"Are you sure?" I ask, because I don't ever want to be oblivious to my privilege in spaces where she feels . . . other.

I don't know what to do sometimes, I feel helpless and angry, but pretending it isn't there just so I can feel better is the opposite of the answer.

And it's not about me. Not about my feelings at all.

"Thanks," Imani tells us. "I'm good here."

"Don't worry," Siggy reassures her. "If we need to run for it I'll trip June."

"Nice," I say, laughing. "I see how it is. All together or . . . not, if there's real danger."

"Just keeping it real." Siggy leans into me, though, giving me a little one-armed hug.

We choose a row in the back, near the doors, anyway.

Honestly, I don't know what to think about preppers. Like, it's cool to know how to do all this stuff? But it's . . . well, the mind-set is maybe . . . um. Well.

Anyway, I'm glad we're in the back.

But when it starts, it's two relatively normal-looking

couples who lead the session. They don't seem that scary. I guess I expected apocalyptic preppers to look more . . . like something out of *Mad Max*? One of the guys looks just a little like a biker, big and burly and bearded. He seems to be the leader of the group, and you can tell he takes all this prepping very, very seriously.

He seems like the kind of person who takes himself very, very seriously, generally. Not just in doomsday scenarios.

Very, very seriously he takes us through a "prepping essentials" PowerPoint.

"The first thing is to know your procedures and know your rules," the biker says.

"Ohh, I like him," Imani murmurs, halfway joking and halfway serious.

"Your love language is rules and procedures," Siggy teases her.

"Shh, I'm taking notes," Imani says.

"Everyone's rules might be different, depending on your prep-group needs," the biker continues. "But you should make your rules and procedures now, before the crisis."

"What crisis?" Siggy whispers the question.

"All of them," I answer.

"For example, my number-one rule is: no outsiders allowed once the crisis hits," the biker says. "Outsiders can be dangerous, and your first responsibility is to your core group."

"That's harsh," Siggy says.

Imani leans over. "Well, think about the show. It makes sense to me."

The biker finishes going over the rest of his rules then tags out to the other man, who looks like an accountant. He tells us how to pack a bug-out bag, and how to safely stash supplies in our houses and offices.

One of the prepper ladies (who looks kind of like Mrs. Claus) goes next, telling us how to make water drinkable by adding a few drops of Clorox to it.

"Two drops per quart, stir, let stand for thirty minutes, and voilà, drinkable!" she says.

Now *that* is really useful to know!

"Speaking of drinking water," the biker guy says, "I'm gonna show you how to set up a solar-filtration system so you can drink your own urine."

"Ew," Siggy whispers.

She's not the only one who has that response, because there's an audible "ew" and then laughter that crests in the room like a wave.

The biker guy looks a bit miffed at the response.

"Real mature, people. Real mature," he says. "But I'm standing here telling you, you can prepare for the worst all you want, you can lay the groundwork for your own survival. You can do everything right. But when push comes to shove, the survivors are gonna be those with mental toughness."

"And those who drink their own pee," Imani murmurs.

Siggy and I convulse in silent laughter. Luckily, we're sitting in the back but omg, Imani just kills me, her face serious as she's nodding along with the biker guy like he is her dude, he is the one, he is saying what we're all thinking, he's the preacher and we're the congregation.

I can't breathe; I'm struggling so hard not to laugh.

The biker guy taps his forehead with an index finger.

"Mental toughness," he repeats.

Imani nods.

"Peeeeeeeeee," she whispers, tilting her head sideways in agreement like the word "pee" is a stand-in for "testify."

Siggy makes a little gasping noise. She's beet red and looks like she's going to bust a gut.

"Stop, Imani." My whisper is pressurized, eking out in front of the laughter that threatens to spill out.

Imani keeps a straight face, just shoots us a glance that says *stop what?* But mirth dances in her eyes and I swear I am going to die right here if I don't make a noise, the pressure of laughter inside me is that strong.

I have to do something.

I can feel the gale of laughter building up in my chest.

Imani turns and thumps me on the back, and a spurt of laughter comes out as a cough. Siggy starts coughing, too.

"You've got to want to survive," the biker guy says. "You've got to want to fight for it and never stop fighting."

Imani bends down to look in my eyes, then she turns to Siggy.

"Y'all need a drink of water or something?" Imani whispers, and we have to choke back more laughter.

Finally, the session is over, and when my stomach rumbles it's a surprise, even though I've been keeping track of the time so we won't miss the podcast or the full cast session on the main stage.

Imani must hear it, too, because she cocks an eyebrow at me.

"Should I be worried? Are you about to turn on me?"

"I mean, if I did, I would make it quick, okay?" I say.

We decide instead of returning to the exhibit hall to eat under fluorescent lights, that we will use the skyway hamster tube to cross over to the luxury hotel for lunch. Besides which, since we are already on the second floor for the prepper session in the banquet room, we're pretty close to it.

We walk down the second-floor hallway, the wall of windows to our left.

"This is a good plan," Siggy says. "I've always wanted to use the skyway."

We reach the tube and walk out into it, over the street. The sun warms us, and I feel like lying down in the tube for a moment, just luxuriating in it.

"Can we stay at the lobby sandwich counter instead of the actual sit-down restaurant, though?" Imani asks when we're about halfway through the tube. "It'll be quicker, cheaper, and we might see celebrities in the lobby, if they're taking a break from the con."

"Yes, let's do that!" Siggy agrees.

We reach the hotel side of the tube, walk past the convention badge and security checkpoint, and take the clear elevators down into the lobby.

As we cross the marble floor, we have to make a small detour around some kind of spill. There are those little collapsible yellow fabric cones spread in a loose triangle around a surprisingly large area of floor.

A maid from housekeeping swipes a large, wet mop across the floor, then lifts the rust-dark mop into her bucket and presses. The red water is vivid contrasted to her white hand.

"Gross," Siggy says. "That looks like blood."

"No way that's blood," Imani says, but she's frowning.

"Maybe the makeup effects team dropped a fake blood packet," I say.

We order sandwiches at the counter, then take a table near the windows, but sit with our backs to the outside. All the better to see the lobby.

We snarf our sandwiches and don't see anybody famous come through the lobby while we're sitting there, just more cosplayers arriving in hazmat suits. Maybe the costume shop had a special group rate? The cosplayers spread into the hotel lobby, stopping and scanning people—swiping those heat-sensitive thermometers across foreheads, sticking a fake chem strip into the maid's bucket water, spreading through the lobby and into the elevators, making people more annoyed than amused.

We're almost done with our sandwiches when Siggy's phone goes off, a cacophony of electric guitars.

"Mark?" I ask as Siggy swipes to answer. "Again? He knows you're here with us!"

I feel my eyebrows pulling down as Siggy makes an apologetic face but takes the call anyway. She gets up from our little table, and takes a few steps away, murmuring low into the phone.

I turn to Imani. "Ugh."

Imani gives me one of those smiles I'm never completely happy to be on the receiving end of. Even though she is my best friend, and even though it's gentle, there's a reprimand in there, too.

"I'm sure it'll be quick," Imani says. "Maybe the mail came."

Meaning maybe there's an admissions letter.

I glance over at Siggy, and it's impossible to tell anything. So I don't think the letter came, because we'd sure be able to tell in an instant if he got in or not.

My fingers drum on the table before I realize I'm doing it. I make myself stop.

Imani scrolls on her phone, patiently, and so I eat the pickle spear left on my plate. My phone just gobbles up power, and it's already low so I'm deliberately saving it for more photos.

We wait. For Siggy to talk to her boyfriend. Which is something she does all the time every day so maybe it could wait.

Ugh.

"June." Imani's voice is gentle.

"I know," I say. "I'm *being* patient."

"She just needs a minute. Relationships take work sometimes," Imani says.

"Should they though?" I ask. I glance over at Siggy smiling and talking.

"They all do," Imani says. "Ryan and I fought, remember?"

Her boyfriend from last year, who graduated.

"Yeah, but you guys broke up," I say.

"Only because he went to college," Imani says. "Not because we fought."

Imani's hand touches my arm. "Besides, did you ever think maybe the reason they fight so much is not because of Mark?" she asks.

"Not really?" I answer, and my tone is defensive for Siggy. Because I know exactly what Imani means. Because I've seen Siggy get into it with Mark.

She's awesome but she goes *off*. And then she doesn't back down, even when she should. When she's completely wrong, or is misinterpreting something he said, she just digs in.

And he's not perfect, but that's not Imani's point.

"I just keep waiting for them to break up for good, I guess," I say.

"I wouldn't hold your breath on that," Imani says.

Finally Siggy comes back to the table.

"Any news?" Imani asks.

Siggy shakes her head. "He just wanted to hear my voice." She tips her chin and pulls a lock of her white-blonde hair, stroking it with a happy little smirk on her face.

Imani smiles at her, and I successfully avoid making obvious hurking noises, so it's finally time to climb the stairs back up to the hamster-tube level. We go through the security point again, showing our badges and opening our bags on the table, and then we're back in the tube, clear to return to *ZombieCon!*

Imani stretches in the sun.

"I feel like a sunbathing hamster," she says.

"Me too," Siggy agrees, doing a deep leg lunge, hands on her hips like she's going to start doing yoga or is posing for a ridiculous Instagram.

Behind us there's a commotion at the hotel side of the hamster tube.

I glance back. Two people in white hazmat suits are there, scanning the guards. A guard shouts as they shove him back into the tube.

"Stop! You have to come through security like everyone else!" the guard shouts.

Me and Siggy and Imani quick-time it out of the tube, moving back into the convention center and stopping along the interior wall. We stand next to one of those red emergency stations, a fire alarm and extinguisher hanging next to a firehose cabinet.

We look back at the drama unfolding in the skyway.

One of the figures in the hazmat suits holds big gloved hands up, in an *easy there* gesture. Another figure is messing with the tables, pulling them back away from the hotel side of the tube entrance.

A third figure is working the mechanism that releases the door hatch to the tube.

"Those guys had better take it down a few notches or they're gonna get kicked out," Imani says.

One of the convention guards is barking into his shoulder radio.

"Yeah," I say. "Let's get going."

I don't want to get caught up in whatever happens next.

10

We go down the escalators and back into the exhibit hall. It's more crowded now, so we have to weave down the aisles a bit more.

Lots of people have visited the various makeup booths and are sporting wounds and scars, or scleral contacts. It's weird and disconcerting to share smiles with these walking wounded.

Although it's also supremely cool.

A drunk, middle-aged man in the center of the aisle lurches from table to table.

"Whoo boy," Siggy says. "Watch out."

The man lurches back across the aisle to another table.

We give him a wide berth as we pass.

The man turns and sees Siggy. He turns jerkily, like his body is a puppet with separate, jointed controls. His shoulders whip around first, then torso, then hips, then feet. He stumbles and crashes into another man.

"Hey!" The man shoves him.

The drunk man hasn't taken his eyes off Siggy. He keeps

moving toward us. His mouth opens, and he tries to speak, but all the noise that comes out is a mangled, garbled groaning.

I . . . don't think he's drunk.

A thick string of saliva pours down his chin. The rope of spittle stretches to his chest.

"You guys." Siggy's voice is tight with fear.

Without thinking, I step in front of Siggy.

Imani must have the same instinct because I feel her shoulder pressed close to mine.

"Cut that crap out!" Imani shouts at the man.

I remember from health class how you're supposed to give people jobs in an emergency.

There's an audience standing around, watching us like this is some kind of performance bit.

"You!" I point to the man who shoved him. "Go get security!"

The man nods and pushes away from the crowd.

A clump of three teens stands in the middle of the aisle. Two girls and a guy, they're just standing there like deer mesmerized by oncoming headlights.

The man pushes the first girl aside, levering on her shoulder like it's a crutch. She gives a little shriek but is laughing, like this is just a joke.

The man hasn't taken his eyes off Siggy, until he careens into the teen boy.

"What the hell?" The boy laughs, and he pushes at the man's shoulder.

The man grabs the boy's arm and pulls the forearm up to his mouth.

The boy yells in pain.

Now the onlookers finally snap out of their daze and several people jump forward, pulling the man off the boy.

The man starts fighting, an uncoordinated flailing, but it knocks some people back.

Blood and spittle coat his chin.

One of the rescuers, a woman, jumps forward. She grasps the man's chin and points it up as she drives her shoulder into his, pivoting him as she shoots a leg straight behind him, throwing him backward to the floor with enough force that his teeth snap closed with an audible clack.

"Badass!" I yelp involuntarily. But day-um!

The woman doesn't look up but instead folds the man's own arm over his throat, a barrier to his teeth.

Three burly guys move in like they planned it, stepping forward to help hold the man on the ground immobile.

A smattering of applause from the crowd.

The burly guys nod acknowledgment for the applause. The badass lady doesn't look up, just frowns down at the man's snapping teeth.

From over here it kind of looks like he's biting his own arm. No way. That's impossible.

Security guards arrive, and the burly men and badass lady start talking to them.

"Let's go," Siggy whispers, still standing behind me and Imani. "I don't want to have to get any closer to that guy."

I've never heard fear in her voice before.

It makes me feel sick. It makes me want to hit something for her. It makes me want to hug her and promise that everything is going to be okay.

Siggy is the freest person I know, and I want her to always stay that way.

"Let's go, then," I agree.

"Okay," Imani says. We turn and start walking away.

We pass the teen boy; he's holding a T-shirt a vendor gave him over his forearm.

"He *bit* me!" His voice is incredulous.

The two girls coo over him. Patting his upper arm and shoulders.

"I should kick his ass!" the boy says, puffing his scrawny chest out.

We keep walking, and at the middle aisle we turn and make our way to the podcast stage.

"That was scary," Imani says. "Good thing that lady knew what to do."

"She was amazing!" Siggy says, her voice sounding a bit firmer now that we've put some distance between her and the man.

"Seriously," I say. "I think I'm in love. Did you see that move? And what she did with his arm?"

"Did . . . did it . . ." Siggy's voice quavers, suddenly small. "Did it look like he was chewing on his own arm to you guys?"

"Yeah," Imani says.

"It looked like it, but that was just the angle, right?" I ask. "It had to be."

"Talk about an intense fan," Siggy jokes weakly.

"He bit that boy," Imani says.

"He was so out of it," I say. "Maybe he was on something."

"I bet he's from Florida," Siggy says, trying to smile bigger at her own joke.

Trying to laugh her fears away.

"Yeah, no doubt he was," I agree, encouraging her laugh.

"The OG Florida Man," Imani says.

We keep walking away from it, putting distance and humor between us and it.

He bit that boy though.

And he was chewing on his own arm.

• • •

The Undead Listen is already recording when we arrive, so we sit in the back row.

The crowd is laughing, so that's a good sign that the trio of friends onstage are on a roll.

"Sure, *you'd* survive," Melinda says into her mic. She cocks an eyebrow at her cohosts, Jilly and Billy, who are twins. The three of them have been best friends forever.

Jilly snorts into her mic.

"I would!" Billy's voice comes out a bit higher pitched than perhaps he was prepared for. He coughs a little, laughs, and speaks again. "I would."

It's one of the running gags that they do on the podcast. Inevitably, after a new episode of *Human Wasteland* airs, Billy will work himself up about a "Pointless Zombie Death" (PZD) on the show that week.

"I don't know," Jilly says. "Since we're live, what do you guys think? Would Billy survive the ZA?"

Imani cups her hands around her mouth and yells, "No!" along with most of the crowd.

Siggy and I yell, "Yes!"

"Sorry, Billy," Melinda says. "Looks like you get et."

"Okay, but at least I would have a *good* zombie death!" Billy argues.

Siggy looks at me, her blue eyes bright. "It's Absurd!" she predicts, bouncing in her chair.

"And with that," Jilly says, and pushes a button. Their original song, "It's Absurd, but I Heard, You Got Eaten by the Herd," plays. It's a chipper 1920s-style song, and the audience sings along.

"Time to rank 'em," Jilly says, fading the song out.

"I'm ready," Billy says, leaning over his mic in readiness.

"Go. Top three PZDs. Is this guy in there?"

I know exactly who they're talking about, even though I missed the start of the show, because in the last episode it was such a glaring PZD.

The guy (an extra in the opposition camp's ranks) had seen the zombie, lying on the ground, just a torso. He'd laughed.

So that told you volumes. No respect for zombies, you become zombie kibble.

And then he'd decided to taunt it, to play with it. He poked it with his baseball bat.

So, it was hardly surprising when, in the middle of his fun, the zombie lunged and grabbed the guy's feet, and he fell on the ground and like a snake the torso was on him.

It was not pretty.

But it had some amazing special effects!

"It was colossally foolish, but it does not go in the number one spot," Billy says.

Number one, a teen girl who asked the approaching

zombie who was her boyfriend, "Adam, is that you?" and "Adam, you're scaring me!" and just stood there while he approached.

I should add that his head was at a gross-disgusting angle and you could see his spine protruding from his neck. Like, that should be mentioned or it doesn't sound like a PZD.

"And it definitely doesn't beat number two," Jilly says.

Pointless Zombie Death number two was a redneck who tried to "wrassle" it. Really. You cannot make this up. Well, obviously someone did, I guess. But I never would have been able to think of that.

But the guy was in mourning for his dead sister, you see. And he was angry and suicidal. And he told the others to go on.

It was the zombie apocalypse version of walking into the sea.

Still ridiculous. And a definite PZD. Infuriated a lot of fans. Because then his friends had to kill him once he became a zombie. It felt manipulative.

Which my mom definitely didn't get when I was complaining about it.

She'd said, "Wait. You're saying a death in a zombie show. Was manipulative."

And then she gave me the *listen to yourself* look.

And I gave her the *I knew you wouldn't understand* eyes.

And that's why I really try not to talk about *Human Wasteland* with her. She doesn't get it.

"Okay, but does it rank as number three?" Melinda asks.

Number three is the worst one, and their numbering is all wrong. But Billy really loved the actress who played Samantha, and said as much, and that's why her death is number three instead of number one.

Also because we know that the reason her character was so poorly killed off was because she was in a contract dispute with the producers.

Talk about a life lesson there. Everyone is expendable in the zombie apocalypse.

But the way they killed her off? So infuriating. And it's hard not to think that was somehow about her being a girl and a fan favorite who tried to use her leverage to get a better deal.

So yeah, we're all a bit PO'd about the way they killed Samantha off. She should have had a hero's death. And it was so much worse than that because it was just so ridiculous.

Imani leans over to me. "Nothing beats Samantha's fighting a zombie with a nail file."

"I know," I moan. "As if she would."

"That still makes me so mad." Siggy shakes her head in exasperation, setting her dangly earrings rocking dizzyingly.

I feel someone looking at me. Suddenly, eyes like a

weight. You know the feeling: you turn to look before you can think. A response to being stared at that is primal, like scenting danger. Somehow you just know.

And so I look.

And so I don't hear whatever Jilly says next, because Scott is standing at the edge of the seats, about thirty feet from me.

And he's staring at me.

The last thing I said to him was "I never want to see you again."

At least he has the grace to look embarrassed. But he's not looking away either.

The problem with Scott is he's charming. He's cute, and he knows it. He knows exactly how far he can push you, or he thinks he does, at least.

I thought his charm was something that was natural to him, like air, like breathing; but now after what happened with Blair, I think it's more calculated than that.

I think he likes to see the way he looks in another person's eyes.

Which means that it never was about how he felt about me, but how I made him feel about himself.

But I didn't know that when we started dating. Even though he went to a different high school, and had a whole other life up there in Peachtree City, I thought of him as mine, when he was with me, at least.

He'd drive down on Saturdays and we'd go out and spend the whole day together, driving around, listening to music, eating picnics in the state park. Making out.

He's not gorgeous. He's cute in an ordinary way. But he's got a . . . way about him.

His hair is sandy brown, streaked with blond and trimmed so short it's almost severe.

I was trying to talk him into growing it out.

I realize I'm meeting his eyes when he smiles and gives me a little shrug.

My eyes jump off him fast.

But not before I see that he's walking over to our row.

"Aw, hell nah," Siggy mutters as Scott scoots into the row near me.

"Hey," Scott murmurs.

What do I say? What can I say? I'm not here to talk to him. I want to listen to *The Undead Listen*, not talk to the boy who I thought was mine. Or was partly mine.

But I also can't help that I still want to talk to him. And that sucks. Because you can't just cut out that part of you. The part that liked a person, and liked what they saw in you, or the person that you were with them. But here you are, anyway, in spite of it all, just wanting to talk to them still.

He looks at me, and his smile is the exact one that used

to make me feel special, the same one that I used to think of as one that was just for me.

Then I realized it was just the way he looked at any girl.

It's like his eyes are saying, "You're not like the other girls."

But I am. I am the other girls. I am exactly, wonderfully, like all the other girls, jerk.

So stop negging us. For once. Just stop it.

I have this whole speech unfurling in my head as he says, "It's good to see you."

But I don't say any of it.

I just point at the podcast stage. And he at least falls silent until *The Undead Listen* finishes.

Imani stares daggers at Scott the whole time. And when Jilly, Billy, and Melinda leave the stage, Imani hisses at Scott.

"Get away from us. No one wants you here."

He ignores her.

"I miss you," Scott says to me. "I wish you'd let me explain."

"Let's go." Siggy stands and reaches across Imani to tug at my arm.

"I did, remember?" My voice should be venom and anger that could etch glass, but it's just a dorky-sounding choke that comes out high, making me sound like a little girl.

High voice, tight with tears. Ugh.

"Did you hear the show?" Scott asks, standing with us, and following as we scooch out of the row. "It was great!"

And there it is. All he ever really liked about me: the way I looked at him.

Tell me how great I am again.

Scott is still talking. "I did a live cast! Not prerecorded like some of these other guys."

"Oh, awesome," Siggy says in a voice so edged it could slice a block of cheese. "That means no one could enjoy it in the moment. Instead of, you know, no one enjoying it later. Woo!" Her finger twirls in a sarcastic whoop-de-doo celebration.

The way she says it; that attitude, perfected, cutting, in the way that I swear to God only Siggy has mastered. A cute blonde stiletto right to the tender underbelly.

I laugh. It launches out of me like a rocket, shooting a shower of pain and anger but also mirth, actual true honest laughter because it's funny, my friend is funny, and I know who Scott is.

I know who he is now.

He's the guy who gets to you by dragging down everyone else. He's the guy who thinks about himself the most, and anyone else second.

He never really saw me. I can play it all back now, and it's embarrassing, like a bad movie montage where the girlfriend watches and listens adoringly as the Guy plays his guitar at her. Plays *his* music. Doesn't ask for hers, doesn't care about hers.

Scott frowns at me as my guffaw tapers to giggles.

For once I'm not embarrassed. I'm not wishing I was smaller, or prettier, or anything else.

Blair can have him. Not that she needs my blessing, obviously she didn't, but hell. It turns out? I think they're a really great match.

"Oh, Scott." I clap a hand flat on his shoulder, like we are frat guys. Chums. Drinking buddies. "Man, it was good to see you!"

I slap his back two times, and press past him.

Scott looks like that dog, the one with spots on his ears, tilting his head back and forth at me in confusion.

Cute, clueless, and ready to go crap on someone else's yard now.

Imani and Siggy fall in behind me, like we're a walking-away dance squad.

"Who's the badass now?" Imani asks, smiling at me slyly.

11

"That was so *epic!*" Siggy yelps after we turn the corner and head down the aisle.

"Yeah!" Imani says, linking her arm with mine.

"*Man, it was good to see you!*" Siggy quotes me. "June, that was perfection." She kisses her fingertips like a chef in a fancy restaurant.

I can't help it, I feel simultaneously proud of myself and a little embarrassed by their effusiveness.

We walk out of the exhibit hall past the volcanic rock waterfall and ride the escalator back upstairs. We file into the shuffling line outside the massive ballroom for the full-cast panel.

We're lucky enough to get inside before they say that the room has reached capacity. It's standing-room only, so we ease along the back of the ballroom, following a clump of people spreading along the back of the room.

As we wait for the panel to start, my feeling of invincibility from seeing Scott fades, and I'm left just feeling a little deflated and a little sad.

"So, I guess that's my first boyfriend, huh?" I murmur to Imani. "Except not even that. Not really."

"Good riddance to bad rubbish," Imani says. "He doesn't deserve you."

"But do you know how it feels to be the only one who hasn't had a real boyfriend?" I ask. "You don't. And Siggy doesn't. And Blair didn't. Just me. I'm the only one."

"That doesn't *mean* anything, June," Imani says, her tone like she wants to grab my shoulders and give them a shake. "High school isn't everything. High school is just a small bowl. You need more fish. Look at you!"

She means it like *you're so cute!*, but she's not really qualified to speak on the subject. She's my friend, and more to the point, Imani doesn't look at me with romantic eyes.

"Don't get trapped in it, June," Imani says.

"Just 'cause he was a jerk doesn't make them all jerks. And it doesn't mean anything about you, either, so stop that crap," Siggy says.

Easy for you to say.

Ugh. Shut up, brain.

"Pretty good view for standing-room only, huh? Even the camera stand isn't in the way." I point to the camera platform, standing in a clear space to the side of one aisle, approximately in the middle of the room.

Siggy and Imani exchange a glance that says they

know I didn't agree with them, but am just changing the subject.

They roll with it anyway.

"Yeah! The video screen helps, though." Imani tips her chin up, studying the row of empty chairs onstage. On the screen we can see through the close-up that each has a name sign taped on, but we can't read who's sitting where.

"Honestly, after this morning I don't know that it would be healthy for me to be that close to either Hunter or James again." Siggy fans herself with her hand.

"Oh lord," Imani sighs.

"Don't hormone-shame me," Siggy says.

"You haven't even seen your favorite actor yet!" I say.

"I love them all equally."

"Okay, you just talk about Linus the most," I say.

Linus Sheppard joined the cast this season. His character, Hugh, was a veterinarian before the zombie apocalypse, so now he's somehow become the medic of the little group of survivors, even if he insists he isn't qualified at least once per episode.

Not only is Siggy absolutely smitten with him, but she instantly and completely shipped him with the trucker's daughter, Shella, played by Annie Blaze. They've got a May-December thing going on, or at least May-October. I try not to think too much about how naturally the audience fell into the ship, when if their ages were reversed people would prob-ably have had a problem with it.

Okay, but having said that incisive bit of social commen-tary, I'm not perfect. I ship them, too. Their chemistry is off the charts.

"He better sit by Annie," Siggy says, her eyes lighting up and her hands balling into excited fists. Like she's going to bang them on a table, yelling, "More! More!"

"He will," I say. "It's what the fans want!"

"You got that right, sis." Siggy holds up a hand for a high five.

It's obnoxious, but I can't just leave her hanging so I give it to her.

Siggy adds a hip bump and a whoop-whoop.

I leave her hanging in that regard.

"Blair's coming." Imani's warning is low.

"What?" Siggy looks worried.

"She's coming to talk to June." Imani passes a hand over her hair, sweeping it to one side and down as she turns away from Blair. "Just let June handle it."

I glance down the aisle and sure enough, my frenemy is walking toward us, a look of determination on her face, which is her usual look, let's be clear, but this is an added determined look.

A determined-determined look. It's the kind of look that

refuses a blindfold at the firing squad. It's the look of the captain bravely going down with the ship. It's the look of someone deciding to wax their bikini area.

"Great." My voice is flat. "First Scott, and now her. Why not. Everything is about them."

Leave it to Blair to make a dramatic scene at the thing I've been saving for all summer. Planning for, dreaming of.

I wish I didn't miss her friendship.

I wish I didn't expect the way she hurt me—what does that say about me? That a part of me knew it all along.

Blair is wearing tight black jeans, ankle boots, and a dark gray shirt. Her blood-spatter VIP collectible lanyard looks like the perfect edgy accessory. Basically, she looks like a rock star, and walks like someone with power, a sexy police officer or something.

Music blares out from the stage. A stagehand with floppy ginger hair is adjusting mics, his shoulders hunched up around his ears like he's shy to be standing in front of so many people, even if no one's paying attention to him.

Blair stops right in front of us. A leg pops out, and her arms cross, like she's waiting to be impressed.

But I know her, so I see it for what it is.

Nerves.

She starts speaking without preamble.

"I'm sitting in the second row, center, and I have a spare

seat next to me. And this extra badge." Her hand pushes out.

It's another VIP badge, platinum level. Blood-spatter lanyard.

Of course. Another one. Her parents probably didn't ask, just gave her the money. I've seen them with her enough; I know exactly what it looked like: *go away*. Or *I give up*.

Two things Blair gets from her parents effortlessly: money and disregard. Her mom, Sherri, is beautiful like her, but cold where Blair is fierce. Sherri's an interior designer and their house is always perfect, and always changing. Almost like a showroom, and not a home at all.

Blair's dad, Mike, is big and tan and wears nice suits. He owns a Mercedes dealership, and when he gets home from that it's like he used up all his words at his job. He doesn't say much to anyone.

Blair's older sister, Emma, is exactly the daughter Sherri and Mike wanted. Perfect, quiet, and contained, a queen bee.

Blair's different, spiky and driven. For good and bad.

It's almost like she *has* to take the things she needs.

In front of me, Blair suddenly drops her eyes, looking at the carpet between her feet. "So I thought . . . maybe you'd like to come sit with me, June."

It's not a question. Is she asking me? This is so Blair. Everything she does she finds a way to frame it so it's up to you to extend yourself. Even if she's the one inviting, it feels like an option you can choose, not something she really wants.

Before I realize I'm doing it, I mirror her posture, crossing my arms, popping a leg out.

Ugh, why did I do that? It looks like I'm imitating her. But I can't change now, or I'll look fidgety, like I have to go to the bathroom or something.

Anger surges through me, so I don't change my posture. Make it mocking. Feel my eyebrow go up.

"Are you asking something, Blair?" I ask, and god*damn* does it feel good.

Of course, she doesn't actually ask it again. She ignores me like she never said anything, and looks at Siggy instead.

So, now I can't laugh in her face at the offer. But I guess I sorta already did that.

"How about you, Siggy?" Blair smiles, a forced showing of teeth. "I'm sitting right in front of Linus's seat."

"Is Annie next to him?" Siggy blurts out. Then she leans back, putting a hand over her mouth, like she's shocked she spoke. "Forget it," Siggy says, her voice firm. She steps closer to me, our shoulders brushing.

"I can see fine from here, thanks," Siggy says. And she crosses her arms like me, and pops a leg out.

A rush of love for Siggy pulses through me.

And so I turn to look at her.

"Are you kidding me?" I ask her. "Take the seat."

"No way," Siggy answers.

"I love you, girl. I want you to take that seat." I tell her.

Siggy leans in, bumping shoulders. "Nope, I'm staying here. I love you, dork."

Blair is watching, eyes cutting between us, forced smile on her face.

And suddenly I'm tired. And sad. The hurt is still there, breathtaking if I think about it. If I stop to notice it.

But I can push it down, can't I?

I have Imani standing next to me, giving Blair a direct, hurt stare. And I have Siggy, still ready to throw off righteously angry sparks for me. True friends. Sisters of my heart. Loyal.

I don't need Blair.

Today isn't about her. It's not supposed to be about what she did to me. So it's not supposed to be about me, either.

I put my arm around Siggy's whippet-waist. My voice is a low murmur.

"It's okay, Siggy. Take the seat. Then come back after the panel and tell us exactly what he looks like from row two, center."

"Are you sure?" Siggy asks, and her voice isn't eager, just worried.

And that alone makes me sure.

"I bet he's even more perfect in real life," I answer.

"Right? It's like he doesn't have pores at all," Siggy says.

"We'll wait here," Imani says, slapping Siggy on the butt. "Go have fun, goober."

I look at Blair. I want her to see it in my eyes: that I'm choosing to let Siggy go. That I'm a good person.

The better person.

That me giving the seat to Siggy means more than her sharing the pass she wanted to give to her boyfriend.

Okay, and that makes me less of a good person than I thought, but I still get points for this, dammit.

Blair acts like she doesn't see it.

But it's plainly obvious, and I might be naive and hope too much of people, but I'm not naive enough not to realize that when Blair got those two VIP passes, they were for her and Scott.

Two passes.

So a part of me has a little jolt of extra life now, that something happened between them, because he's not using the pass. At least not now.

And he tried to talk to me.

Not that he's going to get another chance, it just feels good to know he wants one. That maybe after choosing her over me, he would try to re-choose me again.

Ugh. It sounds gross when I think about it like that, though.

Siggy smiles at us and then follows Blair back up the aisle to the front of the hall. She's keeping a little space between them, keeping her arms crossed so her arms don't accidentally brush Blair.

"That was really nice of you," Imani tells me. "You didn't have to give her your blessing like that."

"Yes, I did," I say. "Siggy wouldn't have minded, but I would have."

Imani gives me a quick hug.

"That's why I love you," she says.

"D'aw," I say, but I can't help smiling anyway.

Siggy and Blair have reached the seats, and Siggy turns and gives two big thumbs-up from the second row.

We're approximately thirty rows and a standing-room-only aisle behind her.

"Besides," I add. "We can't give Blair the cold shoulder forever."

Imani leans into me. "You have such a big heart, June. It's only been like a week."

My shrug shifts the scoop neck of my shirt farther off one shoulder. "Feels like longer, I guess."

Siggy points at the empty chair onstage directly in front of her. She claps and makes a heart shape with her hands.

I send two big thumbs-up back.

"I guess it was nice of Blair, too," I say begrudgingly. "To offer it." Because Blair didn't have to walk back here. She didn't have to offer a spare seat.

"If she really wanted to be nice, or try to atone, she could have offered us both seats," Imani says. "She has an agenda."

The lights in the auditorium dim as the stage gets brighter.

Imani touches my arm, making sure I meet her eyes. "It's Blair, so it's not gonna be straightforward. But it means she misses us. She misses you, June."

Is that the same thing as feeling sorry?

Imani sighs, and her shoulders give a small, defeated shrug.

"It's a start, at least," she says.

What would it take for me to get over the injury?

I can't even picture it.

Because Blair will never be able to cross that distance. She'll never be able to say the right words. Not because there are no right words, but simply because she won't be able to bring herself to say them. Can't bring herself to that vulnerable place.

The flip side of her strength, and her drive, and the intensity I loved about her. That I still love about her.

Which means I'll eventually have to accept the wound,

and move on, accepting the meanings under gestures, somehow have that be enough.

And try not to feel cheated that I never got an actual apology.

Imani's head tilts onto my shoulder as one of her arms squeezes around me. "You don't have to deal with it today, June."

But I will have to. Just not yet.

I squeeze Imani back, grateful for my friend. How can I be more like her? I love her so much it's a physical squeeze in my heart.

Imani looks over, and sends me a sky-wide smile.

She knows exactly how I feel.

12

A cheer ripples through the crowd. The post-show host, Michaela, is back. She stalks across the front of the stage in her high-heel boots and tight blue dress, dreadlocks gathered into a low ponytail, trailing down her back. She's in her element, pointing at fans and waving.

"Okay! Senoybia! Wow!" She claps at us, long nails and dark brown skin luminous under the stage lights.

She's so glamorous. But she's been a zombie on the show a few times, and I could never spot her until she showed us the behind-the-scenes video!

"Okay! All right!" she yells into the mic, and we start to quiet down. "That's better. Children. We've got a lot to cover, but before I start the panel, we've got to go over the rules, again. I'm talking about photo ops."

We cheer reflexively. Photo ops! So exciting!

Michaela nods at us and waits until the cheers quiet down.

"Yes, we're all excited! I want your photo op to be amazing! So just a reminder, okay, because this will get you ejected from the con, and you will not get your photo, and you will not get a refund so . . . *do not bite* the actors."

There are a few laughs from the crowd, but also groans like *seriously?*

"I know," Michaela says. "You would think this would go without saying but. Here. We. Are."

She shakes her head.

"So, since I'm up here saying it, we're going to go farther—no teeth or lips may touch the actor's skin. They're feeling jumpy. They pretend-kill zombies all the time, let's work with them, not against them. This is a no-go zone. So, if you want to pretend to be a zombie, fine! But NO MOUTH CONTACT to the actors."

Imani turns big eyes to me. "Good lord!"

"It better not have been Hunter who got bit," I mutter.

"Any of them! I can't believe anyone would think that's okay!" Imani says.

I get that feeling again. That surge of protectiveness for Hunter, specifically, remembering how he walked out onto the stage, and off it when the girl asked for a hug, pulling his hair over his eyes, but going anyway, an unwelcome part of his job. But should it be?

And now that I've met them, the surge of protectiveness extends to sweet Janet O'Shea, and to James Cooper. He was so nice! So generous!

Did either of them get bit? Or did a fan press their teeth onto their skin, like ha ha, it's just for a joke, right? Get it? I'm a zombie!

Ugh.

It goes all through me. I swear I would tackle any fan who would put their *teeth* on a stranger's skin.

I promise again to be cool. When I have my photo op. I will be cool.

"Okay!" Onstage Michaela relaxes and smiles, strutting forward with slightly raised steps, like an aggressive model on the runway. "Are you *ready* for our full! Cast! PaneeeeeLLL!"

She yells the last word like the WWE announcer says, "Rrrrrrumble!"

We go nuts. We shriek and clap.

Everyone is on their feet. I can see Siggy's white-blonde hair, bright even in the dim light.

Siggy's hands are cupped around her mouth as she shrieks at the stage.

Michaela raises the mic again.

"Did you know we've NEVER had SO MANY of the show actors onstage at ONE TIME?!?"

We shriek again.

"So, let me bring them out!" Michaela walks to the farthest chair, and starts yelling the actors' names. Our shrieks and cheers blend together in a seamless roar.

The actors walk quickly onto the stage in a scattering clump, like a loose firework separating onstage, their teeth and eyes bright, their skin flawless, some of them wearing sunglasses, but the rest just at home under the lights.

They wave to the audience and find their seats as Michaela keeps yelling names and we keep shrieking our applause.

"Simon Wong! Annie Blaze! Linus Sheppard!"

When Linus and Annie step onto the stage, I glance at Siggy. She's bouncing so hard her long hair looks like some kind of scarf, fluttering up and down.

The actors quick-walk to their seats. Annie and Linus are both white, but while Linus is the epitome of a pale Englishman, Annie has a healthy tan that looks golden under the lights. Her dyed red hair falls in luscious curls that brush her shoulders. She pivots in front of her seat, waving like a beauty queen (which she is) before sitting.

Linus smiles and points at Siggy.

"Hunter Sterling!" Michaela yells. "And of course, James Cooper!"

I want to keep watching what's going on with Linus and Siggy, but now Hunter is back onstage and my eyes are drawn straight to him, like he's a bug zapper and I'm a moth.

Yep. Just as gorgeous from the back of the hall. Look at the way he moves.

He shrugs, waves, smiles shyly, and waits for James to catch up to him.

Then, like actual father and son, James puts a casual arm across Hunter's shoulders as they wave to the audience.

We go nuts. I shriek so hard it hurts, but I don't stop because now they're smiling. Then James gives Hunter's shoulder a pat, and a steer, and they turn and go to their seats.

The audience with seats sits down after Hunter and James do. We get mostly quiet, and the panel begins.

Michaela starts reading questions off the card. And just like with any panel I've ever watched on YouTube, the fun isn't in the questions, it's in the actors' interactions with each other.

And it's funny because it's almost like they stay in character. Sam, who plays the old lawyer, Jamison, is wry and wise when he speaks. Cuellar, the actor who plays the abrasive, racist redneck, doesn't come across as racist, but the abrasive energy is still there, though it's covered over like he's just teasing.

It does make you wonder how far down the similarities go.

Michaela turns to Siggy's favorites, Annie and Linus.

"So, newbies! What's it like joining a hit show at the end of the third season?"

Annie lifts her mic and leans forward. "It's awesome! But

I have to say my absolute favorite thing is being shipped so intensely IMMEDIATELY. Thanks for that!"

Her tone is teasing, so it's obvious she doesn't really mind.

Having such a fanatic response to her and Linus's characters together probably ensures they'll stay alive for several more episodes, at least.

Michaela picks up on the tease.

"Well, looking at Linus, I have to say it's a hard job, but someone's got to do it, right?"

The audience laughs. On the video screen above the stage, the camera zooms in as Linus laughs along, and yes, yes, he's quite handsome, with floppy sandy-blond hair and blue eyes that look simultaneously sad, gentle, and happy all at once.

Soulful, I guess you'd call them.

Later I will probably take it to heart that I'm not as good-looking as these people. But right now, it's just too much fun being in the audience with them up onstage.

"But seriously, the reaction to you two together! That was fast, even for the zombie apocalypse!" Michaela says.

Annie laughs, and stretches a hand toward Linus. "Well, I'm lucky."

On the video screen above, I can see in close-up how Linus's eyes go soft and puppy-dog-ish when he looks at her. The audience holds their breath.

"Why lucky?" Michaela asks.

"It's how the Brits put it," Annie says. And her hand extends. Linus takes it gently. "I rather fancy him."

Siggy is going to lose her goddamn mind.

The audience whoops and screams. Onstage Linus and Annie smile shyly, still holding hands.

"Is that so, Linus?" Michaela prompts.

Linus clears his throat, but it sounds shy, like he's nervous. "Yes, I mean, you all saw it. We had instant chemistry. And we spend so much time together."

The audience coos and sighs.

"Oh my gosh, this is a Senoybia *ZombieCon!* exclusive!" Michaela yelps into her mic. "Thank you, Annie, and Linus, for sharing your new relationship with us!"

We shriek and clap.

"Okay, well, now let me ask you two, Hunter and James," Michaela begins, moving to center stage.

James interrupts her. He flicks a thumb at himself, then at Hunter.

"We're not dating," he teases, smiling out at us.

Hunter laughs.

Most of the audience laughs, too, but there are a couple of playful boos.

There are so many ships on this show, let me tell you.

"Well, that's okay. Give it time," Michaela teases back. "Maybe it's a slow burn."

Just the right, fun tone. Makes the playful boos turn into cheers, and the audience laughs along.

She's a really good host.

"What's your favorite part about the new setting and how—" Michaela asks, glancing at her card—but she doesn't get a chance to finish the question.

A man is hoisting himself onstage.

Linus leans forward—holding a hand up in a *stop* gesture—"Hey, mate," he says into the mic. "You've got to stay off the stage."

The man rushes at Michaela, who yelps and takes several steps back.

The man grabs her mic and whirls to us.

He's familiar. Wearing a faded JUST DO IT T-shirt and jeans. A battered backpack slung over his shoulders.

It's . . . I swear it's the same guy who was messing with the crash-bar doors over on Autograph Alley.

"None of you are safe! The virus is here!"

A few people boo and hoot from the audience.

A yellow-shirted security guy on the ballroom floor is yelling into a radio and trying and failing to hoist his bulky self onto the tall stage.

The guy who grabbed the mic is pacing, pulling back a hank of greasy hair in agitation.

"I'm a scientist, a biomedical researcher from the CDC.

You've all been locked in, okay? The whole convention center is in lockdown. There's been an exposure. But I've locked us in here, in the ballroom and the exhibit hall downstairs. It's the only way we stand a chance. Do you understand? The contagion is fatal—always fatal. There's no cure, but if we can isolate—"

"Get off the stage!" a man's voice yells.

Michaela stands to the side, holding out a hand for the mic, smiling with the expression you give a shrieking toddler.

A second security guard in a yellow shirt walks out onto the stage.

The scientist edges away, putting the row of seated actors between himself and the approaching guard.

"The infected are here. We need to establish quarantine procedures," he pants into the mic as he darts to the opposite side of the row of chairs, keeping it between himself and the security guard. "We don't have much time!"

Hoots and laughter scatter through the audience as the scientist runs back around to the opposite side of the chairs.

The security guard chases him like it's a preschool game.

Another security guard trots onstage, then two more. They split and approach the scientist from both sides.

The audience applauds.

"You think you know zombies?" the scientist yelps into the mic, and he ducks under the reaching arm of one of the guards.

He zigs around another set of grasping arms, vaults over Simon Wong in his chair, darts forward to the stage edge.

He stands, looking out at us, his eyes wide, wild. His voice sharp, like a slap.

"The zombie apocalypse is *here now.*"

The audience cheers.

"Listen to me! It's the only way we'll survive!"

The audience hoots and shrieks applause. A guy yells, "Bring it on!"

The guards walk forward, hands up, telegraphing *easy, easy, fella.*

Behind me, there's a commotion, rippling through the pod of us clustered at the back of the room.

People are talking, normal-volume voices, suddenly turning away from the stage.

"What's going on?" Imani asks the man standing behind us.

"Someone said the door is locked," he says, shrugging, like he doesn't really believe it.

The back of my neck prickles.

"This better not be a performance art thing," the man grumbles.

Imani looks at me, and I can tell she feels the same unease.

The guy onstage who says he's really a scientist. Could he be dangerous? He was tampering with that door in the exhibit hall. Has he locked us in? I'm suddenly grateful we all had to go through security, so we know no one has a gun, at least.

"Let's move," I say. "I don't like this."

"Follow me," Imani says, and leads the way, weaving through the crowd at the back, moving away from the doors, moving away from the crowd of people straining to see the stage, working our way parallel to the stage, wriggling through clumps of standing people.

We cut left, Imani's Disney trick, moving through the standing people who line the back of the hall.

We get to the side aisle, where Imani stops and we look around. About ten rows in front of us stands the camera platform. There's a small patch of empty floor on every side. I nod at it, and we leave the wall and head for it. I'm thinking we can put our backs to the platform at least, and we'll be able to look back and see the doors more clearly.

And then it happens.

There's a boom from the central set of doors at the back of the hall. The boom increases to a sudden incessant banging.

The attention of the crowd is splintered, with half swiveling their heads to look at the commotion in the back of the hall, while the others keep hooting and mocking the guy on the stage.

"Here," I say, pulling Imani close as we step into the semi-sheltered space at the front of the camera platform.

"Can you see Siggy and Blair?" Imani asks, straining to see our friends in the second row.

"No," I say. "She's still there, though, right in front of Linus."

Imani keeps looking.

The platform itself is only about five feet tall, just enough of a rise that the camera and its operator are assured a clear shot of the stage.

The camera operator, a woman with wavy black hair and tawny skin, spares a glance down at us. She's dressed in a black T-shirt and jeans like the rest of the crew.

She doesn't let go of the camera arm, but she tips her head at the ground.

"Hey, girls, you can't stand there. See the yellow tape?"

A tape line forms a box-shaped barrier on the carpet around the camera platform.

There's a cheer as onstage a security guy finally gets a grip on the sleeve of the scientist's shirt.

"Okay, we're moving," I say to the camerawoman.

But we don't move.

I'm following my instincts, and my instinct is to keep the

platform to my back, and to stay away from the back of the hall.

The echoing booms continue from the closed sets of doors at the back of the hall.

"It's them! The infected!" the scientist yelps into the mic. He struggles, and his sleeve rips as he tries to pull away from the guard.

Another guard swiftly moves up behind him, unseen.

"There's no cure! It's too late for them, but we can save ourselves if we—"

The sneaky guard jumps at his back, pulling the scientist's arms down and away, then locking them up high, some kind of wrestling move—a Melvin. No, a full Dawson. Something like that.

The mic drags on fabric, amplifying the rustling and thumps of the struggle.

The scientist keeps yelling, but the mic is away from his mouth so I can't make out what he's saying. No doubt more about the infected, how to save ourselves from the infected, or how the door is locked.

Impossible.

Except the doors *are* locked, right?

But he did that.

Then who's banging on the doors?

The mic falls, landing on the stage with a thump so loud it gives a feedback whine.

The barrage of banging on the doors intensifies. It almost sounds like a large animal, a bull or something, running repeatedly into the door.

Two of the security guards have the scientist pinned between them, hauling him across the stage, his arms and shoulders jacked so high by the wrestling hold he's stumbling along on his tiptoes.

Michaela steps forward and picks up the mic. She turns it off, and the shriek of feedback silences.

On the stage, the actors are all looking at each other with concern or amusement, as they once again become the center of attention.

Michaela turns the mic back on.

"Okay, sorry for that disruption. Whoa." She smiles out at us, but on the big screen above her head we can see that her smile is edged with a tension that wasn't there before.

The pounding on the doors is incessant.

"Thank you to con security, you guys are awesome. A round of applause, everyone."

The audience applauds dutifully.

Except for those of us who were standing at the back. We're not really paying attention, not even to the actors onstage.

Instead, unspoken, and en masse, people are all moving into the ballroom, away from the walls.

Away from the doors.

Imani and I stay in front of the camera stand, set near the aisle, away from the clump of standing-room-only audience.

We ignore the dirty looks the camerawoman keeps giving us.

It feels better to have my back to something, even if it's just a black carpet-covered square of low platform.

"Sounds like that guy might have some weirdo friends, huh?" Michaela says into the mic. "Sit tight. Security is working on it."

The banging on the door intensifies, but it has no rhythm, just a flurry of blows, deeply unsettling.

It doesn't stop.

Four security guards make their way down the twin aisles of the hall, moving fast past the approximately thirty rows of seats, converging on the central set of metal doors where the banging is the loudest.

One of the guards is talking into his radio. No doubt trying to call up the rest of the security team outside.

"There's not enough security," Imani murmurs. "Listen to that pounding. That's way more than one person."

We look at each other, eyes saucer-wide.

And the thought registers on my face at the same time I see it reflected on hers . . .

What if it's real?

No. Ridiculous.

You're just scaring yourself.

Where is Siggy?

I crane my neck to locate her. Since we've moved to the left, there's now the entire middle section of seats between us. It takes a moment for me to reorient myself, then I spot her, bright hair shining like a flag.

She's blowing kisses at Linus—so clearly the banging doesn't feel as scary from the front of the ballroom.

"Okay, let's get back on track," Michaela says over the banging. "They'll sort it out, let's just deprive them of the oxygen of our attention, right?"

She hands a second mic into the row of actors on the stage. "Cuellar, a question for you first."

The actor with the aggressive energy nods, reaching for the mic. His dark sunglasses make him look like a biker, or some corrupt cop or drill sergeant. Insectoid and ominous.

I'm sure he's not like his character. He just comes across that way.

"Sure thing, Michaela," he says into the mic. "Whatcha got?"

"What's your favorite—" Michaela begins, voice raised over the continuing disruption.

There's a blistering barrage of bangs on the door.

Cuellar laughs into his mic. "Little pig, little pig, let me in," he chants ominously into the mic.

I wish he hadn't done that.

A shiver races over my skin.

I lean around the platform again, looking back toward the doors.

The security guys batter at the doors from the inside, putting their weight into it, trying to budge them open.

"Imani." My voice is tight. "They *are* locked!"

"Isn't that a fire hazard or something?" Imani asks. Her arms are clenched tight across her stomach.

"Yeah, they should be unlocked," I say. "I don't like this." And that's when the doors suddenly give way.

13

There's a moment of surprised and curious silence as every pair of eyes in the room turns to the center set of doors, now yawning open.

Then someone, no, several someones, lots of them, pour into the ballroom.

There are screams, but I can't see what's happening. Just a mass of people pushing through the doors into the ballroom, moving . . . there's something wrong about the way they're moving.

Fast, but uncoordinated. A herky-jerky, twitching lurch. Like a puppeteer is pulling their strings, yanking them forward in a way opposite to how most people move.

But even from where I'm standing, I can see that audience members are pushing, shoving, screaming to get away.

Without questioning the instinct, I kick at the bottom of the platform, parting the pleated black skirt that covers the spindly struts. My foot finds a point of leverage, and I hoist myself up, pulling at the base of the camera stand.

The camerawoman reaches down and pulls me up.

Then we pull up Imani, scrambling after me in a split second.

A moment ago, the camerawoman was asking us to move away from the platform. Now she's helped us both up onto it. She's looks younger than my mom, with surprise lines grooved into her forehead above wide brown eyes.

We stare at each other in shocked amazement, then the woman points to the doors, behind us.

"They're fighting," she says.

I follow the line of her pointing finger, looking at the mass of people at the back of the ballroom, churning in a pressing ball, like dancers in a mosh pit.

Sorta.

Sorta like that. Except more violent. More shoving, more darting, lunging movement. More bodies falling, actually falling, to the floor, then covered by the next pressing wave of bodies pushing into the ballroom.

They're still coming in.

From the top of the camera platform, I can see what I couldn't standing on the hall floor.

I can see the people who rushed into the ballroom, moving so strangely, jerked along by impatient strings.

I can see what they're doing.

"That's not fighting," Imani says.

It's attacking.

As I watch, a man, one of those who rushed into the

ballroom, makes it through the churning ball of people at the doorway, breaking into the nearly open space at the end of the aisle. He then lunges at a woman. She shrieks and pulls away, into the back row of seats, climbing over people.

The man looks wrong, so wrong. His jaw hangs open as if broken, somehow, slanted and loose. A dark red liquid, a goo, that's what it is, scientific term must be "gross goo," drips out of his mouth steadily, like his throat is somehow a spigot left running in the winter.

A steady drip-thread of . . . goo.

Worse than that, somehow, is his skin. It's . . . mottled like a vulture's egg, gray and white and shiny at once, like a fever or—or—or like—

My rational brain shies away from the thought. From the idea. From the word.

At the same time, that other, panicked part of my brain gibbers the word incessantly, a panicked loop.

Corpse. Like a corpse. A corpse in water, except not bloated. But that color. That texture. Like a corpse. He's a corpse.

A zombie.

The zombie man jerks sideways, shoulders first, then legs, then an arm flings out. His jaw hangs open, but his head lifts, somehow making his mouth wider, as he throws himself at a man, who's just standing there, staring in shocked horror.

The zombie brings him down with an uncoordinated falling attack, with complete disregard for his own safety, the zombie just *throws himself* at the shocked man, bringing him down.

The man shrieks, falling backward hard, his head connecting with the back of a chair.

It must have knocked him out because he doesn't make another sound, or move, as the zombie doesn't pause, doesn't stop, just presses his broken jaw into the man's neck, leveraging and pulling down with his upper teeth, pulling and tearing side to side, like a dog with a rag toy.

A bright jet of blood arcs into the air as the zombie lifts his face. Then he reattaches, sawing more with his upper teeth.

"Oh my God!" the camerawoman gasps.

"We have to go, we have to go," Imani chants, pulling at my arm.

"Where?" I ask, and I glance away from the attacking zombies. I look to the front of the ballroom.

"I'm calling the police," the camerawoman says, pulling a phone out of her jeans pocket.

Siggy. Can she and Blair see what's happening?

The actors on the stage are frowning at the commotion in the back of the ballroom. Some crane their necks to see better. But there's a sea of chairs between them and the back of the hall, row after row of seats filled with at least a thousand con attendees.

All sitting there in the dimness of the room.

They can't see what's happening.

They're not scared.

Yet.

"No signal." The camerawoman jabs impatiently at her phone.

In every row that isn't in the back of the ballroom, the audience just sits calmly, glancing around, some standing, but most waiting for Michaela to tell them what's happening, to get the panel back underway.

But Michaela just stands there, holding the mic below her chin, staring in surprise as more herky-jerky bodies press into the ballroom.

"It's . . . is it . . . ?" Michaela says, squinting at the surging bodies in the back of the room. "Some kind of flash mob?"

The standing-room crowd at the back of the ballroom has started shoving to get away, moving in isolation from the rest of the seated audience like the ripple of a larger wave to come.

And in row two, Siggy is still blowing kisses at Linus, as Blair eggs her on, clapping.

They don't know. They don't see.

This is an attack.

The scientist said *the infected are here.*

Zombies. He called them zombies.

The zombie apocalypse is here now.

I have to warn them. Siggy, Blair, Hunter, all of them. Everyone.

Imani is already ahead of me, of course, her thoughts and mine running together like always, almost as if we're telepathic. She's cupped her hands around her mouth, hollering at the stage.

"Run, Siggy!"

There's too much noise. Too much confusion.

Siggy's head swivels slightly, like she's thinking of glancing back where we were.

Onstage, Linus says something and her head turns back toward him.

On the giant screen over the stage, there's a wide shot of the waiting actors. The shot wavers slightly with our weight as Imani jumps and waves her arms.

"We have to show them!" I tell the camerawoman.

I grab the side of the camera lens and push.

The camerawoman takes ahold of the lever that tilts the camera and adjusts it down.

On the big screen, the picture skims down and across the seated audience, then finally hits the aisle at the back of the room.

The camera must have an automatic focus, or the

camerawoman does it, because the picture first blurs, then pulls in clear on the face of another zombie, a woman with bright blood smearing her mouth and nose, making it look vaguely like she has a muzzle, except for the fact that it's blood, and when she opens her mouth wide you can see chunks of bright red flesh in her mouth.

I recognize her. It's the rude woman with shiny lips from Autograph Alley. The one who pushed in front of me to get Janet's signature.

Something got to her. A zombie. The skin of one cheek is torn—white teeth gleaming through the gash.

Through the close-up of the camera, I can see clearly not just the gray mottling on her skin, the coloring that makes it look necrotic, but also something else.

A writhing, somehow under the skin. As if the musculature of her face is somehow undulating in a wave. It makes her skin look like a snake's egg, pulsating with the movements of the snakeling within.

I recoil instinctively as my stomach lurches. It's disgusting and really, really disturbing, the ripples of the muscles under her gray and mottled skin.

She jerks. Her arms give a spasm, and she falls forward as if tugged, flailing toward a man.

The panic that began in the back of the hall sweeps forward through the seats, like a wave in a stadium, as the rest of the audience sees the zombies on the big screen. As they watch the zombie woman bite into the arm of the man. As they see his agonized, terrified face.

Screams and shouts as people clamber out of their seats, or try to. There's shoving in panic, trying to escape narrow rows and funneling into suddenly crowded aisles.

Imani is still waving her arms over her head, and I see Siggy standing on her chair, searching for us in the back of the hall, where she left us.

Where the zombies are.

She doesn't know to look for us anywhere else.

Even standing on the chair she can't see that we're not there. The back of the hall and now the aisles are a churning mass of panicking people, shoving each other out of the way, rushing toward the exits.

Which, except for the one funneling more zombies into the ballroom, are all locked.

The scientist meant to protect us, but of course no one believed him.

And now only one set of doors is open, and the zombies are erupting in, like ants streaming out of an anthill, angry, hungry, attacking us.

Making this entire ballroom a trap. We're trapped.

"She can't see us!" Imani yells over the screams around us. "She doesn't know where we are!"

Siggy climbs onto the back of her chair, perching there almost impossibly, like a cat—then she takes a few steps, walking along the tops of the chairs like a high-wire artist.

"No!" I shriek. "Siggy! No!"

"She's trying to get to us," Imani moans. "June, she can't go there!"

Meaning back into the aisle. Back where the zombies surge forward, attacking.

Blair jumps onto a seat and grabs Siggy's arm, pulling her back.

The camera platform sways.

I look down. A sea of shoving bodies buffet our spindly scaffold.

"She's got her!" Imani says, relief layering over the fear in her voice. "Good job, Blair!"

I glance back at Blair, pulling Siggy. They're not heading to the aisle anymore. In fact, they're heading in the opposite direction. Instead of rushing toward the aisle, toward the doors, they're clamoring over a row, heading to the stage.

Which means they're facing the screen again.

Imani thinks of it first, moving like lightning. She grabs the camera and swivels it a full one-eighty degrees, to our faces.

It blurs and tightens, blurs and tightens.

"Here." The camerawoman messes with something, and

on the screen at the front of the hall, Imani's face comes into perfect focus, selfie-close.

Blair sees it first, pointing up.

Siggy turns and sees us standing on the swaying platform.

Imani turns, putting her back to the camera so she can face our friends.

"We're okay!" she yells, even though there's no way that Blair and Siggy can hear her.

And even though the platform sways so violently we stumble, gripping each other's arms for balance.

I push my hand at the stage in a shooing motion.

"Go!" I yell.

Imani points at Siggy, then at Blair. Then she makes running fingers and runs her hand to the right, offstage. She pumps her fist in the air twice.

Gestures we know from the show. From James's army ranger character, who's now reaching down to the audience, pulling people onto the stage and out of harm's way.

Blair nods and give a thumbs-up. Siggy frowns, worry stamped on her face.

The platform lurches, and I stumble so hard I nearly totter off into the sea of bodies below us.

The camerawoman grabs my arm, pulling me steady. "We can't stay here!"

All around us, hundreds of people panic, pushing and

shoving each other out of the way, a stampede, headed to the exits, the sets of double doors placed at intervals along the back of the ballroom.

From the platform, the panicking people look like a flock of birds, scattering in different directions from a gunshot.

"We need to get to the stage," I tell Imani and the camerawoman. "There are no zombies that way."

"And there's a stairwell back that way," the camerawoman agrees. "We can get out."

"Okay, let's go." Imani nods.

The only problem is getting down without getting trampled. But then the buffeting crowd thins, suddenly, and rows of empty seats are in front of us.

Screams punctuate the air.

I glance behind us, at the center doors. The infected have stopped pushing in, and the doors hang open, empty.

With a mass of swaying zombies between us and them.

The screams cut off suddenly, and I don't want to follow the sound. I don't want to see why they stopped.

I turn toward the stage.

Most of the actors have exited into one of the wings. James Cooper is only now following after them, walking with an older man he helped onto the stage when the panic started.

Right. They're going right. The exit must be to the right.

I climb down first, straight down the front of the platform. I rush across the small yellow-taped square and climb over the nearest row of empty seats, into the row.

I'm now in the middle section of seats, about ten rows up from the back of the room.

It feels a little safer with the chairs between me and the zombies.

Imani and the camerawoman scramble down off the platform after me, and follow me over the rows of seats heading toward the stage.

More screams and grunting behind us.

I glance back. A pod of about thirty to fifty zombies are approaching a large group of people, maybe a hundred humans, trying to get out another set of double doors.

The doors don't budge, and the zombies hurtle into the scattering people. It looks almost like a football game, just lines of pressing and running people, struggling against each other, indistinct and violent.

Some people have to be getting out, right? They have to be able to run around the zombies, or push them back. We can't all be trapped in here.

It's impossible to tell. There's so much chaos now, and without stopping to really watch, it's impossible to tell how many groups are fighting the zombies, or simply fighting to get away, trampling each other.

The ballroom feels like a bomb went off in the middle of it, the seating mostly empty, bodies and straining people ringing the edge of the room.

We climb over the rows of chairs heading toward the stage, lunging and stumbling like the world's worst hurdlers. Imani is the fastest, her long legs just letting her do these long steps; she's about two rows in front of me. I start to get a rhythm going, though, using this sit-and-pivot move to nearly catch up.

The camerawoman is right with me, until she looks over her shoulder as she's leaning forward to grab the next seat back, misses her grip, and falls forward and sideways.

The back of the chair catches her upper lip as she pulls back and tries to twist to minimize the impact.

It still hits hard, and she falls awkwardly between the rows.

"Hey!" I call to her, and I turn back, lunging over the row to get to her.

Then I see what she was looking at. Why she looked back.

A zombie man has spotted us. It's the man with the broken jaw, one of the first zombies to make it into the ballroom and now one of the first to make it this far into the space.

He throws himself over the rows of chairs with

uncoordinated desperation, without looking at the seats, just throwing himself forward, tumbling, falling, standing, and thrashing forward again.

The camerawoman lies on her back, blinking up at me. Blood gushes down her chin and neck from her split upper lip.

"Get up!" I yell. I pull at her arm, trying not to hear the guttural noises the infected man makes as he advances.

She nods, and sits up, shakes her head like a cartoon character trying to scatter circling birds around their head.

I glance toward the stage.

Imani has just realized I stopped. She's got the fiercest expression I've ever seen on her face—this determined anger.

She's damn near leaping over the rows to get back to where I pull the camerawoman after me, over the next row, and the next.

We're moving too slow.

The zombie man is four rows behind us.

"Come on!" I scream at the camerawoman.

Ten more rows and we'll be there.

It's going to be close.

I refuse to think about what happens if the zombie man follows us onto the stage.

Just get to the stage, just get to the stage.

We keep hurtling forward. Two rows left.

Second row. Where Blair and Siggy sat, my brain comments, like it matters AT ALL.

We're not going to make it.

"Get her on the stage!" I yelp at Imani, and I dash sideways in the row instead of climbing over the next one, trying to draw the pursuing zombie away.

One row behind me, the zombie rushes after me.

I feel the brush of his fingers on my arm.

And then I realize the fatal flaw in my plan.

Because there's an aisle I have to cross to get to the next section of chairs.

And not even the flimsy barrier of a row of seats will be between me and the zombie chasing me.

And there's another zombie, a woman in a loud, jaguar-patterned sequined shirt, stumbling down the aisle toward the front of the stage.

Two zombies converged in a ballroom, and I—I ran right into both of them.

14

ehind me, Imani's voice shrieks like metal on metal.
"JUNE, LOOK OUT!"

At the sound of her voice, the jaguar-print zombie looks away from me toward the stage.

It gives me the split second I need.

If I was coordinated, it would be kind of beautiful.

I burst out into the aisle as both zombies turn.

They flail toward me, but they're heading where I was.

Not where I am, where I've ducked, tucked, and rolled into the world's clumsiest somersault.

But muscle memory takes over and I feel like I'm in elementary school again, wearing pink tights and a black leotard.

The two zombies collide above me. The impact is so hard they spin off each other, knocked back like billiard balls.

I rocket to my feet, spin, then I'm back in the rows, rushing back the way I came, headlong to the stage.

Imani and the camerawoman grab my forearms and boost me so hard I can almost stick the landing on my feet.

Or at least it feels like that as I fall into their arms.

"You jerk!" Imani scolds, giving me a quick hug, as the two zombies chasing me reach the stage. They batter against it with their chests, arms reaching out.

They can't climb it. Or perhaps, like all their movements so far, it's completely uncoordinated, unthought, and they simply can't get enough of their mass to fall forward over the stage lip.

"Thanks," I say to Imani and the camerawoman.

"No, thank *you*," the camerawoman says. "I'm Rosa García." She gently wipes her sleeve across her bloody chin.

"You're welcome, Rosa." I pant. "I'm June Blue."

"I'm-Imani-Choi-and-we-can't-stay-here," Imani says in a rush. She points.

At least ten more zombies from the huge mass in the back of the ballroom have noticed us. They stumble down the aisles toward the stage.

"What happens when they all see us? There are what, two hundred of them? Three hundred? At least. The stage could break or they might find a way up," Rosa asks.

"Agreed," I say. "We need to get to that stairwell."

"Siggy and Blair and the actors went that way." Imani points stage right.

We start moving, behind the row of chairs and toward the edge of the stage. I glance back out at the scene behind us.

The biggest clump of bodies, both human and zombie,

is by the main set of doors. From the stage it looks surreal, like the set of a war movie, or like the carpet is somehow an ocean, and the bodies are the debris of a shipwreck, washing against the walls in undulating waves.

Except the carpet isn't moving, and the movement is only from the zombies now, tearing, pulling, and ripping . . .

There's a second, smaller group of bodies a short distance away from the main entrance, at the next set of doors. Mostly silence, and tearing movement. No survivors.

But at the next set of doors after that, a huddle of around ten humans has rallied and stands in a semicircle. A table has been turned on its side, legs jutting out. Two burly men stand on either side, protecting the small cluster of people behind it.

As I watch, one of the men swings a huge canister at a zombie. It connects to the zombie's head with a resounding clang.

A fire extinguisher. He's armed himself with a fire extinguisher.

The zombie goes down, skull misshapen by the impact.

Past that small huddle of fighters is another group of humans. It's the group of six UGA cheerleaders from this morning, still dressed in their zombified bright-red uniforms. They stand under the curved edge of the balcony. The boy cheerleaders, the stuntmen, are helping the girl cheerleaders up to safety.

Which is impressive, since there aren't any stairs and given that the balcony is at least twelve feet above their heads.

One cheerleader girl is already up on the balcony, running sideways, looking for something, while two of the three stuntmen on the ballroom floor have lifted two other girls expertly, heels in their hands as they carefully launch first one, then the other into the air and at the balcony railing.

It's not pretty, but both cheerleaders manage to make it onto the balcony, although one appears injured, her thighs slamming into the railing as she lands.

The third stuntman spots the other two, guarding them from zombies, but so far none have made it past the group with the fire extinguishers.

For a split second I'm mesmerized, wondering how the stuntmen are going to get up to the balcony.

Two of the stuntmen form a base for the third, the smallest one, to climb up. He puts a foot in the crease of a thigh and hip, then steps on shoulders, then his feet are in their nested hands as the two stuntmen left on the ground send him up.

"We have to go!" Imani says urgently, grabbing my arm.

More zombies are now standing at the foot of the stage, mindlessly reaching for us.

If I look at them too long, at the sickly gray mottling, the disturbing muscle undulations that ripple under their skin, the red-threaded eyes . . .

The gaping wound in one neck . . .

My heart judders, and air is hard to draw, suddenly. Paralyzed, I'm paralyzed with fear. All my life I've heard that expression, and now I know what it means.

I can't move. I can't even breathe.

"Don't look at them! Look at me!" Imani says. Her hands are hot on my face as she turns my head physically away from the zombies.

Behind Imani, one of the two stuntmen left on the ballroom floor is now boosting the other one up from his shoulders. The effort makes his face a series of creases and jutting tendon tracks.

He does one of those really loud, usually obnoxious weight-lifter yells.

But it works, he boosts the other man up, up, up. And now the stuntman he's lifting grasps the balcony rail, pulling himself over.

Every zombie in the hall has turned to look at the last stuntman, even our group bumping against the stage.

How is he going to get up to the balcony?

Then I look at his face, grim and determined as he surveys the mass of zombies coming for him.

He knows. He always knew.

He wasn't getting out.

He feints a lunge in one direction, and the closest zombie

to him falls for it, creating a hole in the line of approaching zombies.

He slips through, no longer looking like a stuntman, but a linebacker in sudden possession of the ball.

He's so brave.

I want to yell and clap. I want to cheer him on.

I also don't want to do any of those things, because the zombies will head for us next if I do.

Me, I'm not so brave.

Imani grabs my hand and tugs, and I follow her, rushing the rest of the way across the back of the stage, past the burned out car chassis set décor, to the curtain at the side, where there will hopefully be stairs down beyond it.

Imani is reaching out to pull back the curtain when I think of it.

The guy swinging the fire extinguisher.

"Wait, Imani!" My voice is a whisper-hiss. "What if they got away but there's a zombie back there now? Behind the curtain?"

PAY NO ATTENTION TO THE ZOMBIE BEHIND THE CURTAIN.

My brain chatters the *Wizard of Oz* joke unhelpfully.

Imani pauses, hand outstretched.

"She's right," the camerawoman, Rosa, whispers behind me.

"So, what do we do?" Imani hisses back.

"We need a weapon." I turn back to the stage behind us. There are chairs, the fancy padded folding kind, a tall stool, an empty microphone stand, microphone on the ground next to it.

"Wait here!"

I dash out, grab the microphone stand, and start to haul it over to the edge of the stage.

The stand is quite heavy, weighted at the bottom by a heavy black disc-weight, and it's bulky, with an adjustable arm coming off the center pole.

As I wrestle with it, I can't help but glance back into the ballroom.

The stuntman has sprinted out into the middle of the hall, dodging zombies and chairs.

He can't run forever.

And that's when I see it, and he does, too.

His squad, the stuntmen and the cheerleaders on the balcony, are waving, pulling their hands silently, urging him back toward them.

They can't possibly help him. They can't reach him, and even if they could, how could they possibly lift him? He's huge—built like if The Rock met The Rock and then absorbed himself, becoming MegaRock.

His friends throw a thick, industrial-weight extension

cord over the balcony. At even spaces, the cord has been tied into loops all the way up, like steps in a ladder.

The stuntman sees it and turns, pulling out of grasping hands and sprinting like a gazelle *back* across the hall to the extension cord.

The stuntman does a running leap and grabs it.

I reach Imani, and Rosa spins the attachment screw threads on the mic stand, pulling apart two separate weapons.

At the balcony, it's like something out of one of those TV athletic competitions. The stuntman just swings and pulls himself, arm over arm, until he's over the top and onto the balcony.

My heart does a happy swoop as his friends hug him, pounding his back, tears streaming down their faces.

Rosa hands Imani the base of the mic stand, and gives me the arm.

The stuntman points down to the other clump of survivors, hiding behind the overturned sound table. The two burly guys down there are still standing, swinging at the zombies with fire extinguishers.

The stuntman and the rest of the cheer squad haul up the extension cord and run along the edge of the balcony until they are standing over the trapped group.

The extension cord starts to lower swiftly.

We can't get there from here. There are far too many zombies now butting against the lip of the stage, and too many more zombies in the rest of the ballroom between us and the extension cord.

But there are already survivors. The cheerleaders and the other people fighting, and more people making it out of the ballroom.

We can do it, too.

I take a test swing with the arm section of the stand. My *ZombieCon!* badge gets in the way, and the shoestring lanyard tangles around the thin metal. I nearly end up clocking myself in the forehead with the abrupt stop of my swing.

"Better take these off," Rosa says, pulling her own ID badge from around her neck.

"Good idea," I reply.

We shove our badges into our bags or pockets.

I take another test swing with the arm section of the mic stand.

Imani hoists the base, the heavy round disc resting on her shoulder like a flat parasol.

Rosa has broken the antenna off the burned-out car chassis.

"Let's go," I say.

I reach out and poke the mic stand arm through the curtains.

Nothing. No resistance, no zombie interest.

So, I reach out and twitch the curtain aside.

15

No one stands on the other side of the curtain.

Imani moves swiftly and silently down the steps and peers around. I pull the curtain back in place.

We can't see the zombies, and they can't see us.

Rosa and I join Imani at the bottom of the stairs. To our left is the tall, floor-to-ceiling black curtain. That curtain and a freestanding panel of chain-link fence are the only things that separate us from the zombies in the ballroom.

It feels bizarre to be protected by something so flimsy. It's like when I was a scared kid, in bed, pulling my covers over my head.

If I can't see it, it can't see me.

Except it seems sort of true. So far.

It's only a matter of time until one of those things blunders into the curtain, and then comes through to the other side.

Or worse, the zombies might knock over the chain-link panel, which would take down the curtains.

We can't be here when that happens.

Right now, all the zombies are preoccupied with the humans who remain on the other side of the curtain. When that distraction ends, we need to be gone.

To our right is the back of the stage. There's a strip of floor between the stage and the back wall of the ballroom. The floor-to-ceiling curtain that runs along the back of the stage makes the area feel like a tunnel.

There's one set of double doors set into the back wall.

And no actors. No stagehands or security.

No Siggy. No Blair.

They got out.

"Those doors have got to be unlocked," I whisper to Imani.

She nods and darts to them.

I follow.

She reaches out her free hand and quietly pushes the crash bar.

It doesn't budge.

She pushes harder. It makes a slight knocking sound, but the door doesn't budge.

"Shh!" I hiss.

"You shh!" she hisses back.

I trade places and try the door. Then Rosa joins me, putting her shoulder against the door.

The quiet bump comes again, but the crash bar doesn't budge.

"Now what?" Rosa whispers.

The tunnel.

"That way." I nod at the curtain-lined walkway.

"Eek." Imani's voice squeaks.

"Yeah," I whisper. "But we have to go. They went. No one's here. We have to go that way."

I go first, and we rush along the back of the stage, trying not to rustle the curtain, trying not to make a sound, unable to see what happens at the next open area on the opposite side of the stage platform.

And trying not to think about hands coming at my legs from the empty space under the stage.

There's so much adrenaline in my blood I don't stop when I get to the edge, just burst out into the second "backstage area" on the other side.

We're still in the back of the ballroom, only separated from the zombies by the black floor-to-ceiling wing curtain and the smaller freestanding chain-link panel beyond it.

But this curtained-off section is bigger. Clearly, it's where the actors gathered to wait for their panels. There's a catering table stocked with snacks and drinks, and a few tall director's chairs, some with coats and bags still sitting in them.

But I'm lucky, because there are no zombies here.

However, there are three people, two of them famous,

standing by the closed double doors, staring at us and blinking.

Linus Sheppard speaks first, his British accent somehow sounding crisper in his urgent whisper.

"Are they chasing you? Are they backstage?"

He sounds like an ultra-posh librarian.

"No," Imani whispers back. "Not yet."

Annie Blaze crosses her arms. "They probably saw you, though." Her whisper is a hiss of anger or fear. Or probably both, but it still sounds like an accusation.

"Take it easy, Annie." The third person is a woman dressed in a rock-and-roll-looking red-and-black business suit. She has sleek black hair in a severe bob; the kind of hairstyle that looks both retro and French.

"Don't handle me, Mia," Annie hisses. "It isn't your job right now."

Mia lifts her hands and scowls in frustration. Her red-soled man-killer stilettos tap quietly as she stalks a few steps away from Annie.

Imani and I cross to the double doors.

"Locked," Linus says, gesturing. "It wasn't locked at first but—"

He pushes. The same rigid bar. The same slight knock as the door shifts in its cradle but otherwise doesn't move.

I'm backstage with two actors from my favorite show:

the veterinarian and the trucker's daughter. And my best friend in the whole world. And Rosa, the *ZombieCon!* camerawoman. And Mia, whoever she is.

And there's an actual zombie apocalypse going on.

It would feel completely surreal if it wasn't for the mortal terror shooting through my veins.

As it is, it still feels surreal, but it's almost in passing, like noticing a giant purple giraffe outside of a train window, and then it's gone as the world whizzes by.

"Where is everyone else?" I ask. "Everyone from onstage? And the others who climbed up?"

"We were all back here. The door was open, just this one." Linus touches one of the double doors. "We were the last to get here, to this side. We were all rushing out but the door fell closed after Sam."

Sam. The older actor who plays the wise lawyer, Jamison, on the show.

"We got to it," Linus continues. "But it wouldn't open and they were already gone."

Imani pushes the crash bar again.

"Dammit!" Imani hisses.

Okay, I don't know what to do now.

What would I do if I was on the show? If I was on *Human Wasteland*?

I rush over to the catering table and unzip my mini

backpack. I stuff in energy bars and several little bottled waters.

I slip the backpack back on and glance back at the others still standing at the locked doors.

Imani's eyebrows couldn't arch at me more.

"Just in case!" I say defensively.

"Uh-huh. Like we're gonna be here long enough to get hungry."

Linus puts his shoulder against the door again and pushes.

"Do you even *watch* the show, Imani?" I ask, frustration making my whisper snappish. But I'm not looking at her as I scan the table. Maybe there's a knife or something. Maybe we could . . . I don't know . . . wedge it in the door thingy and . . .

"We're not on the show! This is real life!" Imani's voice is compressed with effort. I look back. She's pushing the door with Linus and Rosa.

Mia's holding her phone up, trying to find a signal.

Annie's hugging herself, looking like she's about to cry, which makes tears want to jump into my own eyes.

"Feels a lot like the show," I mutter.

Then I see it.

A shabby backpack with a large Mickey Mouse patch.

The guy who jumped onstage, the scientist's bag.

I saw him, crouched at the end of Autograph Alley, messing with the door with some kind of screwdriver.

He put it in the bag.

I turn so fast I stumble on my own feet. I dig in the bag, a bunch of loose tools, bulky military rations, two water bottles, a bandana, electrical tape, duct tape, first aid kit—my hand closes around a screwdriver handle. I have it, it's here.

A key.

Sort of like a key.

I sling the Mickey patch backpack on the front of me like a baby carrier, and rush over to the door.

"Stop pushing." I pull them back off the door, and I hit my knees, okay, so that was a bit too hard, ow.

But I don't stop. I'm looking for the screws or the holes or whatever he was messing with on the bottom of the crash bars.

The screwdriver isn't really a screwdriver. It's more like a hex key, the kind that comes with cheap, assemble-it-yourself furniture, a thin piece of metal that bends ninety degrees at the end and has a flat, stop-sign-shaped tip that slots into special screws.

It's sort of like that, except completely straight and with weird notches and slots cut into the hexagon-cylindrical end. And the whole thing someone put on a screwdriver handle.

I jam the hex-end into one of the round holes at the bottom side of the crash bar. I rotate it, pushing, and feel a sort of sliding-click, and the whole thing pushes in slightly.

I start twisting it, how's it go? Oh yeah.

Lefty-loosey.

Lefty-loosey.

Lefty-loosey.

I can feel the tension releasing. Something is changing at least.

"Hurry," Annie whispers, her eyes on the curtains behind us.

I can't help it, I turn and look.

The curtains are billowing slightly. Swaying, as if being pushed by shoulders or feet.

"I've got your back," Imani says, lifting her disc-ended microphone stand base, cocking it on her shoulder as she faces the curtains behind us. "You just keep going, June."

I turn back and twist some more. The hex-key-on-a-stick stops moving.

I pull it out and shift to the opposite end.

Rosa pushes the bar. It's definitely moving more, but not enough to disengage the lock.

She steps back and I jab the key in the hole and twist until it shifts and indents into place.

Twist, twist, twist.

Annie mutters, "Hurry, hurry, hurry."

Her whisper chants me faster.

My hand hurts, my knees hurt, and my shoulders are wrenched so tight I feel like they're up by my ears, but then the hex key clicks and stops twisting.

I pop the key out of the hole and stand up.

Rosa pushes.

For just an instant, it doesn't move, then it shifts. There's a double clunk of the locks at the top and bottom of the door opening, and a fresh blast of cold air whistles in through the crack.

"Good job, kid!" Mia whispers, tiptoeing closer in her high heels.

Linus steps up, and pushes the door open a tiny bit more. He leans forward, and puts his eye to the crack.

"Looks clear," he says.

"Go!" Annie whispers, and she gives his shoulders a shove.

Not . . . not exactly a friendly move, there, but I guess she's scared.

She doesn't say sorry, not even reflexively, but he's opened the door and stepped forward, glancing around behind it.

"It's clear," he says, and Annie runs.

Imani follows her, then Rosa and Mia. This hall isn't fixed

up like the one on the lobby side of the ballroom. Where that one had fancy, if industrial, carpets and light fixtures, and framed art pieces on the walls, this hall is a tile-and-white-wall expanse. A working, seemingly windowless corridor behind the front-of-the-house formality.

My heart falls that it's empty.

I'm glad there are no zombies, but I was really hoping to find Siggy and Blair there.

The hall is bookended on either side, each long expanse of tile leading to similar exit doors.

I dart through the door Linus is holding open and immediately hit my knees again.

Again, not as smooth as I would have liked, but at least this time it didn't hurt.

Much.

"What are you doing? Come on!" Annie hisses at me.

Linus has braced the open door with his shoulder and foot, holding it steady for me as I jam the key back into the hole.

Righty-tighty.

I twist and twist.

"Good," Imani whispers, encouraging me. "God, you're so smart, June."

Whatever.

But I can't help both the instinct to contradict her, and the charge of pride that rushes through me at her praise.

"Go, June!" Rosa urges.

Righty-tighty, righty-tighty, righty-tighty.

"Have you guys lost your minds? Let's *go!*" Annie takes five steps back toward us.

The hex stops turning. I shift to the other hole.

Linus rebraces the door, and I jab and twist, feeling for the indent and lock confirming that the key is in place.

Righty-tighty, righty-tighty.

Behind me is the empty backstage area.

Well, not precisely empty.

Have the zombies billowed the curtain more? Has any one of them moved through the gap, past the chain link and the curtain?

Can they feel the fresh air from the hall?

Is there a zombie backstage now? Spotting us standing, and me kneeling, like a sitting duck, here in the doorway?

Don't look.

Just turn.

I mean, just turn the key. Don't turn around.

Turn, don't turn.

My inner voice is very helpful.

A huff of humorless laughter puffs a stray hair away from my mouth.

The key stops turning, the ratcheted tightness gone.

I scramble up to my feet and step back.

The backstage area isn't empty anymore.

A single zombie has found his way through the curtain. He's tall with a wide, jutting jaw like an ice scraper.

He looks at us, somehow seeing through the clouded, bloodshot mess that are his eyes. His mouth opens and his arm jerks up and out as he rushes toward us, gasping, a wretched, rattling groan sounding out of his throat.

Linus's crisp, normal speaking voice breaks the spell of shocked fear.

"Not today, thank you," he says, speaking with perfect British diction as he swiftly pushes the door closed.

There's a double clunk as the locks at the top and bottom of the door fall into place.

Then there's a thump, and the thump repeats and repeats as the zombie knocks into the door.

I can't help the titter as it flies out of my mouth, powered by extreme relief, and the fact that it was actually funny.

Imani giggles, too, squeezing my hand, and we lean into each other for a second, a lean that's like a hug, a little.

She puts on an upper-crust accent.

"Not today," she says, and dissolves into helpless giggles.

"Thank you," I finish. And we laugh.

Linus smiles, then laughs, too.

"Y'all are messed up," Annie says, shaking her head at us.

Linus wipes his eyes, and sticks out his hand.

"I'm Linus. Thanks for saving us . . ." His voice trails off, waiting for me to introduce myself.

I feel the blood rushing to my cheeks, and at the same time also draining from my head.

Feeling a little dizzy, I take his hand and shake it.

"June."

"Thanks for saving us, June."

He turns and shakes Imani's hand.

"Imani," she says.

"Pleased to meet you, Imani."

The camerawoman nods at them. "I'm Rosa."

"Mia Fontaine." The woman in the edgy black-and-red business suit steps forward, improbably pulling a business card out of her pocket and handing it to me.

"When we get out of here, give me a call," she says. "I can use quick thinkers like you."

A blush of pride rushes to my face along with the sudden ridiculous image of me bowing out my arms, cowboy-style, touching the brim of my nonexistent hat at Mia in response to her praise.

"Okay, thanks." I look at the card. *Apex Management.* There's an address in Los Angeles, and a phone number.

I slide the card into my back pocket, like the ace it is. I mean, maybe she'll give me an internship or something if college doesn't work out.

After we get through all this.

"And I'm Annie, y'all know that," Annie Blaze says. "And I cannot even believe that we're in some kind of biohazard outbreak."

"Zombies," I say. "It's the zombie apocalypse."

"Sure feels like it, huh?" Linus says, shaking his head.

Imani and I glance at each other. I can feel her wondering at his reticence to call it what it so clearly is.

Maybe it's just too scary? Or he's wanting to be scientific? Precise?

It doesn't matter what we call them. Zombies or infected. It doesn't change what's happening now.

"Well, at least we have familiarity on our side." Mia cocks an eyebrow under her pinup bangs, looking impossibly cool. "I mean, we're all zombie aficionados, right? We know what to do if anyone does."

"Right," Rosa agrees. "I'm sure there are lots of little groups like us all over the center. Fans who know what to do now."

Imani grabs my hand and squeezes, and I know she's thinking the same thing I am.

Siggy. Blair.

"All right, squad, let's get going," Linus says, his voice warm. "I for one want to get out of this scene and into my luxury trailer. You're all invited."

"Right, we're definitely putting that in your next contract," Mia agrees.

I glance up and down the white hall. There's nothing back here, not even a potted plant or a trash can. I wish there was something, anything I could push up to the door to help hold it closed.

We have to rely on whatever mechanism the hex key disabled.

I reposition the backpacks, feeling both reassured at their weight and also completely ridiculous, wearing the Mickey one on the front like it's a baby.

Imani steps close to me, her face drawn in concern.

"Do you think they're okay?" she asks me. "Siggy? And Blair?"

"Absolutely," I say, my voice firm. "They know as much about zombies as we do. And you saw Blair. She knew to get on the stage. I'm sure they're just right up ahead."

Imani nods. Her eyes take on that determined light, the same one from when she was hurdling over rows to come back for me.

"We're going to find them," she says.

I pick the set of doors farthest from the front of the convention center and lead the way down the white-tiled corridor.

16

*M*oving swiftly down the hall, I realize my first impression was correct; there are no windows set into the walls. No windows looking outside, none looking into other rooms. The only window in sight is a narrow one set into the door at the bottom of the hall.

At the top of the hall on the opposite end is a solid door that probably opens into the lobby.

We pass a few other windowless doors with various names or description plates beside them. I don't read any; too busy formulating a plan on the go.

"Okay, that way," I tell the others while pointing to the door with the window at the bottom of the hall. "It's the far, um, left side or Park Street side—whatever direction it is—of the convention center."

"Southeast," Imani says. "That's the southeast side of the building."

Standing next to her, Linus does a subtle double-take, clearly surprised and impressed at the technical precision.

Trust Imani to know it like she has a compass grafted to

her hand. I feel myself stand a little taller, proud just to be her friend.

"Right," I agree. "That's the door to the stairwell. On the ground floor that side of the building has the loading docks."

We rush to the door at the end, and it has a narrow window, crosshatched with wire inside for added security.

It looks out onto the top landing of a wide industrial metal staircase, painted gray.

"Wait," Imani says as I put out my hand to the lever door handle.

"What if they're in there?" she asks, ebony-dark eyes widening.

My hand freezes, hovering in place.

"We don't know where they could be," Annie agrees. "Maybe we should just stay here."

"What?" I whip around. "We can't stay here, we have to find the others—"

Annie interrupts me.

"Why? Who says? We can just stay here. You got us out, you locked them in, there's no windows, this area is safe."

Linus rounds on her with incredulous eyes.

"You can't be serious. Have you even watched the show you're on?"

"What?" Annie says defensively. "What's wrong with my idea?"

"Well, for one thing nowhere is safe," Linus explains.

Huh.

They don't really act like a couple, do they?

"All it takes is for that door to fail, if enough zombies push on it who knows? And what happens then?" Linus says.

"Right," I say, backing him up. "Not to mention that we don't know what's behind any of these other doors, maybe a zombie is there, and what if they come out somehow?"

"Well, we'd run," Annie says.

"Where?" Rosa asks.

Annie gestures impatiently at the stairwell door. "We can go down to the first floor then. Go out the loading docks or whatever."

"Right, so let's at least check it out, huh?" I ask. "Let me just tiptoe out there now, while we're not being chased by anything, and I'll check out the lay of the land."

I don't say that I have no intention of coming back.

Siggy is still out there somewhere.

Siggy, and Blair.

And I suddenly want to see them, *both* of them, with a rush of feeling in my heart like a stretch, like a flood. My friends from childhood, Siggy, my goofy doofus, and Blair.

My prickly friend. Who hurt me.

But it doesn't matter so much now, does it? Not when it's life or death. Not when the chance to mend our friendship might never come now. Not if anything happens to them.

Or us.

Where did they go?

I have to find them or follow them out, if they got out already.

"It's a good idea," Linus urges her. "Better than running into the unknown."

"Oh, shut up, Linus," Annie snaps.

Rosa's voice is measured and soothing. "We can be ready to pull June back and close the door if we need to."

Annie crosses her arms under her chest again.

"Okay," she sighs. "Go ahead. Fine. Whatever."

"Good girl, Annie," Mia says, checking her phone for a signal again.

"Mia, I swear to God—" Annie doesn't finish the threat.

"Let's keep together, everyone," Imani says. "Rule one: We only fight zombies, right?"

I put my hand out to the lever handle, trying to feel steady in spite of my heart hammering in my chest like a runaway train.

Or something that isn't a mixed metaphor or whatever.

Holding my breath, I push the door handle down silently.

It goes, and I feel the metal tongues pulling back into

the door, feel it start to give as I gently press with my shoulder.

Then it stops. A solid stop. Something is blocking it.

"I said you can go ahead." Annie's voice is sharp like an ice pick.

"It's blocked!" I crane my neck, shifting first up on my toes, then down low as I look through the window, trying to get a glimpse of what might be blocking it on the other side.

I push more, and Linus helps.

We try to be quiet at first, but end up slamming it with our shoulders, hard.

A loud bang resounds through the stairwell on the other side of the door, and down the hall for our efforts.

The door doesn't budge.

"Well, that's anticlimactic," Mia quips, her voice dry.

"Okay, so we stay here." Annie pulls her cell phone out of her tight pleather pants pocket, and swipes it on. "I'm going to try 911 again."

We're surrounded by cinder blocks and tile, so I don't need to check my phone to know it's useless.

"No signal," Annie says. "Still."

"No, none of us has one. I imagine it's the corridor," Linus says.

"Try the Wi-Fi," I tell her. "Maybe we can use Skype."

Annie starts rapidly swiping through her phone.

From the other side of the door is a loud groan.

"Oooookay," I breathe, lifting the microphone stand arm, ready to jab.

"Let's hope whatever is blocking that door can't be easily moved," Rosa says.

As a group, we back away from the door.

"The Wi-Fi is down!" Annie snaps in frustration. "This thing is useless."

She glances at me and Imani, seeming to register for the first time that we are armed.

"I need a weapon," she says.

Through the narrow stairwell door window, I see a woman, a zombie, with long hair snarled in clumps in front of her face, almost like someone grabbed her by the hair, trying to stop her. Or trying to bite her.

The zombie sees us and opens her mouth, showing blood-slicked teeth and gray gums.

"Linus should have a weapon, too," Annie says. "You should give him your weapon."

I don't know if she's talking to me, Rosa, or Imani, but it doesn't matter.

Imani and Linus beat my response time.

"What? Why?" Imani asks.

"That's not necessary, I assure you," Linus says.

"He's a *man*," Annie plows forward. "He's stronger and stuff."

"That's regressive BS *and stuff*," I snap.

"Seriously," Imani agrees. "I am not giving up my weapon just because you didn't think of getting one yet."

The zombie woman on the other side of the stairwell door slams her body at the window. So far, the door hasn't budged for her either.

That's . . . *lucky*, I guess.

"If you want a weapon, keep your eyes open for one," Imani says to Annie and Linus, her tone at once scolding and gentle.

"Certainly," Linus agrees. "Here." He trots a few feet behind us to the emergency station.

"This will work." Linus pulls down a fire extinguisher.

"Okay, what am I supposed to use?" Annie asks.

"That." I point to the bright-red box hanging near the fire extinguisher mounting.

"A defibrillator?" Annie scoffs. "What am I supposed to do with that? Hold up, zombie, while I put electrodes on you. Sure. Great. CLEAR!"

She mimics lifting her hands and stepping back from an imaginary body on a gurney, like in one of those hospital shows.

I refuse to let her make me feel foolish.

"It's something. You can get a better weapon later," I say.

"Fine," Annie mutters. She walks to the red box and yanks it off the wall.

"Guess you'll have to wait until we're out of the hall to find something," Annie says to Mia.

"I'm not worried about it," Mia replies, in supreme nonchalance. "I've got mace in my purse anyway."

"Will mace even work on zombies?" Linus asks.

"I guess we'll find out," Mia says, fishing the small aerosol can out of her slim bag.

"We'll find something better soon," I tell her.

"Consider yourself on the payroll." Mia smiles, a gorgeous predatory curve. She really does give the impression that she's completely in control and assured.

Annie hugs the plastic box over her chest, more like the box is a teddy bear, rather than a shield or weapon.

For some reason, we're still creeping backward from the stairwell door. As if a sudden break for it would bring more attackers down upon us.

Or like sudden movement would break the spell of fragile safety we've found in the hall.

"What's the plan?" Linus asks me, glancing back to the stairwell door, where the zombie woman is still going nuts, banging on the door with her arms, face, and shoulders.

"That noise is probably going to bring more zombies," I

say. "More zombies means more chance they'll get through the door, no matter what's blocking it. We can't stay here."

"Agreed," Linus says. "No stairwell means no loading docks. I propose we try the other door." He points to the top of the hall.

"I think that opens to the ballroom lobby," Rosa says.

"We can at least check it out, see how it looks out there," Mia agrees.

"We can't call Siggy," Imani says. "If only we could call or text."

We've almost reached the middle of the hallway, where the closed, labeled doors wait.

They must be offices, or closets, or something like that.

"Hate to inform y'all," Annie says, and her voice is tense with fear, "but that ballroom lobby? It's full of zombies. They came from there."

"Maybe, or maybe they're all in the ballroom now," Linus argues.

"Right," I say. "And if they are all in the ballroom, or if enough of them are, then it's only a matter of time before they're *done* in there."

Unwanted images float into my mind's eye, and the same vision must enter the others' minds, too, because we all get quiet.

Tearing. Ripping. Eating.

Humans.

Humans with bites becoming more zombies, if that's how this particular biohazard outbreak works.

We draw even with the first closet or office door. No name on the sign next to it, just a number, 102. Maybe it's an office, or a meeting room. Or a dressing room.

I put my hand out.

As my fingers curl around the lever, it drops down and the door is yanked open.

I let out an involuntary yelp, which should sound blood-curdling, because I'm that startled.

Instead I sound like that Muppet who speaks in "meep" noises.

Janet O'Shea looks out at me. She's holding a slab of wood, what looks like the front piece of a desk drawer, shoulder high like a baseball bat.

"June!" she gasps, lowering her arm.

The scripted words and bad impersonation come out before I think to stop them.

"We're going to fight our way out, Vivian," I say.

Janet lets out a relieved laugh, and grasps my shoulder.

"Yes, we are," she says. "That we are."

17

E veryone, this is Janet," I say, sweeping a hand from her to the group.

"Hello." Janet nods in recognition to Annie and Linus. Of course, she knows them.

Behind Janet I see *Human Wasteland* actor Simon Wong. He's in his midtwenties and, like all the others on the show, completely beautiful and full of that actorly magic.

The zombie woman in the stairwell lets out an unholy shriek.

"Why don't we step back in here, see if it calms our friend down?" Janet takes a sidestep back, holding the door open.

I glance down the hall at the woman zombie.

Maybe out of sight, out of mind?

Or out of braaaaaiiiinzzz.

My inner voice needs to settle down.

"Good idea," Imani says, hustling past Janet. "I'm Imani Choi."

"Hello, Imani," Janet says as Rosa steps inside the greenroom.

"Ms. O'Shea," Rosa says, sticking out a hand. "I know this is, like, the worst timing, but I am such a huge fan of *Fight the Dead*."

"Oh, thank you!" Janet replies, taking her hand and sounding warmly pleased. "What's your name?"

Rosa's face has flushed a deep red. "Oh! Rosa García! I'm from Miami. I mean I was, now I'm here! I'm in the certification program at Pinewood Studios. You gotta start somewhere, right? But I'm a filmmaker. I mean, I'm going to be a filmmaker. I . . . well. Anyway—"

Her eyes flick over the rest of us, suddenly self-conscious. "When we get out of this," she concludes.

"Of course!" Janet says, squeezing Rosa's shoulder in a bracing, stiff-upper-lip Brittishy way.

"That's so cool that you're in film school," Imani tells her. "My little sister would love to talk to you, I bet, about if there's a makeup program."

"Oooh!" I say. "Tish'd be so good at that!"

"Maybe she can help me out and do the makeup for my student short film," Rosa says, and this frissiony, open-hearted feeling goes through me, just talking about normal things, planning for a normal future.

For a moment, at least.

We all shuffle into the small room. It's one part green-room, one part dressing room. Three separate vanity areas, complete with comically large makeup bulb frames, are on the left; beyond the vanity counter is a bathroom.

"Hey, babe," Mia says, and air kisses over Janet's cheek.

"Hello, Ms. Fontaine," Janet replies, smiling but with a little hovering, quirked corner that seems amused at the familiarity.

I guess Mia has had her hustle on since the con opened.

"Simon," Mia says, kissing the air over Simon's cheek next.

"Mia, thank God you're here," Simon says, moving past air kisses and hugging her properly.

Is it the door closing, or is the zombie in the stairwell actually quieter now that she can't see us?

"Where are the others?" Linus asks Simon.

"I don't know. It was bedlam." Simon gives his head a little shake, tossing his perfect glossy black hair back from his eyes.

I stare for a moment, not just because he's gorgeous, but also because something is very discombobulating.

Beyond standing in a dressing room with some of the actors I love from my favorite show. And Janet O'Shea.

And beyond the fact that actual zombies are trying to get to us.

And then I realize what it is.

Simon's hair is clean.

On the show, they always look sweaty, and their hair is

always swept back in sloppy ponytails or hanging down in greasy hanks.

It's odd what elements the show's producers are sticklers for detail on. Like, it's the zombie apocalypse, yes, so NO GROOMING SHALL OCCUR.

In my opinion it's a ridiculous hill to die on, because it's a television show; just show someone enjoying the last charge of an electric razor they found on a supply run or something . . .

I realize I'm sort of in a shocked, wool-gathering fugue about grooming when I notice Linus has said my name twice.

"Are you okay?" he asks.

"Sorry," I say. "Just tired for a moment."

Linus turns back to Simon.

". . . and that led you to hiding out here?"

Apparently, the group of actors on the panel scattered once in the backstage corridor.

Simon went into the greenroom, where he found Janet waiting. She was supposed to go onstage for an "Interview with a Horror Legend" after the panel.

Together, they waited, thinking that the disruption would be taken care of, not realizing the extent of what had started.

"Did you see a skinny girl with white-blonde hair?" I interrupt Linus to ask Simon.

"Sorry, there was a lot going on," Simon says.

"She came backstage. She can't be far," Imani says, squeezing my arm reassuringly.

"What about the scientist guy?" I ask Janet. "Did he get brought back here?"

"The weirdo who interrupted the panel?" Annie asks, incredulous.

"He's not such a weirdo now, is he?" I ask, but it's not really a question. "This is his backpack." I touch the battered navy backpack hanging on the front of me.

"Hey, I meant to ask, how did you know that key was in there?" Linus asks me suddenly. "Or that it was his?"

I explain quickly, about seeing him messing with the doors in the exhibit hall at the end of Autograph Alley. About how I thought he was maintenance, even without a uniform.

And that makes me sound completely clueless now.

"Hindsight is twenty-twenty," Janet says, squeezing my arm.

"So, what do we do now?" Linus asks. "I take it neither of your phones has a signal, either?"

Janet and Simon shake their heads.

"We should stay here," Annie says.

What is it with this girl and staying put?

"I'm not staying," I say. "Y'all go ahead, though."

Janet meets my gaze, her blue eyes steely. "I want to hear your plan."

I . . . don't have one?

But Janet said I was supposed to trust myself. And my instinct to keep moving is tugging at me like a fire alarm going off in my head.

Move, move, move.

I take a deep breath, and try to put the fire alarm feeling into words.

"I just think we're sitting ducks here," I explain. I point the microphone arm at the door. "That's not a deadbolt, it's a button lock. We don't know if any zombies can get through to this hall, but if they do, we are trapped here. There's nowhere to run."

Linus is nodding.

Imani speaks up.

"We want to find our friends. They came back here, and since no one else is here now, that means everyone who made it out of the ballroom made it out."

I nod and Imani gives me a quick squeeze.

"I don't know what's out in the lobby," I say when she lets go. "But I don't want to wait for zombies to get to me here. And I think that's just a matter of time."

Janet nods, and her mouth quirks to the side, a half smile.

"Okay, but what next? After we get into the ballroom lobby?" Rosa asks.

It's a good question.

On the back of the door is a fire-evacuation map.

I step up to it, jabbing my finger at the diagram. "Okay so the scientist guy said that we were locked in the ballroom. Which didn't work, as it turns out. Probably because the people compromised the locks from the inside, and that let the zombies break the doors down."

Imani steps closer to the map and squints at the doors I'm pointing to.

She still smells nice. Like apples. I probably smell like terror and BO.

"He also said that the exhibit hall was locked down," I continue. "But I'm here to tell you, I think the zombies already got into the exhibit hall."

"Right." Imani nods at me. "That guy who bit that kid."

"Yes," I agree. "And maybe more people besides him? Like what about that girl with the nosebleed? And remember that other woman we thought was a cosplayer? Not to mention anyone else they may have come into contact with or infected."

"So what?" Annie asks. "What does it matter if they're infected? They're locked in, we're locked out."

I turn to her.

"It means that we don't know how many doors are locked through the building, or if someone has established some kind of evacuation method." I shake my head, remembering the scientist trying to talk to the audience. "His plan didn't work, but he had planned *something*."

Imani points a manicured nail at our hallway on the fire evacuation map.

"We're here. This is the stairwell at the bottom. See this hatching up top? That's the escalators. It's not far at all. And from there it's a straight shot either down to the front doors or up to the third floor."

"Okay, I'm following all this," Linus says. "But it doesn't tell me what we should do now."

"Keep up, handsome." Mia's voice has a flirtatious, tough-broad lilt. "It means we should probably make some assumptions. Like that all the exterior doors are locked, for starters."

"Exactly, just like the scientist said," Imani agrees.

"And I think we should assume that there is a single point of exit," I say. "Did you guys see the cosplayers in hazmat suits?"

"Oh God," Rosa says.

"Right. What if they were trying to get a temperature on . . . the spread of the infection, or whatever. And then they made the call to lock us all up to contain it?" I ask.

"He said that. So, the scientist . . ." Linus's voice trails off.

"Was trying to help us!" I finish.

Behind us, Annie lets out a high-pitched giggle.

We glance at her. Annie shakes her head, giving an *ignore me* or *go on* hand wave.

Stress.

Linus's British accent makes the terrifying truth less scary, somehow. "I understand. What's the point of running to a door if the door is locked?"

"Right," I say. "We might be locked in, with our backs against a wall."

"A door that is now a wall," Imani finishes for me, our thoughts running parallel as always.

"So, what do we do instead?" Mia asks, giving me a look like she's a teacher who knows I'm ready for the verbal quiz.

"We go upstairs," I say. "Maybe we can get a signal once we're out of this hall. Or if not maybe we can see out once we're by the exterior windows. And there'll be fewer zombies up there, I bet."

"We can find out where the exit point is." Annie's voice is quavery, but she's with us.

She sees it.

A plan.

"I dunno." Simon winces, letting us see he's not trying to be hostile to the idea, just cautious. "What if going up is just another trap? What if we're trapped up there? What then?"

"There's firefighter roof access up there," Imani says. "It's like a hatch door that lets them come in from the roof but lets us get out, too. If we can find it."

She turns and explains to everyone. "My mom took me all through the construction phase of this place. She's all about learning opportunities and stuff."

"Oh, so that's why you watched the fountain video?" I ask. But really, it doesn't surprise me. Imani's mom is so cool.

Imani nods.

"Hothouse flowers in concrete." She gives me a little hug. "But who cares if it's concrete?"

Janet smiles at us, a gentle expression on her face, like reliving a memory.

"A group of survivors made it to the balcony of the ballroom earlier," I say, running my index finger along the edge of the diagram where the balcony would be on the third-floor layout. "If we get up there maybe we can join forces with them."

"There are no con events on the third floor," Rosa says, her tone growing more certain as she talks. "That means there might not be anyone else up there!"

"Like the kid said. No people means there will be no people who now might be zombies." Mia barely looks up from whatever she's trying to do on her phone.

Linus nods.

"Here's what I would do." I take a deep breath, turning

back to Janet, who asked for my plan in the first place. "Get to that third floor. Either up the escalator, or the regular elevators since the stairs are . . . compromised."

Janet gives me a smile and an approving nod.

"Good. Yes." Mia's agreement is more like an order.

"Okay," Rosa says.

Linus hoists his fire extinguisher.

Annie's chin lifts. Her tear-tracked makeup doesn't take away from her new determination.

"Okay," she says. "Let's go to that damn lobby door."

18

We all cluster behind the door in the white hallway. We can't see into the second-floor lobby area. At the opposite end from us, in the stairwell door, the woman zombie is attacking the window again, banging and thundering at us.

"Remember, to our left is the ballroom." Imani holds up her left hand and gestures a flat circle area. Then she makes her other hand a blade, like a wall, and holds it perpendicular and solid. "To our right is a wall that is part of the banquet rooms. We're running along that wall all the way to the end where we'll reach the escalators."

Sometimes I wish I could just download Imani's directional awareness straight into my head, like an upgrade.

But right now I'm just glad she's right here with me, keeping us all on the right track.

"Got it." Linus nods at Imani, a crisp motion that conveys both appreciation for the reminder and assurance that we have got this, as a group, we have got this, by Jove.

Somehow the nod conveys all that.

Linus volunteered to lead the way with Janet; and Simon

and Mia (now armed with a drawer front piece of her own) agreed to bring up the rear.

I stand with Imani and Annie and Rosa, in the middle. Ready to run. Or to fight.

But mostly to run.

Discretion is the better part of valor and all that.

Now that we're standing here, at the doorway, getting ready to leave the temporary safety of the backstage hall, my heart is thundering in my chest and my palms are slippery and I'm more than a little bit terrified.

What's on the other side of the door?

Simon has a vanity stool he'll swing at any zombies behind us, and Linus has his fire extinguisher. Rosa traded her antenna for a metal table lamp. Imani and I have our microphone stand pieces, and Janet and Mia have drawer planks.

Annie has her defibrillator case.

Oh Lord, what are we doing?

Linus looks over his shoulder back at us.

"Are we ready?" he whispers, but doesn't wait for an answer.

He pushes the door open, as quietly as possible, while still trying to go fast.

He rushes out, followed by Simon.

Simon takes the door, holding it open for us.

We run out in a clump, following Linus and Janet into the lobby.

So far, so good.

Behind me, I hear Simon let the door fall closed with a bang. Which means . . .

"Run!" Simon yells, like we're not already running.

But we kick it up, because now we know that we don't have to be quiet.

Because we're being chased.

We get to the escalators. They've been turned off.

At the top of the escalators is a makeshift barricade. A heavy potted tree, several upholstered chairs, and a sofa, as well as a janitor's rolling trash-can cart have all been wedged into the openings at the top of the up and down escalators.

"Dammit!" Linus glances between the barricade and the approaching, shuffling zombies.

I really, really, *really* want to get up there with whoever had the presence of mind to do that already.

"Go," Linus says, and he moves aside, letting Janet lead the way onto the escalator. "See if you can climb over it."

Simon arrives and whirls to face our pursuers.

My breath won't come, my heart freezes as I see them, lurching, stumbling, coming at us, closing in from the lobby outside the open ballroom doors.

Four zombies. The first, the closest, is a short teenager, reaching toward Simon with clawlike fingers.

Simon shoves him back with the stool.

"Go!" Linus urges me, his voice firm but not loud.

Because if they can fight off this group, and not draw any others, maybe our plan can still work.

I nod and dart up the motionless escalator, falling in at the very back of the group, behind Annie.

We rush up the steps, trying not to listen to the struggle behind us.

At the top of the escalator, Janet is already climbing the barricade.

There's a sickening drop to the right of the escalator. If the barricade shifts, or if she loses her grip . . .

Janet straddles the top of the barricade, the upended sofa, and reaches down to help Imani.

A clang sounds behind me, the solid metal thunk of a fire extinguisher hitting a skull.

I look back in time to see one of the zombies fall over the edge of the railing. I make the mistake of looking down to the first floor, where another zombie lies still.

The drop makes me woozy, so I look away fast.

Linus stands in the entryway of one of the escalators. Simon is in the other, both of them using the curved escalator sides to shield themselves somewhat, with their backs to the steps behind them.

Another zombie man stumbles forward, reaching for Linus.

There are only two zombies left, the one reaching for Linus and a final zombie behind him.

Simon hits the second zombie with the seat of the vanity stool, two of the tripod legs held in Simon's hands.

The zombie falls, but pops up onto his feet again, fast.

Linus swings the fire extinguisher at the zombie clawing at him. There's a dull clang as I look back to the barricade.

Annie clambers over, helped by Janet.

"Come on, June!" Janet urges.

I shove my mic stand arm through the straps of the scientist's backpack. I put a hand on the potted plant, a naked-trunk spiky palm, and pull up to put a foot on the trash can, then shimmy, telling myself it's not moving, it's not shifting, it's not about to fall over into the three-story drop to the right.

Janet has a leg hooked over the sofa armrest. She catches my hand and hauls with surprising strength.

My foot kicks off the cart, and I'm scrabbling over the top of the armrest, pulling and kicking into the empty air under the jutting armrest, like a swimmer struggling to boost out of a deep pool.

I get my stomach on the armrest and hook a leg up and then over.

"Good girl," Janet says, patting my shoulder.

The clang sounds again, and I look back down to Linus

just in time to see him fall backward on the escalator steps, as the zombie falls on top of him.

"Linus!" I shout.

Simon glances over, but he has to look back at the fast zombie he's fighting. Simon flips the vanity stool around, shifting his grip to the circle of the seat. Using the feet of the vanity stool like a lion tamer uses the legs of a chair, Simon rushes at the zombie and boosts him up and over the escalator edge.

The zombie falls, landing on top of the others that Linus and Simon threw down while we were climbing.

I don't watch to see if the zombie at the bottom gets up; my eyes are drawn back to Linus.

He's beneath the zombie, but somehow crouched between the metal steps and the zombie's bulk. The zombie's head snaps around, unable to reach Linus.

"Hey!" I call to the zombie. "Hey, zombie guy! Nom nom!"

The zombie looks up at me.

"That's right, look at this tasty goodness!" I stretch my arm out. "Nom nom!"

"Cut it out!" Annie hisses. "Stop calling to it!"

"I'm trying to help your boyfriend!" I hiss back, and don't hear if she responds because it's working, the last zombie on Linus has opened his mouth and is crawling forward, up over the metal steps, over Linus, who lies motionless beneath him.

Simon rushes up behind the zombie, grabbing Linus by the hand and pulling him up.

Linus stands, looking dazed.

The zombie man claws at the barricade, bloody, discolored hands grasping at the potted plant, the spiky palm, pulling, tugging, without thought.

The sofa I'm draped across sways.

"Get down!" I order Janet.

She looks like she's going to argue for an instant, then she nods and shimmies down fast.

I'm going to have to follow her or try to find a longer weapon. There's no way my mic arm will reach. I could throw it? Maybe there's something else I could throw.

I look around—what's within reach?

An accent pillow on the sofa has been smooshed into the crease at the back.

I grab it and hurl it at the zombie's head.

It bonks off his head like a marshmallow.

It's a pillow.

What the hell was I thinking?

Something brushes my elbow, tickling like spiders walking on my bare skin.

I twitch away and glance down.

The strings of a mop brush against my elbow. Standing at the bottom of the barricade, Janet holds the handle, boosting the weapon up to me.

I grab the strings, lift it up, and shove it, mop end down, into the zombie's face.

He swipes at the mop strings covering his eyes. I lift the mop back up before he can get a grip on it.

He's a big guy. Tall.

His center of gravity is several inches higher than the escalator's handrail.

I push the strings into the zombie's face again, then dangle them.

The zombie swipes again, a wild swing of his arms at the obstruction.

But I'm too fast, I pop the mop back, then shove it in again.

This time I tilt the strings in front of his eyes, and to the side slightly, causing him to twist on the stair, ever so slightly.

The zombie lets out a grunt and throws his arm wide, an uncontrolled arc.

Simon yells and swings the vanity stool like a baseball bat, connecting with the back of the zombie's head.

The huge zombie tilts, then falls over the handrail like a sack of cement potatoes.

Behind Simon, Linus winces as he looks up at me.

"Thank you, June," Linus says, in his impeccable accent, like we're sitting in a garden and I've just handed him a cup of tea.

"You're welcome, Linus," I reply. I don't *think* I was mimicking his accent. Was I?

19

Linus has a little trouble getting over the barricade; he's either winded or injured. Maybe both.

"Excellent work, lads," Janet tells him and Simon, giving them both a hug after they join us.

"Thank you. Both of you," I say.

Linus nods and looks around. We're all huddled at the top of the escalators on the third-floor landing.

I've discarded the mop on the landing. It was too hard to maneuver. Instead I've pulled the shorter mic arm back out, just in case. The makeshift barricade blocks much of our sight line into the large third-floor balcony lobby area to the right. So far, everything's clear, but we keep our voices low, just in case.

Annie is working her phone next to the exterior windows. She barely even looks at Linus.

"Are you okay?" I ask him.

"I took quite a fall," he says. His hand goes to the back of his head. "Cracked my head."

His hand comes away bloody.

"Oh," he says conversationally. Like *would you look at that?*

"How about we take stock of the area, but you hang in the back. When we know it's clear, you can get cleaned up and rest properly," Janet says, but she looks at me for permission. For some weird reason.

"Good idea," I agree. "Catch your breath first, though."

Linus nods gratefully and leans over, his hands on his knees.

Imani's voice next to me is low, pitched only for me to hear.

"Did you see that zombie fall on him?"

"Linus? Yeah," I whisper back.

"Do you think, I mean, how do people get infected, anyway?" Imani pushes her hair back behind her ear. "On the show, it's bites, right?"

"Yeah, bites only. On the show."

"Did he look like he was limping to you?" Imani's eyes look pained, like she's hoping against hope.

But fears the worst.

"He fell on the escalator. Of course he's limping." But I glance over at Linus again, standing next to Janet.

And is a bite the only way to get infected? What if it's just particulate, like a cough, or sweat getting into a cut?

Or in your mouth?

"I don't want everyone to turn on him, or each other," Imani whispers. "But we need to find out if he's been bitten, don't we?"

"Yes," I agree. "I'll take him aside and ask in a minute." The pleading enters my whisper. "We can give him a moment, right? After all, he covered our escape. And we have to make sure there aren't any zombies up here."

My hand sweeps out, encompassing the third-floor lobby beyond us.

Imani glances back at Linus, smiling ruefully at something Rosa has said.

Imani nods.

"Okay, but keep your eye on him," Imani instructs me. Then she steps over to the windows where Annie and Mia are already trying their phones.

"Any luck?" I ask them, even though Annie's scowling, and jabbing her fingers on her phone like she would stab it if she could.

"No signal," Annie says. "Anyone else want to try?"

Imani holds her phone up, first at one corner of the window, then another, before shaking her head.

"There must be a dampener," she says. "Or maybe it's just the steel or the atmosphere today."

"Wait, why would there be a dampener?" Mia asks. "Aren't those illegal?"

"Not if you're military, or police," Imani replies. "SWAT and special response teams use them."

"That's good!" The corners of Rosa's eyes crinkle with her relieved smile. "That means help is on the way!"

"Or it could mean it's happening everywhere." Annie hugs the defibrillator case tighter. "What if the zombies are outside, too?"

"No," Janet says, with absolute conviction. "No way. Otherwise we wouldn't be locked in. If it's a dampener, it means they're out there working to contain it."

"*If*," Mia says. "We have to face that we don't really *know* anything."

"I wish I could call my parents," Imani says. "They'd know what we should do." Even though her voice is steady, I can tell she's feeling it, and I'm feeling it, too.

The edge of tears, honed on the sharp longing to be out of here. To be safe in the circle of our parents' arms.

I reach out and give her a one-armed hug. Imani leans down and rests her head on my shoulder for a moment.

"Do you really think everyone else onstage got out?" Simon asks us. "James, he was helping people. Hunter was with him. And Sam, he moves slow sometimes, because of his knees . . ."

Simon's voice trails off, and I can see him picturing more of them: his fellow actors, castmates he's worked with for the past three years. People who he's come to call friends.

"They're fine." Mia's voice is tough. No nonsense. "They're just like us, fighting their way through this mess. That's what we've got to keep doing."

"Yeah," Annie says. "Sam's a tough old bird. Remember that day he had to film the fight scene with the barn zombie? He wouldn't quit until it was right."

Imani stands up straight. She smooths her tunic. "We're not the only ones who got out of that ballroom. We're going to find others. We keep looking," she tells me.

Simon picks up his vanity stool and shifts his grip.

"Let's go," he says. "We should clear this level, for safety. We should check the bathrooms for zombies, then the lobby and sitting area, then we can try to make contact with those survivors in the balcony and figure out about the dampener or what's next from there."

I nod, and we form an impromptu phalanx—me and Simon in the lead; Janet and Linus in the rear; Imani, Mia, and Annie in the middle.

Around the corner from the escalators is a wide, extremely long lobby. There are upholstered chairs set in conversational groups at intervals beside the railing that runs alongside the escalator area. More chairs and sofas are set down the exterior window wall beyond that.

Bathrooms are up near us, catty-corner to the escalators. At the far side of the lobby, on the wall opposite the bathrooms, a long bar stands. Barstools are bolted to the floor in front of it, and a small flotilla of tall cocktail tables is scattered before them.

The balcony of the ballroom is separated from the lobby by a large semicircular wall bowing out in an arc. Four pairs of closed double doors are set in the curved wall.

Behind those doors is where I think other survivors are: the cheerleaders and stuntmen I saw climb up, and any others they managed to save from the ballroom floor.

Simon and I lead the way to the first set of balcony doors. I put my ear to it, but can hear nothing.

I reach out to the handle. My fingers curl around it.

The rough voice echoes out across the lobby, shocking me so hard I jump.

"I wouldn't do that if I were you, sister."

My head whips to the right, toward the bar.

Cuellar Tucker, the actor who plays the tough redneck, stands with an elbow on the bar, foot up on the rung of a barstool like we're in a western and he's about to mount his horse.

"Cuellar!" Simon's voice is tinged with relief.

My hand drops from the balcony door. We step back from the doors and cross to the bar.

"It's okay to come out," Cuellar says to the bar behind him.

Then, sprouting over the top of the bar like a cautious lily, the bright white top of Siggy's hair. Blair is close to her, both their eyes wide as saucers, wider still to see us standing there.

"Siggy!" Imani rushes forward, meeting Siggy at the corner of the bar. They hug, and Imani reaches out to grab Blair's elbow.

Blair clasps Imani's arm back, both looking surprised, and relieved, at the contact.

I'm right behind Imani, so Siggy hugs me next, squeezing tight across my shoulders. "Oh, June! I thought you were—I thought—"

She can't say it, and she doesn't have to.

"I know. Me too," I say.

Imani and Blair look at each other, almost like there are words waiting to be said. Instead they hug quickly, once, and then draw apart.

Siggy and Imani stand between me and Blair. But that doesn't stop my hand, reaching around instinctively behind them, and touching Blair's shoulder, briefly.

"I'm glad you're safe," I tell her.

"Me too," Blair replies. "Glad about you guys."

We smile at each other awkwardly, but don't hold eye

contact for too long. The relief I feel that Blair is okay is real. But so is the lingering hurt from before the zombie apocalypse started.

Mia's stilettos click as she crosses to the bar.

"Cuellar, you big lummox, good to see you."

Cuellar laughs and puts down his drink. He holds his arms wide and then lifts Mia off the ground in a bear hug.

"I shoulda known barracudas would be okay," he teases her.

"Still a charmer." Mia squeezes him back.

Cuellar puts her down. Rosa and the others come forward, and we take a moment for rushed introductions.

"Hey." I motion to Blair and Siggy. "You might wanna take those badges off. Take my word for it."

Siggy and Blair nod and don't ask why, they just hurriedly pull the lanyards over their heads.

Then Simon asks Cuellar, "How'd you end up here?"

"Well, it wasn't planned exactly," Cuellar says, his rough voice lilting in humor. He turns and rummages behind the bar, bringing out another glass. He tips a bottle of whiskey at Linus.

"How about it, limey? Looks like you could use it."

Linus winces but nods.

Cuellar pours another drink for himself and one for Linus.

"Anyone else want one, sing out or help yourself," he says.

Mia immediately steps behind the bar and grabs a glass.

"Backstage was awful, and confusing," Siggy says to me. "Everyone rushed to the exit, but only one door opened. I fell, and Blair helped me up, then we ended up near the back of everyone running out."

Her eyes start blinking rapidly. "I can't believe this is happening!" Her voice is small, and incredulous. "Is it anywhere else? I can't get a signal, can't text my parents or Mark."

"I'm sure he's okay," I tell her.

Siggy grabs my hands, squeezing tight. "Do you really think so?"

"Absolutely. He's safe," I say, putting as much conviction as I can muster into my voice.

Siggy's big blue eyes start to shimmer, but she takes deeps breaths and fights the tears back. It's almost like I can see the love she feels for Mark radiating from her, like how heat lifts off pavement.

I rub her shoulder in a way that I hope says I'm sorry I ever gave her a hard time about Mark.

Emotions. Woof, they're hard.

I glance at Imani. Her eyes are glistening, too, and I know she's thinking about her parents. And Tishala.

"Okay," Imani says, blinking fast. "So you're in the hallway. Then what happened?"

"In the hallway there was one of them already. The infected," Blair says.

"A zombie," I say.

"Yeah," Blair answers, nodding.

"It attacked the first group who ended up in the hall. Then they split," Siggy says.

"She means the group split in half," Cuellar interrupts. "Into two groups."

I would like to tell him that I knew what she meant, and he doesn't need to explain for her. Like anyone says "split" to mean "leave" anymore.

I keep my mouth shut, because Siggy doesn't look upset with him.

Instead she's looking at him like he's her hero.

But Blair catches my eye and gives a slight eye roll. I tip my chin to let her know I saw.

Cuellar picks up the story.

"Half of 'em went one way, into the stairwell with the zombie chasing them, the other half ran out the lobby doors in a panic."

He takes a big swig of the whiskey, making a face around the bite of it in his throat.

"Pointless, of course, because there was still a mess of

zombies in the lobby. They ran right into them." He shakes his head, scrubbing a hand over his beard stubble. "But it's not like anyone was thinking. And anyway, it gave us at the back the chance we needed to get up here."

"Why'd you come upstairs?" Linus asks, sipping from his glass like a gentleman in a club.

"No other option," Cuellar admits, shaking his head. "I saw some in the atrium, maybe five or more, and sounded like a helluva lot more down there. I turned off all the escalators at least, so hopefully none of them will end up here by accident. They don't seem too smart with climbing stairs or what have you."

"We saw a group of survivors get to the balcony," I say, pointing at the nearest set of doors. "We figured all the doors leading outside are locked like the scientist said, and so we decided to come up here to try to join forces."

"Well, sure, but the problem with that is, they're infected. Zombies, like you said."

Somehow, Cuellar doesn't look sad to say it.

Instead he's got one of those looks on his face, the kind that only some men sometimes get. That makes me want to take a step away from him. This look that he's somehow satisfied, no, that it somehow satisfies something *in him*, to be right.

To tell me that I'm wrong.

To be right over a girl.

That's what it feels like.

Maybe I'm just being paranoid. I've been through a shock, and right now I'm overreacting.

I take a small step back anyway.

At the same moment, Imani moves behind Siggy, and comes around slightly in front of me, standing close.

She felt it, too.

"How do you know they're zombies?" Simon asks, friendly tone, not suspicious like I would sound. But I'm glad he asked because I have the same question. Even if the last stuntman up the extension cord got bitten, it's not been that long. He might still be fine. We were just downstairs, everything happened too fast—

"I saw them, the zombies in the balcony," Cuellar says.

It sounds like the title of a deeply inappropriate picture book.

The Zombies in the Balcony.

I wrench my brain back to focus completely on what Cuellar's saying.

"First thing I did when we got up here was turn off the escalators, then I barricaded the top of 'em."

"Good thinking," Janet says.

"Thank you, ma'am."

"Then what?" I ask.

"Well, then me and my two little hitchhikers here—" He tips his head at Siggy and Blair indulgently, but something in his eyes is like a guy ogling a waitress.

"We'd be dead if it wasn't for Cuellar," Siggy interjects, her voice completely sincere.

Blair doesn't say anything.

I meet her eyes and she gives me a look, the smallest of shakes to her head.

"—we went around to make sure it was safe, you know. So, I say wait here, girls, behind the bar. Then I go to that door right there and I ease it open. Perfectly silent."

He drains his glass and puts it down on the bar quietly. It doesn't fit with his self-satisfied air, the gentle motion, when it feels like what he wants to do is slam it down like a trophy.

"He didn't see me," Cuellar says. "Big guy. Infected now. He was attacking whoever else was up there. It's sad, but at least he can't figure out how to open a door, right?"

He grabs the bottle of whiskey and tilts another helping into his glass.

"They're dangerous, but they're mindless," Cuellar says. "They can hear better than they can see, I think. Some of them are faster than the others, did you notice that?"

"Yeah. Zoombies," I reply.

Rosa lets out a rich laugh. "Zoombies. That's good."

"What do we call the slow ones?" Mia asks. "Slothbies? Slowbies?"

"Walkers," Janet says.

"We need to secure the balcony doors," Linus says, but his voice is flat. I glance at him, and he looks pale.

"Hey, sit down, Linus," I urge, gesturing at one of the barstools.

"You hurt or something?" Cuellar asks.

Linus gives him a wince-smile, and touches the back of his head.

Cuellar reaches behind the bar again and grabs a handful of square cocktail napkins, hands them to Linus.

"Hey, girlie, wanna help your boyfriend here?" Cuellar asks Annie, who just rolls her eyes at him. She drifts back toward the wall of windows, trying with her phone again.

Cuellar laughs.

"What's so funny?" Blair asks, and her sudden voice must startle him, because he looks around as if he's surprised by the source. Maybe he wasn't expecting how sharp it sounded. How assertive.

But that's Blair. She can be utterly fearless. And I can tell from her tone that she doesn't really care what Cuellar is laughing about, but is just challenging the aggressive taunt underneath it.

"Nothing, just it's all fake," Cuellar answers, giving Blair that up-and-down look that makes me want to throw a drink in his face.

"Can it, Cuellar," Mia says. "PR's my job, remember?"

"It hardly matters now," Linus says, but there's apology in his voice.

"You're . . . not dating?" Siggy's voice is small, her tone like a little kid asking if Santa is real.

I can't help it. After everything.

This.

This is what breaks me.

A laugh burbles up from my chest into my throat. I cough to choke it out, because I don't want to hurt my friend, don't want to hurt my Siggy.

I'd probably be disappointed, too, if I hadn't already seen with my own eyes how very NOT into each other Linus and Annie are.

"Sorry," Siggy says. "Never mind. It doesn't matter. None of my business."

"We all made it your business," Linus says. He gently repositions the stack of cocktail napkins on his head. "Mia thought it might help keep our characters on the show longer, you see."

Siggy nods, and waves her hand like *of course, of course.*

"I wasn't wrong," Mia says. "Can you keep it confidential, kid? When we get out of here?" she asks Siggy.

Siggy nods.

Linus winces again, but it doesn't look like it's from the injury on his head.

We seriously have such bigger fish to fry, but it's encouraging that Mia's so confident we're getting out.

"So, what do we do now?" Simon asks.

"Right," Janet agrees. "We need to formulate a plan."

They both look at me.

Linus turns on his seat to look at me as well.

Cuellar looks at me, too, in absolute disbelief, looking from them to me, back to them.

"What, you think y'all are in the army or something?" Cuellar asks, his voice scornful. "What you gonna do, just go out there and reconnoiter?"

He laughs, a dismissive huff, but still friendly. Like he expects us all to laugh along with him.

No one else laughs.

I don't say it, but yes, we should absolutely "reconnoiter" or whatever. We already know there are zombies on the balcony, but where else might they be? Before we can do anything else, we should secure ourselves here—which mainly means taking a moment to make sure we won't be surprised by zombies—which sounds like a soap opera, *Surprised by Zombies*—either coming out of the balcony, out of a bathroom, around the hallway corner, or anywhere else.

Like out of a maintenance closet or whatever.

We should check the utility stairwell door, too.

I think that's all that's up here.

But we should try to find a fire evacuation map for the third floor, like there was in the dressing room. Then we'll know for sure if there are any other rooms up here.

Then we can decide what's next. Try to get a signal, or try to find roof access.

"Safety first, right?" I say to Linus and Janet. "First we should try to secure those doors, or perhaps confirm how many zombies are up there? In the balcony? I wouldn't want to be surprised if they suddenly blunder their way out."

Linus nods encouragingly.

Siggy puts her hand a little ways into the air, like she's in class and I'm the teacher. I nod at her. "We should check all our phones over by the windows in an organized way," she says.

"Great idea," I tell her.

"None of 'em are gonna work, but go right ahead, chickadees." Cuellar knocks back the rest of his drink like I've personally offended him somehow, and he has to knock a bad taste out of his mouth.

"What's your problem, buddy?" Blair asks, and I have a rush of gratitude—that she's backing me up and that it's not just all in my head.

Then I remember about Scott. About running around behind my back, instead of just telling me. And the gratitude slips away like a receding tide, quick, leaving gross flotsam on the shore.

"Nothing," Cuellar says. "I just don't think we should be taking orders from a teenager."

The teenage "*girl*" part is unspoken.

"No one's taking orders," Rosa says. "We're all strategizing, here. And she thinks clearly, and we can all use a bit of that right now."

Simon nods, arching an eyebrow at Cuellar's empty glass.

Cuellar's eyes tighten.

"Someone should check the bathrooms, and that balcony door," Mia says, defusing the moment. "We hide out up here long enough we'll want the bathrooms, plus we can see if they lock from the inside."

"Right," Simon agrees. "And we can control the access now. Take out the zombies one at a time if there are any."

He hoists the blood-and-goop-spattered vanity stool.

"Cuellar, how about you come help me?" he asks.

"Sure thing, Wong," Cuellar says, a bitter undertone to his voice. But he lifts the empty whiskey bottle in his hand and flips it around, grasping it by the neck.

"I like bashing things in the head," Cuellar says as they walk to the bathroom doors.

20

*C*uellar stands behind the door, waiting. Simon nods his head, and Cuellar pops it open.

No zombies rush out. Simon eases into the men's room to make sure it's clear.

"I'll go test our phones by this window," Imani says to me, pointing to the window on the exterior wall close to the bar. I hand her my cell. Blair and Siggy move over to the windows with her. Annie is already walking along the wall farther up by the upholstered chairs, holding her phone like a dowser's wand.

They hold their phones up and start slow-walking forward along the window wall, watching their screens.

"Is anyone wearing a belt they don't need?" Linus asks. "I can start with the doors."

Rosa nods and takes off her belt, handing it over.

"No belt, but I have this." Mia digs in her sharp-edged, small purse. She pulls out a braided nylon strip. She gives it an expert tug, and it twirls open into a thin cord.

"That's . . ." Linus trails off and laughs. "That's paracord, right?"

Mia smooths her bangs. "Yeah, it's one of those survival bracelets. Bear gave it to me."

We all just kind of blink at her for a moment.

Then Linus thanks her and drapes the cord over his shoulder alongside Rosa's belt. He lifts his shirt and goes to pull his own belt off.

Which is when I notice his hands.

They're shaking. But more than that, they're . . . off-color. Paler, and lightly mottled. Like the vessels under the skin are faintly bruising. Or like blood is becoming sluggish, pooling somehow.

Or starting to.

"Linus?" I ask. My heart feels crouched in my chest, tiny and frightened.

"Yeah," he says. "I was waiting for the right moment to tell everyone." He glances around, making sure no one else other than me, Rosa, and Mia is paying attention.

Then he rolls up one sleeve.

A bite.

Ragged and still bleeding, or more like oozing, with teeth marks clear.

"But he didn't get you." My voice is a whisper. "You fell under him and he couldn't reach you."

Linus smiles at me.

"The tall guy? No, he didn't get me," he agrees. "This

was from the first one, while you were climbing. I recognized him, well, sort of, from today. A fan."

His tone is self-mocking as he pulls his sleeve back down.

"I couldn't hit him, not fast enough at least. Or not hard enough." He shakes his head, dragging a hand through his still perfectly floppy hair. "He's lying on the floor of the atrium now."

My voice is quavering when I speak.

"Maybe, when we get everything locked down, we can get a cell signal. And then—"

Linus stops me, shaking his head.

"June, I heard that scientist. He said there's no cure, remember? And I'm on a zombie show. I know what this means."

The scientist's voice echoes through my memory, words he huffed into the microphone as security chased him around the stage.

Too late for them and *fatal.*

"Oh, Linus." Mia's voice is soft. She puts a hand out to him.

"So, don't argue with me if I decide to act like a hero, okay?" Linus says. "Just let me go out in a blaze of glory, right?"

I swipe at my eyes.

"Okay." I try to match his light tone. "Only if you promise it'll be a bonfire."

"Yes ma'am." Linus sketches a salute at me. "And if I start to . . . change before then, you have to take me out. Or be sure you lock me up or something."

"I'm sure we have time," Rosa murmurs, her voice small.

"Well, only if you don't tell Cuellar," Linus says. "He probably won't want to wait to bash me in the head."

It's supposed to be funny.

Over Linus's shoulder, I see Cuellar and Simon come out of the men's bathroom and take up the same ready pose outside the women's bathroom.

Rosa gives Linus a hug. Together they carry their weapons and the belts over to the first set of balcony doors and begin tying the handles.

No zombies emerge from the women's room, so Simon and Cuellar go inside, then come back out in a few moments.

Clear.

Good.

The two men turn left, heading past the curving balcony wall as they walk down to check the stairwell door.

The girls looking for a signal aren't having any luck, so I decide to recheck back by the windows above the escalator, just in case. If I stay low, any zombies who might be on the second-floor level below won't be able to see me over the railing or the balcony.

I grab my cell from Imani, and, hunched over like a crone, I scuttle to the top of the escalator. I sit cross-legged on the floor by the windows, and get out my phone.

It's dead, the battery gone from low to empty. I shove it back in my pocket.

Out the window I can only see rooftops of downtown, and the sweeping covered walkway that runs alongside the convention center.

I crane my neck, trying to see if there's a sign of . . . well, anything. Police, or ambulances, or army trucks.

But from this vantage point I can't see. And the road could be closed.

They have to be out there. After all, they locked us in here with the infection, right? To contain it.

I glance back to check on the others. Rosa and Linus are trying the handles of the second set of balcony doors. Everyone else: Janet, Annie, and Mia, and Siggy, Imani, and Blair are moving in a loose clump across the windows—holding their phones up and out.

Cuellar and Simon turn and head back up the hall from the stairwell door, giving a thumbs-up.

The stairwell door they've just checked is just like the one that's one floor down, metal, white, and with a long, narrow window set above the crash-bar handle.

Between the elevators and the stairwell, we might have access to the whole building. If we can deal with the zombie in the stairwell. Assuming there's only one or even if there are two, we can probably make it down to the second floor again or even the exhibit hall ground floor, if we need to.

We should try to find the roof access next. It might actually be in the balcony. That would be a problem.

Okay, but we're in a pretty good location right now, all things considered. A barricade, a mostly okay emergency escape route, two if you count the elevators, bathrooms and water . . . I have a weapon and snacks . . .

And no zombies. Well, if we can completely secure those balcony—

Electric guitars wail into the quiet, a hard rock-and-roll riff made tinny from Siggy's phone speaker, but still plenty loud.

Siggy looks simultaneously horrified and reflexively happy, standing on one of the cushioned chairs, holding her phone high in the air.

It's Annoying Mark's annoying ringtone.

She has a signal, he's calling, and it's making a god-awful racket.

Siggy lowers the phone and swipes mute or answer, as the balcony doors closest to her flap and strain against the belt tied around the handles.

There's a bang as one of the unsecured doors flies open and bashes into the wall, and zombies push out, maimed and groaning, jerking along on the tugging strings of their unnatural hunger.

The one in front is the stuntman from the cheerleader

squad, the last one who made it into the balcony by climbing up the thick orange extension cord. Now his eyes are cloudy and crisscrossed with burst capillaries. His skin has the writhing ripple of twitching muscles, and the mottled, necrotic coloring all the infected have.

Other zombies pour out the door behind him, the rest of his cheer squad and the others they rescued from the ballroom floor. They're all zombies now, some with horrific, gaping, torn, and bloody injuries, and all of them with jerky, flailing movements, as if they're being yanked toward our movement and our noise.

Annie lets out a shriek and everything starts happening very, very fast.

I leap to my feet and run around the edge of the barricade toward Imani, Siggy, Blair, and the rest of the group.

Simon sprints down the hallway toward us, vanity stool raised. Cuellar spins on his heel and runs *away* to the stairwell door.

The stuntman zombie in the front of the pack lunges at Rosa.

Linus jumps in front of her, swinging his fire extinguisher up in a short arc.

"Run!" he yells, then gives Rosa a shove toward me. "Hey! Come at me!" he calls to the zombies.

He moves back, away from us, toward the bar, yelling,

whooping, thrusting his fire extinguisher up and out.

Most of the zombies follow the noise and the movement. No, all of them. They all follow Linus.

"Move it!" I hiss to Imani, Siggy, and Annie. "Stairwell!" I point down the hall.

I rush to the bathroom alcove and wait for the rest of the group to get past me, standing like a guard with my mic arm cocked like a bat.

Simon takes up a similar pose with his vanity stool, facing me from the curving wall across from the bathroom like a matching bookend.

Or a gate.

Annie, Imani, and Siggy rush past us to the door at the end of the hall.

Blair and Mia run past. Mia is taking the lightest, shortest, fastest steps I've ever seen, keeping her stilettos from clacking on the floor.

Rosa and Janet are last. Janet is pulling Rosa, tears and horror plain on the camerawoman's face.

At the bar, Linus is surrounded.

Simon grabs my shoulder, pulling.

I can't watch.

I spin on my heel and sprint down the hall with Simon.

Behind us, a piercing scream, and then other noises I don't want to hear.

21

*W*e crash through the door and turn.

I drop the mic arm and grab the hex key from the backpack.

"Hold the door!" I urge Simon, and I start twisting the hex key in the crash-bar holes.

"No time!" Simon urges.

"Just do it or they could follow us into the stairwell!" Janet orders.

I glance up the hall, and sure enough a single cheerleader zombie has stumbled into the top of the hallway.

She turns her face toward us.

Twist, twist, twist.

The cheerleader sprints—she's one of the fast ones, a zoombie; she rockets down the hall.

I get one side locked down as she reaches the door, grasping for me, where I'm still kneeling on the floor.

Simon shoves her back with the legs of the stool, shoves and keeps shoving. Janet props the door for me, holding her vanity drawer front by the pull handle, holding it over me like a shield.

Another cheerleader zombie surges forward behind the fast one.

Suddenly Imani is there, pushing out at the second zombie with her microphone stand, yelling with the effort.

"Fall back! Fall back!" I yell, feeling the crash bar lock.

Simon and Imani jump through the door and together with Janet help me shove it almost closed as more zombies arrive and stack up, trying to push through the narrow gap to get at us.

Blair rushes to us, shoving at the door as we all grunt with the effort to force it closed.

With a perfect, efficient pivot that would make most people dizzy, Imani spins to the side and jabs her microphone stand into the gap, shoving.

It's the shove, not the stab, that clears the door. Imani pops the mic stand back and the door closes with the double thunk of the long bars locking into place.

"Way to go," I pant. "Imani."

Imani sags against the door next to me.

"Thanks," she pants back, holding up a hand.

I slap it lightly, weak with relief.

I land on my haunches, only meaning to go down after it's already started. The post–adrenaline dump makes my hands shake.

"Dammit, Linus!" Simon curses, hitting the door. "Aghhh!!" he screams at the faces of the zombies pressing against the narrow window.

I glance down the first flight of stairs to the landing in between floors.

Annie looks like she's trying not to cry, as she hugs her defibrillator case against her chest. Mia's there, with Siggy next to her, unarmed with a shell-shocked expression.

"He saved us," Annie says.

"He was bitten," Mia murmurs, rubbing Annie's back lightly. "He knew he was infected already."

We're going to have to find Siggy a weapon. Blair, too.

My voice is croaky when I speak. If I wasn't so scared and tired, I might be thirsty.

"We have to get ready—there's a zombie in the stairwell."

Something about the phrase makes me want to laugh. It's another title. A fancy BBC TV show. It makes me want to pretend to be British, announcing the zombie in the stairwell like I'm a butler.

Oh.

It's Linus's voice I'm imagining.

Tears prickle in my eyes.

"Already took care of it," Cuellar announces, climbing back into sight from the stairwell below us.

"Okay," I say. "Thanks."

"Oh God, poor Linus." Mia swipes at her eyes, and then smooths her bangs, an unconscious habit.

"He saved us," Rosa says.

"Now what? It can't be for nothing," Janet says.

"I don't know," I say. "But I think—"

"I'm done waiting around like some sitting duck," Cuellar interrupts, his tone accusing, as if he wasn't just standing around when we found him.

"Right," I say. "I agree."

"So where do we go?" Annie asks.

"Here's what I know," I say. "That scientist who got on the stage said—"

"That guy!" Cuellar scoffs. "Yeah, sure, let's base our plan off *him*."

"Let her talk!" Blair snaps. Her dislike of Cuellar is palpable.

"Go on, June," Imani says, giving me a nod.

Cuellar lets out a curse, but he props himself against the wall and crosses his arms.

"What do you think, June?" Siggy encourages me.

I take a deep breath, and try to ignore the way that Cuellar's lip curls as he listens.

"Here's what I know," I start again. "We made it up here, we found our friends and tried for a signal. We don't have one, and we can't see anything from those windows. As for the roof access, we can't locate it unless we want to fight a bunch of zombies while we look."

Siggy shakes her head, a gesture echoed by Mia and Annie.

"Right," I continue. "But we're in the stairwell now. We can make it all the way down to the first floor in safety. If the exhibit hall is locked like the scientist said, we can maybe make it to the atrium and the front doors."

Cuellar's lip has stopped curling. His eyes are sharp, calculating.

"I know Cuellar saw zombies when he looked down the escalator, but that was right after it all started. Maybe they were drawn up to the second floor. If any are left, maybe we could fight our way out past them. Or sneak past them! I think we should head down to the ground floor, and try to get out the front doors."

"But what if they're locked, like the scientist said?" Mia asks.

"Maybe they are," I concede. "But maybe not. I think there's a team of people trying to contain this infection."

I turn to Siggy.

"Remember those people in hazmat suits?" I ask her.

"Those were cosplayers, weren't they?" Siggy asks, turning her luminous eyes from me to Imani to Blair. "Weren't they?"

"No way to tell, I guess," I say. "But I don't think so. Not with all this."

My hand swirls around—an all-encompassing gesture that takes in the whole mess we're in.

"If there is a government agency here trying to contain the infection, they'll have a triage area set up. Like in the show. Remember? There'll be hazmat gear, scanning sections, probably secure trucks or whatnot—but they will have a plan that could be in action right now! They're probably out there as we speak!"

My heart suddenly thunders in my chest at the thought of it: freedom, safety, and my mom coming to get me.

My mom? Oof. I better not think of her, or my dad. Or even Summer, far away at college. Is she safe? She has to be.

If I keep thinking of her and my parents, I'll start to bawl, and Cuellar will stop listening to me.

Ugh.

"Maybe it is as simple as the chosen exit point is the front door. Maybe we'll get there, and the doors will be unlocked, will be the exit point, and we can get out."

"Or maybe not," Blair says, but her voice is not needling. It's just firm.

"Or maybe not," I agree. "In which case we break out."

I point at Imani's disc-weighted microphone base.

"We take out the glass. We can grab another fire extinguisher. We bash the hell out of the glass."

"What if it's shatterproof?" Janet asks.

"All glass is breakable," Imani says. "Shatterproof just means it won't pulverize or break jaggedly."

"Oh yeah?" Cuellar pops off the wall. "What about bulletproof glass?"

"There's no such thing as bulletproof glass," Imani explains. "The correct term is bullet resistant, but all glass breaks. Besides which it's mostly used for armored vehicles. The glass in the building is probably just extra thick and shatterproof."

We stare at her, my gorgeous, brilliant friend. I feel like our collective demeanor is either impressed, confused, or fondly amused by her.

Imani waves her coral-tipped fingers in a let-me-get-through-this-quickly twirl.

"I know because I like studying the—" she begins to explain.

"It's okay, don't hurt yourself," Mia interrupts, cocking a hip out. "You've got my vote."

"So, we break the glass," Rosa says. "But then the zombies can get out, too."

"The army has to have set up a perimeter by now," Simon says. "Locking us in was to buy time to set it up."

"So, they'll be ready to take out any zombies that get out?" Siggy asks.

"I would think so," Simon answers.

I take another deep breath, and the words are there, spooling in my head.

"I don't know what those zombies are, or how they happened exactly, but I know that I'm going to try to get out of here. And we will do better together. There's no guarantee of safety. There's no guarantee that I'm right about the atrium or ground floor being mostly empty. There's just no guarantee for any of it. But all we can do is try, and I'm asking you to try with me. We fight together or we end alone. I'm asking you all to fight with me."

There's a heavy moment of silence, when I look at each of them, reading their faces. Janet smiles slightly, and I can hear her voice in my head, saying to trust myself. Imani, a fierce determination in her eyes, then Siggy, scared but sure. Annie, more determined than I expected, honestly. Simon, resigned but ready.

Mia nods. Rosa, standing beside her, frightened, but she nods, too.

Blair, as fired up as me. I can see it in her eyes. She's ready to fight.

Good old Blair.

The spell of silence is broken by a rough guffaw.

Cuellar is bent over at his waist, hands on his knees, laughing. He screams *ha ha ha* at the ground.

Before I can begin to process it, or feel truly angry, or hurt, he holds up a hand, trying to signal through his laughter *wait*.

"Oh lordy," he laughs. But he stands up, flipping the bloody bottle around to a ready position. "You're a trip, kid. For a second there I thought this was one of those prank videos. Honestly."

He swipes at his eyes.

"*Here's what I know,*" he says, mocking me. "You're not my leader. So, no. I ain't *with* you. I ain't *with* anyone. I'm out for me. But sure. Let's go down to the atrium. Try those doors or bust 'em out. But this isn't a team."

Annie starts to protest, but Cuellar keeps talking over her half-formed words.

"Don't get me wrong, girls. Or you, Wong. If I can help you get out I will, but this ain't some kind of hero TV show. I'm for me, no one else. And I'm going first."

"Just like you led the way back there." Janet repositions her drawer plank, tucking it under her arm. "Turning tail and running. June and Simon had more courage than you. And Linus. He saved us."

"Bra-freaking-vo," Cuellar mocks. "Where did it get him?"

Linus. It lances through me, a guilt that cuts directly into my heart. Linus's courage, his sweet demeanor, his humor. I barely knew him, but he was a whole person, a good person, no, a great person, and now he's dead.

It was my idea, leaving the hallway and going to the third floor.

Cuellar keeps talking.

"Don't for one minute think that I'm gonna be pulling a hero move. It's survival, not social niceties. Got it?"

He flips the bottle around, whirling it forward, then backward. He stabs at the air, his opposite arm coming up to drive extra force behind the jagged glass.

"Any of you killed one yet?" he asks. "I've got three."

He points the bottle at me, then drags it across, pointing at the others, a sweep like the slice of a knife.

"We leave together. We end alone. Everyone dies alone, no matter where they are or who they're *with*."

Simon Wong shakes his head.

But no one speaks.

Embarrassment floods my face that I said anything to start with. That I thought I knew what to do. And even though a part of me is screaming at myself to say something, to deny the harshness of his words, I also can't help but recognize the truth.

Linus is dead and I was the one who said . . . I was the one who said we should keep moving, we should go up. It's my fault, it's my fault he got bitten, it's my fault he died. It's all my fault.

A tightness grips my shoulders and a wash of nausea sloshes in my stomach. I'm ashamed, suddenly.

"All right." Cuellar flexes his shoulders and rolls his neck. "Just so we're all on the same page."

22

We take the steps down, stopping at the second-floor landing. I lean over the railing and look down. The woman zombie that Cuellar killed is one level down, lying crumpled against the wall.

I stand back up and cross to the second-floor stairwell door. I finally can see what is blocking it, what I couldn't see when we couldn't open this door from the other side.

A thin rubber doorstop has been wedged into the base of the door.

I glance through the window, looking into the long white hallway behind the ballroom.

It's still clear. No zombies have managed to get through. Yet.

I hang back and gesture for Siggy to wait. Imani stops and so does Blair.

"We need to get you both weapons," I tell Siggy and Blair. "There's an open dressing room on this hall. We can grab something."

Janet and the others have stopped only a few steps down the next staircase. Janet climbs back up.

"Good idea," she says.

"I should grab something, too," Mia says, following Janet.

I guess after Linus, being armed only with mace and confidence doesn't feel like enough anymore.

Cuellar plants a hand on the wall and flips his broken bottle around. "Wouldn't mind getting something a bit more substantial myself."

Great.

"The rest of you can all wait here," I tell them. "Rest. Besides, the fewer of us who go, the quicker, and probably quieter, we'll be," I say.

Mia sits on another step and pops her feet out of her stilettos. She flexes them, rotating the ankles and putting her feet flat on the landing.

"I don't suppose you'd grab something for me? Anything would be fine."

"Sure, Mia," I reply.

Janet sits on another step. "You think it's safe for us to wait here?"

"As safe as anything else. There're no zombies in the hallway yet. If we're quiet we can come back lickety-split."

Simon sinks down to the step next to Janet.

"Annie, do you want a new weapon?" Imani asks.

Annie shakes her head, hugging her defibrillator case tighter.

"Maybe this one is good luck," she says.

"Okay, here, share these." I pull two water bottles out of my backpack. I reposition the two backpacks on me so their weight is evenly distributed again.

I hand the water to Rosa.

"Be careful," she tells me.

I bend and wiggle the rubber doorstop out of the narrow gap.

Imani puts a hand on the stairwell door handle and pushes it slowly, silently, down. She pulls the door inward.

"Let's go," Siggy whispers.

Cuellar pushes to the front. He walks, cat-quiet, into the white hallway.

"Blair, Siggy, let me and Imani go first," I whisper.

Blair nods and takes the door. Imani and I creep into the hall with our microphone stands raised, ready to swing or jab.

Janet takes the door and holds it open a crack. She watches as the five of us tiptoe-rush down the hall to the dressing room door.

It's déjà vu all over again, as we reach not only the dressing room door, but the double doors that lead into the back of the ballroom.

The noise coming from the ballroom beyond the doors is both unmistakable and unmistakably louder.

Zombies. Groaning, shuffling, knocking against the doors, making them shudder in their frames.

"Shit," Imani whispers, glancing at the doors, which are moving and knocking.

"Keep going," I hiss.

Cuellar is already standing at the closed dressing room door. He points at it with his thumb, eyebrows raised.

Checking with me that this is the place.

I nod.

Cuellar holds his bottle up, bracing his wrist with his other hand, ready to jab. He tips his chin at the door handle for one of us to open it.

Like clockwork precision, as if we've planned or somehow rehearsed it, Blair jumps forward and grabs the door handle to the dressing room. She twists it and lunges silently into the room. Simultaneously, she plasters herself flat against the door, getting out of the way of our weapons should we need to fight.

But the dressing room is still empty.

We hustle into the space. Blair closes the door silently behind us, muting the noise from the zombies across the hall.

Cuellar wastes no time. He quietly puts the bottle down on a dressing table counter and grabs the other vanity stool, the match to the one that Simon has.

"Don't take too long," he murmurs to us.

He slides silently back out the door into the hallway.

"What a jerk," Blair whispers. She looks around the dressing room.

"Seriously," Siggy says.

"I didn't like the way he was talking to you," Blair says, glancing at me with that ready-to-brawl light in her eyes.

"Thanks for backing me up," I say. And I mean it when I say it, but at the exact same time, the partner thought spikes out, and lodges in my throat.

Wish you were always so loyal.

I don't say it, but there must be a residue of the emotion in my eyes, because Blair winces slightly, and moves to explore the small bathroom attached to the dressing room.

Imani doesn't say anything, just waits by the closed door.

Siggy goes to the drawers set in the middle of the vanity table counter. There's only one left that has a front piece, the top drawer, narrower than the other two.

Siggy opens the drawer and starts tugging at the front.

I walk over to a metal table lamp on an accent table, unplug it, take off the lampshade, and tuck it under my arm for Mia.

"Why didn't you argue with Cuellar, back there?" Imani asks, her voice a low murmur when I lean against the door with her.

I shrug.

"Because he wasn't wrong," I whisper. "Linus is dead, and it's my fault."

Tears jump to my eyes, but I can't hide from it, can't hide from the guilt and the shame that I ever thought I knew what to do.

"What?" Imani's whisper is pressured with incredulity. "No! Don't you dare think that, June!"

Blair comes out of the bathroom carrying a heavy driftwood sculpture.

Siggy has the drawer front loose, but not completely off.

"Need a hand with that?" Imani asks her.

"I got it." Blair walks over to the counter, puts her piece of driftwood down, and grasps the opposite side of the narrow front piece. Together they strain to quietly pull the drawer front the rest of the way off.

"It's true, though," I say to Imani. "Maybe he'd still be alive if—"

"That's bull." Imani's whisper cuts over mine. "If it wasn't for you, we'd already be dead or we'd be zombies. In the ballroom, remember? You found that bag. You opened the door."

It helps a little to remember that.

"But—" I start.

"No buts!" Imani loops her free arm around my shoulders, squeezing me tight. "Sure, we might have made some mistakes, but they didn't look like mistakes when we made them! No one's psychic! No one's right all the time, no matter what it looks like from the outside."

She squeezes me again.

"We didn't make the zombies. We didn't cause this. We're just doing our best to get through it. So, don't you dare say that any of it's your fault."

I take a deep breath and nod. The tight feeling gripping my shoulders and chest loosens.

"Guys, we're going to have to make a little bit of noise here," Siggy says, standing up and panting, her breath moving a loose lock of white-blonde hair.

"No, we'll try it all together," Imani says. She looks at me, an eyebrow cocked, like a challenge. "All together, or none at all. Remember?"

23

All together we managed to pry the drawer front off without making too much noise. We rechecked the hallway, which was thankfully still empty, so we rushed to rejoin the others in the stairwell.

I gave Mia the metal lamp. We all stood, stretched, or put our shoes or backpacks back on, and climbed down the stairs, past the dead zombie, to the ground-floor stairwell door.

Now we're piled up behind Cuellar, waiting as he cranes his neck, trying to get a clear view out the narrow window into the ground-floor hall that leads to the lobby and atrium.

Annie's pressed so close to him, it's like she wants to be grafted into his side.

But I can't blame her. Ever since his speech when he trashed the idea of self-sacrifice or even teamwork, it's like he's grown larger somehow.

Become a person you could see surviving.

Not because he's good, or particularly smart.

But because he's pragmatic. Unhesitant.

Even though Imani consoled me, and did make me feel

better, I'm still exhausted and a little dispirited. I feel like I'm underwater, somehow. My brain feels like when I took the SAT the first two times.

Swollen and sluggish. Like a computer that just keeps spinning that "loading" wheel . . . but nothing is happening.

"I don't see any of 'em." Cuellar's voice is a low gravel whisper. "So. All yer shoes tied? Weapons ready?"

We're all standing, almost on our tiptoes like sprinters, various makeshift weapons held in tight grips.

"Then let's go. Quiet and slow down this hall, then we'll stop." Cuellar opens the door.

Since I'll be last out, I step forward and hold the door open for the others. Simon goes next to last, and I let the door fall after myself, then catch it at the doorframe, easing it closed as quietly as possible.

Our motley crew tiptoe-rushes after Cuellar, down a tan-and-white hallway, industrial carpet silencing our steps even more.

This hall runs along one of the interior walls of the exhibit hall. We pass a set of closed double fire doors. If the scientist guy made all his rounds, then this set of doors and all the others will be locked tight.

And I have the hex key.

We pass a series of framed paintings, tranquil and bland scenes of lakes and trees, pass another set of fire doors, go a little farther, and stop at the corner where a large potted fern and some trees in massive ceramic containers stand in a row, like soldiers standing guard.

Cuellar crouches behind the fern, glancing around the corner into the lobby that connects to the atrium.

Waiting in the back of the group, all I can see are the escalators and a few motionless or twitching zombies lying on the tile around them.

Linus and Simon's zombies, thrown down from the fight on the escalators one floor above.

Behind the escalators is an open space, then the window wall, the polarized glass filtering the bright afternoon sunlight.

Except there's also a glare, reflected from the large, white piece of fabric that has been hung up outside, blocking the view out.

But also blocking the view in.

My heart does a happy little leap in my chest at this confirmation that there will be help outside, that already military or police or whoever have started assembling a plan, cordoning off a quarantine zone, and blocking the windows so the zombies inside don't bash themselves against the glass trying to reach the humans outside.

Before I can point out the cloth to Simon, Cuellar stands all the way up and shifts his grip on the vanity stool.

"Now!" Cuellar says, and darts out into the lobby.

We move out, running behind him, less in a line now, and more in a clump, as we dash between the front of the exhibit hall and the escalators.

There are only a few zombies on the ground level at all, apart from the incapacitated ones Linus and Simon threw down. So, it would seem that our reasoning was correct—when the outbreak started, most people were locked into the exhibit hall or were attending the panel session in the ballroom one floor above us.

Which means that there are not currently a lot of zombies on this level, or at least not many we can see right now, between us and the atrium front doors.

A group of eight zombies stands on the opposite side of the escalators from us, facing the whiteout windows, seeming oblivious to our presence.

They start groaning and reaching toward the glass as we rush past on the opposite side of the escalators.

At first I'm confused; then I realize they're like a cat chasing a shadow.

They're reaching for our reflection in the whiteout windows.

We run silently past the front of the exhibit hall, past the tiny security booth beyond that, and then we're almost there, rushing around the back of the volcanic water feature, onto the tiled floor of the three-story atrium.

Where some of our more fashionable shoes start to make noise.

Blair tries to rush quietly, taking shorter steps, trying to keep the back of her boot heels from landing so hard.

Mia runs silently, those amazing, tiny tiptoe steps.

Annie doesn't bother. She clatters as she runs in her wedge sandals.

She doesn't let a gap form between herself and Cuellar.

Miraculously, it looks like we have enough of a lead. Even with the noise now drawing their attention, we're going to make it, all of us.

Behind us, the zombies trying to reach our reflection turn at last in the direction of the noise.

Cuellar reaches the doors, the center set, modern glass and steel with wide crash bars.

The doors are also swathed in white fabric or canvas, no doubt for the same reason the window wall is wrapped in white: to stop zombies from trying to reach the teams of people on the other side.

Cuellar thrusts an arm out, and the crash bar goes in smooth, just like it's supposed to, like no one's tampered with it.

Even though I can't see outside past the white, I know they're out there.

People who know what to do. The army. The police. Anybody.

Cuellar bumps into the door with a grunt.

"Go!" Annie urges.

As if spurred by her voice, the group of zombies behind us makes a sort of roar, a guttural cry as they stumble forward, flailing toward the atrium.

They're not zoombies, at least. All moving more slowly, more jerkily, lurching as if from injuries or other damage.

Cuellar throws his shoulder into the door, jumping at it. There's an echoing bang that bounces up the atrium.

He falls back, rubbing his shoulder and cursing.

"No!" Annie yelps. "It has to open!"

Simon runs up the semicircle to the next set of doors and pushes. The door doesn't budge.

I run past Cuellar, down to the last set of doors on the side closest to the exhibit hall.

Behind me there's a tremendous echoing crash as Cuellar swings the metal stool legs at the glass door.

I push at the bar and it goes in, but the door doesn't budge.

Cuellar swings again, and again. Imani runs next to him and hefts the heavy disc end of her mic stand. She swings it like a sledgehammer.

The glass cracks. Cuellar slams his stool into the same spot. He and Imani swing and draw back in rhythm, as the glass fractures into spiderwebbing, peeling away from the metal frame, crumpling but not falling outward.

Something's wrong.

The glass should be falling outward.

The guttural noises of the zombies have changed, becoming amplified.

Which means I know without looking that they've reached the atrium.

"It won't work!" I yell, turning to look back where I came, up the semicircle of the atrium entry. "The doors are blocked!"

Simon stands at the opposite edge of doors, my mirror image.

"They're boarded up!" he yells back.

As if confirming whatever Simon could see out his set of doors, the spiderwebbed glass at last folds, like a shutter, and falls back toward us, onto the floor.

Cuellar rips the white cloth, revealing a broad plank of wood, completely covering the door.

They hung the cloth to stop the zombies from breaking the glass, then they boarded up the doors.

"Dammit!" Cuellar shouts.

"We have to fight!" I call. "Then retreat!"

Someone yells, "RUN!"

The first zombie, a man, rounds the edge of the water feature farthest from me and closest to Simon. The zombie man moves in a twitching lurch, dragging one half-eaten leg behind him.

Two more zombies emerge behind him, another man and a woman, jerking and lurching from their own injuries that happened before they . . . changed.

The woman has a torn and bloody calf and lower leg, white bone and torn tendons showing through the shredded meat. She has to lift and throw that leg forward first, propping back on her good leg.

The third zombie, a short, bald man, is not injured, that I can see. But he has the same twitching jerking on his unseen virus-strings, tugged forward faster when he sees Simon, bloody mouth opening, spilling chunks of raw meat.

More zombies shuffle forward behind these three, stumbling sluggishly, then with increasing speed as we come into view.

The bald zombie breaks into a lurching run toward Simon.

Simon lifts his vanity stool.

Annie screams, and the bald zombie turns, shoulders, then head, then hips, in her direction.

Cuellar tears Annie's grip off his shirt.

And he runs back the way we came, toward the stairwell.

Annie follows, and so do the rest, Rosa, and Imani, and Siggy. They run instinctively, like gazelles leaping away from a lion. As a group, they press between reaching zombie hands, shoving their weapons out.

Simon rushes after them, arcing the seat of the vanity

stool sideways and into the head of the slower zombie reaching for him, knocking her sideways.

Simon sprints ahead of the others, stands guard at the top of the hall, and yells.

"Hurry!"

My group runs and I'm still standing here, frozen against the boarded-up doors so the rest of the zombies won't notice me.

Except, no. Rosa isn't running *away*.

As the short, bald zombie reaches for Siggy at the back of the pack, as his fingers twist at the edges of Siggy's scarf of trailing hair, and as his lurching rush amps up another notch . . .

While I stand helpless and rooted to the floor with my heart in my throat—

Rosa pivots and runs *back*, toward the bald zombie, and then diagonally down, toward the exhibit hall and where I stand, even though she's about twenty feet away from me. Her voice lashes out.

"Hey! Mr. 305!"

Okay, I hadn't really thought of it, but yes, he does sort of look like the zombie version of the Miami-based rapper Pitbull.

The bald zombie spins away from Siggy in that disjointed way again, first shoulders, then hips, then feet, and runs toward Rosa.

Rosa takes a wide stance and cocks the metal lamp on her shoulder, holding it upside down in a choke-tight double grip. The felt-covered base rotates in small circles by her ear, as she watches, and waits.

It's a thing of pure beauty, the way she steps forward, the lamp's whistling arc, composed of hours spent in the batting cage or on the field. So, I guess Rosa must have been on her high school or college softball team, because that lamp swings out like whip-crack poetry in motion, and it catches the Pitbull zombie mid-run.

The lamp hits him square in the throat. His legs keep running, as the top of him is knocked back, held in sudden place by the impact. His feet run right out from under him and up into the air, almost like he's trying to run up an invisible wall.

The bald zombie slams onto his back, a horrible, wet choking noise rattling out of his throat as he scrabbles on the ground.

A piercing shriek sounds from the opposite end of the convention center ground floor, coming from the direction of the hallway where Simon was standing guard moments ago.

Rosa whirls in the direction of the scream and sprints toward it, as Mr. 305 struggles up to his knees, and falls over again, arms and legs thrashing.

I step out to follow Rosa, which is when I realize there

are more zombies streaming around the opposite side of the water feature, the lower half of the circle, moving between the waterfall and the exhibit hall.

Way more zombies. Ten? Twenty?

And I realize I'm too far behind Rosa. And far, far too far behind the others.

Time slows, for a split second, like in a movie, or a football replay. In the taffy-slowdown, I have a math epiphany.

Or something.

A perfect image appears in my mind, plotting the graph of the variables—two groups of zombies, some fast and some slow, one group of survivors, fast, but way ahead of me. And that scream is a giant unknown symbol, no, a variable, dammit. Wait. Is it. An exponent? Is that the thing it is? Get it right, June.

I don't have time to solve for X.

But it doesn't matter, because I can see it, clear as day. The water feature, the locked doors, the security booth and one long wall of the exhibit hall, boarded-up doors and no time to break them open. And the zombies, inexorable, all vectors and quadrants—my mind predicting and following arcs and parabolas, point-to-point-to-line-to-conclusion— suddenly, with perfect clarity.

I am not going to make it.

Even if I run like an Olympic sprinter. Even if I call out

to Rosa, and she waits for me, and tries to whack some of the zombies away with her lamp, and just ends up eaten for her trouble. Even if I dodge and weave, dip and slide, flip around like a superhero on steroids who's made of pixels and CGI instead of flesh and bone.

I'm simply too far away.

There are too many of them, funneling around the bottom of the water feature—plus the group at the top fixated on Rosa and the scream.

But if I don't yell for help . . . if I don't try to follow the others . . . if I just think clearly, if I can think clearly—

A single flower flutters down from the mound of fake volcanic rock, waterfall, and orchids. The flower lands in the small, surrounding pool.

And I know what to do.

I run up the semicircular entryway, looping behind the first group of zombies, the mangled group of injured and slow, one uninjured and faster, stumbling after Rosa. The woman zombie with the chewed-up leg is up again, from when Simon knocked her down.

Only Mr. 305 sees me. The others are distracted by the scream.

Mr. 305 is up, sorta, falling and crawling and standing again, making his unsteady way back toward me as he registers my movement.

My friends, my group, can make it back to the stairwell and safety. I think they will. Even though I don't know who screamed or why.

They have to be safe.

Imani and Siggy and Blair have to be safe.

I run toward the smaller group of zombies, but off to one side. If they were normal people, there's no way they wouldn't see me in their peripheral vision.

But their eyes. The bloodshot hemorrhages in the eyes of all the infected. The occluded black of impact cataracts, or clots, or whatever incredibly gross thing has happened in their eyes means . . . maybe it means . . .

They won't see me yet.

Of course, it's only a matter of time and field-of-vision until they do.

As if hearing the thought, the other zombie man with the dragging leg turns toward me, a zigging motion, whip-sawed away from the noise of the scream.

I rush at him, silent, although I want to yell, swinging the microphone arm with all I've got. It catches him on the side of the head, connecting with a resounding impact I feel up my arms, and throws him sideways into the woman zombie.

They fall and I leap into the fountain, splashing with huge steps until I reach the base of the volcanic rock, actually poured and stained concrete.

I shove the microphone arm through the loops of the backpack I'm wearing on the front and I grab the rock, seeking a foothold alongside the smaller waterfall on the side of the feature.

My feet squish in my Converse and my fingers fumble at the rock, but I find a foothold, and push myself up, jutting my other foot out to find another rock ledge.

It's there, almost where it would be if it were a step and the entire water feature had a built-in ladder.

I climb and climb; by the time I'm halfway up I realize I *am* on a ladder or stairwell, of sorts, because the entire water feature is man-made, and therefore allows for easy, if mostly hidden from the casual eye, maintenance paths.

Behind me the zombies I felled are growling and roaring again. I glance back. They're straining against the bench-like ledge of the water feature, as if they don't understand how I got where I am.

Just like on the stage.

Then the woman zombie with the floppy foot falls into the water, thrashing around in hectic spasms as she tries to stand, bashing her head and arms against the rock, the ledge, the next zombie that falls into the water.

It's only a matter of time before they manage to get to their feet and come at the rock wall. Hopefully they won't be able to find the steps I used to climb.

I'm actually counting on it.

That, and the fact that so far the noise of other zombies doesn't seem near as entrancing as the sounds and sight of regular humans.

Which means, even as I strain to listen over my own labored breathing and the rushing fall and gurgle of the water-falls around me, that I don't *think* the other pod . . . group . . . whatever of zombies has seen me, or even knows I'm here.

They turned like a flock of confused birds when they reached the atrium, moving almost as one, the scream and the flutter of movement drawing the entire pod back the way they came, focused on the rest of my group. But they hope-fully had enough of a lead and are safe back in the stairwell.

Except for whoever screamed.

Please, please, please don't be Imani or Siggy or Blair.

I reach the top of the water feature, just short of being able to see into the second-floor ballroom lobby, but I can see down all around the atrium and entryway.

I was right, the larger group of zombies hasn't looked my way at all, even as the trio in pursuit of me moan and gurgle their frustration at the rock or the ledge.

Movement catches my eye. I crouch and lean, craning my neck to see down. Reaching out from behind the security booth's door, there's a frantic pale hand and dark-sleeved arm waving at me. I can't see the rest of the body that belongs to the hand, but it keeps pulling, urgent and somehow curt *come here* gestures.

Behind me all the zombies are now in the fountain, Mr. 305 thrashing in the water, the others on their feet, straining and reaching up to where I sit perched on the top of the concrete rock.

A central pump feeds all the waterfalls from the top—a cauldron of water in the middle with four spillways, one in each direction. I hook my leg over the cauldron edge, praying I won't get electrocuted somehow if I dislodge a light or something, and I splash-fall across the knee-deep water, and lunge over the opposite edge, clinging where I think the hidden access steps would be, if I were a maintenance worker.

Sure enough, I find a toehold and I slip down, out of sight of the zombies trying to learn how to rock climb.

The acid test. Are they like zombies on the show? Or in movies? In other words, are they inexorable and terrifying, but also completely mindless?

Can they think?

If so, will they think to walk *around* the base of the volcanic rock?

If yes, how long will it take them to do it?

If no, how long will it take for them to forget I was ever there, and to start their aimless, shuffling meandering like fish in an aquarium, but that might result in the same thing—

The zombies moving around the edge, and able to see me again.

My foot slides, then loses its perch. I fall several feet, one cuff of my jeans gets pushed up by the jagged concrete, and it gouges into my lower shin. I let out a quiet noise at the pain as the other foot shoves on a step, and my hand grips a thick tuffet of hearty green fern.

I breathe a curse and finish climbing down, into the pool, trying not to splash more than the waterfall behind me as I turn to face the security booth.

The door stands open, but there's no gesturing arm anymore.

I sit on the ledge of the fountain and lift first my banged-up leg over, then the good one. The water slaps loudly on the tile, running off my clothes onto the floor as I lurch across the floor to the open door.

I fall in, ducking under the desk, beneath the window line.

Under the desk there is a bank of angled screens showing footage of the security cameras positioned all around the ground floor of the lobby and atrium.

Nearby a voice hisses, "Shh!"

I scoot back on my butt, pivoting to face the door while simultaneously pressing my back against the wall under the desk.

Hunter Sterling is crouched behind the door, holding a finger to his lips, begging me with his eyes to be quiet.

24

*H*unter Sterling is sitting right there.

Hunter Sterling basically just saved me.

I was doing okay without Hunter Sterling, more or less. But I am appreciative, because Hunter Sterling is apparently an all-around good guy. Yay!

Look! It's Hunter Sterling.

Hunter Sterling watches the angled video monitors next to my head, and I understand how he knew where I was, what I was doing, and that he could signal to me.

Not taking his eyes off the screens, Hunter Sterling gently eases the booth door closed, painstakingly slow, gentle push, pause, gentle push, pause, almost like he's making a stop-motion movie.

Then it clicks, quietly. And he reaches up to shoot the deadbolt. Then he glances at me.

I mouth the words.

"Thank you."

Hunter Sterling nods, and looks back at the screens. He crawls nearer to me and sits with his back against the wall that meets mine in the corner, so we're nearer and also perpendicular to each other.

There's not much space in the security booth.

Hunter Sterling picks up a small handheld radio. Probably a guard snuck it in to listen to a game.

Hunter Sterling puts it to his ear and turns it on. He's quiet, listening.

"Anything?" I ask.

"Just the usual stuff," he whispers back.

Our knees are close enough to touch, so I'm careful not to accidentally bump his as I stretch my injured leg out, flat on the floor.

The injury is kind of impressive.

It's gratifying when something painful looks as bad as it feels. As opposed to, say, heartbreak. Which feels like hell and looks like self-indulgence or worse. Mopey songs and mopier face.

Not the raw bleeding pain that it feels. Or the sinking, sucking weight in your chest.

Or the humiliation. If you're me.

"I can see them on the monitors," Hunter Sterling whispers, gesturing to the screens next to my head. "I saw them coming, the second group. I tried to warn you guys."

The voice that yelled "Run!"

"Thank you," I say.

Even in a whisper, I can tell his voice is raspy, cracked. "I couldn't think of how to warn you before, then when you started making noise, I could see them coming, and that's when I yelled."

"I think it helped," I tell him. Then I remember the scream. I glance as the angled TV monitors under the counter.

There's a fat streak of blood on the floor at the top of the hall. As if someone got injured and then dragged.

"I heard a scream," I whisper, and I can't take my eyes off the screens because the zombies are suddenly there, shuffling back, aimlessly, under the lenses of the cameras.

"I'm so sorry," Hunter says. "I couldn't see much, but I think someone in the group got bitten. Or worse."

My heart clenches. It wasn't Imani. It couldn't be Siggy. Certainly not Blair.

I will not believe it.

And with my heart, I can't believe it. My Spidey senses reach out and I swear I can feel her, I know she's okay. Imani is okay.

And if she's okay, Siggy must also be okay. And Blair, too. They're okay. I know it.

"We're getting outnumbered," I whisper back. "But we thought we could get out."

Hunter nods, and glances away from me, checking the monitors again.

I carefully pull the microphone arm out of the straps of the backpack I'm wearing on my front and place it on the floor alongside my leg.

Then I slip the backpack off my chest and slowly, silently unzip it and dig inside.

"Here." I hand Hunter Sterling a water bottle.

The appreciation in his earth-green eyes makes my stomach do a little flip.

"Thanks," he says, twisting the lid off and taking an enormous chug.

I try not to watch the way his throat works, with his head tipped up, as he swallows.

I mean, I watch. Appreciatively. But I tell myself not to make it weird.

Myself is not listening.

In myself's defense, this whole thing is weird. Endorphins from my scraped-up leg are zinging through my body, endorphins, and hormones, okay—what does he smell like? I will have to make a note of it when I calm down a bit—Siggy will demand to know—

All of it is a bit much. I'm here hiding out from zombies and I'm with the star of my favorite show, a zombie show, and it's as if nothing is real anymore.

Or it's real, but it's not real in the same way.

There's probably a word for it. Hyperreal. Surreal. TV-real.

I shake my head and make myself look away from arguably the most beautiful human to ever walk the earth.

"I'm Hunter Sterling," Hunter Sterling whispers, putting his hand out in a *pleased to meet you* shake.

It's kind of adorable.

I smile like a dork.

"I know," I say, but I take his hand anyway, trying to ignore the ZING! that shoots through my body at the touch of his skin on mine.

"I'm June Blue," I say.

Then I let go and dig in the backpack again. I find a bandana in the scientist's backpack. It looks clean so I lean over and start tying the bandana around my injured shin. My hands are shaking, adrenaline and pain and low blood sugar, probably.

"Let me help," Hunter Sterling says. "Watch the monitors."

I twist my neck to see the screens. So far, the large group of zombies hasn't wandered back this way; they're clustered around the hallway, their backs to the camera. The smaller pod hasn't found their way around the volcanic fountain.

"So far, so good," I report as Hunter Sterling cinches the bandana tight.

"Sorry," he says.

I must have made a noise.

"It's okay. I'm just hungry."

Did I just crack a joke?

Hunter Sterling lets out a quiet laugh as he sits back against the wall.

"Too bad we don't have a catering truck for the actual zombie apocalypse," he says. And it takes me a second to realize he joking, too, and then I snortle a laugh out my nose.

I glance back at him.

Aaaaaaaaand he's smiling at me.

Actually smiling.

At me.

I smile back and hear the goofus "dur-heyuck" laugh in my head as I snortle quietly again.

Smooth, June. Real smooth.

Snap out of it.

"Well, it's not a catering truck, but—" I reach into the backpack and pull out two energy bars.

I hand one to Hunter Sterling.

"Wow, what *don't* you have in there?" he asks, voice tinged with honest amazement.

And I feel like an actual badass.

We open and eat the energy bars. I'm flexing my calf and my foot, seeing how bad the injury is—now that it's covered up it doesn't seem so rough.

"So, how did you end up here?" I ask, tilting my eyes to the desk surface over our heads.

We exchange our stories. Establish we were both in the

ballroom when it started, and how we got out, who was with us. Who we lost.

Hunter was with James. Of course, the actor who played his father figure very much seeming to fill that role in real life.

I don't tell him that I met James as a fan mere hours before the apocalypse started. Or how nice he was to us.

But I listen as Hunter's whisper urgently explains how he, like me, got separated from the rest of his group.

It was basically the same thing that just happened to me, how I ended up split off from the others by the sheer bad luck of zombie pack (horde?) dynamics.

Except Hunter, James, and the other actors and audience members with them actually got to the doors after they were locked, but *before* they were shrouded in white cloth.

And saw out the chained glass doors, as they banged and hammered and yelled.

There were people in hazmat suits. Whole platoons of them, as well as tenting being set up, military-grade weaponry and barricades, a double-ringed perimeter, and a woman in a hazmat suit standing right on the other side of the door—trying to communicate with them.

She'd waved, yelled, and gesticulated, but then the zombies had arrived, chasing Hunter, James, and the others trapped inside.

It was chaos, terror, screams, people were attacked, taken

down, the group had scattered, James leading the rest up the escalators to the second floor, not realizing until he got somewhere safe, if he did, that Hunter had been isolated behind the rest, cut off by the same water feature and a smaller pack (contingent?) of zombies.

Until he'd managed to dodge and weave his way here, under the desk, behind the locked door, and stayed there until the zombies at the door had been drawn away by something else.

Us. Our group.

And he'd seen on the monitors how that played out, and how I'd become isolated, how the pack (flock?) of zombies had split. As in into two groups. So Hunter was able to signal to me.

And here we both are, hiding. With no way out.

"We're in a lockdown," Hunter whispers. "Impossible as it seems, with actual zombies, or whatever they are."

"That scientist guy that jumped onstage said he was a biomedical researcher, so it's probably like a rage-virus or rabies kind of thing," I say. "They're not reanimated corpses, technically."

I remember the look of them, graying, necrotic flesh, bloodshot, capillary-burst eyes. Herky-jerky locomotion like looking at a dancer attempting to perform a piece inspired by neurological damage.

"I mean," I add, "I don't *think* they're actual reanimated corpses."

Hunter cocks an eyebrow.

"How reassuringly technical," he whispers, a rueful grin skewed sideways at me.

I grin back.

"That's me, Miss Overly-Accurate-in-Life-and-Death-Scenarios," I joke. I grab the air beside my eye and reposition fake glasses. "Actually," I whisper in a quasi-nasal voice, "they're not reanimated corpses." I give a little sniff and simultaneously slide my index finger up the bridge of my nose, pushing the pretend glasses up.

Hunter snorts a laugh, then lifts a fist in a sky-punch of celebration.

"Death is still real!" he whisper-cheers.

I glance at my leg. I flex my leg gently, roll it side to side.

"How's it feeling?" Hunter asks.

"Better," I answer. "Thanks for helping with the bandana bandage."

I don't mean to, not consciously, but I'm feeling punchy and so I do it without thinking.

I repeat the phrase "*bandana bandage*" with over-enunciation.

Hunter curls slightly away from the wall, stifling a laugh.

"The only thing that would be better," he whispers, "is if there was a fruit motif on the handkerchief, then you'd have a *banana bandana bandage*."

I feel a fizzing laugh build in my chest. My hands flap in front of my face in a *stop, I'm gonna bust* universal gesture.

We don't look at each other, taking deep breaths to disperse our overstressed, completely inappropriate given the situation, punchy laughter.

I can't help it.

"It would be so great if you had that fruit motif handker-chief while you were on vacation," I start.

"Staaaaaahp," Hunter hisses, snorting.

"—by the beach," I continue, and we're both curling, trying to keep our laughter as quiet as our whispers.

"Don't you dare!" Hunter gasps. "Don't say *cabana!*"

We both eke out hisses of near-silent laughter, sounding like that old animated dog, Mutley, with his asthmatic *heh heh heh*s.

It must be stress, and the laughter must be some kind of stress relief, because apart from the stitch in my side from trying to hold the laughter in, I actually do feel better.

We agree to a truce on the bandana thing, so we take deep breaths and get ourselves back under control, carefully not looking at each other until the jag subsides.

When we're quiet for a full minute, I take the lid off the water bottle and take a drink.

Hunter clears his throat.

"If the bandage got torn," he begins.

I laugh-choke water into my nose.

25

After the laughing jag, we share another energy bar and the rest of the water bottle.

Hunter hands the last bite to me.

"I guess we can't sue a zombie convention for having an actual zombie apocalypse," he says. "But it does seem a little on the nose."

"I just wish they would've put it on the promotional materials."

I yawn.

"What time did your day start?" I ask.

"My driver picked me up from the hotel in Atlanta at seven." Hunter repositions himself, propping his elbows on his knees. "How about you?"

"My driver dropped me off at six thirty," I say.

His eyes narrow in concern. "I wasn't trying to sound like a jerk. The driver was a convention volunteer named Cindy. It's just an industry term to call it 'my driver' or 'your driver.'"

I put a hand on his forearm.

"I was just kidding," I say. "My driver was my mom."

Hunter smiles. "She sounds nice, getting up early on a Saturday to drive you down."

"Not only that but she bought us a drive-through breakfast on the way," I tell him. "Me and my friend Imani."

"I didn't stop for drive-through breakfast," Hunter says. "Just coffee."

He sounds so adult. I don't even like coffee unless it's the sugary frozen kind.

"Imani didn't really eat her breakfast," I say. "But that's probably because she had so much pizza last night."

"So, you had a slumber party, too? That sounds like fun."

I stop, carefully checking his eyes, because maybe it sounds silly. Makes me seem like a little kid. Maybe he thinks I'm younger than I am.

Maybe I am younger than I am, but that's not the point.

But Hunter's still smiling, this wide-open expression on his face, not like an adult at all but like a kid listening to story time.

"Yeah, we have sleepovers all the time," I tell him. "We grew up in each other's pockets, as my mom says. We live on the same block. If we cut through backyards it's like only three houses away."

Hunter's expression turns wistful.

"I don't have any friendships like that," he says. "I mean,

I have friends and stuff, but it's not the same. We moved around too much and then when I got cast—"

His voice trails off. He catches himself, and looks down.

"It's just hard to do long-distance friendships, and everyone on the show is older than me."

I nod. Then I narrow my eyes at him.

"Tell me the truth, Hunter."

"Okay, what?"

"Do you even like coffee?"

Hunter chuckles, and shakes his head. "It's okay."

"Put a lot of sugar and milk in it." I wink at him. "Pro tip."

Hunter laughs and sketches a salute at me.

I flex and lift my leg, then straighten it out again.

"I think I'm good," I say. "And as restful as this has been, we should make a move."

"Few issues. First: go where?" Hunter asks.

"There's got to be a way out."

"I don't see how, if they have it all locked down and blocked from sight." Hunter shakes his head. A lock of wavy hair falls over his eyes.

"That woman, the one outside, in the hazmat suit—where was she pointing? She was trying to tell you all something, what was it?"

"I've been replaying it in my mind," Hunter says, his eyes closed. "Behind us. She was pointing behind us."

"At the zombies coming, maybe," I whisper, although no. It had to be something more.

Or is that just my own desperation?

"No, it was behind us and up. But not the escalator. I don't think . . ." Hunter's whisper trails off, a self-doubt that is so familiar to me under the soft tone. "I don't know."

"No, go on. What were you going to say?" I urge him, and touch his hand.

"It's just . . . the angle was off." His words are urgent, as he turns his hand up to squeeze mine, tight, like the pressure of his fingers can tell me more than his voice, what he means.

I would like to take a moment, right now, outside of time or mortal terror, to observe in my body the way it feels to hold Hunter Sterling's hand. Surreal as it is, and not-really-a-hand-hold-kind-of-holding-hands as it is.

It feels nice. Really, really nice. So warm. So tingly.

"What was the angle?" I ask. "Where?"

"Up and outside," Hunter says. "It doesn't make sense. I can't figure out where she was pointing. I would say down the street, but it was up."

He lets go of my hand and points over his own shoulder and up at the desk surface above us.

Outside. Up. Down the street.

"The hamster tube!" My voice is quiet yet still louder than I intended. I glance back at the monitors. The group of zombies standing at the fountain haven't really moved from their location, although their arms are now lowered.

The other screens are blank, the horde or pod of zombies having wandered into a blind spot.

"What?" Hunter asks.

"The walkway thingy! The skyway!"

"There's a skyway?"

I see our town and Hunter's experience with it for a split second, through his eyes. He probably watched fields and houses, trailer parks and denser subdivisions out his car window as the driver brought him in from Atlanta.

Depending on where he was dropped off, he wouldn't know there was a skyway. Especially with as small as the town must seem to him.

As small as it actually is.

Midsized is what our mayor likes to call it. Midsized so that it doesn't sound like "not as small as some." Or "bigger than many!"

Tiny to Hunter Sterling, though.

And, like, we know, the hamster tube is ridiculous.

"It leads to the hotel," I say.

And of course. The tube makes the most sense as a point of exit. It's tiny. And I saw them, I saw the people in hazmat suits; we thought they were the same cosplayers from before but they weren't, they were from the army or whatever group is trying to deal with all this. They pushed the security into the tube, they closed the entry into the hotel.

I tell all this to Hunter.

Maybe the hotel is in lockdown, too. The elevators locked, the army waiting in the lobby at the multiple points of exit or entry, and an orderly, safe, manageable quarantine and screening area.

"It makes sense," Hunter agrees. "Too bad we can't get there."

"But we can!" My voice is a hiss, so I open another water bottle. "All we have to do is try to reunite with the others. With my friends Imani and Siggy and the rest who ran to the stairwell. And then the stairwell is already clear, I know that much, so we go back up to the second floor and then we make a break for it."

"A few little hurdles," Hunter says, and his voice is gentle, like he doesn't want to be mean or deflating.

"Go ahead." I take another drink.

"First, can you 'make a break for it'? With your leg?"

I flex my toes, rotate my ankle, and lift my knees.

"Yes," I say, ignoring the discomfort. "Absolutely."

"Okay," Hunter continues. "Second hurdle, Cuellar. What if he won't let us in?"

I shake my head, although I guess he knows how Cuellar is better than anyone.

"He will," I say. "And if he doesn't, Imani and Siggy will. They'll have our backs."

Hunter nods.

"And if no one is there and the door is locked I have this." I hold up the hex key. "It can open a disabled crash bar."

Hunter shakes his head, but he doesn't say anything about the possibility of no one being there, of the door being locked.

He clears his throat.

"Last hurdle," he says, and he looks away from the screens into my eyes. His gaze is powerful, the green of his eyes pulling at me, like gravity.

"How do we get to the stairwell without the zombies getting us? Like, where even is that second . . . group? Herd? What is the collective noun for a group of zombies?"

"I know!" I whisper. "I've been wondering the same thing. I'd think a devouring but that doesn't really trip off the tongue."

"Sounds good though, *a devouring of zombies*."

"Yeah. How about a shamble?"

"Doesn't sound scary enough. A hunger?"

"Nah, sounds like a good snack would fix them."

"I've got it, June," Hunter says, and he smiles at me. "A killing of zombies."

I try it out.

"A killing of zombies." I smile.

I like it because it's scary, but it also sounds like not just something they do, but something we can do.

"So how do we clear the hallway so that we can reach the stairwell door?" Hunter asks.

"I have an idea for that," I say.

26

"This is so dangerous. So dangerous. This is dangerous, dangerous, dangerous," I chant, because it is, but I'm doing it anyway.

Because we can't just stay here forever, and we have a place to go, and then another place to get to.

The stairwell for Imani and Siggy and Simon and Janet and the others, and then the hamster tube.

I mean, assuming they're all stuck in the stairwell the way we've been stuck here. But if they've moved to another floor, I'm hoping we can follow them somehow.

Either way, it's better than hiding under the desk in the security booth.

Assuming this plan works.

"This is such a bad idea," I whisper to myself, a goad but more just fear, plain fear, the edge of panic, and acknowledging it makes me feel a little less . . .

Panicked.

What I'm doing is carting the small, old-fashioned radio out to the front of the atrium.

Then I'm going to put it on the ledge of the fountain and turn it on. The zombies will be drawn to the sound and we'll make a break for it.

So far, they haven't seen me.

So far, it's working.

So far, so good.

Before I can turn on the radio, though, it all goes sideways.

"Run!" Hunter urges, behind me. I take off and I hear him skidding on the tiles at the edge of the hallway; the squeak-then-slide of his shoes is almost comical.

I turn back to make sure he's upright.

"Go!" he yells, as his legs slip and he practically pinwheels in place, almost like a cartoon character as he tries to get traction.

It's just a split second, then he's moving fast beside me.

And we don't have time to notice, but we both saw that what he slipped on was a long smear of fresh blood.

We sprint down the first-floor hallway. Behind us, the frenzied groans of the zombies chasing us echo into the hall.

We're almost to the stairwell door. Through the narrow window I see Janet's surprised face as she looks out at the noise. She breaks into a huge smile, then her mouth moves and I see it almost in slow motion, as she's calling to the others.

The door gets pulled open before we reach it. Imani

reaches out, pulling us in, then Janet slams the door closed again.

The zombies chasing us crash into the closed door. The bangs of their impact echo up the stairwell.

Before I can even breathe, Imani's there, hugging me and saying, "I knew you were okay. I knew you were okay."

Siggy hugs me, too. "Oh, thank God, June!"

We all start crying but it's relief.

Blair hugs herself, standing a bit back, but she smiles at me, so I return it.

"Hey, this is Imani and this is Siggy, my best friends," I say to Hunter. "This is Hunter Sterling."

"Well, duh, June," Siggy says, but in a whoa-dude tone, her eyes wide.

"This is Blair," I say pointing. Blair shakes his hand and says, "Nice to meet you," like Miss Manners.

"So glad you're okay, June," Janet O'Shea says, and she hugs me like my mom would and I try not to think about my mom or my dad because if I do, I'll start crying real actual sobs.

"Good to see you, kid," Cuellar says, his voice strange, changed somehow, and he grabs Hunter by the scruff and gives him a little one-arm hug that Hunter seems more to endure than enjoy.

Simon and Annie come in, and it's an actor group hug, mirroring my friendship-hug with Imani and Siggy.

I look around. A sinking feeling washes through me, with the memory of the long smear of blood at the hallway entrance.

"Where's Rosa? And Mia?"

"Mia's gone," Cuellar says, and his voice is rougher than usual. "Dead or one of them now."

He turns his body partly away, bringing a hand to his eyes.

"Mia's shoe broke," Imani says softly, looking between us and Cuellar. "She fell when we got to the top of the hall."

"We were too far ahead," Janet says, dropping her eyes. "We didn't realize she'd fallen."

"It was so fast." Tears spill down Siggy's face. "The hall was like a bottleneck, and the only thing that kept the zombies off the rest of us was Mia's scream."

"We all kept running," Janet says. The little group seems to shrink, arms coming up, hugging themselves.

"Of course we kept running." Cuellar's voice is a knife, cutting off the subject.

But his eyes are round, shining.

I remember him bear-hugging Mia.

Mia gone, and no one able to help her.

"But what happened to Rosa?" I ask, because she had sprinted in their direction the minute she heard the scream.

After the scream.

So she was on the other side of the bottleneck.

"I saw her at the end of the hall," Simon says, hopeful

dark eyes moving between me and Siggy. "She was too late to help Mia, but she didn't get caught."

"Not that we saw," Cuellar says, voice rough.

"She couldn't get down the hall, presumably," Janet interjects. Simon nods.

"She paused for just a moment, then kept running that way."

Simon points in the opposite direction from the atrium, away from the front doors.

Rosa ran down the hall past the escalators, past the hallway with our stairwell, and beyond in the direction of the first-floor bathrooms and meeting rooms.

"I bet she made it," I say. My voice grows firmer when I say it again. "I think she made it."

"Maybe if we wait here, the zombies will go away, and she can make it back here, just like you did," Annie says.

"We can wait here for a while," Imani agrees. "Give her that chance, at least."

Janet reaches out and touches first my arm, then Hunter's. "I'm glad you're both okay. So glad."

Hunter leans down to hug her, and then so do I.

"How did you get through the zombies anyway?" Annie steps closer, like we are all somehow huddling around a fire instead of standing under the fluorescent stairwell lights.

"June's idea," Hunter says. "I was just hiding in the security booth."

"You waved at me!"

"We both ended up there, under the desk."

"At least the door locked!"

"And finally June says, 'We have to go!'"

"Well, yes, but you also said, 'Let's use the cameras!'"

"I wish we had them now. Or, like, a drone or something."

"June crawls out to put a radio on the fountain as a decoy."

"Hunter's watching the security monitors, but the zombies saw me, I guess?"

"Right, so we ran here when they ran there."

"Anyway, that's how we got away, and ran down the hall." I turn to Imani, who's watching me with a bemused expression.

"What?" I ask.

"Nothing," she says lightly, but she's covering a smile as she turns away.

"What?" I ask Siggy.

Siggy leans over and speaks just to me in a low voice.

"You guys are finishing each other's sentences."

"What?"

"Just telling you."

Huh. I mean. What?

But something about our telling of the story must have lessened the tension somehow because Imani and Siggy aren't the only ones giving us amused looks.

"So, does anyone have an idea how many zombies were

actually out there?" Blair asks. "Because I would say at least ten? Maybe fifteen? It was too hard to tell when it all started to go bad."

"How many zombies were chasing you?" Hunter asks Cuellar, then winces at the flash of anger in his eyes.

Hunter puts up his hands in a placating gesture. "I'm just trying to figure out how many were loose on the first floor," he says.

Cuellar shakes his head.

"I don't know, if I try to think about them too much my brain goes all . . ." His hand comes up by his ear and wobbles there. "It probably felt like more than it actually was. But it felt like a lot."

Hunter nods. A muscle jumps in his jaw, and I swear he looks like a poster of himself, except moving. A determined look enters his eye, and it's his character he looks like, Clay Clarke, ready to face the odds.

"If this was a filming day," Hunter murmurs to Cuellar. "And they were just extras on the show? How many are on the call sheet?"

Cuellar huffs a laugh, but his voice has lost its tight edge when he speaks.

"Twenty, I think. Yeah. Right around that."

"And we had those two groups by the fountain," I say.

"It's the second floor you've really got to worry about,"

Blair says. "That one set of ballroom doors is open, and there were almost a thousand people in there, easy."

"Right, but there's nothing to draw them out. They're like flies in a bottle lying sideways." I illustrate with my hand. "There's only one entry and exit, and they have no lure to go out. Sure a few of them will be out, just due to sheer numbers and chance, but I don't think it will be insurmountable."

"Why does it matter?" Blair asks. It's not confrontational, but more like she knows me, because she does. She used to be one of my closest friends.

"It matters because that's where we're going next," I say.

27

I just wish we had those security cameras with us now," Hunter says, but there's no edge to it.

And we *are* about to run into the unknown.

We had waited in the stairwell, out of sight of the zombies in the first-floor hallway, until they wandered off, while we rested, hoping that Rosa might find her way back to us.

Eventually we had to admit that she might not come back. Probably wasn't coming back, even if she wanted to. There was no telling where she was, or what situation she might be facing.

Janet said Rosa might have barricaded herself in a room, or met up with another group of survivors.

No one wanted to say what else might have happened.

But we had to keep moving, had to go on to our next plan. We're hoping Rosa is, too.

We can't wait in the stairwell forever.

We stand ready in the stairwell, behind the second-floor hallway door.

The others are ready; well, Annie's as ready as a girl armed with a defibrillator case can be, I suppose, and the others are ready to get the hell out of here, after hearing about the woman in the hazmat suit pointing to the hamster-tube-skyway thing.

So, we're going to rush out of our safe zone again. Out there.

Where zombies are.

But we have a plan, and I know if we can just get to the hamster tube . . . this whole nightmare could be over. We can get out, get screened, get quarantined, whatever.

And I can call my mom.

"Yeah," I agree. "Everyone ready?"

I try not to put an overemphasis on *everyone*, but it's there, unspoken. After the loss of Mia and also probably Rosa, I can't think about them right now, or I won't be able to do anything. And we have to go. We have to get out.

To do that, we have to stick together.

Cuellar must have been shaken by the loss of his barracuda, Mia, because in spite of himself and his harsh words before, he's not insisting on going first anymore, and he seems content to follow along with our group.

Then again, what are his options?

The only thing he asked was, what happens if we get to the tube and the opposite side is blocked again? Like the atrium doors were.

So, I told him that unlike the atrium we can lock the zombies out of the tube by closing the hatchway behind us. And on the way to the tube we'll stop at the fire-safety station for the ax.

Cuellar's mouth flattened and then rose into a tight grin at that.

Janet made us all stop and practice a formation, of sorts. She said it was the way the ancient Romans used to be so good in battle; they would form a turtle shell with their shields close together, then fight while being protected and protecting each other.

"We don't have shields, but we do have long weapons, most of us anyway," Janet said, smiling gently at Annie and her defibrillator.

"If we practice and stay close together," Janet continued, "in a sort of turtle formation, we can protect each other's backs."

So, we practice, lining up in pairs, moving tightly together in a circle on the landing, like an imitation of an elite SWAT team or something.

Then we break and get ready, stretching or rolling our necks, checking our shoelaces and stuff.

Siggy makes quiet little "Vvvv! Vvvv! Cssssh!" lightsaber noises as she practices swinging and jabbing out with her drawer plank. She catches me watching and strikes a big Jedi pose, like a movie poster.

She holds the pose and nods her head.

"Ahhh yeeeaah," she says, drawing it out like a surfer. "Dead-leeee."

I snort and she laughs back.

We're as ready as we're gonna be.

I ease open the door, and peer out. It's clear, so I lead the way down the hall.

The white hallway is the same, just as we left it. We move silently. The double doors that exit from the back of the ballroom still flap and strain from the zombies moving on the other side.

There's no telling how long this hallway will remain passable.

We pause at the dressing room for Hunter to arm himself with a heavy wooden lamp, bigger than the matched pair Mia and Rosa had used.

I look at Annie and tip my head at the dressing room.

Annie shakes her head, clutching her defibrillator case like a talisman.

It's gotten her this far, I guess. Plus, to be fair, she looks pretty shell-shocked.

We go back into the hall and rush down to the double doors that lead out to the second-floor lobby and escalators.

"Okay, no one left behind," I whisper over my shoulder. "Remember the turtle defense thingy."

We cluster together with each other at our backs, our weapons bristling outward.

If two sections of a microphone stand, two vanity stools, front pieces of drawers, a lamp, a sculpture, and a defibrillator case can be said to bristle.

The point is, we're going to work together this time.

Hunter stands to my right. We're the front of our little phalanx.

"Yay, rah, turtle defense thingy!" he cheers, a low murmur so only I hear, then he shoots that crooked smile at me.

I smile at him, just a full-on beam of teeth and gums, I'm sure, and my heart does this squeeze-trip-skitter-lunge thing. Like it's warming up for more work to come, if I ever get more of those smiles.

Which, like, how ridiculous am I for thinking about how nice the shape of Hunter's lips are? Right now? When we're going out to face certain danger and possible death?

Get it together, June.

Okay, except his lips are *so* nice. Call it a focus object.

A gal could go to war for a pair of lips like that.

We push open the door and run out into the second-floor lobby. Our turtle is basically two by two, Janet and Imani behind me and Hunter, Siggy and Blair behind them, Annie and Cuellar and Simon bringing up the rear.

The ballroom lobby is very bare compared to the balcony area upstairs on the third floor. There's no bar and fewer seating areas. It's just a wide sweep of carpet and entry points to the ballroom.

A single zombie, a man, stumbles haphazardly around the second-floor lobby.

He doesn't see us. At first.

We don't stop, simply rush across the carpet, across the area at the top of the escalators, turn down the side hallway.

Behind us, the zombie lets out an unholy roar.

"Don't stop! Don't look!" Cuellar calls, so we hightail it, bounding like deer toward the escape of the hamster tube.

Which means we have to run away from the top of the escalators, past the small banquet rooms, another set of bathrooms, another banquet room, and it's there—clear and glinting in the late afternoon sun.

The hamster tube.

We back up, putting Cuellar's side of the turtle formation beside the emergency fire station.

Cuellar drops his vanity stool. He opens the cabinet and pulls the fire ax out of its brackets.

That zombie's roar must have drawn others; the noises behind us are . . . intimidating, but I'm not looking back until the turtles in the back tell us to turn and fight.

And yes, it looks like my hope and the hazmat lady's

gestures were right—there's a barricade at the far end of the tube, the hotel entry side.

It's a mostly round door, or rather a hatchway cover, a lid, shaped to fit exactly over the hamster tube entry. It's flat only on the floor edge, and it looks like it fits over the hotel side of the tube sort of like the lid on a can of Pringles, a larger lip-edge stretching beyond the frame of the tube, but on the hotel wall side, keeping the whole thing from falling inward.

A duplicate lid is on the convention center side of the tube, stowed immediately to the side of the skyway, in a discreet, wallpaper-covered recess.

We run into the tube.

At the back of our phalanx, Cuellar and Simon grab the convention-hall side hamster tube cover from its stow position and haul it into position behind us.

Except something immediately goes wrong, or the convention center–side lid is broken, because it tilts inward at an alarming angle, only seeming to catch on the frame edge of the tube in two places, pivoting inward like a quarter held between two fingers.

Cuellar and Simon push it up, hard, just as the zombies arrive. Gray, vein-mottled arms tear at us.

The disc of the hatch lid slams upright into the zombies, thumping into place, but unsecured, held by the strength of Cuellar and Simon.

"We got a problem here, girly!" Cuellar yells.

"I see it, sonny!" I yell back. "Hold it!" I point to Janet, Blair, and Imani. "Stay here, help hold the lid. We'll get to the hotel side and get help."

"Done," Janet says, as Imani nods. Blair presses her hands flat on the lid.

Hunter and I sprint across the tube, over the distance of the three-lane street below us. The back of my neck prickles at the yawning distance between us and the others, between me and Imani and Siggy, and yes, even Blair, and the thundering pounding on the hatch behind us magnified by the tube.

We reach the hotel-side hatch and pound on it.

"Hey! Anyone there? Help! Help! We're normal! Let us through!" I'm yelling and pounding, Hunter is doing it, too, our voices booming back with the sounds of our banging on the lid

Nothing. Not a sound, not an answering call, nothing.

It's growing hotter in the tube, the sun beating down onto the film-covered glass, cooking us like bacteria in a test tube.

"Where are they?" Hunter asks. "She pointed here. She was pointing here!"

He steps back into the tube and cranes his neck, looking farther up the street below and behind us.

"Help!" I yell, and kick the hatch with my foot.

Sweat pools in my armpits and butt crack. I feel a droplet run down my temple.

"Cuellar! Bring your ax!" I yell.

Cuellar pivots away from the broken convention-side hatch, leaving the others to hold it, and comes running.

"No one's here," I say. "Or if they are, they aren't coming."

Cuellar wastes no time. He lifts the fire ax and starts chopping.

The first impact splits the plastic coating of the hatch cover, showing the wood beneath.

"Good, keep going!" I say.

Hunter looks at me, frustration, anger, and apology in his vibrant eyes.

"I guess I got it wrong," he says. "She wasn't pointing here." Both hands drag hanks of dark hair off his forehead.

"Maybe, maybe not," I say. "But she was pointing somewhere."

We look at each other, and have the idea at the same time. We leave Cuellar working frantically with his ax, and we pivot and run back out into the center of the tube, and stop in the middle.

"Any luck?" Blair calls over her shoulder toward us.

A crashing, battering of knocks and thumps against the broken hatch.

"Not yet," I yell back.

Hunter shields his eyes against the sun and peers out, up the street, toward the front of the convention center.

But I look the opposite way, down the street, toward the back of the building.

And that's where I see people.

"Hey! Hey!" I yell, jumping up and down, waving my arms at the soldiers and scientists, whoever it is out there, in hazmat suits erecting barricades and more tents. There are what look like security trucks, and prison buses, more orange plastic barricades, and fully armed soldiers standing behind it all.

None of them look up, or even down the street.

Where are they? What part of the convention center is their staging area? If that's even what I'm looking at?

I mean, when you think of it, that's not really that many people. For what's going on.

There should be way more people.

Unless I'm looking at the back of it, the rear, and around the corner, in the back parking lot of the convention center, there are more people.

Hunter keeps waving and yelling, even after I stop.

"Where are they setting up?" Frustration makes my voice sharp. "There has to be an exit point, a screening point. That's what she was trying to tell you. So where is it?"

"On the back of the building," Hunter says. "The loading dock to the exhibit hall."

"Why there?" I ask.

"It's wide, there's room to set up, I don't know, a funnel or something."

"I don't know, this whole thing is starting to feel particularly mismanaged."

I'm thinking of the scientist, how he didn't appear to have any backup, not even a PR liaison to break the ice or vouch for him before he jumped onstage. It was almost like he had gone rogue, was acting on his own or something.

Trying to save us.

What if there is no actual exit point? No screening point? They just want to keep us all locked in?

Hunter says it.

"They're going to just let us die in here." His eyes are wide, shocked.

The pained disbelief on his face hurts me to see. Maybe because I know now: his goofy sense of humor and his loneliness. His consideration, his kindness. It shoots through me, goes all through me, as my mother says. Pulses like a lightning stroke of pure rage and protectiveness.

I feel myself grow in power. In fury. In energy, a dump of adrenaline making me feel invincible, making me refuse it.

"We're not doing that," I tell him, voice strong as a mountain. "We're survivors. If they locked us in, we'll break our way out."

Somehow.

Hunter locks his eyes with mine, and there's a look in them I've only seen on the show, when his character Clay Clarke looks at his surrogate father, Captain Cliff Stead.

Awe. He's looking at me with awe. And something like hope, and something like worship.

Admiration.

The sun glares onto my back, and sweat is literally pouring down my face, under my hair, as I cook in the tube.

There's no AC in the ZA.

It's just a clear tube. Who designed this? Haven't they ever been outside in the South? Lord. It's so hot. Like we're in a greenhouse or something, the only thing above us film-tinted Plexiglas and sky.

Nothing between us and the sky.

A sudden picture pops into my brain, swooping in there like a fancy zoom-special-effect camera shot.

A communications satellite, bleeping and zipping by, high in the atmosphere above us.

"Hunter! Go trade with Imani!"

Hunter doesn't ask why or hesitate. He sprints to the embattled hatchway and takes Imani's place.

"Here!" Imani rushes up next to me. She's holding out her phone. I try 911 and get a recorded message.

How many people are calling?

"No answer." I hand the phone back.

Imani opens the Code Blue police scanner app. The spinning wheel connecting to our local frequency is aggravatingly slow as it loads.

I glance down at Cuellar. The hotel-side hatch is splintering, but not broken yet, in spite of how he's attacking it.

Imani and I huddle close to each other, bent over her phone like it's a sacred flame as a fusillade of booms echoes from the hatchway into the convention center.

"We've got to make a move soon!" Simon's voice is part yell, part grunt of effort. Blair repositions herself, shoving her back against the lid.

The phone connects, and a man's voice blares into the tube.

". . . dock. We are prepping for SRT entry and extraction at 1800 hours. Consult the building map from the fire inspector. Ground team A will clear the loading dock area. SRT will enter and proceed to the first-floor exhibit hall. Clean and sweep."

"Roger."

"Roger."

The first man's voice returns. "SRT, you copy?"

"Heading to position now," a young man's voice answers. "Ready by 1800."

"No, no, no!" I moan, picturing it now, just like it would be if it was on the show. If it was *Human Wasteland*, this plan would go horribly, horribly awry. There would be mass carnage. Mass death.

The infected would erupt from the exhibit hall, into the loading dock area, out into the world.

That scientist. That rogue scientist, and maybe even the hazmat not-actually-cosplayers . . . they locked us in here, but they also locked *them* in here.

It doesn't matter how it started; well, I mean, of course it matters. But it doesn't matter to me, here and now.

All that matters is I am not ready to die, and I'm tired of sweating in this hamster tube, and I'm mad, dammit, because I'm supposed to be having the Best Day Ever and instead I'm fighting for my life.

"Can you hear me?" Imani talks into her phone, pushing an on-screen button. But the app isn't designed that way, doesn't actually have the frequency to send directly back to the police. Instead she's trying to talk to anyone who's listening, kind of like a CB, except both it and the police band signal are actually rerouted.

And we don't have time to hear if anyone has their ears on, so to speak, because at that moment the embattled hatch tilts inward, a sudden spill of arms and fingers clawing around the top edge.

Simon screams a curse and shoves back. We rush to him, and all push at the arms and fingers, bashing them, trying to get the zombies to pull them back.

But their pain response isn't there. So, the arms don't draw back, even though Siggy stabs one clean through with the pointed corner of her drawer plank.

"We have to get out of here!" Simon pants, shoving at the bottom edge of the hatch, struggling to keep it from tilting farther inward.

No one has to say it, we just push against the hatch, our faces grim.

If Cuellar can't break that other hatch down in time . . .

There's no way out.

28

There has to be a way. I got us in here, I can get us out.

Except, my plan, such as it was, kind of hinged on the idea that someone would be waiting on the hotel side of the hatch.

And that the convention-side hatchway would actually lock behind us.

And that we'd have time to break down the hotel hatchway with the ax if no one was there.

"Can we ever catch a bloody break!" Janet yells.

If it was an SAT math question, it would be something along the lines of a ticking clock.

How long will it take the zombies to break down the hatch and kill the humans trapped inside?

"Now what?" Hunter says, as we strain to hold the tilting hatch in place. His voice isn't angry, just scared.

And seeking inspiration.

What would Clay Clarke do?

Can't hide. Can't run.

I yell down the tube to Cuellar.

"Out of time! We have to fight!"

Cuellar stops his attack on the hatch and runs back toward us.

"If someone can lift me or Siggy, we can take a few of them out through the gap."

I make a downward stabby motion with my microphone stand.

Which, okay, we *try* that plan. But then the microphone stand isn't exactly sharp, and the hatchway is already tilted too far, and then it's chaos as the hatch spins in place, tilting in, and zombies fall over the hatch and each other, grasping for us. Then the hatchway comes away from the wall-edge completely. It tips onto its rounded edge and wobbles in a slow roll into the tube before falling flat.

Imani swings the weighted disc-base of her microphone stand, and it impacts a zombie head with a crunch.

I jab upward, and my microphone stand arm goes into the gut of a zombie woman. It feels like it . . . might have impaled her? But I don't have time to check, I just yell and shove her back into the zombies behind her.

Beside Simon, Blair lunges at a zombie with her driftwood sculpture, knocking the zombie back while Simon swings his vanity stool in tight arcs, impacting the approaching zombies as we retreat into the tube.

"Duck!" Cuellar yells, and Hunter and I drop to our haunches.

There's a blur, and a whistling, as Cuellar leaps over us, ax swinging sideways across the line of approaching zombies.

We pop back up and compress back into our loose turtle shape, but there are just more and more zombies stumbling into the hamster tube. At least ten, no, twenty, no, more.

My heart thunders like a locomotive.

And then instead of fear, I get another jolt of pure anger.

It powers through me like a charge of gathering electricity, and I almost feel like it could lift my hair or crackle through my fingertips.

"Lift the hatch!" I yell to Hunter and Imani. "You stay in turtle!" I yell to the others, and I rush forward, jabbing and swinging and pushing.

And I definitely impaled that woman zombie, because she's slumped over against the curved wall of the tube, weakly swiping at me as I zoom past her.

Good to know. The mic arm did the trick.

I jab it into the face of a zombie man, his gray, seething skin my only target, but it catches on his cheekbone, then slides up and into the jelly of his eye, like a perfectly lined-up pool shot, so clear I should have called it first.

Eyeball, corner socket.

The zombie man falls like he was pole-axed straight in the brain. Which, I guess he sort of was.

The mic stand is stuck in his eye.

I make a high-pitched keen at the absolute grossness, the kind of noise I make when I smoosh a cockroach, except more, and I stand on his face to yank the end of the mic stand out of his eye socket.

Next to me, Imani lets out a yell like a warrior princess, and she swings that mic stand like it's an extension of her own arm. Is there anything my beffie cannot do? I contend there is not, for lo, she fells two lurchers with one blow, head into head into hamster tube. *Crunch, smush, crumple.*

Smear of fluids.

I'm perilously close to peals of unhinged giggles or screaming.

Maybe that's a healthy reaction, but I honestly can't spare the oxygen, so I stifle it and jab my mic stand arm into another zombie face.

It doesn't go as well as the first time, just tips the zombie back on her heels, and her fingers catch at my arm and she yanks me forward.

I stumble but bring the mic arm up in between us. The woman pulls me in closer, trapping my arms and the mic stand between our bodies.

Her gaping mouth strains toward me.

I rap her with the mic, like a teacher with a ruler, or an old-timey lady slapping a suitor.

You cad.

Then Siggy is there, she must have left the turtle with us even though I told her to stay back. She's yelling "Ew! Ew! Ew!" as she stabs with the sharp corner of her drawer. It sinks into the lady's neck first, then her cheek, then her eye.

The woman zombie lets go of me and falls.

"Thanks," I tell Siggy.

Siggy's making the most disgusted and appalled face I have ever seen.

"Ew," she says softly. She's pale, and there's fountain spatters of blood on her, but she doesn't faint. Doesn't look like she's about to, either.

Ahead of us, Hunter and Imani have propped the hatch up on its flat side.

We skid over to them and all crouch close under the angled edge of the hatch.

"It's a rolling shield," I say. "So roll it!"

Hunter and I take the front handle, set into the flat side of the hatch, while Imani and Siggy take the back one, and we push.

Tilted at about a forty-degree angle, the hatch acts like it's one-part shield, one-part bowling ball, aimed at the ankles of the zombies trying to reach us.

It rolls smoothly, knocking over zombies, until the rounded edge becomes the flat side. But we just hoist it and set it rolling again.

Speed is more important than taking out the zombies behind us; the ones we've set spinning and falling over our shield. So, I don't turn to stab them, or face them, just glance over my shoulder once as we keep going.

"Hey! What do we do?" Cuellar yells as we keep barreling forward, knocking zombies ass-over-ears behind and over us.

"Take them out!" I yell back.

And then we are there, pushing into the hallway, where more zombies turn to see us, our rolling shield, and the meat of our arms, legs, and faces. They come, running, stumbling, or shuffling.

"Fall back! There!" I yell, and let go to point straight ahead. We rotate and drag the hatch backward with us, putting our backs to the wall directly across from the hamster tube. The same place Imani, Siggy, and I stood earlier today, watching the hazmat suits close the hatch.

The wall by the bathrooms. Where the fire-safety station is.

Missing an ax, but with a fire hose behind a glass cabinet door.

Imani doesn't hesitate. She lets go of her side of the handle, and spins, all in one movement, like a dancer; she keeps spinning, grabbing the handle and pulling the cabinet door open.

The move would make me dizzy, but Imani stops on a dime and yanks the hose out, popping it out of its zigzag stow pattern, pulling it arm over arm like a cadet in basic training, or like a magician with a really heavy scarf coming out of their sleeve.

When she gets enough of the hose out, she turns on the fat faucet on the top of the case. Then she plants her feet wide, and puts a hand on the lever running along the top of the hose nozzle.

"Drop now!" she yells, and so Hunter, Siggy, and I shove forward, letting the hatch door push out. Then we fall back, ducking.

A wide jet of water pounds into the zombies, pushing them away.

Hunter and Siggy and I scurry on our heels, back behind Imani and the jet of water. We crouch against the wall.

A loud clanging draws my eyes, and I glance up in time to see the remaining loops of the stowed hose flapping and expanding with the water pressure, popping free from the brackets holding it.

"Watch out!" I yelp to Hunter and Siggy, but it's too late.

A falling, flapping loop of wide canvas hose clocks Siggy in the back of the head. Siggy falls forward, dazed.

I haul her back and shield us, pulling the rest of the hose out before it can pop loose again.

Imani steps forward, sweeping the zombies with the

increased water pressure. She's aiming at their chests, not sweeping their ankles. I want to tell her to take them down, then we can run out and stab them or something. Then I realize what she's doing.

She's pushing them back in a row, like the hose is a leaf blower and the zombies are the leaves, nudging them toward the interior bannister. Toward the one-story drop to the hard tiles below.

They start toppling, first one, then another, over the rail. Imani steps forward and sweeps again, keeps sweeping as the zombies spill over like bowling pins.

Hunter lets out a whoop beside me, and Siggy joins in with a wobbly-sounding yippee, and I'm screaming with them and at the zombies, screaming at all of it, and then they're all gone, literally washed overboard, propelled by a jet of water.

I grab Imani's arm and we rush the few steps forward to the hamster tube, Siggy and Hunter right behind us, helping to drag the heavy hose.

"Get down!" Imani yells, and Blair puts out a hand, tugging Simon down beside her as the others also duck. Then Imani washes the zombies in the tube back, back against the opposite, ax-scarred, locked hatch.

We advance in, and the others scrabble toward us, low or crouched under the jet of water.

To my surprise, Cuellar comes last, slinging the ax around him like he's some kind of medieval knight, knocking the last of the zombies away from the retreating group and into the jet of water.

Janet and Annie take the hose as Hunter and Siggy come forward to spell them in the fighting.

Cuellar, Simon, and Blair stand with their weapons raised, and wait for Imani to turn off the jet.

Hunter, Siggy, and I join them, standing tight in a row, ready to sweep in.

"When you say go, I'll keep the ones down on the right," Imani says, and she gives the plume of water a twitch, indicating the direction so there will be no confusion.

"Got it," Simon says.

"Go!" Cuellar yells.

Blair nods, determined.

Imani aims the jet at the zombies on the right side of the tube, keeping them down.

Hunter, Siggy, and I follow Cuellar, Simon, and Blair in a rush down to the zombies sprawled on the left side of the tube.

We're getting splashed by droplets from the hose impacting the other zombies, and I'm desperately trying not to think of the words *blood borne* or *bite borne* or *virus* or *atomized* or whatever, as we take out the zombies struggling back to their soaking feet.

When those zombies are dispatched, Imani turns off the hose and we rush to finish the job off. All the zombies are down, and I think they're all dead, but one behind Cuellar surges up, screaming a hissing, pressured noise out of his mangled throat.

Behind the zombie, Siggy lets out a pissed-off shriek and leaps forward, swinging her drawer plank down on the back of the zombie's head. The zombie falls like a tree, but it's still making those horrible noises.

Siggy steps onto its neck and makes a *gimme* motion with her hand. I hand over my mic arm. With a repeating "Ew!" keening noise, Siggy stabs the pointy end of the mic arm into the zombie's ear.

The zombie goes completely slack.

With a violent tug, Siggy pulls the mic arm out of the zombie's ear and hands my weapon back to me. She picks up her drawer plank again and tosses her long blonde hair back behind her shoulders.

Cuellar leans over panting, broad, square hands planted on his knees.

"Gotta hand it to you, girls," he says, eyes sweeping over Imani, then me, then Siggy. "You've got some helluva will to live."

I can't help the crooked smile.

Imani slings the fire hose up, cocking the nozzle on her shoulder. "You got that right," she tells him.

Siggy simply gives one long shiver of disgust. "Ew."

"You're not so bad yourself," I tell him.

Cuellar salutes us with the ax.

29

*W*e clean our weapons on the clothes of the fallen zombies and cautiously move back into the long hallway that leads to the top of the escalators.

We have to decide what to do next, because now that we've cleared the zombies currently loose on this level, we have a window of opportunity.

Before other zombies in the ballroom find their way out the wide-open double doors.

We could go back in the tube and take the ax to the hotel-side hatchway again. But there's the small issue of the SWAT team or whatever it was called getting ready to a mass of zombies, and unleashing them into the sleepy downtown of Senoybia.

My hometown.

Sleepy, small, nice-place-to-raise-kids Senoybia.

We need to tell the others what we heard.

Imani and Hunter and I explain to the others what we saw outside, and then heard on the Code Blue app. About how it sounds like the military or police are preparing to enter the exhibit hall through the loading dock.

"Man, if that don't just sound perfect," Cuellar says, his whisper so sharp it should be weaponized. "1800 hours, that's 6:00 p.m. An hour." He shakes his head. "Bet you dollars to donuts there's some wannabe heroes down there all excited to shoot their weapons. Go all Johnny Hotshot."

He sounds exactly like his character, and also, incidentally, exactly right.

"All it will take is just one zombie to get out, and everyone we know could be infected. Hell, the whole world," I murmur.

"They're going to be overrun," Hunter says.

"Can you imagine if someone who was bitten got on an airplane?" Janet whispers.

"We have to do something," Simon says. "We have to warn them."

"How?" Imani asks. "The phones are jammed, and my app wouldn't send."

"Maybe there's a radio," Hunter begins. "A walkie-talkie, I mean. Downstairs in the security booth."

"I didn't see one, did you?" I ask.

Siggy's blue eyes go wide.

"I saw one," she says, turning to me. Her hands rise to her face, like she's about to yelp in excitement, jumping up and down.

"Where, Siggy?"

A smile rises on Siggy's mouth, pure as a sunrise. Her

expression is happily thunderstruck, like she bought the winning lottery ticket and just now found it in the bottom of her purse.

"The preppers."

We explain to the others about the Apocalyptic Preppers panel, and how the preppers might still be in the same banquet room, just down the hall.

"They had an afternoon session on the schedule, too," Siggy says. "We nearly decided to go to that one, but we worried it cut too close to our photo-op time."

At the mention of the photo op, this thing from earlier today that now sounds like something from an alternate reality, Simon Wong smiles, Cuellar Tucker scowls, Annie Blaze unconsciously fluffs her hair.

And Hunter Sterling gives me a speculative look.

"What?" I whisper.

"Just wondering who your photo was with, that's all," he teases.

"Like I'll ever tell you," I sass back, but I also wink.

Siggy's still talking excitedly to the others, telling them about the session and about the big yellow radio that was standing on the table to the side of the preppers.

Hunter bumps his hip against mine.

"So, it *was* with me." His whisper is somehow also a crow, self-satisfied and jubilant.

"Don't get too cocky." I hip bump him back. "You still don't know the props we were gonna make you hold."

Which, okay, we weren't going to, but you never know and some fans get very, well, shall we say elaborate.

Hunter lets out a little laugh, and smiles at me, this direct, almost admiring-feeling gaze? It beams right into my eyes.

I return it. I swear his eyes just sparkle, somehow.

I might get an anime nosebleed if I keep looking at him, I swear. He's *so* handsome.

Siggy turns back to me.

"Right, June?"

Even though I wasn't paying attention, her tone isn't asking, it's showing everyone else that she's right.

So I don't hesitate.

"Right," I agree, backing her up.

"Well, let's go, then," Janet says. "Sounds like that radio could solve all our problems."

The rest of the group agrees, so we move swiftly down the hall, away from the escalators and past a set of bathrooms, to the banquet hall.

It's a strange sense of déjà vu, almost like we're going to walk right back into another session. Like the zombie apocalypse hadn't started at all.

Except, well, the door's closed now.

One of the doors was open, propped open, so that late-comers to the sessions could ease in and find a seat without disturbing the rest of the audience.

But now both of the doors are closed. Siggy reaches out and tries the handles.

Locked.

"They're in there for sure," Siggy says. Her voice is still bright, and I can't blame her. I'm excited, too. That radio could save us, could save everyone. It's the link we need.

Siggy knocks on the door, three swift raps.

Behind us, Hunter, Simon, and Janet stand guard with Annie and Blair in between.

"Hello?" Siggy calls. "Are you still in there? Preppers?"

There's no answer from the other side.

"It's okay, there are no zombies here right now," Siggy tells the door. "It's just a few of us survivors, you know. Out here survivin'."

She laughs, a "ha ha" of hopeful camaraderie.

With a door.

Is anyone even in there?

"If you could let us in, that would be rad. You have a radio, right? We saw some troops outside." Siggy glances back at me and shrugs.

Imani steps forward and bangs her fist on the door, *hard*.

"We know you're in there!" she says, her voice raised.

A low voice responds from the other side of the door.

"Keep it down!"

Siggy nods in victory.

"Talk to us and we will," Siggy promises.

There's a pause where there should be the sound of the door opening.

The door doesn't open.

"Are you gonna let us in or what?" Siggy hisses, frustration spiking her words.

"No way. We talk, that's it."

"You can't be serious," Imani says.

"Damn straight we are. So talk or git."

Imani steps forward like she's about to start pounding on the door, or kick it in.

"Hold up." Cuellar's whisper is pitched for just our ears. "Let me talk to him."

Siggy turns those hero-lit eyes to him.

"Okay," she says, giving him her place by the door.

Imani moves a slight step back and crosses her arms, waiting.

Cuellar steps up to the closed door, puts a smile on, and scrubs a hand over his bristly hair.

"Hey," he says to the door. "This is Cuellar Tucker, you know, from the show."

He cocks a smile at the door handle, unconsciously,

like it's a peephole or a camera. Like they can see him.

"No shit?" The man's voice from inside is interested.

Cuellar smiles at Siggy, then me. He whispers conspiratorially, "Preppers love me."

Janet lets out a little snort-laugh, nothing mean, just the ridiculousness of our situation, and the weirdness of fame, that Cuellar knows his demographic like that.

"Yeah," Cuellar says to the closed door. "And I got Simon Wong with me. And Janet O'Shea. And . . ." He pauses, and cocks an eyebrow at Annie.

Annie nods, and steps forward.

". . . and Annie Blaze!"

"Hi!" Annie's voice is high and bubbly.

"Dang!" The man's voice is impressed. "I gotta say, I love the show."

Cuellar nods sagely at the door. A *yep, yep* kinda gesture, like a quarterback methodically moving the ball down the field.

"Thanks, man," he says. "We work hard on it."

"And we love our fans," Annie chirrups. "You're all so supportive."

Cuellar nods at her, like they're two business hotshots in a well-worn scene: closing the deal.

"So, listen, if you could let us in, man, we'd really appreciate it."

Cullar leans back, like he expects the door to be opened that moment.

It stays closed.

There's what feels like a long moment of silence, like we're all holding our breaths.

Finally the man on the other side of the door replies.

"I just can't do that."

Annie cusses under her breath and steps away from the door.

Cuellar smiles in disbelief.

"What?" His voice has lost its honeyed, wheedling tone.

"I know," the man says. "It sucks, right? But we just can't open this door. Rule number one of survival is—"

Cuellar cuts in.

"I don't know where you get off, buddy, but there ain't no rules now. Got that? So open this damn door. Now."

There's another silence that somehow feels affronted.

"No." The man's voice isn't regretful anymore.

Cuellar turns to the rest of us, clustered around the door.

"Y'all *move*." Cuellar hefts his fire ax.

We all make a hasty retreat, four or five steps back. This time Cuellar's voice isn't soft anymore.

"This is your last chance! Open this door or I'll bust in there."

"Start that crap and we'll retaliate." The man's voice is every bit as pissed off as Cuellar's.

"Oh yeah?" Cuellar taunts. "I got an ax."

"We've got an improvised bomb and Molotov cocktails."

Cuellar looks surprised for a moment.

"Bull! You're bluffing!"

A cheerful woman's voice comes from behind the door. It sounds like the lady who looked vaguely like Mrs. Claus.

"No, we do, really! You can make them out of normal household chemicals, and for the explosive device all you need is—"

"Margaret, hush!" the man's exasperated voice snaps.

"Sorry," she says to him, then she raises her voice to us. "Sorry we can't help y'all!"

Her tone is like if we'd knocked on the door looking to borrow a cup of sugar.

"Listen, okay, we don't have to get in the room," Siggy says, both to us and to the preppers on the other side of the door. "We saw troops outside, they're going to come in. We need to warn them. Do you have that radio?"

"Already tried it," the man says. "It won't work, they got a dampener."

"Right," Siggy says, her tone conspiratorial. "But we got a signal when we went out into the skyway. Maybe if you give us the radio we could actually communicate with—"

"No."

Just like that.

"You don't understand," Siggy begins, but he cuts her off again.

"Oh, sure. I get it, kid. And maybe you're even telling the truth about the signal. But then what? I open the door to give you the radio. You guys try to force your way in here. Next thing you know you're in, or you're not. But at what cost? People could get hurt. My people. Then undead come. It's a real snafu."

Siggy's mouth just drops open, the expression almost cartoonish. She's just gaping at the door, head shaking gently in disbelief.

Then she swipes at her eyes with a hand. Shakes her head more forcefully, and steps back.

And I'm furious suddenly. White-hot rage at the obnoxious preppers on the other side of the door. Who wouldn't even try to figure out a way to work with us. To help us.

And at how they just knocked her back like that. My Siggy. Stealing her hope, like taking candy from a baby. Like it didn't matter.

Like she didn't matter.

Janet repositions her drawer plank, resting it across the tops of her shoulders. She tips her head away from the door.

"Let's go." Her voice is tight with anger.

"Where?" Annie asks.

"Away from this toxic BS," Janet says. "We'll regroup, make a new plan."

Cuellar nods. Simon moves out farther into the hall, like he's on point.

Blair follows Simon, and the rest of us move into our turtle shape, our energies either dejected or infuriated.

Imani stays at the door; her body is rigid with fury.

I go stand beside her.

"Let's go," I say.

"These . . . these . . ." Her voice is so tightly wound it's like she's fighting to control the low words.

"*People*," she hisses. And somehow it's the worst insult.

"I know," I tell her. "The worst."

"What's the point of rules?" Imani crosses her arms over her stomach, almost like she's cradling an injury.

She looks at me.

"What's the point of rules if there's no empathy underneath?"

And it's easy to forget, sometimes, that Imani needs rules so much because they're protective. Because they make her feel safe.

Because underneath everything, her calm, strong demeanor, her academic gifts, and her beauty . . .

She's a kid. My best friend in the whole world. And even

though sometimes I put her on a little pedestal, with love, she's human.

She's scared, too.

"I know," I tell her.

Siggy touches her arm. "It's all right, Imani," Siggy says, and her voice is so strong, it makes me feel stronger just hearing it. "We know better, they don't. They have to live with that."

"With themselves," I add. "If they survive."

Imani nods, and lifts her chin. Her hair shivers over her shoulders when she gives her head a clarifying shake.

"Okay," she tells us.

But she steps up to the door again.

Her fist bangs on the door once.

There's a startled curse, almost like the man on the other side had his ear pressed to the wood listening when she banged it.

Imani smiles, this gorgeous curve of righteous satisfaction. Her voice is just loud enough to carry to the preppers hiding in the banquet room.

"Enjoy your piss-water, assholes."

Cuellar lets out a guffaw. Janet laughs that gorgeous villainess laugh, as Imani and I join the rest of the formation.

30

Since the preppers wouldn't let us in, we decide to return to the stairwell to talk over our next move. For one thing, it feels like a space we can be marginally secure in, and for another, no matter what we plan next, it gives us access to the other floors.

And maybe we might find Rosa there, in the stairwell waiting for us. Even though it's unlikely, it could happen, right?

"We have to figure out something," Siggy says as we move down the hall. "How to stop the zombies before the army comes in the loading dock. We can't let them out after all this."

The second-floor lobby balcony is still a ways off, at the end of the hall past the escalators.

"I know," I say.

The sudden image of the zombies being released by the SWAT team, swarming into the sleepy downtown of Senoybia, causes my heart to stop in my chest, a physical ache.

"I know it's dinky," Imani murmurs. "But I kinda like this town."

"Me too." I think of the park with the duck pond, the playground behind the cemetery, the cute downtown streets, and the hardware store with one of the first Coke murals ever painted.

They all seem almost indescribably precious now. Maybe they are. Maybe they always were.

"Not to mention, like, the people," Siggy says, her voice a bit croaky, as we draw even with the water fountains and bathrooms. "Lots of good people in this town. You know. Our parents and siblings. And Mark."

Her voice breaks on his name.

"Absolutely," Hunter agrees, putting a gentle hand on her shoulder.

"Tishala could be anywhere," Imani murmurs. "And Mom. They're out on their girls' day. Shopping and looking for—"

She looks at me, her eyes agonized at the jagged line of her thoughts.

"What if they're close by? Looking at the Japanese bridge or the gazebo? And they don't know, and the zombies get out?"

"We'll save them," I say, my voice steady, even if my heart is goldfish-out-of-the-water floppy. "We'll save all of them. We'll save Senoybia. And, like. The world."

There's a moment where we silently look at each other,

acknowledging the task. And not knowing how we can do anything. But knowing we have to do something.

"Yeah," Annie agrees. "But first, can we get some water?" She steps up to the fountains set between the men's and women's bathrooms.

We all stop, forming a protective ring around the water fountains and whoever's turn it is to drink.

Imani takes a big drink. "Ahhh!" she exclaims, exaggerating. "That's nice."

We all laugh, thinking of the preppers.

Hunter steps up for his turn at the water fountain. He takes a long drink then lets the water run over his face for a moment.

He stands, swiping a hand down his face, scattering water droplets.

His eyelashes are bunched together by the water, looking impossibly darker. Thicker.

Imani nudges me with her elbow.

"Jeez, girl. Thirsty much?" she whispers, just to me.

I smirk back at her, then step up for my turn at the water fountain.

I've just taken my first big gulp of chilled water when I notice movement in my peripheral vision. The door to the women's restroom is opening.

I react on instinct, lunging forward with the mic arm raised.

"June! It's me!" Scott falls back against the open bathroom door with his hands up.

There's not really a word for the stew of emotions that churns in my gut at the sight of him. Relief is in there, not just that he's not a zombie, but also that he's alive. By which I mean, I *am* glad he's not dead or a zombie. I'm not a total hate-monster.

So, yes, there's relief there. But also anger, annoyance, betrayal. The usual ingredients.

Plus a fun! Bonus! That feeling? The one where you want to curl up and die and never have anyone look at you again? That level of embarrassment so strong it's practically visceral horror?

That's there, too, when Blair steps forward.

"Scott!" She opens her arms to hug him.

I guess my shunning of him at the back of the podcast session a few hours ago (it feels like another life now, honestly) must have made some impression at least, because he glances at me uncomfortably while returning her hug with one arm.

"Where are the zombies?" Scott asks, stepping back from the hug and glancing past me. His eyes take in the others.

"They're around," I say, because who has time to get into it all, right now right here, when we have to figure out how to warn the military or police or whoever is outside readying to try to come in.

Scott looks around at the others, and his eyes lock on Hunter, Annie, Cuellar, and Simon.

"Hey, hello," Scott says, and he nods at them in greeting.

"Everyone, this is Scott," Blair says.

"Hello," Janet says in her polite, sweet voice.

"I'm a big fan," Scott says, ignoring Janet, just completely zeroed in on the other, bigger stars. "I run a little podcast, *Wasteland Stans*, maybe you've heard of it?"

Cuellar cuts him an expression that if voiced would say, "Kid, are you serious with this crap right now?"

"If . . . I mean . . . when we get out of here would you—"

"Sure, buddy, sure." Simon smiles at Scott and lays a reassuring hand on Scott's upper arm. His demeanor is like he's a) used to pushy fans, b) in the middle of a zombie apocalypse and doesn't have time for podcast hosts right now, and c) both a and b.

"One thing at a time, okay?" Simon says.

"We should keep moving," Janet says.

"Do you have a weapon?" Annie asks Scott, and is it just me, or is she holding her defibrillator case proudly?

Scott nods and produces a pristine fountain pen.

I mean . . . sure.

"How did you end up in the bathroom?" Blair asks him.

"I was in the first-floor lobby when it started. I ran upstairs and tried to get to the hotel through the skyway, but it was locked, then I tried to get in with the preppers."

Imani snorts, but it's a supportive-of-Scott's-plight comment on the preppers more than anything.

"They wouldn't let me in, so I avoided some more zombies, mostly, and ran to the bathrooms. The door didn't have a lock, but I was able to hide there until the zombies forgot me and wandered away."

"Well, that's lucky," Simon says encouragingly. "You're lucky you didn't get trapped in there."

"Yeah, I know," Scott says. "I know I should have come out; the first time you walked by, I heard you. But I just . . ."

His eyes drop, his chin drops, his whole demeanor gets smaller.

"I was too scared."

Annie steps forward, lifting a hand from her defibrillator case.

"It's okay." She places the hand on his shoulder like a parent talking to a child. "We all get scared."

I wasn't sure at first, but Annie Blaze is all right. She's more than all right. She's awesome. It doesn't matter who she's consoling, it doesn't matter that it's Scott, just her instinct to do it, when we're all so stressed out, is amazing.

It's official. I'm an Annie Blaze fan.

Our group leaves the water fountains and continues creeping down the hall toward the escalators and the stair-well. We're in our loose turtle shape, with Scott sort of absorbed into it near the back.

I pick up the thread of conversation from before my ex-boyfriend showed up.

I really am glad he's alive. Really.

I'm also glad he's behind me now, literally, muttering at the back of the group with Blair.

"So, you want to go down to the first floor, do our whole water feature schtick again, and check out the security booth for radios, just in case?" I ask Hunter.

I'm distracted but it almost seems like Scott and Blair are arguing.

"No, I wouldn't say I *want* to do that." Hunter shoots a side-long glance at me. "Just it's a thought. I don't have any others."

Call it nerves, but I'm speaking before I think about what I'm going to say.

"Well, don't worry your pretty head about that, little mister," I say, a joking bravado in my voice. "I'll look after ya."

Hunter laughs, and I steal a glance to find him smiling shyly back at me.

"You think my head's pretty, huh?"

Ladies and gentlemen, I do believe the boy is flirting with me. In the middle of the zombie apocalypse.

Although I guess, technically, I flirted with him first.

In front of us, Cuellar stops short and drops low, although there's no potted plant to hide behind this time.

We all freeze, just in time to see a teeming swarm of zombies gathered at the far edge of the second-floor lobby.

31

Then some of the zombies see us, and all hell breaks loose.

It's like in the movies again, with that impossible time slowdown, in a way that it totally wouldn't in real life, you would think, but you'd be wrong, because here we are, and there's a mass, no, a horde, no, a killing of zombies ahead, and so yeah—time slows down.

My insides turn into Jell-O because there are so many. Too many, just a huge, huge number. If it was the SAT, the word question would be "How many zombies will be left with nothing to eat after our group is devoured completely, down to bones and gristle," because it's that many. Fifty? Eighty? A hundred? More?

Cuellar cusses.

Then several things happen at once.

A man wearing a maintenance uniform, one of those big zip-front jumpsuits made out of thick navy material, turns from the side of the herd closest to us. He's wearing a welder's mask with the visor up. Jaundice-yellow and blood-streaked eyes see us, somehow, because his jaw opens, no, it *unhinges*.

He's terrifying.

I can't take my eyes off him as he puppet-jerks forward, a single arm flailing toward us.

But he's not the only one, and at least one other zombie is faster, a zoombie, because suddenly the welder is knocked slightly sideways by a guy in a yellow shirt, a security guard, just zooming up from behind.

Cuellar pops up from his crouch and steps forward, swinging high with his ax.

The blade impacts the jaw of the security guard zombie, a crunch of bone and spray of blood, and the ax stroke lifts him up and back, throwing him into the zombies behind him.

Our defense-turtle shape collapses as we stumble away, flattening into a row of sitting ducks just waiting for which zombie from the horde will reach us first.

Annie yelps in fear; Simon moves forward next to Cuellar, his stool swinging.

Hunter rushes to stand with his costars, lamp raised.

Two voices gibber in my mind.

This is it. This is it. This is it.

and

We have to . . . we have to . . . we have to . . .

Then Janet steps forward. Amazing Janet. *There's no stopping them, Vivian!* Janet O'Shea. Looking like the coolest older lady you ever saw in your life, with her short, spiky white hair, and her drawer plank raised. She yells at me, her piercing blue eyes capturing mine.

"The elevators, June!"

Because if we fall back, what do we fall back to? Just barricades that will be overrun or doors that will give way against the onslaught of the horde.

And we have to stop them. *We have to.* They can't be released into the world. Into Senoybia. Into our sleepy little Saturday downtown, they just *can't.*

I nod at Janet, and spin on my heel, darting behind the line of zombie defenders, real life imitating reel life. Who is better suited to survive the zombie apocalypse than those who've done it before?

Even if it was only make-believe.

I sprint around the corner and along the wall and start mercilessly jabbing the elevator button.

Without thinking, I've just picked a direction; I've picked up.

Up up up.

Up and away.

I don't look over my shoulder. Why would I? It's just a matter of time now. Which will arrive first . . . the killing of zombies or the elevator?

"Hurry, hurry, hurry," Imani chants next to me, watching

the doors like she could summon the elevator with her mind if she just focused hard enough.

Siggy stops on my other side.

I dart a glance behind. The others have followed me: Blair and Scott standing right behind Imani and Siggy, with Annie behind them, still clutching the bright-red case to her chest.

Between us and the zombies, standing in a loose semi-circle of defense, are the actors, Simon, Cuellar, Hunter, and Janet. Swinging and shoving with their weapons, pushing the zombies back as best they can, holding out for just moments, just moments.

We only need moments.

The elevator door dings.

The stainless-steel doors part, revealing a single zombie man, turning to stare at the door with blood-fogged eyes.

"Oh, for f—," I curse, and continue cursing a blue streak as I lunge forward into the elevator, mic arm raised.

Imani jumps in beside me, and holds the doors open for the others.

Siggy follows me with her pointy plank.

Together we stab and jab the zombie, over and over, until he falls.

I'm grunting as I jab. Siggy's making her "ew, ew, ew" energy-up noises as she jabs.

The zombie falls dead, and we shove him back against the back wall of the elevator.

I spin to the control panel.

"Come on!" I yell to the others. They fall back, still fighting, into the steel-framed cube.

"Go, go, go!" Imani yells.

I jab the third-floor button, then the door-close button.

It is the door-close button, right? I get confused by those drawings, sometimes.

I glance down and confirm, yes, it's the door-close button.

The button makes a rapid clicking noise as I press it frantically.

The doors start to close, and our line of four defenders pull their weapons in.

But then a zombie pushes into the closing doors, triggering the safety bar.

The doors start to open again.

"Dammit!" Cuellar yells. He pushes the ax head out, into the zombie, pushing him back.

I jabjabjab the door-close button.

The doors start to close again.

But the same problem happens again on Hunter's side, a woman zombie reaches an arm through, triggering the doors to open again.

I glance over the heads of the fighters defending the

breach and the zombies trying to reach us in the elevator, to see the rest of the horde advancing. Soon they'll be too many. Soon we won't be able to hold them back. The sheer weight of the zombies in the back will push the front row forward, first onto our weapons, then into us.

"I know what to do," Janet pants, turning to look at me as the others push and shove.

Her bright eyes are determined.

"Make sure you stop them. This stops here, with you."

"No! Wait!" I yell, but it's too late.

"Move!" Janet yells, and she pulls Hunter's shoulder back roughly. He stumbles and falls into me. I catch him, but the wind is knocked out of me as we careen into the wall behind us.

Janet has grabbed Imani's longer base of the mic stand and flipped it sideways in both of her hands, holding the pole with the grip of a weightlifter, high on her chest, crosswise to her body.

She yells and digs with the balls of her feet, like a sprinter when the starting pistol fires, and runs *into* the line of zombies trying to get into the elevator, pressing the bar of the mic base into their arms, then spinning and sweeping it down, pivoting, knocking a zombie back with the sweep of the mic base, knocking the welder zombie aside with the impact of her own back, and then she throws *herself* at the third zombie, the woman.

"No!" I sob.

But it works.

The zombie arms are clear of the elevator doors for a split second.

I jab the door-close button, and try not to see the determined grimace on Janet's face when the zombies grab her. When the woman zombie bites.

"Janet." My voice is shivering with tears. "Janet!"

The doors, unimpeded, start to close.

Janet keeps her eyes squeezed tight, then I can't see her anymore as zombies cover her, as they—

"Dammit!" Cuellar shouts.

The welder zombie pushes forward again, trying to get to us. As he reaches the closing door, his lunge into it knocks the welder's visor closed over his face.

The elevator starts to protest, pinging and bonging. An automated voice sounds.

"Please clear the doors."

Then repeats the instruction in Spanish.

"Jesus! Close the doors!" Scott yells to the ceiling, like the elevator voice is an AI of some sort, and can hear him.

It'd be funny if I wasn't hoping it might somehow work.

Hunter and Simon put their palms flat on our side of the doors, straining without a handhold, trying to slide the doors shut, quicker, faster, and in spite of the fact that the huge welder zombie is now filling the closing gap.

I'm sobbing, tears streaming down my face for Janet, and out of anger; she didn't deserve this, none of us deserve this, and we have to stop it, we have to stop it!

But all I can do is keep jabbing the door-close button.

Something must be working, maybe the button abuse, maybe Hunter and Simon straining against the doors, trying to keep them from opening, because even though the welder zombie has pressed a snatching arm and a bit of his shoulder and head through the gap, and even though he's pressing against the automatic emergency-open bar, the doors don't open.

They can't close, but they don't open.

And the welder zombie's bulk is sufficient to close up the gap so no other zombies can reach us.

Cuellar tries to stab him with the legs of his stool, but it doesn't seem to affect the zombie and his face is now protected by the welding mask.

Annie and Scott stumble back from the swipes of his muscular arm.

Blair tries to follow, but the welder's thick fingers tangle in her hair.

Scott cringes against the farthest wall. Annie steps forward, one hand lifting from the red case.

Blair lets out a yelp as the zombie hand yanks.

The zombie's face and body are trapped in the door, but his hand pulls inexorably back.

Even though his mouth is covered by the welder's mask, with enough force he could yank her out.

I lift the mic arm and jab his neck, his throat, and it doesn't change a thing. He doesn't flinch, doesn't totter, doesn't seem to be affected at all.

So, I attack his arm instead. I break his finger, dislocate his thumb, and tear at her hair.

Blair yelps and strains, ripping her own hair even more to get loose.

We fall down, leaving hanks of hair in his grip, but she's free.

We scrabble like crabs, backward, up against the opposite wall.

The welder zombie still strains toward us, faceless and huge, and the doors start to open again.

"Excuse me, please." Annie's voice is airy and just a bit unhinged, like a determinedly upbeat airline attendant who's been awake too long, but she's stepping over us, around us.

She expertly dodges the sweeping hand, and turns to look at me.

"Can you keep his hand up, please?" she asks, voice bright but with a terrified light in her eyes.

"S-s-sure . . . ?"

I step up, shift my grip to Janet's weightlifter hold, then jab the mic stand up under the welder zombie's arm and press it up, up, up.

Imani grabs one side, and I shift my arms in, so we're both lifting his arm up, and away from Annie, who now kneels on the tiled floor of the elevator.

"What the hell?" Cuellar grunts.

Annie opens the defibrillator case and squints at the contents of the case, at the instruction card, then she shrugs and pulls out a broad electrode pad, yanks the paper off the sticky side, and stands up, slapping it on the welder zombie's exposed throat.

She quickly slaps on two more, one next to the first, and the third on the visor.

She flips on the defibrillator base, and the unit makes a high-pitched whine.

An automated man's voice comes out of the unit.

"Heartbeat irregular or absent, please reposition the contact pads, and press to detect again."

"No, thank you," Annie says, and her hand hovers over the red shock button.

"You guys get ready to let go," she says to . . . all of us, I guess.

"And you better get away from the walls, too. Just in case," Annie continues, calmly.

It's a stainless-steel box, so yeah. Blair and Scott scooch in on their butts.

"Okay!" Annie's voice is officious and cheerful. "Clear!"

Imani and I duck and drop the metal mic stand. Hunter and Simon step back from the stainless-steel doors, which start to grind open.

Annie presses the button.

A bolt of sound, a zap, a *ka-chung*, and you can actually see where a small ridge of electricity arcs over the visor.

The welder zombie convulses once. His arm collapses like . . . like . . . well, like he's been shocked in the head with enough voltage to stop a heart.

The zing of electricity quiets.

Blair stands with her driftwood sculpture. She plunges the wood into the welder zombie's chest, shoving him back out of the door gap.

The defibrillator's electrode cords pop out of the unit as the zombie falls.

I push the door-close button. The doors close all the way.

The elevator starts to lift.

There's a crackle in the speakers that wasn't there before as the elevator lifts, and Muzak drifts down.

32

it the stop button," Hunter pants. He's bent over partway with his palms planted on his knees.

I hit the stop button.

"What if the elevator stops working?" Blair asks, her
hands raised in a *wait a minute* gesture.

Oops.

Well, too late now. The alarm is a separate button, so
while the elevator has stopped we can at least rest in peace.

Not *rest in peace*.

Rest, you know, in peace.

Ugh.

I dig in the backpack and pass around the last water bottles and energy bars. Cuellar and Simon sit and press their
backs against the doors.

Annie packs up the electrode- and cable-free defibrillator.
The red case closes with a gentle snap.

"Annie, that was brilliant," I say. "Thank you."

Hunter stands, pushing his hair out of his eyes. "Seriously!"
he agrees. "Brava."

Annie simpers. There's no other word for it. She twists her head, tilting one ear a little toward her shoulder, smiling, eyes up then lowered, a pleased-yet-shy smile on her face.

"Thanks," she says as the others echo our praise. "Thanks, it was nothing. I just saved the day, that's all."

We laugh, but Annie's eyes grow dark and glisten with gathering tears. "Me, and, uh, and Janet."

A lump gathers in my throat. I want to say something about Janet. About how lovely she was to me, about how she made you feel the warmth in her eyes, in her smile. How she was a real person, and how Vivian was a great character.

But even if I could think of what to say, my throat won't work, thick with emotion and choked with the fact that nothing feels like enough when someone has sacrificed themselves for you.

I still don't know what to say.

Cuellar, of all people, says it for us.

"She was one in a million," he says, swiping at his cheek with the knuckles of one hand. "A total class act, a true-blue broad." He lifts the water bottle. "Let's not let her down. She died for us. Let's make it worth it."

We all nod, lift our water bottles or mime holding a glass, and toast Janet O'Shea.

• • •

Once we've rested, we all agree there's literally nowhere to go but up. The first floor is already a dead end, and besides, those exhibit hall doors didn't seem all that secure. The second floor we just left is absolutely not an option, it's overrun with zombies, so that leaves only the third floor.

Which, we know, will have the zombies from the balcony. But that's still way fewer zombies than on floors one and two. If the barriers at the top of the escalators hold.

If.

Our plan, such as it is, is to explore the back-office hallway of the third floor. It's the only area of the third floor we haven't tried, to see if we can find an office window to signal the army or SWAT team, whoever is massing at the loading dock to try to get into the exhibit hall floor.

Plus, as Simon has noted, the freight elevator might go all the way up to the third floor, in which case it would be somewhere back in that hallway, given the layout of the building. And that makes sense because it would allow the convention center staff to not only bring all the heavy stage scaffolding, theatrical light rigs, cameras, amplifiers, and stacks of speakers to the second floor, but also continue up to the balcony level to deliver the sound and mixing boards.

And if we can find the freight elevator, we can take a direct ride down to the loading dock.

Even so it will be better to try to signal first, so we don't all arrive just to get shot.

So many things can go wrong with this plan, but it feels so much better to simply have one, to be making a move.

I hit the stop button again, which starts the elevator.

The elevator rises, and we all stand in the bunched turtle formation that Janet taught us, weapons bristling toward the doors.

Imani has Janet's drawer plank.

"If we pass another defibrillator, I wanna grab it," Annie says, hugging her used defibrillator to her chest.

"Okay, Annie," Simon says. "That'd probably come in handy."

"When we get to the third floor, we might see Linus." Annie's voice is smaller now, shrinking into itself, emotion squeezing it tight.

We're all silent, and I'm certain our minds are all in one of only two destinations. One, thinking about Linus, the horrid yell he made—the sight of him disappearing in the bodies that converged to feed on him. The noises—

Or two, we're imagining what he might look like now. Either truly dead, or infected, stumbling along on fed-upon legs, cataract-fractured eyes, seething snake-egg skin.

"Be prepared for it, but try not to dwell," I say. "He'd want us to save . . . everyone."

Annie nods, and hugs her defibrillator case.

The elevator voice says, "Third floor," and the doors slide open.

At first everything looks clear. We move out onto the landing in front of the elevators.

The barricades at the tops of the escalators have been partially dismantled. Not as if they've been cleared intentionally, more as if a battering ram has struck at them. Chairs and cleaning products and even the plant have fallen over.

"Not good," Cuellar whispers.

We hustle away from the lobby, away from the escalators and semicircular wall smattered with sets of balcony doors.

We arrive at a wide swath of carpeted hallway and framed art. At the end of the hallway is the stairwell door, and set into the right wall, where the back of the building will be, is a single door, with no crash bar.

We rush to it. A sign reads STAFF ONLY.

The offices where we can signal. That will lead to the freight elevators.

The staff door is locked.

"No!" Siggy tugs at the handle.

Through the slight gap in the doorframe, I can see that the door is locked with a deadbolt.

"Got anything in that bag for this?" Simon asks me.

"No."

Cuellar puts his shoulder to the door, but it doesn't budge.

If the hinges were on our side, we could try taking them off and get in that way, but as it is, the only thing we could try to do is break the wire-thread-webbed narrow window.

Which, if it worked, would still make a huge amount of noise.

"I'm not staying here," Cuellar says, and we feel it, too. That feeling of being bottled up, in a dead end with our backs to the wall, like in the hamster tube, no way out, nowhere to run.

So, we all act on instinct, fear crawling up our necks, and rush back out to the third-floor balcony lobby where at least we can move in a few different directions.

But in the moment, we simply rush away from the tunnel-trap of the hall.

The curve of the balcony wall sweeps out away from me on the left.

One set of balcony doors yawns open.

I break from formation to ease up to the open doors, while the others either creep forward with Cuellar, to look down the hall that parallels the street and leads to the bathrooms, or stand waiting near the elevator, weapons outstretched.

I put one eye to the hinge-gap at the back of the door.

I'm afraid I'll see the big cheerleader stuntman, or Linus, dead on the floor, or worse, lurching around aimlessly on the balcony with empty, blood-rimmed eyes.

But there's nothing, at least not in my narrow eyeline. No zombies, just rust-stained carpet and a few overturned chairs.

I'm easing forward to crane my head around the edge of the door for a better look, when Cuellar yelps.

A zombie man holds Cuellar's arm, pulling and lowering his mouth to bite.

The zombie was just right there, hiding in plain sight. He looked like part of the barricade, the upended sofa with the loud splashes of color across the back.

Which doesn't really speak well for this man's fashion sense when he was a normal human.

For a moment my brain can't process it, and I wonder if the zombie was waiting to ambush us, getting sneaky.

Impossible.

Is it?

Can they learn?

But the zombie's moving slow, so slow, was he just . . . tired? Or powered down? Fading from the virus, or whatever?

How long until the virus really kills them?

Maybe the man was too injured or maimed before the virus turned him. Whatever the reason, we weren't prepared for him, we didn't see him, and now it's too late.

Cuellar punches the zombie's head, but he doesn't let go, and he's too close for the ax to swing enough.

He bites, and Cuellar shrieks.

Simon rushes forward, pushing out and back with his vanity stool—lion-tamer moves down now, and efficient.

Simon pops the legs of the stool into the zombie's chest.

The zombie in the loud shirt falls backward into the barricade, sending the planter sideways, crashing into the shatterproof-glass protective railing at the top of the landing.

"Run!" Cuellar yells, his eyes bulging over Simon's shoulder, as he sees before the rest of us, the gnashing, slavering group of zombies drawn to the noise.

They're coming from the long hallway that leads away from the balcony. No zombies are coming from the balcony lobby itself. Then I realize why.

They'd been drawn away from the balcony and its lobby by *us*. By the noise we'd made one floor below, when we were in the hamster tube. Banging the hatch with an ax, yelling, fighting.

They'd probably even been able to look down and see us. Or see movement, at least.

We should have thought of it.

The balcony is clear.

"This way!" I yell, pulling my hand to myself then swinging around the door.

Here we go again. This move, at least, I know.

Third verse, same as the first.

I pull one door closed with me, and hit my knees on the

other side. The hex key is stashed in climber webbing on the front of the backpack.

I pull it out and jam the end into the crash-bar on the balcony side of the doors, turning turning turning as fast as I can, as the others rush toward me, and as the group of zombies chase.

And then I think . . . *okay, but is the balcony really clear?*

Just turn, turn, turn.

The others will be here in a minute, they can clear it.

But only if we can *lock it first*.

I try not to feel it, the exposed expanse of my back, unprotected, undefended to the space, to whatever might be left here.

I'm a turtle without a shell.

I glance back at the others. Imani's drawer piece jabs out and lodges in a zombie's neck. She gives it one tug, but it doesn't come out.

She lets go of it and lunges for something, comes up spinning a stick, no, it's a mop from the barricade. The one Janet handed up to me when Linus was being attacked on the escalator.

It whistles in a twirling arc, knocking the plank-necked zombie into another zombie.

Imani jabs the strings out like a spear tip, shoving them back. Then she pivots, and still holding the mop like a spear she sprints toward me, overtaking Blair and Scott, and nearly reaching the front of our group.

Simon arrives first, and he sweeps his eyes around, then turns to put hands on the open door's crash bar.

"Come on!" he yells.

Imani and Siggy jump through the door next, followed by Annie.

Cuellar is . . . not coming.

He's spraying blood with one arm, ripping it out of the zombie's mouth. He swings the ax around and around his head, like a Viking.

Its fast-arc cleaves into the heads of the zombies approaching him.

"That's right!" Cuellar whoops. "Get you some!"

"Blair!" Imani shrieks.

I glance up from my work, hex key gone still in my hand.

Blair is standing with Scott, trying to help him. She's pulling him. Is he falling? Why? More important, *why is he dragging her down?*

Hunter takes the hex key from my limp grip and starts turning it in the second hole.

I stand and step out from the doorway.

"Blair! Scott!" I yell. "Get your butts moving, NOW!"

Blair gets Scott to his feet. He takes one step and falters, tipping backward over his own heel, like he's fainting in slow motion.

A trio of zombies is distracted by the motion, turning away from where Cuellar fights.

Scott tries to right himself. He grabs at Blair's helping arms, but instead of pulling himself up, he yanks her violently down.

"Hey, numbnuts!" I shriek, taking three steps out. "I'm the only one who gets to do that!"

I don't even know what I'm saying, but I know what I mean, because it goes all through me, the sight of Blair being jerked so hard it knocks her hair back, like the whipping of a horse's tail.

Don't you dare hurt her, asshole.

A cluster of images fires in my brain as I run out, ignoring Siggy and Imani yelling *No, June!* Ignoring Hunter pleading *Don't!* Ignoring the incoming trio of zombies, with their malignant skin, the mottled, bloated-corpse patterns of veins dark with pooled blood, and the fine muscles somehow twitching, writhing under the lingering sheen of a fever-popped sweat.

But I'm not looking at them as I sprint silently to my friend.

I'm looking at Blair, and remembering instead.

Blair, on the day I met her in kindergarten. This cute brunette with an upturned, freckled nose and a wide satin ribbon pinned in her hair.

Which she pulled out the minute her mom left. Just as she ignored the girls her mom tried to introduce her to, when they walked into the room, girls with ribbons of their own and smocked-bib dress fronts, or ruffles upon ruffles upon ruffles.

Instead she walked up to me. And she said, "I'm Blair. Will you be my friend?"

Like she saw something in me she liked, right away.

I felt like a flower in the sun.

When I puked on Brandon Huckabee in third grade she said he deserved it. When I got drunk for the first time at Chastain Walker's barn party the summer before our junior year, she took care of me and wouldn't leave me alone for a second. A kid fell out of the hayloft and broke his collarbone that night. I always knew it would have been me who got hurt if it wasn't for Blair.

Sure, there was always other stuff between us, the competitive stuff I didn't understand, and still don't, and try not to feel, but even though it's there, and even though it hasn't changed and probably never will, it doesn't change *everything else*.

She can always get a rise out of me.

Because she's Blair. And I guess I'll always love her, okay?

If we get out of this alive, I should end the ice-out. I should at least hear what she has to say.

I'm not sure if it's a baby in bathwater, our friendship, but there's something there, something important that can maybe be saved or salvaged, and I am *not* going to let Scott or anyone else drag her down to be zombie kibble.

If this was an action movie, I'd skid to a stop next to Scott, and I'd deck him, or something, and I'd have a cigar jammed into my mouth and I'd say, "Not on my watch, pal." And I'd pull Blair into a bridal carry and we'd run back to safety.

But instead I sprint up and sling a sloppy punch down at his wrist, his hand still closed around Blair's arm.

Scott is making a horrible choking sound, like his throat is swelling, or like water is pouring into it.

He doesn't let go of Blair's wrist, so I start peeling his fingers back, one at a time, like when I was a little kid and my dad dared me to get the quarter out of his fist.

"Run, girls!" Cuellar yells, his voice raw and ragged.

I glance up as Scott's hand finally slips off Blair's forearm.

The trio of zombies is almost on us, arms outstretched.

I drag Blair up. One of her arms comes up behind my shoulder as we turn.

"Wait!" Scott coughs. His voice somehow submerged.

I look down at him.

Blood courses down his face, pouring out of his nose like a spigot.

No one hit him.

He's infected. I remember the girl on the floor of the exhibit hall, before it all started.

Selfish, scared Scott. He had to know he was already infected, when he was bitten. But he chose to hide it.

"Run!" Blair says, giving my shoulder an urging shove with her hand.

We run.

I expect to hear the ugly sounds of the zombies attacking Scott, but they don't come.

When I reach the balcony doors, I turn to look back.

Hunter works furiously at the last lock.

The trio of pursuing zombies is close; they've ignored Scott, just moved right past him, something about the virus already making him seem like one of them.

Not worthy meat.

We're going to get to the balcony in time, though. We're faster. I stop once inside the balcony door, and glance past Scott to see Cuellar.

He's climbed atop what's left of the wavering barricade. Sitting up there, watching us leave, waiting for it. Making sure we're safe.

Annie is crying.

"I'll never forget you!" she yells to him.

Cuellar holds up a hand, puts two fingers to his lips, then holds the fingers out to us.

He lets himself fall, headfirst, off the barricade and over the guardrail.

Annie sobs as Hunter pulls the door closed behind us with a resounding bang.

33

Annie hides her face in her hands, not trying to stifle her tears so much as abandoning herself to them.

Simon touches her shoulder gently, and she turns to him, pressing into his consoling hug.

"Thank you, June," Blair says. "For coming to get me."

She's looking at me with big eyes, and I feel a self-deprecating grimace crawl across my face.

It was all for nothing. I might have saved us temporarily, but now we're trapped, zombies behind us, zombies below us, and there's literally nothing else we can do. Nowhere else to go.

If we leave, we'll just lose more people. And what would we even leave to do? All our plans are for nothing.

"You're welcome," I tell her anyway. "Wish I could have done more."

Linus and Mia. Janet and Cuellar. And Scott. All gone.

Blair looks like she wants to say something more, to argue, or tell me it's not my fault, and honestly, I don't have the heart for any more reassurance in this moment.

I give her an apologetic smile that I hope she understands, that I'm not trying to cut her off, I just *can't, I really can't,* in this moment, I can't think about it, can't replay what happened to exonerate myself, I can't. I need a minute to sit with it, literally.

I walk over to a cushioned folding chair, lying where the back row should be, knocked onto its side. I pick it up, set it back on its feet, and collapse into it.

I hear murmuring behind me, the others discussing, perhaps, what we do now, if anything, when the fact of the matter is we're trapped. Boxed in. There's nothing left to do.

The roof access, if there is one, isn't here. Isn't in the balcony.

There are zombies literally everywhere but this one balcony space.

A presence approaches me, and I know without looking who it will be, then confirmation as I smell her lovely, familiar scent. She still smells like fresh apples.

Imani turns another chair onto its legs and sits next to me.

Our arms brush.

She understands my need to be silent. Is there anything as pure and consoling as a friend sitting with you silently? Sharing your grief?

No. There isn't. I'm sad to say I know that now, empirically.

Time passes, maybe just a few minutes, maybe a half hour. I don't know and I don't care. I feel untethered from everything, lost, until Imani's voice calls me back.

"I love you," she says.

She turns that beautiful, wistful smile to me. A smile that communicates that nothing has changed with us. With our friendship. That it's steadfast, like a compass point. Like her ability to always find our way forward.

"I love you, too," I tell her.

Another chair gets placed on the other side of me. Siggy sits and presses into my space, the three of us huddled together like kittens in a basket.

"I'm proud of us," Siggy says. "I'm proud of you, Imani. I'm proud of you, June."

Siggy's blue eyes shine with tears, but she doesn't look away. She doesn't flinch or blink.

And she doesn't crack a joke.

"I'm proud of us, too," I reply. "I'm proud of you, Siggy."

Imani leans around me. "Yeah. You didn't even faint or get nauseous once, Siggy. When you fought them."

Siggy sits up straighter, the praise making her grow from within.

"I'm still squeamish," she says. "I'll probably throw up later."

"That's okay," I tell her. "You've earned it."

I didn't mean for it to be funny, but it is.

A small laugh ripples through us at the image, the thought of a well-deserved hurkening.

Imani and Siggy wrap their arms around me and each other, and I do the same with them, a group hug.

Then Siggy lets go and stands.

"I'm going to go look around. See what all's up here. Just to be sure."

Checking that there's nothing else we can do, that there's no surprise cache of supplies or a stowed prepper bugout bag. The instinct still there, keep searching. Keep trying.

Maybe there's something.

I nod.

Imani stands, too. "I'm going to see if there's a way to reinforce the doors."

I nod again, and want to tell them I get the message.

Don't give up yet, June.

I don't want to steal their hope, or tell them it's pointless.

So I just nod.

My friends walk off, my strong, beautiful friends. I want to cry, a mix of love and sorrow and I don't even know what, a longing.

Instead I just sit some more.

On the ballroom floor below, zombies seethe, their guttural growls and the automaton clacking of their jaws rising into the air, like a buzzing of devouring bees.

Hunter puts a hand on Imani's chair, then sits down next to me.

"A swarm," I say, waving my hand at the zombies below us. "They sound like a swarm of zombies."

"I think they sound like a saw," Hunter says, like this is a normal conversation. Like the zombies below us are performing. "A band saw of zombies."

I nod. Then I glance at him.

"I was going to ask you a question," I say. "When this day started. At your opening session."

Hunter shakes his head gently. "Feels like a lifetime ago."

"A whole other world," I agree.

He crosses his arms over his stomach and stretches out his long legs, crossing them at the ankles. He tilts that crooked grin at me.

"So, you're a fan, then?" he teases.

"Oh yeah." I push my hair back off my shoulders in an exaggerated gesture of preening-pride. "I was Clay Clarke's biggest fan."

Hunter's eyes cloud slightly. His eyebrow inches up.

"*Was?*"

"Wellllllll." I draw the word out. "Let's just say I've decided that I like Hunter Sterling the person more."

Hunter gives a little laugh.

"Oh," he says. "That guy."

His tone is joking but there's something underneath, small but noticeable, like a sliver of splinter under the skin.

I touch his arm, just once, because it feels like I should be able to telegraph the truth to him through my fingertips.

"Yeah," I say. "That guy."

Hunter clears his throat, a little shy cough.

I smile, and he smiles back, and below us the zombies buzz like summer cicadas.

"What was your question, anyway?" Hunter asks.

I laugh. Why not?

"In that interview, you said you identified with Clay because he was searching for something." I sit up and lean forward slightly, then glance back over my shoulder at him.

"What is it that you're searching for?"

Hunter laughs, and shakes his head, the movement causing hair to fall over his eyes.

His default shy-gesture.

"I don't know," he says.

I wait.

"That's the answer." He glances at me. "I honestly don't know. But sometimes I feel like there's something out there, calling to me. Something I should find. Something that will make everything make more sense somehow. Like finding the key to a test. Does that make sense?"

"Oh yeah," I answer. "That makes sense."

I feel a light brush on my hand. Hunter's knuckles rest tentatively against mine.

Hunter smiles, sweet and sad, and I smile back. In spite of everything.

It's confusing, but no one cares, so I smile back.

I turn my hand over, and Hunter takes it, pulling it onto his leg and threading our fingers together, squeezing just so.

My heart does a little skitter-jump, and I can't help it, but here it is anyway, this swelling-to-burst feeling in my chest, like a bubble of doomed happiness.

"What a way for the world to end, huh?" I ask. "Ridiculous old world."

"There were parts of it I liked," Hunter says.

"Me too," I say. "Kittens and stuff."

"Ice cream," Hunter says.

"Weighted blankets."

"Drive-through food," Hunter says. "And . . . you're pretty cool."

A flock of butterflies launches itself into a swirling victory lap in my stomach.

"You too," I say. "Also I like butterflies. All the butterflies. Heaps of them, a flutter-by, or whatever they're called."

"A kaleidoscope," Hunter says, smiling at me shyly. "A kaleidoscope of butterflies."

Yep. Exactly.

Only losers fall in love during the zombie apocalypse.

• • •

After a while, the others drift over to where we sit, in our little theater row. First Imani and Siggy, who adds her seat next to Imani. Then Blair, pulling up a seat next to Siggy, then Annie and Simon next to Hunter.

And then there were seven.

Annie leans forward, gently depositing her defibrillator case on the floor in front of her.

The hard plastic shell is Red Cross red, blaring out help that we won't receive.

Behind us, the doors knock incessantly. The zombies, trying to get in.

"How long do you think the doors will hold?" Simon asks.

"Pretty long?" Hunter guesses. "It helps that they open outward."

"They're still weak at the middle, though," Imani says. "I didn't see any way to strengthen them."

"I wonder if anyone else made it out?" Hunter asks. "Maybe they did, and they're telling the army to try a different route right now."

It's a hope. But it doesn't seem likely, given everything we've seen.

"Maybe there are little groups of survivors," Imani says. "Hunkered down in places like the preppers. Waiting to be saved."

It's a nice thought, if only the end of the world wasn't at hand.

Zombies, rushing into the army, overrunning and attacking them, keeping going past the barricades, into Senoybia.

We stare down at the horde of zombies, easily over five hundred of them, and only some of whom have seen us and are flailing claw-handed arms impotently at the air.

"I guess we're just gonna sit here," Siggy says. "When it all hits the fan."

The army or SWAT team, unleashing the zombies into the unsuspecting world.

It doesn't feel good. Just waiting for the inevitable. As if that's our only choice.

"Well, I don't even have a weapon anymore," Annie says, but her voice is light, she's making a joke. "If I had found that new defibrillator, I'd give them what for." The teasing tone falls out of her voice. "Like Linus would have said."

The defibrillator.

"Damn right you would," Simon says. A low, exhausted laugh rumbles out of his chest. "That was just about the best thing I've ever seen, Annie."

"It was pretty badass," Annie agrees.

At the front of the ballroom, the giant screen hanging above the stage glows a digital blue. Under it are preamps and speaker stacks, scattered chairs. Above it are the glowing lights of a theatrical light rig, suspended on a long pole at the front of the stage.

The defibrillator.

If only there was a way to zap them all at once.

It takes me a minute to realize someone is saying my name.

"June?" Hunter's looking at me with a question in his eyes. "What is it?"

I give my head a little shake.

"Nothing. It's just a brain fart." I smile at the others. "It was nothing."

"Bullshit," Imani says, leaning into my face, her eyes searching.

I let go of Hunter's hand and work my fingers into my hair.

"It's nothing—just—" I wave at the red case. "Defibrillator. What Annie said. If we could only shock them all. I was thinking, I don't know . . . if we could somehow get on that stage and electrocute them."

"One at a time?" Annie asks, her eyebrows coming together in a frown.

"No, all together," I say.

"The defib's not that strong," Annie says.

"I know, I was thinking, the lights. Or the speakers. They must have those really fat plugs. Draws a huge voltage."

The others just look at me, and I feel silly.

"I know it won't work," I say hastily. "I mean, if there was one of those fire hoses in here, maybe we could soak them all from up here, then do it."

"The water would conduct the electricity," Simon says, nodding.

"But there's not a hose up here," I say.

Siggy points up.

"We have those," she says.

As one, our row tips our heads back.

34

"his is the worst idea in the history of ideas," I say. "It started as mine, so I get to say that."

I'm wrapping electrical tape around the handle of the hex key, winding it around and around a wooden mop handle and the hex key, an infinity, figure-eight loop-de-loop.

"Well, I'd rather die with a bad idea and moving than no idea and standing still," Annie says.

"That's the spirit!" I say, giving her a little hug.

Simon jogs back to where I stand. He's been running back and forth at the edge of the balcony, waving his arms and shouting.

"It's going to work, June," he says. "But I still think you should let me be the one to climb down."

"Why, because you're a guy?" I shake my head. "Besides, I need you up here if anything, you know . . . goes wrong. You'll have another shot at it."

I hand the mop to Blair.

"Wait till I go before you start."

"Do you have a minute?" Blair asks, tipping her head to the side, indicating that she'd like privacy.

I follow her a few steps away from the others.

I know what this is going to be. A Blair version of an apology. Words that feel regretful, but which don't take ownership, don't take the sting away, and filled with these voice-trailing-off gaps that take the place of actually saying *I'm sorry*, which she has never been, will never be, able to do.

But I owe it to her, and to the entire history of our friendship, to hear her out.

And I'm ready to accept her for who she is, and that includes her flawed apology.

"I just want to say I'm truly sorry," Blair says.

My heart stops, and then it speeds up, and I feel blood rush to my cheeks and ears in shock.

She said it. She actually said it.

And she's still talking.

"—for everything. I don't really know why I do the things I do, sometimes. And it's not like he was that great."

I feel my lip push out in a *wasn't he?* expression as my heart rate calms back down.

Call it the zombie apocalypse, but I decide that I really don't care why anymore.

"It's okay, Blair," I say. "Thank you for saying that. It's okay."

Forgiveness is a gift you give yourself. Or something like that I saw on a mug sometime. But pithy as it sounds, it must be true, because the minute I say it, I actually do feel better. Not because it doesn't still hurt about Scott, not because suddenly all is well, or that I somehow magically can trust her again, but maybe just simply because I don't feel poisoned by my anger. I'm just letting it pass through me, and letting it go.

I'm not going to nurse it anymore. Not going to fan its flames, or push out with that feeling of being wronged.

And suddenly I feel bigger. Stronger.

"Thanks for letting me off the hook, but I have to say it." Blair's hand opens and bobs at me, pleading.

"Okay," I agree.

"Can we sit?" Blair walks to the front of the balcony, and sets up two chairs behind the rail.

She's not done?

I sit next to her, looking out at the blue screen hanging over the sea of groaning, straining zombies below.

Blair takes a deep breath. "I've . . . I guess I've been jealous for a long time."

I want to say *Aha!* Or *Eureka!* Or something that a scientist might say. I also want to argue, because what? Why?

What I say is "Me too."

Blair looks at me. She tucks long, honey-brown hair behind one ear.

"Really?" she asks.

"Yeah," I reply. "Of you, or parts of you. Things that I'm not."

"Yeah." Blair smiles a little, and then she's turning on the seat, twisting sideways so our knees nearly touch. "And I don't like the way that makes me feel."

I nod. "Me either."

"I don't know why it started, or how," she says, words rushing out. "But it did and it's been there for so long. And then I was just reacting to it . . . and then Scott. I'm so sorry, June."

Scott. A jerk. A charming guy. Dead now, and does any of this matter next to that?

I try not to flinch but it's there, it must be, because Blair looks distressed, almost like she wants to pat at me or hug me.

"I wish I could take it back," she says, her voice urgent. "But I did it. I knew how you felt about him, but I wanted . . . I wanted to take him. I liked him, but I also wanted to take him from you. I didn't really think when it started, we started flirting online, and I haven't had that many boyfriends—"

"Gee, I wonder what that's like." It comes out harsher than I mean it, but it's there, the truth.

We are the same in so many ways.

"Sorry," I say. "That was a knee-jerk."

Blair sighs. "It's a fair point."

There's a moment of not-silence, but not talking, as we sit and try to process what we want to say, what our emotions are doing.

The moans of the zombies stretch up to us, life-and-death context.

"Listen," I say, turning to Blair, meeting her eyes for the first time. "I want to be friends again. But I want to feel safe with you."

Blair is nodding rapidly, her eyebrows up in a *yes!* expression.

"I understand," she says. "I don't know how I can fix it. Except to tell you the truth, and to keep saying it."

She takes a deep breath.

"I have to find a new way. Because I can't just feel better about myself when I can do better than you." She looks down. "And I don't know why we should feel—why I should feel . . . competitive. Like there's only so much to go around, attention, or whatever."

"Control," I whisper.

Blair glances at me.

"I do it, too," I continue. "I don't like it, but I feel . . . like I have to compete with you. Like we have to struggle for . . . control. Which is ludicrous. It doesn't even make sense!"

"Right?!" Blair grabs my wrist, squeezing it in agreement. "What even is that?"

We meet each other's eyes, shaking our heads in mutual dismay and confusion.

"Is it the patriarchy?" I ask.

"I mean, I would like to blame the patriarchy?" she answers.

"Let's blame the patriarchy," I suggest, and then we're laughing, small little huffs at the ridiculousness of the place, the patriarchy, the zombies below us, but also laughs of relief.

It feels like we've climbed over something, this huge obstacle, together.

Blair lets go of my wrist to hold up her hand, making a promise. "June, I swear to you. I swear, when we get out of here, I'm going to be a better friend to you, I promise. Cross my heart and hope to die."

She does the hand gesture, drawing an X over her heart, and it doesn't feel ridiculous, the childhood oath.

It feels like a summoning of our past, the whole of it, playground games and spend-the-nights, that time we went to the beach together, playing with Barbies, whispering secrets in each other's ears.

How I knew she had to feel left out sometimes, hell, lots of times, with me and Imani.

Everyone plays their part.

"I'm sorry," I tell her. "I'm sorry I ever hurt you, and I'm sorry for not letting you talk to me. To us. I'm sorry for the cold shoulder."

"It's okay." Blair waves it away with her hand.

"No, it wasn't right either." I shake my head, embarrassed of how it had felt *good* to punish her.

"Okay." Blair nods. "Thank you for saying that." But when she glances up at me again, her eyes are shining.

I've never actually seen her cry before.

"Hey!" It's my turn to want to pat-pat at her. To dab away impending tears with the press of my hands. "Don't cry."

Blair lets out a sob.

"Hey! What did I say?" I fret.

"I can't help it, I love you," Blair says, her voice a warble of tears.

"I love you, too." My voice is frog-strangled, too.

We hug, and it feels like wringing out all the bad, and then soaking in the good, okay, except more elegant than that, but that clean feeling, at last.

We sit back, smiling.

"Friends again. Forever," I say.

Blair stretches out a hand, and I put mine in hers.

"Damn straight," she says.

Below us, the zombies groan and seethe, but up here there is space and air.

. . .

After we recover ourselves, Blair and I stand and walk back to where Siggy and Imani are waiting, a little separated from the rest of the group.

Imani runs up and touches Blair's arm, smiling because we are.

Siggy is frowning, not in anger but in skepticism, and I want to kiss her cute mama-hen heart.

"It's okay," I tell her. "We had it out."

"Yeah," Blair says. "I'm sorry. I guess I hurt us all, huh?"

Siggy watches Blair's eyes closely.

Imani opens her arms and Blair steps into them. "Oh, good," Imani says. "I couldn't stand it. Either of you hurting. Or fighting."

"It's not gonna happen again," Blair promises.

Siggy doesn't look hostile, but she's not warming up completely, either.

"Siggy?" Blair asks, when Imani lets go of the hug.

Siggy takes a deep breath. "I just want this to be real. To last."

"I promise, you'll see," Blair says. "I am gonna be like Scrooge, you know? Better than my word."

"Me too!" I promise.

Siggy studies our faces for a moment, and then she can't help the smile that tugs at the corner of her mouth. The lingering tension in her forehead relaxes.

"Well, okay," she says. "That's better."

And you know, it actually does feel better. Like we've opened a window, somehow.

Hunter's voice calls to us from the mixing board. "Okay, we're all set!"

Siggy hugs Blair and then Blair lets go and turns, pulling me into a hug, squeezing me way, way too tight. And that's why I can't breathe. That's why my eyes are tearing.

Whatever.

We pull apart, and I swipe at my eyes. We walk back to the others, Hunter, Simon, and Annie, waiting for us in the center of the balcony.

Everyone is ready, determined looks on all our faces.

"Okay. Go time," I say.

But first everyone moves in, the same unspoken instinct. To hold close, to huddle up. So we all hug, not just me, but each other, a standing puppy-pile of arms and elbows and heads.

Team Turtle is going in, one last time. All or nothing, baby.

35

"You got this, June. You can do this," I chatter under my breath.

The others are all standing at the opposite side of the parabola-shaped balcony, yelling, hollering, making noise.

Attempting to draw every bloodshot eye up, and away from me, huddled below the railing of the balcony, hands wrapped around the thick extension cord the balcony-escape group had tied into loops to make a rescue rope.

"Hey, zombies!" Annie screams. "Look up here, yummy!" She drags her hands up her arms, like a game-show model demonstrating cold cuts.

"Hey, zombies! Zombeeeeeez! Zombies!" Siggy and Imani call the zombies like they're on a farm calling hogs.

Simon whoops and yells.

Hunter prances back and forth at the extreme front of the balcony, his hands planted in the small of his back, elbows jutting, an imitation of Mick Jagger.

A snort of laughter sounds at my shoulder. I whirl.

"Blair!" I hiss. "What are you doing?"

Blair shrugs, hands up.

"Helping you, aren't I?" she says. "Someone's gotta watch your back."

I smile.

"Friends again, forever," I say.

"All together or none at all," Blair agrees, like it's a call-and-response.

Which is how I end up climbing down the extension cord with one of my best friends, while our other friends do their part to distract a room full of zombies.

I land awkwardly, stumbling on my bad leg when I do, but Blair catches me, and we rush forward to the stage.

One of the zombies at the back of the crowd turns at our movement.

Blair vaults herself onto the stage like a stuntwoman, with agile grace and coordination.

I jump at the stage after her and catch the edge with my solar plexus, knocking the wind out of myself. I kick my legs, hoisting my tummy up and onto the lip of the stage like a seal.

But it works, and we're up before the row of zombies at the back can see us.

Now here's hoping they still haven't figured out how to climb.

I give the balcony a thumbs-up while Blair starts searching through the folds of the curtains at the edge of the stage.

Hunter gives me a thumbs-up in return, and runs to the soundboard table in the middle of the balcony, and the only reason I wouldn't let him come with me when he tried to insist was because he was the only one who knew how to work it.

Showbiz kids.

Time for phase two of our plan: lure.

Suddenly the screen above our heads changes from blue to a picture of Hunter Sterling as Clay Clarke, bright and clear and in close-up.

And silent.

I make a *what the?* gesture to Hunter in the sound booth.

He makes a *wait* gesture, then pushes a few more buttons.

Sound blares out, loud, then louder, as Hunter turns the volume up.

"I don't know what those things are or if they're everywhere." It's Captain Cliff Stead's speech from the first episode.

The zombies on the floor of the ballroom, all five-hundred-plus of them, stumble toward the stage, drawn by the voices of the actors, and by the sight of me and Blair, standing on it, waiting.

Up in the balcony, Imani and Siggy begin the third step.

Imani runs back and grabs the mop from where it rests against the back wall. She approaches the edge of the bal-cony and leans out.

Simon holds her around the waist, and Siggy helps support her uplifted arms as she stretches.

The end of her mop handle, tipped with the hex-key screwdriver, connects with the sprinkler head.

Imani jabs.

The thin plastic stop-toggle breaks off, and a twelve-foot circle shower of water falls on just the edge of the balcony; the rest of the water lands on the zombies below.

Several zombies rush headlong at the front of the stage. Two fall back. A third falls onto it, arms out.

I pick up a microphone stand from the stage and bash the base into his face, pushing him back.

"But I know one thing," Cliff says from the screen.

Imani and her helpers rush along the front edge of the balcony to the next sprinkler.

The water landing on the hardwood floor of the ballroom spills out into a wider and wider area; as the heavy shower continues to fall, the water spreads outward, toward the side wall, toward the front of the ballroom, toward the back doors.

"I'm gonna fight."

I hear a thunderous boom, and my eyes jump to the back of the ballroom.

The single set of open doors has slammed back against the walls, pressed by the massive influx of zombies.

It's working.

The sound lure is drawing them, from the hallway, up from the first-floor lobby, over the barricades, and with those numbers, probably from the exhibit hall itself.

I feel triumphant, then tiny, then terrified as hundreds more zombies press into the ballroom.

The zombies at the front of the stage are buffeted by others arriving. I can feel the vibrations through the stage floor.

The curtain behind the stage billows against the chain-link set dressing. The zombies that found their way backstage to the double doors now trying to find their way back, following the noise.

How many zombies can press in until there are enough to collapse the stage? Or to climb over each other to reach us?

I lift my eyes, looking for Imani, and clever Siggy, who had said, "Haven't you been in a hotel and seen those little *No hangers!* signs below the sprinkler heads? When they're set in the wall? That's because you can set them off just by trying to hang a shirt there!"

Imani's taller and so she has longer arms; that's the reason we chose her to do the sprinkler-jabbing. She's working fast now; three more sprinkler heads have been set off and she's working on another. When that one pops open, water gushing out in its wide circle, Imani, Siggy, and Simon sprint around the soundboard, ignoring the two sprinkler heads in proximity to it, and rush to the opposite side of the balcony and start again.

I run to the edge of the stage and grab a white hard-sided briefcase. I open it. Inside it's filled with foam rubber, with little nests for battery or broadcasting packs.

I carry it out to the center front of the stage again, and look out over the sea of straining, grasping bodies. More and more push into the hall, tracking through the rapidly pooling water.

The front edge of spreading water isn't far enough yet.

Almost. Almost.

I open the case and place it, rubber side down, on the carpeted part of the stage behind me.

"Got it!" Blair yells from the side of the stage.

She pushes the curtains back, revealing a square aluminum truss that runs up and over the front of the stage. Hanging off the center top piece of the truss is a huge light bar, easily ten feet in length. It hangs out just slightly beyond the front edge of the stage.

Blair has her hand on a lever of some sort. She gives it an experimental crank.

The lights lift an inch.

Blair steps back and looks up, taking in the cables.

At the front of the stage, the movement of the zombies piled up, trying to reach us, has changed. Instead of reaching, and ineffectively pushing their chests against the edge, they're starting to rise, somehow.

It's uncoordinated, nothing like a predetermined movement. A susurrating noise under their groans, a slight rise and fall, like a wave.

Like popcorn in a pan, as kernels expand beneath kernels.

The stage shifts, I can feel it start to slide slightly backward.

They're being pressed so hard against the front edge that it's rupturing lungs, breaking ribs. Several of the zombies start to pour blood and other effluvium out of their mouths, noses, eyes. The pressure of the mass of bodies behind them is quite literally crushing them.

And causing others to rise, squeezed in and up, like . . . like . . . like—

Okay, like a push-up bra? Except grosser.

Like a pimple.

My stomach lurches with nausea. I take a deep breath and look away so I don't hurl.

It's only a matter of time before one of them, through the combined lift and squeeze, tips over onto the stage.

If it doesn't simply collapse first.

"Ready when you are!" Blair yells.

There are too many bodies in front of me. I can't tell if the water has reached far enough forward. It must.

We can't wait much longer. The stage shifts again, like a raft on an ocean, drifting back. Shuddering.

I glance up at Hunter. At Imani and Siggy.

I lift the microphone stand and wait at the front of the stage.

"Get ready to jump!" Blair yells at me.

"Wait for it!" I yell back, rolling my shoulders and jabbing the heavy mic stand out in front of me experimentally.

On the balcony, Imani makes a hand gesture like water, a snaky wave. Then she gives a thumbs-up.

The water has reached far enough.

Thank you, Imani.

"Get ready, Blair!" I yell.

Blair wraps her arm, then a leg into the curtains at the side of the stage, winding it around herself like an aerialist on webbing.

She pulls herself up, off the metal stage, but tilts sideways, still keeping a hand on the ratchet lever.

At the very back of the hall, I see the silhouette of two shuffling zombies, turning *away* from the stage, from the room, running out into the hall.

What the hell?

Maybe the SWAT team has arrived. We have to light this thing up *now*.

"Three, two, one, GO!" I yell.

There's a whizz of wires as Blair releases the lights.

I lunge forward with the mic stand, and heave with all my strength, knocking the aluminum light bar out that tiny, extra, necessary little bit.

Over the zombies. Over the water.

I'm supposed to jump up and back now, in the split second it will take the lights to drop, hit the water, and send out deadly bolts of electricity.

I leap up and back, extending toward the open white case.

From the balcony it looked like it was made of fiberglass-type plastic, white like a construction helmet, so it shouldn't conduct electricity. Plus, bonus, it's lined with that foam rubber to hold the battery pack things.

And I'm hoping between those two things, and the thin carpet that lines the plywood square top of the stage, that it will be just enough of a dampener, that in killing the zombies, I won't also be killing myself.

But if I do, well.

It was an honor serving with me.

My brain is so inappropriate, but that doesn't stop it from cracking the joke as I stretch my toes down to try to stick the landing on the case.

The light bar falls into the zombies, hard. The bar snaps in two, crashing heavy spotlights blaring out red and blue beams of light into the zombies, then past them, into the water.

There is an audible pop and sizzle as arcing power bolts through the crowd of bodies, backward, sideways, and forward, all at once, like branching lightning.

My feet don't ever get to connect with the case to test my theory. Electricity shoots into the air, twisting up metal and aluminum, through the air and into me.

The bolt goes in my ankle, shoots up my leg, and comes out on my outer hip in an instant; a simultaneous, painful shock, like it's one motion, not two moments, the lightning like a gunshot. I'm blown forcefully up and back, rotating around the axis of my jolted hip, flying off the stage, over the edge, into the chain-link set dressing and heavy backdrop of curtain that stops me, catches me, drops me.

And everything goes dark.

36

*I*f I'm dead, it shouldn't hurt, right?

So, I'm probably not dead?

There's a ringing in my ears, and everything hurts, especially my leg, somehow both novocaine-numb and shooting pain at the same time.

I feel like a cartoon, like there's still a draining, drifting power pinballing in me. My hair should be twisting from static. If I held a lightbulb between my teeth, it should light up.

". . . oooon?"

The voice is like a muted whale song. I can't discern words, just noises. Swooping ups and downs of tone.

Scared. Urgent.

A finger pokes my ribs. A hand rests on my sternum.

The warmth of a body close to mine.

Leaning over mine?

"Joo-uuun?" the voice repeats.

A girl's voice. High.

Another, deeper voice whale-songs next.

"Tss oooaaak," it rumbles. "Eeee iiiiid iiiit."

Opening my eyes is a struggle. Then when I get them open, my vision is all haze, darkness and haze, until I blink it away.

The sounds clarify when I see lips, or when I wake up fully, I'm not sure which.

I'm lying on my back, on the ground, no, on a waffle iron. It's the chain-link, now flat on the back of the stage. It's dim-dark; we blew out the circuit, I guess. Only the lights in the balcony are still on.

There's a glow of a cell-phone flashlight in my face. It tips sideways when I try to lift my hand to shield my eyes.

First, I see Hunter's gorgeous mouth, and then face; he's leaning over me, eyebrows drawn together in concern, but also, he's smiling.

His hand rests, warm, on my sternum.

"We did it," he repeats. "It's okay."

He smiles at me, like a sunrise: it lifts across his face, lights it, and warms me like a blanket. A really lovely, soft, heavy blanket.

I like him as much as blankets.

"As much as that, huh?" He's laughing.

What?

"God, you scared me," Blair says. One of her hands is on my arm, the other swipes tears off her face. "Don't ever do that again, okay?"

My voice sounds weak, and a bit furry, cotton-wrapped.

But I know I'm speaking this time.

"Deal," I say.

Footsteps rush in, and Imani and Siggy are there, hugging me tight, lifting my shoulders, not listening to Hunter's "Careful!"

"It's okay," I say, moving my toes, lifting my knees. Wrapping my arms around my friends.

"We did it," Siggy sobs, part laughter, part exhaustion and relief. "We saved the goddamn world."

We stick to the edge of the ballroom as we help each other out.

Okay, so basically everyone's helping me. But with each step I feel stronger, and by the time we get to the doors into the second-floor lobby, I'm only holding on to Hunter, and that's really for another reason.

I don't look at the dead zombies. I keep my eyes away from the inert, infected bodies splayed across the ballroom floor.

The scientist's voice replays in my head, a self-comforting reel. "Too late for them" and "no cure," he'd said.

Simon opens the door first, sticks his head out.

We're all still carrying our weapons. There might be stragglers, plus we're not foolish. And we've all become a little bit attached to our weapons.

Annie even trades her used defibrillator for a new one.

"Okay. Now all we have to do is find the SWAT team. Get to the loading dock. Make sure there's no chance a loose zombie can get out."

I nod tiredly.

"Even if there are stragglers, it's not a herd. We lured most of them up," I say.

"Yeah, at some point, we have to trust the professionals to get it right," Hunter says. "Now that there're not hundreds and hundreds of zombies."

Still, we sweep our eyes around as we make our way to the escalators, then clear the rest of the barricade to walk down.

On the ground floor, Annie crosses to Cuellar's body, and covers his face with her jacket.

Two sets of doors to the exhibit hall hang open. I was right, that boom was the zombies breaking out.

We turn away from the locked doors of the convention center, and away from the volcanic rock waterfalls.

"Hey!" the whisper-call startles me so much I nearly drop the mic stand.

Rosa rushes up to us from the hallway that stretches along the window wall and continues past the escalators, to the meeting rooms beyond. A huge smile is on her face. Her arms are held open.

"Rosa!" Simon whispers in surprised joy.

She hugs first Simon, then Annie, then me, Hunter, and Imani, Siggy, and Blair.

"I knew you made it!" I say, but the relieved tears spilling down my face tell the truth of my fears.

"I'm so glad you're okay!" Siggy nearly cries. "You saved me!"

Rosa gives Siggy another hug, and Siggy squeezes her tight in thanks.

"Where are the others?" Rosa asks, frowning at our smaller group. "Janet and Cuellar?"

So we tell her. About Janet, sacrificing herself so we could escape in the elevator. We tell her about Cuellar, getting ambushed and bitten, then letting himself fall.

And she tells us about running down the meeting room hall after we got separated. About how she managed to lock herself into a maintenance closet.

The first time she could no longer see the shuffling shadows through the gap at the bottom of the closed door, she cracked it open, only to hear a commotion above her head, from the second floor.

Then when she opened the door wider, first water, and then zombies started falling.

She was one level below us, almost exactly in the same spot that we were one floor above, when Imani hosed the zombies over the balcony railing.

Rosa waited in the closet a long time after that, only daring to come out when the lights dimmed, then flickered.

She thought it was the army, cutting the power, getting ready to come into an unknown situation.

It was us.

We explain about our electrocution plan as we walk toward the backstage hall.

We turn the corner and see two zombies standing in the hall, facing the backstage door.

"Not today, jerks," Imani says, dropping her bag and swinging her mop-handle-hex-key spear up.

Suddenly I remember, from before we dropped the lights, two zombies rushing out of the ballroom.

"Wait," I say as the zombies turn.

The man zombie is grimacing, wide red-shot eyes and hanging mouth.

When he looks up, his wide-hanging mouth transforms into a smile. "Oh, thank God," he says.

The woman zombie lifts her head.

"Seriously," she says. "I *have* to take these contacts out already."

"—the hell?" Simon breathes, his weapon still up.

I can't help the peal of laughter and relief as I recognize them.

"Hello, young lovers," I say. "Imani, Siggy, remember them?"

Imani's eyes widen. "No way."

"Way," the woman says. They're staying back, a wise move until Simon believes what his mind is trying to tell him, instead of his eyes.

"Simon, Hunter," I say, holding a hand out to the zombies, "these are *cosplayers*."

"Oh," Simon says, lowering his vanity stool somewhat.

"Uh, hi." Hunter gives them a little nod. "Sorry," he adds. "It's just a bit disconcerting after everything."

"Think nothing about it, my good fellow," the man zombie says, waving away the apology.

"Tell me about it," the woman says at the same time, her voice overlapping his as she stretches her neck. "But it saved our lives. I've got to tell the world. Write a book, *Cosplay Saved My Life*. No hyperbole. They didn't know we weren't one of them."

"Wow, that's lucky," Annie says.

"Not just lucky, smart, too," the man says. "Rachel here realized it. Other cosplayers panicked and ran screaming. Rachel made us blend in."

"Aw, thanks, babe," Rachel says. "But it was you who realized what their plan was, with the water. Good one, by the way, guys."

But she's not looking at us, as she smiles adoringly at the man.

Their foreheads come together, as they start cooing "You're awesome," "No, you're awesome" love-talk to each other.

"Jeez, you guys," I say. "Get a morgue."

• • •

In the end, the army found us.

It was all very exciting, being surrounded by shouting, riot shields, and guns, but we were able to pretty firmly establish that we weren't zombies, and the cosplayers had taken off most of their makeup by then.

There were more survivors, too. James Cooper and his group managed to make their way to the office areas behind the ballroom balcony hall, and locked the Staff Only door with the deadbolt. Michaela, the aftershow host, led a large group of at least thirty survivors, in an orderly, no-pushing fashion, up to the roof, and then signaled for help from up there.

And there were more survivors still, pockets of them hunkered down, or finding their way from dangerous place to dangerous place, fighting to survive like we had.

One of the SWAT team guys said we probably saved a bunch of people by drawing the zombies up to the ballroom when we did.

Of course, the preppers survived also, although one of them was promptly arrested for possessing an illegal weapon.

While we were learning who all made it through, we

were sitting in the medical tents. Waiting to be checked out, waiting for the area to be secured. And I realized that we could use our phones at last.

It was fun telling Siggy she should try calling Mark. It was even more fun hearing her absolute joy when he picked up. And hearing him sobbing with relief that she was okay, and then how he immediately patched her parents into the call so they could feel the same relief, well . . . I decided not to call him annoying anymore, not even in my head.

He's not so bad. Not So Bad Mark Not So Bad Carson. More important, Siggy loves him like whoa and maybe they'll figure their stuff out. If they both end up at the same college, or maybe even if they don't.

All I know is I'll be here for her either way.

Imani called her mom and Tishala, and it was like I was sitting with stereo headphones on, Siggy on one side, Imani on the other, both of them crying and saying *I love you*, and *I know*, and *Me too*.

I asked for a phone and a soldier gave me his. Mine had long since died, but they plugged it into a rapid charger for me.

When I heard my mom's voice, and my dad's, I lost it for a little while, I'm not going to lie. There's nothing wrong with tears, certainly not tears of relief and love and all those near-death clarity emotions that burbled up in my chest and knotted in my throat.

Also, Mom was crying, too. And that always sets me off. I can't help but cry when Mom is sobbing big fat *I love you*s and *I'm so proud of you, baby*s and *Thank God you're alive*s into my ear.

So yeah, in spite of the cell phone dampener, word had gotten out that something bad was going down at *ZombieCon!* Not just because of the military presence and barricades, but because one of the podcast stage hosts turned his T-line linked feed on, left it streaming as the zombies attacked.

At first people thought it was a hoax, a *War of the Worlds* thing. But then the news started reporting the quarantine and blockade, and everyone got glued to their phones or TV screens.

James Cooper came looking for Hunter, and rushed across the tent to grab him into a bear hug. Hunter hugged him back and they were like actual father and son, so happy to be reunited. Hunter actually introduced me to James, who remembered me from before. It was pretty surreal.

Simon hugged James, too. Rosa was hugging a fellow crew member who'd made it into James's group of survivors, and it was teary and sniffly there for a while.

In the good way.

We explained to the army officers about flooding the ballroom and our trap, warned about the danger of restoring power to that area. Apologized about the water still running.

A tight-eyed commanding officer called us "tough little grunts" and said something about a commendation.

I leaned over to Imani, and elbowed her in the ribs.

"A commendation!" I whispered. "Eat your heart out, Harvard! Imani Choi is getting a freaking medal."

• • •

After a while the convention center was secure; even local news was allowed to set up outside the front of the main entrance. The army command told us we'd have to report to the base hospital tomorrow for more debriefing.

But until then, we could go.

I stop right outside the tent, remembering.

"Hang on, I gotta get my phone." I turn to hobble back inside.

"Wait here," Hunter says, and trots back into the tent for me. He reappears a few moments later, holding my phone, and with an amused expression on his face.

"Nice lock screen," he says, handing my phone over.

Oh no.

I look down. The fake-prom selfie I took with the life-sized poster of Hunter Sterling positively blares out from my newly charged phone.

I feel like a large blinking sign should appear over my head: DERP.

"Okay, laugh all you like," I say.

"Oh, I'm going to." Hunter moves next to me, and pulls my arm around his shoulder, even though it's not strictly necessary to help me walk anymore.

"For the record, we had a great time," I say.

"I clean up good, huh?" Hunter says, and I can't help but laugh, because as Clay Clarke in that poster he's sweaty, grimy, and unkempt.

Also, you know, completely gorgeous.

But the boy standing next to me is way better.

"I told you to rent a tux," I say. "But nooooooo."

"Next time," he says. "I demand a do-over."

"This doesn't count as a promposal, for the record," I say.

"Noted, Ms. Blue. Noted." Hunter smiles at me, humor in his hazel-green eyes, and my heart does a skitter-lunge.

I smile back.

We make our way out of the triage area, past the loading dock, around the corner under the hamster tube skyway, and back around the front of the Senoybia Convention Center.

It's dark, full night, but you'd hardly know it from the large, generator-powered klieg lights on poles.

We walk together, me, Hunter, Imani, Siggy, and Blair, out toward the farthest edge of the containment area, where our parents and news vans and a crowd of onlookers wait.

James Cooper is ahead of us, talking to a reporter in a pool of bright light from the camera.

We stop to take it all in, still behind the orange plastic barriers.

Voices shout at us, other reporters seeking exclusive interviews.

"You made it!" The voice is somehow familiar, yelling from across the broad swath of concrete in front of the convention center.

I turn, and see the rando guy from this morning, the one who said he was a survivor. His ZOMBIES HATE FAST FOOD T-shirt's a little worse for the wear now, torn and spattered like all our clothes, but he's got a huge smile plastered on his face.

"You did, too!" I yell back. I give him a big thumbs-up. He does a slow clap for me before going back to his interview.

"Hey, I have a question," Hunter says, touching my elbow.

I turn to him, smiling. Movement catches the corner of my eye. I glance behind us.

It's the *ZombieCon!* banner, dangling loose, falling across the lower half of the convention center windows. Fluttering in the wind.

The slouching front of the loose banner obscures the start of the words, so now it reads YOU SURVIVE.

"What?" I ask.

Hunter puts his hands at my waist.

"What are you doing next weekend, June Blue?"

I smile up at him.

"Oh, I'm killing the SAT, dude. Definitely." I frown and nod my head like a serious student.

Hunter laughs, so I put my hands up to his head, in his hair.

"Better give me a kiss, though. For luck."

I tug gently, and he lowers his lips to mine.

The kiss is like a fission of everything that's good in this world. Everything, yes, but mainly kissing, which is very, very good, and Hunter Sterling's lips, which top the list right now at the present moment.

A fusillade of flashes snaps us out of it.

Our picture has been taken by the photographers waiting to report on the scene.

"Who needs to get a room now, June?" Siggy drawls. But she's smiling.

"Seriously," Blair teases, but her eyes light up with her smile.

"No, keep going." Imani is holding her phone up, like she's recording. "When I sell this to TMZ it'll pay for our summer trip to Cancún."

Siggy squeals.

"I love that idea! Oh, we should definitely go!" She jumps, clapping, her hair pluming out behind her.

"Absolutely!" I agree, meeting Blair's eyes. "We should all go."

Blair smiles at me, a big, easy grin, spreading across her face, wide open like she's a little kid.

Like it's the first day of kindergarten again.

A rush of love glows through me, an actual physical rush, at the sight of my friends smiling back at me. I drink in the sight of Siggy, Imani, and Blair, standing there, arms crossed and legs propped out, their hips cocked to one side, almost like they're simply over everything, so casual and so cool.

Complete badasses.

We did it. We survived, in spite of everything, and here we are, on the other side. All together.

Imani—always attuned to me, or me always to her, or both of us somehow on the exact same page, or feeling, with perfect empathy—reaches her hands out at the same moment I do.

My group of friends huddles in and we hug tight, laughing with pure joy at life, at each other, with each other.

I point toward the barricade, where the flash pops haven't stopped since the moment survivors started walking out.

"You know what time it is, right?" I ask.

Imani laughs, then Siggy, and Blair, and we holler, all together, "*Special Memories!*"

Our huddle opens up, and still laughing, with our arms around each other, we smile for our photo op.